The Unforgettable One

Also By Nikki A Lamers

The Unforgettable One

The Unforgettable Series #5

By Nikki A Lamers

Copyright

Second Edition

Cover design by Jessica Scott, Uniquely Tailored

Photograph by Violette Wicik, Violette Wicik Photography

Cover Model Kerry Mannix

Frey Dreams an Imprint of Nikki A Lamers

ISBN 978-1-951185-23-7 (paperback)
ISBN 978-1-951185-22-0 (ebook)

Table of Contents

Prologue

Sadie

Looking at myself in the mirror, I question whether my whole life is a mistake. I wonder how I have messed up so many times to find myself here. Did the fear of being a single mom cause me to ruin my best friend's life, as well as my own? Did I want to be in love so bad that I just imagined I love Micah as much as he loves me? Did I try so hard to change my life and my reality that I ignored everything my heart told me to remember? Am I the reason he's changed so much in the past few years that he's now become a completely different person? Would it even matter if he were the same man he was when he became my best friend?

I don't know when I started to live someone else's life, but sometimes I feel like that is exactly what happened. I'm living in a town that should feel like home after spending my whole life here, but I no longer have any real friends. I no longer have a family who claim me as part of their own, except for the one I've built. I'm working at a local gift shop instead of teaching like I had planned. I'm living with my husband, my best friend, someone who no longer knows me. Sometimes I wonder if he even likes me anymore. I have a one-and-a-half-year-old that screams...a lot. I have never felt more alone in my life, but I have no idea how to change it, or maybe I'm too scared to try.

Then again, maybe I'm the one who has changed. Maybe I'm the one who let myself become who he wanted me to be; even though I knew it wasn't me. I thought having a family would make me happy. I thought marrying my best friend and raising my little boy would be all I needed.

Unfortunately, I crave more. I forgot to tell myself that the family I build, can't be with just anybody, not even if he's my best friend. A genuine family has to be created from love, not my hopes and imagination. No matter how much I wish for the happily ever after, I can't just force it to come true.

"Sadie? Where are you?" Micah calls from the living room as he slams the front door.

I frantically shove myself off our bed and attempt to rush towards the kitchen as I yell out, "I'm here! I was just putting some things away." I bump into him in my rush and he looks down at me skeptically.

I hold my breath as I stare into his flat blue eyes that used to hold so much life. I wait for him to speak feeling numb. "What's for dinner? I'm starving," he finally grunts.

I try to hold back my sigh of relief when he doesn't question me. "There's a chicken potpie in the oven. It should be about done." I brush by him towards the kitchen. "How was your day?" I ask on autopilot.

"It was fine," he mumbles. "Where's Holden?" he questions, walking over to lean against the gray Formica counter.

"Sleeping," I answer robotically. I hear him sigh with relief as he steps up behind me. "He should be awake any minute," I add as I peek through the oven door to check on dinner. He wraps both of his arms around my waist, brushes my dark hair to the side and presses his lips softly against my neck.

"I have to grab this out of the oven before it burns," I inform him quietly. He sighs again and slowly backs away from me.

I feel his eyes on me, studying me before he finally speaks. "Why don't I take you out tonight after dinner? I think you could use a night out. My parents can watch Holden for us," he suggests.

"Did you already ask them?" I blanch. He winces at my reaction, so I take a deep breath and try again. "If it's ok with them, that would be nice. I can't be out too late though; I have to work at ten tomorrow morning." He smiles genuinely and nods in agreement.

Micah grins at me looking completely relaxed for the first time in a while. He's giving me the same smile he could always give nearly any girl to make them practically fall at his feet. We eat in comfortable silence before we both change into more appropriate clothes to wear for our night out. I quickly touch up my dark hair and make-up as part of my lame attempt to make both Micah and I happy. As soon as his parents arrive to take care of Holden, we both kiss him on the forehead and wave goodbye as we walk out the door.

Micah drives us to the local pub and inevitably spots a few of his friends the minute we step through the door. He grins and immediately strides over to join them. I roll my eyes as I trudge behind him to their booth. They're all guys I grew up with too, but they're definitely his friends, not mine. His three friends nod to me in greeting as Micah relaxes back into the booth. He pulls me in beside him, wrapping his arm possessively around me. He grabs a glass and pours himself a beer from a pitcher sitting on the table. He doesn't offer anything to me, but then again, he knows I don't like beer all that much.

I instantly tune out the conversation, not wanting to hear about the girls his friends are hooking up with. They all talk like I'm not there unless they're harassing Micah about me. Instead of listening, I sit quietly, watching them laugh and drink together. I try to remember what it was like to hang out with friends like this, but it's nearly impossible.

For as long as I can remember it's been Micah and me, but my other friends never stayed the same. Once middle school began, girls looked at me differently and I never understood it. After a while, I realized to them I was the only girl Micah would fight for and their jealousy showed me a very different side of my friends, especially through social media. That's when my friends became whomever Micah's friends were dating at the time. Unfortunately, once we hit high school, it also included whomever Micah was screwing around with at the time, which made for uncomfortable situations for both of us. He never really had a serious girlfriend though, so he would always take my side. His friends would joke, "Sadie's like the perfect girlfriend. You can screw around with whoever you want and she's always here waiting for you." For Micah and me though, we have always been best friends and that's all that mattered to me.

I glance up at him with a stiff smile and he pulls me in for a loud smacking kiss making his friends laugh. He grins down at me, then over to his friends. "I always told you assholes I'd marry the hottest girl in town one day." His friends groan in unison and Tim throws his napkin at Micah before quickly changing the subject.

I sigh and tune them out again. I can't help but feel like I'm on the outside, even with Micah's arm around me. Every few minutes he kisses me or tries to pull me into the conversation. I feel guilty for how hard he tries to make me comfortable and attempt to smile and remain polite. But my mind keeps drifting away from the people around me to Holden. I'd honestly rather be on the outside of this world and home with my little boy. Then again, even with Holden, I've been struggling to find a place where I truly feel like I belong.

Fortunately, Micah remains satisfied as long as I'm by his side. I accept his kisses, no matter how sloppy he becomes, hoping not to make a scene. He loves to kiss me in public even though he knows it makes me uncomfortable. As the night goes on and he downs more beers, things only become more awkward for me. He paws at me, trying to snake his hand up my skirt, making me squirm and blush crimson red. I gently shove his hands away, trying not to make it obvious. He grips my thigh tightly just above the hem of my skirt, not letting go. I soon become more and more eager for the night to be over so I can drive us both safely home.

At least Micah doesn't argue with me when it comes to drinking and driving. When I can't stop Micah from pushing my limits anymore, I decide it's time to encourage him to leave. I place a few sweet kisses to his neck and whisper in his ear, "Can we go home now?"

He turns to me and grips the back of my neck, tugging my head to his. He kisses me hard before he pulls back with a salacious grin. "It's time to get my girl home boys. We'll catch you later," he broadcasts to his friends, waving as we stand. I ignore the crude remarks from his friends, pretending I can't hear anything. He quickly guides me out of the bar and hands me the keys to drive home.

The drive is short and I release a grateful breath the minute we walk in the door. I smile at his parents watching TV on our worn brown leather couch. "We're back. How was he?"

"He was an angel," his mom replies smiling. "Did you two have fun?"

Micah nods. "A great time. Thanks Mom," he states giving her a hug. "Thanks, Dad," he adds and shakes his hand. "We'll be over tomorrow," he adds.

"You know we're always happy to help," she smiles and steps towards me.

She gives me an awkward hug as I paste on my smile. "Thank you for watching him," I express to both of them. His dad gives me a nod and Micah locks the door up behind them. "I'm going to go check on Holden," I inform Micah. I spin on my heel and head upstairs.

I slowly sneak into Holden's room and hold in my sigh of relief when I find him sound asleep. I slowly take in my beautiful little boy, with his chubby arms and legs, his little round face and his perfect blonde curls. I have to admit, nothing is more precious than when he's sleeping peacefully.

I feel Micah move in behind me. "Good, he's sleeping," he mumbles into my ear. He wraps his arms around me clumsily and grabs my breast making me wince. He murmurs, "I want you, Sadie. Let's go to bed."

I hold in my sigh and tighten my jaw to hold in my tears as I follow him to our room. I let him take my clothes off. I barely register the kisses he covers my body with. I keep telling myself, "He's a good man. He's my best friend. I chose this. I chose him. He deserves to have a wife who loves him and treats him right."

I feel him push into me and I try to relax so it doesn't hurt so much. He squeezes my breast and grunts, "Come on, baby." I turn my head to the side and grab on tightly to his shoulders as I let the tears fall and he slams into me while I keep praying for it to be over and then it is.

He rolls off me with a satisfied moan. The ping of his phone sounds and he reaches for it, grabbing it off the nightstand. He glances at the text that just came through and groans with annoyance. His fingers fly over his phone in response before he stands up and throws his pants back on. "It looks like Tim is still at the bar and needs a lift. The dumbass doesn't have any money left for a cab. I'll go and pick him up and be back soon," he informs me. He leans over and gives me a kiss not even noticing my dried tears. "I love you," he yells followed by the door slamming shut without a response from me.

I don't even bother getting up to clean myself. Instead, I pull my pajamas on and curl up into a ball, hugging my legs tightly. I desperately try to relax and go to sleep. I know Holden will be up soon. Eventually, my body drifts into sleep from pure exhaustion.

I wake up to loud pounding a couple hours later. Completely disoriented from crying and sleep, I finally register that someone is pounding on our front door. I glance over to the other side of the bed and realize Micah isn't back yet. I kick off the covers and push myself out of bed.

Grabbing my robe, I quickly wrap it around me and stumble out into the hall. I pick up a crying Holden on the way who seems to have heard the pounding as well.

"Daddy must have forgotten his key," I mumble rubbing my son's back gently in comfort. "I'm coming, Micah!" I yell right before I open the door to two uniformed police officers and flashing red and blue lights.

"Mrs. Rossi?" I nod my head, suddenly feeling dizzy as a whooshing sound takes over my ears. An older officer opens his mouth with a solemn look on his face, but the only words that register are "Micah...accident...I'm sorry." I feel one officer reach for Holden as my body begins to collapse and everything goes black instantly.

Chapter 1

Matt

2 ½ Years Later

"I can't believe I'm back here," I grumble as I park my dark red Chevy Silverado in my parents' driveway, filled with the last of my things from Texas. I stare up at the large white farmhouse with a sprawling front porch. Beyond the house, evergreen trees are interspersed with various other types of trees and scattered everywhere throughout the property as well as all the way down the hill to a beautiful blue lake. The lake looks incredibly peaceful right now, not even a ripple from any wildlife or the wind. I watch as a loon pops his head up disturbing the calm waters as it calls out to his family.

I take a deep breath of fresh air smelling nothing but pine, admitting to myself I love it here in Maine. The house is incredible and has a fantastic view, but my parents living here is the only reason it actually feels like home. My parents only bought the house a little over five years ago. I only lived here on summer vacation from college or when I flew home over breaks and while visiting when I could after I graduated two years ago. For me, I guess it feels more like a summer vacation home than anything. We moved around every couple years for my dad's job while growing up. The only time we ever stayed very long in one place was when my oldest brother, Jason, was in high school. He was a fantastic football player and I assume the coach helped to convince my parents to stay so he could stick with his team. The rest of us never had that luxury.

A knock on the window near my head startles me and I glance over to my little brother Christian, who's not so little anymore, grinning widely. "Are you ever going to get out of your truck? I'm sure it smells much better out here," he taunts. "You have been in there for days!"

I shake my head and smirk at him. I push my door open, quickly jumping out. "Aw, did you miss me, little brother?" I prod, giving him a quick hug and a pat on the back.

He chuckles and shakes his head, but declares with a genuine smile, "Welcome home, Matt."

I step back and grin. "Thanks, Christian."

"Need some help?" he offers.

"Sure, I don't have too much. I got rid of all my furniture down there, so it's mostly just clothes, books and stuff," I inform him.

"What are you going to do when you find your own place?" he asks with a raised eyebrow.

I shrug and smirk at him. "I guess I'll find some new shit. I just had to get the hell out of there," I add as my explanation.

"So, are you gonna' tell me what happened to finally drag your ass home?" he probes curiously.

"Nope." I grin and slap him on the back harder than necessary. I saunter to the back of my truck to unload my things. "So, where's Bree?" I question, changing the subject as I pull down the tailgate. Bree is Christian's fiancée whom we all adore.

"She's back at her house studying for her finals," he informs me. "She's trying to take advantage of any time she has not doing last minute wedding shit."

I nod my head like I understand when in reality we both know I have no clue. "Is she back in Portland or down the road?" I inquire and slide Christian two large boxes.

He grins. "Just down the road. I'm not going to be too far away from her anymore if I can help it," he adds.

I laugh but know better than to give him a hard time about it. After everything Bree and Christian have been through, that's the fastest way to piss him off. I grab two boxes of my own and turn towards the house when Christian stops me. "What the hell is that?" he asks, nodding with his chin towards my left bicep.

I glance down at my arm and notice my black t-shirt rode up on my arm when I picked up the boxes to reveal my black armband tattoo. It's waves about an inch thick all the way around my bicep. I look over at him defiantly, quirking my lips. "It's a tattoo, genius."

He chuckles, shaking his head. "I can see that smartass. Mom is going to flip," he states with a smirk.

I roll my eyes and continue striding towards the house, although I'm tempted to stop and pull my shirt back down. He's right. She will flip, but she's going to see it eventually, anyway. I'd rather deal with the fallout now.

Just as I get to the front door, it flies open. "Matt, you're here!" My mom grins, her green eyes shining bright as she gives me a hug around the boxes and a kiss on the cheek.

"Hi, Mom." I smile sweetly at her. She's dressed in a pair of dark blue jeans and a pale, yellow t-shirt with her blonde hair in a ponytail. "Were you planning on helping?" I ask looking down at her with a grin.

She shrugs. "Well, I figured your brothers would help you. I just thought I'd make all of you something to eat while you unpacked."

"Thanks, Mom." I smile and give her a kiss on the cheek as well. "I need to set these boxes down before my arms fall off," I joke.

Christian is already down the stairs and passing me by when I hear my mom's gasp. "Matthew Emory! What did you do?" she asks accusingly, making me visibly flinch. Christian chuckles, clearly amused, as he heads out the door to grab more things from my truck.

"It's a tattoo Mom, no big deal," I answer, sounding exasperated, although I hate disappointing her. "I have to go put these down," I reiterate and walk towards the stairs, feeling her glare on my back.

"I'm not done with you, Matthew!" she yells after me. I nod my head in understanding, knowing it's true, but I keep walking.

I step into the bedroom I stay in when I'm here and immediately drop the boxes to the left of the doorway. It has lemonade yellow walls with the bed, dresser, and nightstand all in oak. The bedding is a blue and white comforter with matching pillows. I don't really have any personal things in my room except for a couple books and a few pictures.

I walk over to the dresser and pick up the small stack of pictures I left here and flip through them. Most of the pictures are me with my brothers and sister. Then I come across one from my first summer here with *her,* and my heart instantly clenches, even when it has no right to do so. She has a huge smile on her face like she's laughing, lighting up her blue-gray eyes. Her hair appears so dark it's nearly black and it's blowing in the wind against her pale skin.

"What are ya' lookin' at?" Christian prods, startling me as he attempts to glance over my shoulder.

I jump away from him and stuff the pictures into the top drawer of the dresser. "No one," I grumble.

He smirks, his eyes dancing with laughter. "I said what, not who." He stares at me for a minute before he contemplates, "That couldn't be the ex. You said you didn't have any pictures of her here, unless you just took them out of the box or you lied," he teases me. I narrow my eyes and bite my lip to suppress my retort. "Maybe those are pictures from our first summer here when you disappeared all the time and never told us where you were," he adds the corners of his mouth twitching upwards.

Ignoring him, I stride quickly out of the room. I descend the stairs swiftly with Christian on my heels chuckling. My mom is standing alongside my dad at the front door. He has his arms crossed over his chest and he has that intimidating look on his face he always gets right before we (mostly me) would get in trouble. My blonde hair and green eyes come from my mom, but I'm built like my dad and both of my brothers, right down to the confident smile. Both Jason and Christian look almost identical to my dad with their blue eyes and brown hair, although Christian's hair is much lighter with his natural blonde highlights. When the three of us are together, there's no mistaking we're related, although I'm the shortest of all us boys at five-feet, ten-inches. "Hi, Dad," I greet him, waiting for the lecture.

"Welcome home." He smiles and gives me a quick hug with a firm pat on the back. He tugs the sleeve on my t-shirt up, before looking down at me arching his eyebrows in question.

"I got it last fall," I offer them as my explanation. He just shakes his head, gives me a familiar look of disappointment before he walks out the door towards my truck, passing by Christian. I heave a sigh feeling defeated. "I like it, Mom. I'm sorry I didn't tell you until now, though."

"You didn't tell me," she reminds me. "You probably wouldn't have said anything at all if I didn't see it," she admonishes. She grimaces, always hating to be angry with any of us. I know the moment she gives in as she opens her arms wide with an exaggerated sigh. I step into them and give her a big hug. "I guess if you like it, I'll deal with it," she groans in resignation. "I'm just really glad you're finally home Matthew," she whispers, sounding slightly choked up.

I swallow the lump in my throat with her words. For my sister, my brothers and me, home has always been where our parents were living, not necessarily a specific place. I'm the only one that was still living more than an hour away since Theresa moved home after her accident. "I'm glad I'm here too," I murmur.

My mom's forehead wrinkles with worry as she asks, "You don't have any more you didn't tell us about do you?"

I chuckle and shake my head, insisting, "No, Mom. I promise." I watch as she breathes a sigh of relief. I give her another quick squeeze before I step out of her embrace. "Thanks Mom." I appreciate they didn't blow up at me like they would've if I were still in high school, or maybe they still would've if it were before Theresa's accident. Everything changed after that happened. Either way, I'm grateful for their reaction. I'm not about to explain I got it when I lost a bet with one of my friends down in Texas. I really do like it, and I've actually contemplated another one. I just haven't gone through with it yet.

I step around my brother and pass by my dad on the way out to get more things out of my truck. It doesn't take long for us to finish. I'm just closing up my truck as Jason pulls into the driveway with his girlfriend, Sara. He steps out and gives me the same brotherly hug and pat on the back as Christian. "Welcome home, Matt!"

"Thanks, Jason. Did you plan to get here right when we finished unloading?" I ask with a quirk of my eyebrow.

He smirks. "Nah, just had something important to do before we came."

I shake my head, laughing as I step over to a blushing Sara to give her a hug. "Good to see you, Sara."

"Thanks, Matt, you too. Welcome home," she stammers, her eyes narrowing on Jason.

"You know I'm a couple years younger than Jason, and better looking too," I flash her my best smile, "and I know how to treat a girl right," I tease.

She giggles and shakes her head while Jason glares at me. "I'm here two minutes and already you're hitting on my girl and annoying the shit out of me."

I chuckle in response. "That's what brothers are for," I claim, grinning playfully.

He grabs Sara's hand and walks towards the house. I'm about to follow when Theresa and her boyfriend Jax pull in the driveway right behind Jason's truck. I release a sigh and walk over to my little sister as she steps out of the car. I immediately wrap her up in a tight hug, lifting her off the ground. "It's good to see you, T." After her accident, I admit it's always a relief to see her. "At least this time you're not climbing your boyfriend in front of me," I joke, trying to cover my emotions.

She blushes and shoves at my chest. "Matt, put me down!" I set her on her feet with a grin covering my face. "Welcome home!" She smiles at me and shakes her head at the same time.

I turn to her boyfriend, Jax. "Good to see you again."

He smiles and offers me his hand. "You too, Matt."

We shake hands as Christian steps up to us. "Did I just hear something about climbing? Pretty sure that's not in your job description, T," he teases her, and she blushes again. We all love to give each other a hard time, but I have to admit, I probably do it more than anyone with Christian right behind me. After all, he is younger than me, even if it's only by a year. "Do you mind moving your car, Jax? I'm going to take Jason's truck to go pick up Bree since everyone is here and we're done with moving Matt's shit back in."

Jax nods his head and slides back into his car. I wrap my arm around Theresa and walk with her towards the front porch. "How have you been feeling?" I ask sincerely.

"I'm doing great, Matt. The only days I seem to be sore are when it's cold or rainy outside." I tilt my head to the side and assess her closely, hoping she's telling me the truth. "I promise," she adds with a small smile.

"Jax is good to you?" I prod, observing her face for the truth.

She blushes again and my jaw twitches. Her reaction tells me more than I want to know. She nods her head and smiles, her eyes lighting up. "He's really good to me."

I sigh. "Okay, T."

"Do I really get to see all of my brothers in tuxes in a couple weeks?" she asks giddily. My head drops back, and I groan in response, making her laugh. By the time we reach the front door, Jax is right behind us, and we all step inside.

Theresa and Jax walk in first. They turn and stride through the second doorway on the left towards the kitchen, where we can hear our parents talking. Instead of following them, I walk straight ahead towards the back of the house. Just beyond the foyer sits a large, open living room with high ceilings. The whole room is covered in old wood with a massive stone fireplace against the wall near the center of the room. The entire wall of the house facing the lake is covered with windows from the ceiling down to the floor giving us an incredible view with a lot of memories.

I step up to the windows and look out at the green in front of me running down to the lake; the lake that always reminds me of *her*. I wonder if she still lives here. I wonder if they have kids now. I close my eyes and sigh, the familiar painful ache in my chest returning as it tends to do when my mind drifts to the memory of seeing her with her husband. Then again, she never knew she was anything to me; at least that's what I always told her. I grimace at the thought, regret weighing heavily on my chest.

"Matt! Are you coming?" Christian yells from only a few steps away, hand in hand with Bree.

"Hi, Bree," I greet, striding up to her and giving her a quick hug.

"Hi, Matt. Are you okay?" she asks hesitantly, giving me a strange look.

I nod, insisting, "Yeah, I'm great. What's up?"

Christian chuckles, informing me, "Mom has been calling you to dinner."

"Oh, okay," I mumble, shrugging. "It's been a long couple days," I throw out, trying to excuse my behavior. I turn and stalk past them. We stroll into the connecting dining room with a large oak dining table as I try to shake my thoughts away. I sit on the opposite side I normally do, facing the connecting kitchen so I don't have to look at the lake. Theresa and my mom both narrow their eyes, looking at me curiously, but everyone else ignores me.

I laugh humorlessly and grumble inaudibly, "Nothing ever changes."

Chapter 2

Sadie

5 years ago...

I glance down at my phone and notice I only have a few minutes before my best friend, Micah, will be here to pick me up. We're going down to the lake to swim and enjoy a bonfire with a bunch of our friends. There's a perfect spot for swimming near an old bridge. It's on the way out of town, so there's not a lot of traffic. It's both a little grassy and sandy near the beach area. A rope swing hangs from a giant oak tree I choose to believe has been there forever. The tree has large branches hanging over the water and we all use it to jump in. My favorite part about this spot, though, is probably that we're able to light a small bonfire without any problems. I love relaxing in front of a fire.

I take one last look in the mirror, assessing myself. I'm wearing a white bikini which contrasts great with my black hair and a faded pair of very frayed jean shorts making me wonder if they're getting shorter by the minute. I pull on a pair of white sneakers, so it's easier to walk on the trail by the bridge down to the beach. I think I've slipped down the trail every time I've worn sandals or flip-flops. I apply some red lip-gloss and throw it in my backpack just as the doorbell rings. "Sadie, Micah is here!" my mom calls down the hall.

"Coming!" I yell back. I slide my phone into the side pocket of my backpack and throw the strap over my shoulder. I hurry out to the living room where Micah stands talking with my dad. "Ready?" I ask Micah without preamble.

He turns towards me and his eyes grow wide as a slow grin covers his face. He quickly schools his features with my dad standing in front of him and I have to hold back my laugh. Micah is a good-looking guy, but he's not my boyfriend. We're just friends. He's my best friend, but we're just friends. He probably looks like my brother when we're walking side by side. We both have black hair, blue eyes and with our Italian skin we both tan easily. "Hey, Sade," he mumbles.

I smile. "Hi, Micah. Let's go!" I urge, grabbing onto his hand and heading for the door. He chuckles and lets me drag him. "Bye, Mom! Bye, Dad!"

"Have Fun!" my mom proclaims, waving us away.

"Be good!" my dad demands just as we walk out the door and Micah closes it behind him.

"In a hurry?" Micah asks. I just smile in response and walk to his silver Toyota Corolla. He laughs and opens the passenger door for me. He drops my hand as I slide into the car. By the time I buckle my seat belt, he's backing out of my parents' driveway. "You look good, Sade."

"Thanks, Micah." I grin, knowing what's coming next.

"You know you could always change your mind and stay here for college. I don't know about being so far away from my future wife," he teases.

I laugh. "You know I'm not staying here or marrying you."

He grips his chest like he's in pain. "That really hurts!" I shake my head at his antics. "Besides, I know you'll change your mind one day. Since we were meant to be and all," he claims. He smirks making me laugh. Pulling the car off to the side of the road, he parks on the grass just before the bridge. I jump out of the car with my backpack and wait for Micah to grab his things out of the back. He walks over to me with his backpack thrown over his shoulder and wraps his other arm around me. "Let's go celebrate graduation a little early," he announces, grinning. Tilting his head down, he kisses the side of my head.

He drops his arm and jogs down the trail in front of me to greet his friends. I move down the trail much slower, hoping I don't fall this time. My toe catches on a rock, causing me to trip just before I make it to the bottom. I ungraciously flail my arms and stutter step to catch myself just before I land on my face. "Are you okay?" an unfamiliar deep voice rumbles, giving me chills.

I look up to find the owner of the sexy voice and my breath hitches when my eyes meet the brightest green eyes I've ever seen. "Um, I...I'm...I'm okay. Um, thank you," I stutter as I blatantly stare at the guy standing in front of me. He pushes his blonde hair away from his eyes as he grins at me. "I'm just a little clumsy sometimes," I murmur and smile up at him. The top of my head barely reaches his shoulders, but I am barely over five feet, so that's not saying much. My eyes drift down to my eye level, finding his broad chest on display. He's standing in nothing but a long, dark blue bathing suit. I've never seen abs like his on any of the boys I know. He clears his throat and my eyes dart back to his face to find him smirking at me. I feel my face instantly heat with embarrassment.

"Coming Sade?" Micah calls. I peer around the guy standing in front of me. He turns to follow my gaze as well before his eyes come back to me narrowing slightly.

"Um, yeah," I stammer. I move to step around the guy to follow Micah, but he doesn't budge an inch, blocking the end of the path. "Excuse me," I say and smile politely with my heart pounding erratically inside my chest.

He grins and takes one step back holding his arm out for me. "Of course, Sade."

Goosebumps cover my body when I hear my nickname cross his lips. I look up at him, my eyebrows drawing together in confusion. "Do I know you?" I would think I'd remember meeting a guy like him.

~ 26 ~

He chuckles and shakes his head. "Not yet." My eyes narrow further and he quickly explains himself, "Your boyfriend just called you Sade."

I slowly release my breath, and without thinking, I blurt, "He's not my boyfriend."

His eyebrows rise in doubt as his eyes flick over to Micah and then return to me. He probes, "Does he know that?"

I ignore his question and inform him, "My name is Sadie."

The corners of his mouth curve up further as he rumbles, "Matt."

"I haven't seen you before. Are you from around here Matt?" I ask curiously. He looks older than me. Maybe I've just never seen him.

He shakes his head. "Nah, I'm just here visiting some family for the summer." I nod my head in understanding. We're always meeting tourists around here, especially in the summer. "How about you?" he prods.

I nod in confirmation. "Yeah." I gesture to the people behind him. "Most of the people here are graduating high school with me next week."

"Ah, so I stumbled onto a celebration of sorts," he states, grinning and making my heart skip a beat.

I shrug, mumbling, "I guess. It's a great place to hang out. We'll probably get a bonfire going in a couple hours," I tell him hoping he'll stay, but I'm not sure why. That's a lie. I want him to stay so I can stare at him some more. The boys I know aren't built like him.

"Are you inviting me?" he asks playfully.

I shrug, trying to act nonchalant when Micah's arm drapes over my shoulder startling me. "Come on, Sade," he grumbles and kisses me on the cheek. "You're too slow," he complains.

I blush and allow Micah to drag me away. "Stay," I call out to Matt, very aware his eyes remain on me.

He cocks his head to the side, glances at Micah and then back to me again. *"Maybe I will."* I grin and turn around stumbling slightly. I hear Matt's chuckle behind me as Micah helps me remain on my feet.

Micah and I walk over to our friends and we both toss our bags on the sand. *"I'm going to jump in,"* Micah announces. *"Anyone want to come?"*

I shake my head no, as I simultaneously hear a string of, *"Yes's."* Both guys and girls jump up and head to the lake, following Micah like always. I sigh and pull my pink and white striped towel out of my backpack. Shaking it out, I lay it down on the sand in an open spot.

Kari sits up on her towel and gives me a small wave. *"Hi, Sadie. Did you just get here?"* she asks.

I smile, confirming, *"Yeah. Were you asleep again?"*

"I didn't get much sleep last night and it's just so comfortable here," she claims, grinning sheepishly. *"Is Micah with you?"* she prods, looking around like she's searching for him.

I grin knowingly. Everyone always wants to be around Micah. He's the guy every girl chases. He's smart, athletic, handsome and charming, but I don't tell him that. He's confident enough without an ego boost from me. I'm really the only girl he's ever been loyal to, but the girls around here keep trying, hoping they'll be the one to tie him down. *"Yeah, he's already in the lake,"* I answer. Micah's howl echoes across the water as he jumps from the rope swing, making me laugh as I flop down on my towel. I lean back on my hands and stare out at my classmates swimming in the lake.

"I think I'm going in," Kari announces as she walks towards the water.

A gentle nudge to my shoulder is my only notice as Matt sits down next to me. He pulls his knees up and loosely wraps his arms around them, linking his fingers in front of his knees. *"You don't want to swim with your friends?"* he prompts.

"You stayed," I state the obvious, ignoring his question.

He chuckles softly. *"A beautiful girl asked me to. How could I say no?"* I feel myself blush and I take a deep breath, attempting to shake it off.

"You're here for the whole summer?" I ask again for clarification.

He nods his head, his lips twitching in amusement. *"Yeah, I'm just visiting. I leave to go back to college mid-August."*

"Where do you go to school?" I inquire.

"Baylor," he informs me.

"That's in Texas, right?" I prod. He nods in confirmation, giving me a crooked smile. *"Very cool. Do you like it?"*

"Yeah, it's a great school and good friends help too," he declares, nodding. *"What about you? What are your plans after celebrating your graduation?"*

I giggle. *"I'm starting at Johns Hopkins University in the fall. I leave around mid-August too,"* I enlighten him.

He glances over at me, his eyes widening in appreciation; I assume for my choice of school. Butterflies take flight in my stomach with the way he assesses me, my whole body warming from the inside out. *"Congratulations,"* he proclaims. *"It's a wonderful school and beautiful campus, too."*

"Have you been there?" I ask.

He nods, elaborating, *"I used to visit family there."*

"You seem to have family everywhere," I joke.

His smile wavers as he answers, *"Yeah, something like that."* I study his strong profile as he stares out at the lake and feel a need to cheer him up. He sighs and asks casually, *"So, Sadie, what do you guys do around here for fun in the summer?"* I smile and gesture towards the lake. He chuckles in response, the sound causing goosebumps to erupt over my skin. "Well, what do you say about maybe showing a tourist around sometime?" he proposes casually. "To maybe pass the time before you leave?"

"You mean me show you around?" I squeak, my eyes widening in surprise. He laughs wholeheartedly, making his green eyes sparkle and causing my breath to hitch at the gorgeous sight. He nods his head in affirmation, grinning. "Sure," I reply, trying not to sound too excited. "Is there something you want to do?"

He shakes his head. "Nah, I'm just looking for a beautiful girl to hang out with once in a while. I figured I'd ask instead of taking my chances trying to chase you down at this swimming hole next time."

I laugh and shake my head. "Sounds like just what I need," I finally admit.

"Really?" he asks doubtfully.

I purse my lips and narrow my eyes, curious as to just how much he's asking for, but the anxious feeling I have in my belly makes me feel like I have to take advantage of the time he's offering. Micah will work a lot anyway. Plus, there's just something about this guy smirking playfully in front of me. I want to spend time with him even though I have no idea who he is. I might as well enjoy my last summer here. It will be over soon.

"So, you said you're visiting family?" I prompt and he nods his head in confirmation. "Are they from around here?" I question, trying to figure out if I might know them.

"Nope..." he mumbles dragging out the word and popping his p. Then he laughs and gives me an easy smile. "No pressure, Sadie. I'm just looking for a friend to hang out with once in a while. You seem like someone who might know their way around, so I don't have to drive around aimlessly looking for something to do."

"You don't want to ask one of the guys?" I question stupidly.

He laughs loudly, the amazing sound echoing through my insides, giving me chills from the inside out and causing me to blush. "I'd rather ask you," he admits, grinning. "But if you're not interested..." he trails off.

I answer on reflex, "I'm interesting, I mean interested, I mean..." I pinch my lips tightly together and look away as his laughter again heats me from the inside out. I roll my eyes and smirk at him trying to pretend I'm unaffected by him when it's so obvious that I am. "I mean, I'd be happy to show you around and be forced to hang out with you."

His smile grows and his green eyes sparkle with mischief like they're trying to verify he's trouble for me. Then again, I don't really need any more proof of that. All I have to do is look at him and I know I'm in trouble.

A soaked Micah suddenly ambushes me, making me shriek. He picks me up and throws me over his shoulder. I scream louder as I try to get away. "If you want your shorts to stay dry, I'd start shimmying your cute ass out of them right now," he warns and smacks my ass. "Just checking for your phone," he jokes in explanation.

"Micah," I screech, "Put me down!" He just laughs, ignoring my request as he hauls me towards the water. I immediately wiggle out of my shorts and kick them to the ground, knowing he's not about to stop. Seconds later, his feet hit the water, and he pulls us both under. I come up laughing and squeal, "It's freezing!" I splash Micah, then cross my arms over my chest, knowing white isn't the best color to get wet, but I didn't think I was going swimming today. I shake my head at him, trying to decide what I should do when my eyes drift to where Matt is now standing with his arms crossed watching me with Micah. His protective stance makes my stomach flip and I immediately try to shake it off. "We have to start the fire now," I insist. "I'm freezing!"

Micah laughs, "I wanted you to play with the rest of us." I glare at him, and he chuckles, "Well I wanted you to *play with me," he grins flirtatiously, and I roll my eyes. He kisses my cheek and smiles. "I'll go start the fire for you, Sade."*

I follow him out of the water, keeping my arms across my chest and go straight for my towel. Matt remains standing right where I left him, holding my towel up for me. I quickly step into it and wrap it around me. "Thank you," I chatter.

He rubs my arms up and down quickly to help warm me up. "You look like you just did the Polar Bear Plunge. The water wasn't that bad," he claims, grinning.

"I get cold easily," I explain, grimacing. He chuckles and my eyes snap to his. My body instantly warms with the look he gives me. "You're trouble," I mumble inaudibly.

"What?" he asks innocently.

I shake my head. "Nothing. I just think it's going to be a fun summer," I proclaim instead.

He grins, his green eyes shimmering as he agrees with me.

Chapter 3

Matt

Present Day...

"Aren't you sick of this place?" I ask my brother Jason as I accept a mug of beer from him.

He laughs and shrugs, nonchalant. "I don't really work here anymore. Jax is here more than I am," he adds, gesturing back towards the bar.

I put my hand up in greeting to acknowledge my sister Theresa's boyfriend working behind the bar. "At least I don't have to watch you trying to jump him again with him back there," I tease, making Theresa blush.

"We were alone and fully clothed," she attempts to defend herself.

I grimace. "We all know that doesn't mean anything, T!" Both Christian and Jason grumble in agreement. "And you obviously weren't alone, or I wouldn't have that horrible image burned into my head," I add as if I'm in pain. She glares and sticks her tongue out at me, making me chuckle.

"Ugh, I can't hear anymore about T doing dirty things with Jax or I'll lose my damn mind," Christian groans.

"I wasn't doing dirty things!" she tries to clarify. We all ignore her, and she huffs and groans in annoyance, crossing her arms over her chest.

"Let's hear about what happened in Texas instead," Christian prods, smirking at me. "I thought things were going well down there for you. Then, all of a sudden, you finally take us up on our offer to move back and help us out with the business full time."

My brothers started a local recreational business. They offer different activities to people throughout the year, such as kayaking, paddle boarding, hiking, snowmobiling, fishing, cross-country skiing for groups, families, or individuals. They also offer limited instruction, training and education depending on the activity, and act as guides on trails or in the water since they know the area in all four seasons. Fortunately, they've been doing really well, and they asked me to come back and help with both their marketing, which is my specialty, and out in the field. "I know you missed us, but…" he trails off, waiting for me to fill in the blank.

I groan in aggravation, not wanting to talk about it. Theresa adds, "I'm guessing it has something to do with the mysterious Natalie who never wanted to meet us."

Clenching my jaw, I cringe at her assessment, knowing I have to give them something or they'll never stop harassing me. I heave a sigh and take another sip of my beer before I relent to their questions. "It's not that she didn't want to meet you exactly, it's that I didn't want her to meet you," I clarify, hastily stuffing a French fry in my mouth.

I watch as three sets of eyes narrow on me instantly. Jason crosses his arm and leans back in his chair giving me his intimidating big brother pose. "Talk, Matt," he demands.

Heaving another sigh, I drop the fries from my hand. I look down at the table to gather my thoughts, before bringing my eyes back to them, knowing they're all growing impatient with me. "I don't know," I grunt with frustration. "She may have been my girlfriend, but it was never serious for me. For lack of a better word or phrase, I guess she was like a placeholder for me," I attempt to explain.

"What?" Theresa gasps in horror, dropping her hands to the table. Ignoring her, I glance at Christian, knowing if anyone will understand this, it's him.

His expression turns soft instantly, now more curious than anything, but he remains quiet, waiting for me to continue. I shake my head at Theresa's exasperation. "Don't feel bad for her, T. She used me a hell of a lot worse than I used her. She always knew where she stood with me." Her glare turns more furious, and she crosses her arms again like she doesn't believe me. I groan, knowing I have to explain myself a little better. I don't ever want T thinking I'm an asshole to women. "Let's put it this way," I begin, ready to throw any positive image of Natalie away, "she was screwing one of our full-time clients. I walked in for a meeting I thought I was invited to, along with another one of our colleagues. I guess they thought they had more time before everyone showed up or they just didn't care." I shrug like it doesn't matter. "I walked out and turned in my resignation. It was time anyway."

"What?" Theresa gasps, her mouth now sitting open in both shock and disgust.

I try to comfort her, insisting, "It's fine, T. I'm better off. I knew it would never go anywhere with her. Now all of you get to enjoy my company," I tease, fanning my hands out. I need to lighten the mood somehow.

"Sorry, man," Jason concedes. I nod my head in acceptance. I glance over at Christian, finding him still eyeing me thoughtfully. With the way I worded that, he knows there's more to the story, but I'm not ready to talk about *her* yet with all of my siblings. I'd share a little with Christian because I know he'll understand, but not with everyone yet. Jason's too perfect and Theresa will just tell me how I messed up and how to fix it, but this can't be fixed. Luckily, Christian doesn't ask me anything else before I'm able to change the subject.

"So, how about a toast?" I propose, raising my glass.

"It's your turn," Jason reminds me.

I nod as my siblings hold their glasses up and wait for me to continue. "Here's to the ones we love, here's to the ones who love us. If the ones we love don't love us, then fuck them and here's to us." I grin and take a drink of my beer.

My brothers chuckle, shaking their heads in amusement, while Theresa rolls her eyes at me, but they all drink along with me despite what they may think. "Where'd you hear that one? I admit it kind of works for you at the moment," Jason states, smirking.

"Some hot girls I used to hang out with all the time in college. They would say it quite a bit and it kinda' stuck," I confess.

"So what's the plan for next weekend, Christian?" Jason questions as he sets down his beer.

Christian finally looks away from studying me as he answers, "We're going to have a combined bachelor and bachelorette party at 51 Wharf Nightclub here in Portland. Bree has been asking me to go check it out with her and go dancing, so we figured it would be the perfect time. Are you going to be okay with that T?" he asks, suddenly worried. Theresa used to dance growing up and then she was on a dance team as she got older. She loved it. After her accident, she has not only stayed away from dancing, but she has also had trouble watching other people dance.

She smiles shyly and nods. "Jax has been encouraging me to dance more. We've gone out dancing a couple times now," she admits. "Nothing crazy, but we've been having fun." She grins anxiously around at all of us, awaiting our reactions.

"That's great, T!" Jason and I exclaim at the same time.

Christian looks at her like a proud father, but they always were really close. We all are, but since they're the youngest, they were the last two to leave the house. "I'm so happy for you, T," he declares, grinning.

She looks down at the table and then over towards the bar to search out Jax. We all know that's probably her sign, asking us to change the subject, so Christian does exactly that. "We reserved a VIP area for our group. Then, we can all stay at either my place or Jason or T's. A couple of the girls will sleep at Bree's place," Christian continues.

"Why are you combining them?" I inquire, more curious than anything.

"We've been through enough. We don't really need this. We just figured it would be a fun night to hang out with close friends and family," he explains. "Plus, Bree needs a break before the wedding with finals and graduating and everything else. This way, I won't be the only one making sure she actually relaxes. I don't want her to get too stressed out!"

"So, it's not a lot of people?" I probe inquisitively.

"Nah, all of us, Jax, Blake, my roommates Joe and Dean. Then Bree also invited Sara and Blake's girlfriend Liz, of course, as well as a couple girls she's worked with at the gift shop in town up at the lake and Amy," he adds, grimacing. Christian briefly dated Amy when him and Bree were broken up, not realizing her connection to Bree. It's uncomfortable for everyone sometimes, but they do what they can to get along for Bree.

I nod my head, mumbling, "Sounds good." I pat my full stomach and stretch my arms above my head. "Well, I'm going to head back to mom and dad's since I'm the only one that has to drive back to the lake tonight. Thanks for dinner big brother," I declare, giving Jason a crooked smile.

He shakes his head, mumbling, "I'm not buying dinner."

"Sure you are," I insist. "At least you are for me," I clarify. "I know how much you want to welcome home your brother that's been away on and off for the past six years," I state, smirking.

He shakes his head at me, but sighs, letting me know he already conceded. "Welcome home, Matt," he grumbles. I give him a pat on the back and Theresa stands to give me a hug.

I walk over to Christian, and he stands. "I'll walk out with you. I have a question," he adds.

"I'm not paying for you, too," Jason complains.

Christian waves him off and walks towards the door calling, "I'll be back."

I trudge out the door after him as I wave goodbye to Jax behind the bar. I make it to my truck without him saying a word, but I'm prepared to answer him now. "Who is she?" he asks simply.

I swallow the lump forming in my throat. "I don't know," I respond. His eyes narrow, calling me on my bullshit answer. I heave a sigh, elaborating, "It's not like you and Bree. We hung out a few times. I don't even know her last name," I admit, laughing somberly. I shake my head, disgusted with myself. "For some fucked up reason, I couldn't forget about her, but she sure as hell didn't miss me when I was gone. She didn't wait for me. She moved on, so it wasn't mutual. It doesn't matter," I add.

"How do you know?" he implores.

"Because she married someone else," I utter, feeling like I just stabbed myself in the chest. Christian winces and I laugh humorlessly. "It's okay. I'm not meant for a happily ever after. Place holders work just fine for me."

"Matt, you can't..." he begins, before immediately trailing off. I remember what he was like without Bree. He knows better than anyone how I'm feeling. He won't try to change my mind. He sighs in resignation, mumbling, "I'm sorry, Matt."

I nod my head slowly in acceptance. Taking a deep breath, I pat him on the back. "I'll see you next weekend, Christian." I step towards my truck without another word from my brother.

The drive back is dark and depressing. I pull into the local market so I can grab a few beers and some snacks to bring back to the house on the way. "I need a life," I grumble to myself as I step out of my truck.

I stride across the parking lot and pull the door open as a woman is exiting with two large bags full of groceries. "Thank you," she murmurs softly as she looks up. Shocking, yet familiar, blue-gray eyes meet mine with a gasp. My heart stops and restarts as I struggle for breath. "Matt," she huffs as if in pain just as all her groceries tumble to the ground.

The fallen groceries startle me into action. I crouch down and begin picking up her food and returning it to one of the bags. I slowly rise with the bag in my arms, taking her in. She's more gorgeous than ever. She's still petite with curves in all the right places. She has her long black hair twisted up on top of her head with several loose strands falling around her face. Her skin appears so soft and delicate with her rosy cheeks. Her blue-grey eyes stare back at me, wide-eyed, jolting me to the core with their contrasting intensity. "How are you, Sadie?" I ask, my voice sounding much stronger than I feel.

"I…I'm fine," she replies, her voice cracking. At least I know I'm not the only one affected by this unexpected run-in, even if it will do so much more damage to me when I have to walk away.

We stare at one another for a few moments, not knowing what to say or do, when I notice tears form in her eyes, catching me off guard. To save both of us from anything further, I know I need to escape. "Let me help you bring these to your car," I stammer and turn back towards the parking lot. "Which one is yours?" I inquire, looking over the cars in the lot.

She appears like she's about to argue, then changes her mind. She shakily points to a green Volkswagen Jetta and stiffly walks towards it. When she reaches the car, she fumbles with her keys. I grab the other grocery bag from her to give her another free hand, but she continues to stare at the keys in her hand like her life depends on it.

She finally mumbles, "Thank you," as if the words cause her pain. Her hands tremble as she unlocks the door and pulls the back door open.

She takes a step back for me to set the groceries inside the car. Crouching down, I place them on the seat, flinching at the sight of a car seat on the other side of the car. I clear my throat and stand up straight, slamming the door shut. "Drive home safe," I mumble, offering her nothing but a stiff smile.

I spin on my heel and stride quickly back to the entrance of the store, trying to remember my reason for coming. "Matt," she calls, sounding desperate, just before I reach the door.

My steps falter, but I keep going without turning around. I storm through the market as quickly as possible. I reach for some chips, pretzels, and a case of beer to have just in case. I throw my money at the cashier, probably scaring the poor girl half to death if the look on her face is anything to go by. I stride out to my truck, scowling at the now empty parking space where her car sat only moments ago.

"She's still here," I mutter. "She's still here and she not only has a husband, she also probably has a kid." I hit the steering wheel hard with an open palm three times before I drop my forehead to the same spot in defeat. I've never regretted not giving a girl more until Sadie came along. With her, I wish I had done everything differently, but by the time I figured it out, it was already too late. If I have to run into her all the time knowing I can't have her, I no longer know how long I'll be staying here.

I sigh and start my truck. I lift my head, suddenly feeling completely drained. I back out of the parking lot and turn right onto the nearly black country road towards my parents' house. I think it's time to look for a place of my own again because I don't want to be around anyone right now. There's too much going on and my mom will ask too many questions just before she'll try to fix everything.

Unfortunately, she can't fix anything this time.

Chapter 4

Sadie

"I can't believe Matt's back", I mumble to myself as I stare at my son. He's pushing a red matchbox car along the wood floor and crashing it repeatedly into the legs of our old pine coffee table, making appropriate sounds as he goes. He's a beautiful, almost four-year-old boy, who received nearly all his looks from his father. He has wavy blonde hair, bright green eyes and a smile that melts my heart every single time I see it light up his face. Unfortunately, I also feel guilty every time I look at him because he doesn't have a father. I wish more than anything I had done things differently but wishing won't make it come true. My heart aches, sending the pain up my throat and into my gut. I sigh, knowing I'll probably never be rid of it.

As I watch him play, I let my mind wander to the first time Matt kissed me…

5 years ago

"Hey Sade," Micah stalks into my room and flops down onto my bed. I watch his eyes widen through my mirror as I finish brushing my hair. He whistles low and deep. "Where are you going?" Micah asks. "Thought we had plans."

I turn to him with a guilty smile. "I was hoping we could reschedule. I promised that guy, Matt, I'd show him around." His eyes narrow on me, making me roll mine. "He's only here for the summer Micah."

"Yeah, but so are you," he emphasizes as he sits up on the edge of my bed. "When will you have time for me?" he prods softly. I feel an overwhelming sense of guilt at his words.

Taking a deep breath, I gulp down the lump in my throat. "You're right, I'm sorry. You can come with us," I offer, taking a step towards him.

He chortles. "I don't need a pity offer Sade."

"It's not a pity offer! You're my best friend!" I defend.

He sighs and runs his hand through his dark hair. "It's fine. I can go catch up with the guys or something. We'll do something tomorrow?" he prompts, arching his eyebrows in question. "I have to work the day after that."

I nod immediately. "Of course!"

He looks at me critically, grimacing. "Are you sure you want to wear that dress?"

My eyebrows scrunch together, and I screech, "What's wrong with my dress?" I look down at the sunset orange sundress that flares at my waist.

"Nothing, except maybe it's a little short," he teases and pinches me in the back of the thigh. I smack his hand away and he laughs. As his laughter subsides, he looks up at me with resignation. "You look hot. Just be careful. You don't know anything about this guy!"

"That's why I'm meeting him in town," I inform him.

"I still don't like it," he protests with a grimace, "but have fun and call me if you need anything!"

"I will, I promise," I concede, grinning. I roll my eyes, pretending I'm annoyed with him.

Sighing, he shakes his head and pushes off my bed with a smirk. He quickly wraps me in his arms. "Be safe! I love you," he adds and kisses me on my cheek before he stalks back out of my room.

Grabbing my car keys, I stride towards the front door. "Bye Mom," I call as an afterthought. I hear her *distracted goodbye just as I pull the front door shut. It's only a few minutes before I pull up to the bookstore and combination coffee shop in town.*

Climbing out of my car, I shut the door and walk inside, immediately spotting Matt sitting at a table eyeing a book about Maine. He moves to turn the page and glances towards the door. His eyes begin returning to the book when they quickly snap back up and meet mine. The pages flip closed as he smiles wide, taking my breath away. He pushes the chair back, taking two long strides to meet me. "Hi," I whisper shyly.

His grin grows as he mumbles, "Hi, Sadie." His eyes roam over me quickly from head to toe, making me blush. "You look beautiful," he whispers with awe.

"Thank you," I reply, playing with the hem of my dress. Of course, since Micah mentioned the length, I'm self-conscious about it because what teenage boy doesn't like girls in short dresses? I decide to change the subject instead. I gesture to the Maine tourism book still in his hand. "Thought I was going to stand you up?"

He laughs, making my chest tingle with warmth. "Nah, but it's always good to have a back-up plan," he jokes.

"Well, you have already seen most of it." I shrug, teasing him right back. "You've seen the swimming hole and now you've seen Main Street. I guess there's nothing left for me to do."

His eyes sparkle with mirth as he takes a step closer to me and says breathily, "I guess that means we can get to the good part of tonight."

He traps me in his green eyes momentarily. My breath speeds up and I feel the rise and fall of my chest. "Um, I..." I stammer. I shake my head and take a step back to pull myself together. He chuckles softly, but I ignore him. I clear my throat and try again, "Actually, there's live music outside at the clam bar tonight. I figured we could walk through town first. There are a lot of great little shops. Then we could go check it out."

"Is that the place with the outdoor bar and seating by the water?" he inquires. I nod my head in confirmation, and he smiles. "That sounds good."

I feel myself relax with his agreement and smile back at him. "So, are you ready?" I prompt.

He glances back at the table he was just seated at, holding only the book about Maine. Then he looks back at me with a shrug. Holding his hand out, he gestures for me to walk in front of him and I do, pulling at my hem as I go. He smacks my hands away, making me gasp. I spin on him, my face instantly going red. He smirks, claiming, "You were obstructing my view." I raise my eyebrows and my mouth drops slightly open, taken aback by his forward demeanor. He just laughs in response before walking in front of me and sauntering out the door with a swagger as I watch him go.

Shaking myself out of my stupor, I catch up to him. Glancing at me, he teases, "See, if I had my hands covering my ass, you wouldn't have been able to ogle me." I feel my face turn beat red eliciting another chuckle from him. "Relax," he encourages. "I just want to have fun, Sadie. If I'm too much for you to handle, you just let me know."

I square my shoulders and step past him, lightly smacking his ass on the way. I watch his eyes widen in surprise, giving me the courage to add, "Nah, I'm good."

We reach the clam bar quickly without going into any of the stores. I'm thankful for the bluegrass type music flowing throughout the area as I begin fidgeting, not knowing quite what to say to Matt. He's definitely different than the guys I'm used to. I peek up at him and smile when I catch his eyes. "Grab a table anywhere that's open," a waitress calls out as she rushes past us, pulling me out of my head.

Matt gestures for me to lead the way and I go right to a table for two next to the water. "Is this, okay?" I ask him as I sit down. He answers by taking the seat across from me.

"Hope you like seafood," I mumble, trying to think of something to say as I look out at the water. He doesn't reply, and I glance over at him to see if he heard me.

The corner of his mouth twitches up and he nods his head in affirmation. Taking a deep breath, his eyes never waver from mine. He opens his mouth like he's about to say something when our waitress steps up to the table. "Hi, I'm Char. I'll be your waitress tonight. Can I get you anything to drink?"

"I'll just have a Coke," Matt replies, still staring at me.

I tear my eyes away from him and smile nervously. "Hi, Char. Can I have a Diet Coke?"

"Oh, hey, Sadie. I'm sorry, I didn't even see you. Where is Micah and who's your friend?" she prods, throwing Matt a flirty smile.

I blush uncomfortably. "Um, Micah is out with the guys." I glance at Matt who continues watching me intently. "And this is Matt..." I trail off.

He finally turns towards our waitress and grins, making both of us melt. "I'm just Matt."

Char giggles. "Okay, just Matt. I'll go get your drinks." Then she turns and walks towards the bar to do just that.

I look back at Matt and find him still staring at me like he's trying to figure me out. "What?" I ask, trying to keep any exasperation out of my voice.

He sighs and admits, "I'm just trying to figure out what's going on between you and your friend, Micah."

"Nothing is going on with us," I insist. "We're just friends. It's just he's my best friend. We're together a lot," I attempt to explain my relationship with Micah. He nods his head, biting his lower lip in contemplation and still not quite responding. Sighing, I ramble on, "Besides, I'm leaving for college and he's going to college close to home. I won't be seeing much of him after this summer anyway, unless I'm

home on break." I shrug like it's no big deal, but that thought really makes me sad.

"It's okay if there is something. I just don't want to step on any toes. I'm barely here and then I'll be gone," he reminds me. "You probably won't even remember me." He smiles and I can't help but laugh like he's lost his mind. I don't think Matt's the kind of guy who's forgettable. "I just want to have fun, Sadie," he insists again.

I nod my head in agreement. "That's good because like I said, I'll be gone soon too. I don't need anything more than fun this summer." My mouth tastes bitter as the words leave my mouth, but it's the truth because it has to be.

Our waitress steps up and sets our drinks down in front of us. We order steamed clams and two bowls of New England clam chowder. "A beer would really taste good with that," Matt grumbles.

"How old are you?" I ask curiously.

"I'll be twenty this fall," he informs me. "Please tell me you're legal," he jokes.

Grinning, I answer, "I'm eighteen." He smiles, then leans back in his chair, turning towards the source of the music. Two guys, both in jeans and t-shirts playing guitars, belt out a song into their microphones. They sit atop a small raised section on the deck opposite the bar. I haven't really paid much attention with my focus on Matt, but they're pretty good.

A girl with pale blonde hair and creamy, flawless skin, wearing a long white skirt and a black tank top sets a stool down between them. Stealing a microphone from one of the guys with a smile and a kiss, she looks out at the crowd, making me laugh. She closes her eyes and takes a deep breath. When she opens her mouth, a beautiful sound comes out as she sings a beautiful version of "At Last" by Etta James. "I love this song," I mumble to myself.

My view is suddenly blocked as Matt stands in front of me, offering me his hand. I tip my head up and look at him *curiously. He raises his eyebrows and prompts, "Dance with me?"*

I'm not about to say no, so I take his hand and let him pull me up into his arms. He takes a couple of steps away from our table and towards the music as he spins me in his arms, pulling me closer. I rest my hands comfortably between us on his upper chest, just below his shoulders. I'm fully aware of his hard chest under my hands, causing me to struggle as I try to control my breathing. I attempt to gulp down my nerves and peer up at him. He's staring intently at me, his green eyes seeming to grow darker, as my own breathing picks up again. My heart beats in my throat, making it hard to breathe. I think I feel his heart pounding against my fingertips, but that could also be my heartbeat vibrating through every inch of me.

His fingers lightly trail along the bottom of my jaw until they reach my chin where they still and hold me in place. He slowly lowers his head towards mine until our mouths are only inches apart and I can taste his breath mixing with mine. I feel like I might pass out if he doesn't kiss me now. He searches my eyes, asking for permission before barely brushing his lips across mine and making me gasp. In the next moment, his lips crash into mine like he can't wait another second to taste me. His lips are soft and warm as they move with confidence over mine. My entire body floods with heat from my lips to my toes as his kiss nearly shatters me but I'm not quite sure why. I feel the tip of his tongue run over my lips just before he presses his mouth firmly against mine one more time before he pulls away.

He holds me captive in his eyes as we both catch our breath. I want to lean on my toes and kiss him again, but my head reminds me to be careful. I'm leaving soon and so is he. Applause breaks out around us, reminding me of where we are as the song comes to an end. We break away from each other, still breathless, and swiftly return to our table.

Present Day

"Mommy, I'm hungry," Holden whines. He taps me with one of his matchbox cars, snapping me out of my daydreams.

Heaving a sigh, I smile down at my handsome little boy. He will always hold my heart. "Well, I think we better get some food into your tummy then, little man!" He jumps up and runs into the kitchen as fast as his little legs will carry him with a cheer. "He's what's important," I remind myself. I don't have time for anything besides him. Matt coming back can have no bearing on my life.

The time for us has come and gone, no matter how much I want it.

Chapter 5

Matt

Striding through town with my hands stuffed in my pockets and a scowl on my face I can't seem to wipe away, I huff in frustration. I have no idea how I'm ever going to get through the next couple weeks. My brothers and my sister are all so fucking happy and then they look at me with what I can only describe as pity when they realize I'm in the room with them. I don't blame them. And honestly, I am truly happy for them, but it doesn't make it suck any less for me.

I had to get away before any of them said anything else about forgetting Natalie; that she's not worth it. They're absolutely right. She's not worth it. Unfortunately, Natalie is not what eats at me. Regret consumes me, even more since I saw her. I know I should've done things differently back then, but what I know about my mistakes doesn't do a damn thing to help me now.

Sighing in annoyance, I finally lift my head to pull myself out of my depressing thoughts. I need to figure out where I want to go, anyway. I've gone up and down Main Street four times now without even glancing at the stores I'm passing by. I need to buy a wedding gift for Christian and Bree. I want to buy something that will mean something to them instead of just giving them cash. Besides, they didn't want to register for gifts. They decided they already have so many things they use at their house from both her mom and her grandma's deaths, so they didn't want to ask for anything. I guess that's all the more reason I think they deserve something special. It also made for the perfect excuse to escape from the overwhelming happiness at my parents' house for a while.

I turn and open the door to one of the many gift shops in the area. This one describes itself as having a variety of "All things Maine". There's pottery, signs, pictures, clothes, lighthouses, shells, and even a blueberry pantry section. The blueberry syrup quickly became one of my favorite things the first summer I spent here.

Weaving around the displays, I make my way over to items that might be more appropriate for a wedding gift, when a picture hanging on the wall stops me in my tracks. It's a colorful painting of the lake at Sunrise. The view is between a couple evergreen trees with a clear blue sky and the sun just beginning to sparkle off the lake. The only ripples on the surface are from two loons who have popped up from down below. On the slightly rocky shore sits two kayaks with their paddles sticking out, one red and one blue, near a worn wooden dock. Anyone who knows about Christian and Bree's first summer together knows this painting looks as if it was made just for them. It even almost appears like it was painted with the view from Bree's house in mind; the house left to her by her grandmother.

I turn and walk to the register, pulling my wallet out of my back pocket. "I'd like to buy that painting," I tell the gray-haired woman behind the counter as I point to it on the far wall.

She nods her head. "Absolutely. It's beautiful isn't it?" I nod my head in agreement. "It was painted by a local artist too."

Looking up as I hand her my credit card, I open my mouth to ask about the artist, when a startled gasp from behind me causes me to stiffen.

The hairs on the back of my neck stand at attention as I slowly turn around, already knowing whom I'll see. Sadie stands in an aisle filled with hand painted vases staring at me wide-eyed and blushing a deep shade of red. Her dark hair is pulled up in a ponytail with several strands hanging loose. She's wearing kelly-green short-shorts that make her legs look longer than they are, along with a ruffled white tank top. She looks utterly gorgeous. Her skin already has a touch of golden tan with her Italian genes. I can't help but remember how velvety soft it felt under my fingertips. The simple thought makes me drop my head in annoyance with myself. I curl my hand into a fist and grit my teeth, feeling my jaw click.

Taking a deep breath, I avoid looking at Sadie again as I turn my attention back to the saleswoman. "Is there any way you can gift wrap that for me and I can pick it up later today?"

"Oh, of course!" she exclaims. "It's a gift then?"

I give my head a quick nod, mumbling, "Yeah." She hands me back my credit card along with a receipt to sign. I quickly scratch my name across the bottom before giving it back to her. With a kind smile, she hands me my receipt, adding, "Just bring this in when you come in, just in case I'm not the one who's here." I nod again stiffly and stuff the paper into my pocket as I turn to flee.

Keeping my focus on my escape route, I attempt to stalk past Sadie. Reaching for me just as I pass, she calls desperately, "Matt, please wait!" She wraps her hand around my bicep, causing my breath to catch. I instantly halt, struggling to hide my reaction to her. Gritting my teeth again, I turn to her. I let the corner of my mouth pull up in a sneer, raising my eyebrows in question. She blushes an even deeper shade of red and immediately drops her hand from my arm. "I just…I mean we just…I mean can we talk?" she stammers. My mouth drops slightly open and before I respond, she adds, "I just mean that I think we should talk. There's…" she trails off.

Holding my breath, I wait to see if she's going to continue, but when she doesn't, I release my breath and slowly let my smile grow. I cross my arms over my chest, attempting to control my erratic pounding heartbeat. I want to take her up on her offer, but I can't. She's married to someone else. Why in the hell would she want to talk to me now anyway? We may have been the very definition of a summer fling, but I realized too late that wasn't at all what I wanted from her. She may not have a fucking clue, but that doesn't change how I felt about her or the fact that I never met anyone else who made me feel the way she did, and I sure as hell tried. Why would I torture myself by even talking to her when she obviously still has an overwhelming effect on me?

I drag my eyes over her from head to toe and back up again as I watch her squirm uncomfortably. Tilting my head to the side, I finally open my mouth and ask snidely, "Problems at home?" Her face scrunches up adorably in confusion, making me laugh humorlessly. She doesn't need to tell me about him. I don't really want to know. "No worries, *Sade*. We were never really good at talking anyway, were we?" I taunt sarcastically.

A hurt gasp leaves her lips and tears gather in her eyes, bringing an ache to my chest. "I just thought…" she trails off. I watch her Adam's apple bob up and down as she attempts to swallow the obvious lump in her throat, making me feel like complete shit. My fingers itch to grab her and pull her close to me, wrapping her up in my arms to comfort her. Instead, I dig my fingers into my arms, trying to keep them from moving. She shakes her head in disappointment, dismissing me. It feels like my heart drops to my feet and spills right out onto the floor at her feet. "Just forget it Matt. It doesn't matter what I thought," she spits out. Then she spins on her heel and storms past me and out the door.

I drop my hands, feeling like an asshole. I don't want to be that guy, especially not with her. The last thing I need is something else to regret. I quickly rush out the door and follow behind her. "Sadie, wait! I'm sorry," I plead. Her steps slow and I repeat my apology, "I'm sorry. Please don't run away from me again," I beg. When she doesn't reply, or stop moving, I continue, "Besides, it looks like we might run into each other now that I live around here. It would probably make it easier on all of us if we could be civil. I'm really sorry."

My words finally make her freeze. I watch as she rigidly turns around, looking both cautious and slightly terrified. She catches my eyes and clarifies with evident shock, "You're not just visiting family this time? You live here now?"

Gulping nervously at her reaction, I don't take my eyes off her as I nod my head and admit, "Yeah. I just moved last week." I watch as her hands begin trembling and her face turns a ghastly white. "Are you okay?" I prod, confused by her reaction.

She shakes her head and then changes her movements to nod. "Um, yeah. I'm okay. I'm fine. I'm good. I'm great. I just...I um...I just have to go," she rambles, obviously flustered by my news. "We'll talk later. It will be fine. You're fine. I'm fine. I mean..." she trails off with a wince, and I notice her eyes fill with more tears.

I take a step towards her, my heart aching for her, yet I'm not even sure what's going on. "Sadie," I choke out her name. I need her to tell me what's wrong. Is it me or is it something else? Or maybe it's someone else? Maybe I hit a nerve asking her about trouble at home? Or maybe it's just a bad day? She shakes her head vehemently and puts her hand up to block me from coming any closer to her. Without saying another word, she spins on her heel and runs down the sidewalk and away from me as quickly as possible.

Standing in the exact spot she walked away from me, I watch her go. I feel so completely confused and helpless. I know I was an asshole at first, but I tried to make it right. Staring after her, I feel like I'm waiting for her to come back and tell me what's going on long after she's entirely out of my sight. I have so many questions even though I know anything with her is none of my business and really never has been. Groaning in frustration, I eventually force myself to move. I try to shake off our encounter, already going over ways in my head to keep myself busy. It's always worked for me in the past.

I'm not ready to go back to the house yet, especially now. Instead, I turn around and walk back into the store we both just left. I might as well pick up the wedding gift I just purchased for Christian and Bree now that I'm not in such a hurry. Plus, I have something else I believe I need to do sooner rather than later. I grab a copy of the local newspaper on the way up to the counter. "You're back already?" the woman asks as I approach.

"Yeah," I grin. "I thought I'd sit outside and look through the newspaper. I just moved here and I'm staying with my family right now. I need to find a small place available to rent for a while," I respond.

"Oh, okay. Welcome! I hope you like it here. If you have any questions about the town, I'd be happy to answer them for you. Unfortunately, I don't know of any rentals. Most of them are already taken by now this time of year, but that should help," she replies with a genuine smile.

"Thank you," I murmur, grinning. "I appreciate it."

"Why don't you give me about twenty minutes, then and I'll have this gift all set for you," she replies with a genuine smile.

"Thank you, again," I reiterate. Having lived in so many different places growing up, the friendly people and how helpful they can be is definitely one thing I've always noticed about Maine. It's something I can't help but like for a place I'll be calling home, for now anyway.

I step outside and find a bench a few stores down. Sitting down, I open the newspaper just as my cell phone vibrates in my pocket. I pull it out to see a message from my brother, Jason. "Could you come back home to talk about the marketing plan with Christian and me? We also want to go over what you'll be covering while he's out for his honeymoon. He'll be out for a couple weeks starting Thursday."

Besides looking for a new place to live, this will be the perfect distraction for me until the wedding. My fingers fly across the screen, typing out my reply. "I'll be back to the house in about an hour." I tuck my phone back in my pocket and begin going over some ideas I already have in my head as I search for a few places to check out. I'll search on-line for apartments too, but this is a good start. There's no way I can stay there for too long.

"Thanks bro," comes Jason's reply.

Chapter 6

Sadie

I'm a mess. I can't believe I just stormed away from him like that. I sounded like a complete fool. I can't even imagine what he must think of me now. I shake my head, still in shock after finding out Matt is going to be living here. I can't help but wonder why, even though it's not my business.

I don't understand why he was so cruel to me at first. He's never been cruel. Was everything I knew about him all a lie? No, I rationalize with myself; he did run after me to apologize. Does he know I was married to Micah? No way. How would he know and why would that even matter to him? My heart flips painfully, aching from all the loss I've endured, all the loss Holden has to live with because of me. He needs his father. I whimper into my hands with the strongest urge to hold my little boy.

Cautiously, I tiptoe into my son's room like I do every night. Sometimes I need to just look at him to remind myself of the good in my life. He's lying on his back with one arm above his head and one arm wrapped tightly around his small lion stuffed animal. His little lips are slightly parted just above the lion's mane. I smile down at how innocent he looks, wishing I could keep him this way forever. His green safari comforter has been kicked down to the bottom of the bed. Reaching for his blankets, I carefully cover him up. I lean down and gently press a kiss to his forehead, breathing in his fresh scent. "I love you," I whisper as my eyes again fill with tears. Taking a step back, I quickly and quietly slip out of his room.

I hold my breath, letting the tears fall silently down my cheeks as I make my way down the hall to my room. As soon as I cross the threshold, I shut my door and release my breath along with the sob I have been holding in. Leaving my lights off, I crawl onto my bed, curling myself up in a ball and let myself cry. I cry so hard, I can barely catch my breath, knowing I should have done so many things differently.

I should have insisted on going to pick up Tim that night instead of letting Micah go. I'd known Micah had been drinking. Or maybe I shouldn't have married him when I didn't love him like he deserved. Maybe I should have never gone out with Matt the summer before college when I knew I couldn't have him. Maybe if I could go back to that summer when everything changed, Micah would still be alive. I sob into my legs until I can't cry anymore. My sobs eventually lighten enough that I'm able to reach for the Kleenex box on my nightstand and clean up my hands, legs, and face.

Groaning, I crumple up the dirty Kleenexes, tossing them into the garbage on my way to the bathroom sink. I splash some cool water on my face without daring to look at myself in the mirror. I don't even want to imagine how bad I look right now, even though it doesn't matter since I'm going to sleep, anyway. It's not like I'm going to see anyone in my room.

With Matt here, I'm afraid he's all I'll think about besides Holden. I sigh, "What am I going to do?"

I brush my teeth and make my way back to my bed in the dark. Lying on my side, I hug my pillow to my front for comfort. They're the only hugs I get besides my favorite ones from my beloved little man, Holden. I close my eyes, remembering the day with Matt that everything seemed to change, and I let it happen.

4 Years and 11 Months Ago…

Matt and I haven't gone on any more dates, but he always seems to end up where I'm hanging out with my friends. Granted, I usually tell him where we're going to be, but I'm hoping to go out with him again, instead of just catching up with him at the swimming hole or at the clam bar.

Tonight, we're all hanging out in Micah's back yard. Micah has a huge white sheet hung between two trees and when it gets dark later, he's going to screen a movie on it. Lately it's been an action or horror movie, but either way, I could care less. I'm too nervous to care, wondering if Matt will even show up.

I attempt to keep my mind occupied and walk over to sit on a wooden bench next to the fire-pit. I listen to the chatter around me as I stare at the rising orange flames dancing freely. "Hey, Micah, want to play football before it gets too dark?" one of the guys calls to him.

I glance up just as he tosses a football right at his chest. He spins it absentmindedly between his fingers as he looks down at me. I raise my eyebrows in question, and he grins in response. He turns back and throws the ball back. "Nah, I gotta' spend some time with my girl first." The guy chuckles and walks away just as Micah flops down beside me, wrapping his arm around me. I roll my eyes at him, and he just grins and pulls me closer. "What?" he asks innocently.

My eyes narrow as I look over at him teasing, "It's kind of hard to be your girl when you were making out with Clarissa yesterday."

He waves his hand like it's no big deal. "You know all the other girls don't mean anything to me. You're the one I'm going to marry some day," he jokes.

I giggle, shaking my head at him. "You're crazy," I laugh.

He pulls me in close for a hug, laughing. When he lets me go, he has a funny smile on his face. He kisses me on the cheek and adds playfully, "You know I love you, Sade. You'll always be my girl."

"Whatever," I mumble, brushing off his comment. "But I love you too," I add, dramatically rolling my eyes.

He tucks a strand of hair behind my ear, giving me a look I can't quite decipher. "Hey, man." Micah nods at someone over my head.

I turn around to find Matt standing behind me with a conflicted look on his face. I feel myself blush, wondering if he overheard any of my banter with Micah, but it's not something I really want to ask him. He clears his throat and smiles awkwardly down at me. "Hi, Sadie."

"Hi, Matt." I blush even deeper and attempt to wiggle unnoticeably away from under Micah's arm. Micah chuckles, I'm sure knowing exactly what I'm trying to do.

After torturing me for a few more seconds, he finally stands and lets his arm slowly fall from my shoulders. "I think maybe I will go play football for a while, or maybe I'll go find Clarissa." He smirks and winks at me. I watch Micah jog away as his arm wraps around both Kari and Clarissa, making me giggle at his antics. I have no idea why they let him get away with it.

Matt clears his throat and my eyes snap over to him. He has his hands stuffed into the pockets of his olive-green shorts. Appearing unsure, he asks, "Can I sit?"

My eyebrows scrunch together in confusion as I reply, "Of course." Pulling his hands from his pockets, he sits down next to me on the bench. He clasps his hands together and leans forward, placing his elbows on his knees. His knee begins bouncing, his whole body following suit. I'm not sure what's going on with him, but I need to ask, "Are you okay?"

He drops his hands and sits back, turning slightly towards me so he can face me. "Yeah, I'm good." He glances over towards Micah, then back to me before he takes a deep breath and releases it slowly. The butterflies in my stomach *are going haywire as I try to figure out what he's thinking, although I'm afraid to find out. "Sadie, I really like hanging out with you," he begins.*

The butterflies go into an even bigger frenzy, making me think I might throw up. I have a really bad feeling about this, but I'm not ready to stop spending time with him. I really want to be able to kiss him again. Just the thought of kissing him drives me crazy. I don't want him to walk away. "I love hanging out with you too," I whisper, barely able to get the words out.

He sighs and runs his hand through his blonde wavy hair, just like I wish I could. "I told you before I don't want to step on anyone's toes," he reiterates, his gaze flicking over to Micah again before settling back on me.

My breath rushes out of my lungs in a near panic. "There's nothing going on with Micah and me. He's not my boyfriend. He can do what he wants," I say, gesturing towards him with his arm still around Clarissa. Turning towards him, I look him in the eyes and insist, "I can do what I want too and what I want is to hang out with you."

Matt's eyes narrow and he bites the corner of his mouth as he stares at me. My whole body remains tense. I feel like I'm waiting on pins and needles just to hear what's on his mind. He finally takes a deep breath and releases it before he speaks. "We're both leaving soon, anyway. What happens really doesn't matter," he states.

I gasp, slightly hurt by his words, but I still don't want to lose time with him when it's going to be so short, anyway. I don't understand how he can already mean so much to me, but the fact is, he does. I'm not sure how to convince him that nothing is going on with Micah and me, either. Micah is just my best friend, that's it. I shake my head in frustration, knowing I can't let us end like this. "It matters to me," I whimper.

Matt's features instantly soften. "I'm sorry, I didn't mean it like that. I just meant that we both know, no matter what, this can never work out for us in the end. We're going to different parts of the country for college. I don't want to say this is more than it is. It's not fair to either of us."

I nod my head in understanding, knowing he's right, but I'm still not ready for him to walk away. Covering his hand with mine, I ask, "So what if we just keep it fun? No promises. We both know it can't be more and I'm okay with that," I insist, trying to hide my wince at my own words.

Matt still has a look of uncertainty as he shakes his head in disbelief. "Are you really okay with that, Sadie? Even when it's more than likely we'll never see each other again after this summer?" I hold my breath and nod my head, even though everything in me is telling me this is wrong. His eyes narrow and he prompts, "So if I tell you I'll delete your number after this summer and I expect you to delete mine, you'll do it?" I nod my head, holding my breath so I don't flinch. "And if I never tell you anything else about me, even my last name, and say I don't want to know yours, you're fine with that?" Nodding my head again, I fight back the pain at his words, but I can't let him go, not yet. "So, you want me and you to just be what, a summer fling?" he prods, sounding surprised at his own words.

I glance over at the fire, my mouth hanging open in shock at our conversation. "I..." I trail off not able to form the words and Matt shakes his head.

"You don't want that, Sadie. You're too good for that," he contends.

I shake my head and insist, "I don't want you to walk away." He sighs and leans towards me, pulling me into his arms. I relax into him, feeling relieved. Wrapping my arms around his waist, I rest my head on his chest. I listen to his heartbeat, feeling safe and at home in his arms, even though I'm fully aware that's not reality.

"How about we both take a couple days to think about this?" he suggests. I open my mouth to protest, but he shakes his head and asserts, "Really think about this, Sadie."

I heave a sigh in resignation, knowing he's not about to change his mind. "I don't want to be the one to ruin anything for you," he whispers, making my heartbeat even faster. He kisses me on the forehead just before releasing me. "I'll see you around, Sadie," he rasps just before he stands to walk away.

I jump up, feeling panicked. "Matt, wait!" Throwing my arms around his shoulders, I stand on my tiptoes, pulling his lips down to meet mine. I kiss him with everything in me. Weaving my hands into his blonde waves, I hold on tight, trying to keep him there. I lick the seam of his lips, nearly begging for him to let me in and he does. His arms hold me to him as his mouth covers mine and our tongues tangle together, licking and tasting one another. Our mouths move together in a perfect rhythm, and I quickly get lost in my desperation not to lose this guy I barely know.

He groans and pulls back, lightening the kiss and turning it soft and sensual. Tearing his mouth away, he rests his forehead on mine and cradles my face in his hands. "Damn girl," he whispers before placing his lips gently against mine once more. Pulling back with a sigh, he holds me in his gaze. He searches my eyes like he's looking for something before he demands again, "Just really think about it Sadie. I'll see you in a couple days for coffee and we'll talk." I nod my head unable to speak right now. Licking his lips, he sighs, biting the corner of his mouth as he turns to walk away, again running his hand through his blonde waves.

I watch him go feeling sick to my stomach. I can't believe I just did that. That's so unlike me. There must be something wrong with me. The moment he's gone, I turn around finding Micah standing behind me with a sly grin. "That was hot! Wanna' practice with me?" he jokes.

I shake my head and laugh. "Go find one of your girls." I stride past him quickly, trying to hide my blush as I walk back towards the fire.

Present Day

I roll over on my bed and try to push both Micah and Matt out of my head. Thoughts of them only make me feel guilty. I need to stop wishing for things to be different. That won't change anything. I need to figure out how to deal with Matt living here. Glancing over at the clock, I groan, knowing I have to be up in a couple hours for Holden. I close my eyes and attempt to stop my flurry of thoughts and get a little more sleep before morning.

Chapter 7

Matt

After taking two different groups out on the lake kayaking today for Christian, I'm exhausted. The second group was three young families, and the kids had an abundance of energy, wanting to see and do it all. After working in an office for so long, this is a lot harder than it used to be. It doesn't matter that I work out almost every day. This was different and the first time I've ever felt old. I'd honestly like to do nothing but go to sleep. Kicking my shoes off, I drop on my bed with a groan filled with relief.

My door suddenly flies open, startling me. "How'd it go today, Matt?" Christian asks as he steps into my room.

"Don't worry about knocking, I'm decent," I say only half joking. There's another reason I need to go find a new place to live. I sit up as my brother drops on the bed beside me.

Christian grins and slaps me on the back, harder than necessary. "Wouldn't even think of it."

I shake my head in annoyance and sigh. "Don't you have a fiancé you can go annoy the shit out of now?"

He ignores my question and raises his eyebrows, wanting his own answer. "How did it go today?" he repeats.

I shrug my shoulders. "It was fine. The first group was a group of guys up here camping. They were easy. The second group, as you know, was three families. There were two seven-year-old boys and an eight-year-old girl who kept having water fights with their paddles, with me in between them. They thought they were hilarious."

Christian chuckles. "I would've loved to see that!" The corner of my mouth twitches up now that I'm able to admit to myself it was pretty funny. I'm just a little bit more tense than normal since I can't stop thinking about Sadie. Actually, saying I'm only a bit tenser is an overwhelming understatement, but I'm not surprised. Sadie has always increased my blood pressure in more ways than one right from the start. "Please tell me you didn't tip their kayak?" he jokes, jolting me out of my self-pity and making me laugh.

"I was good, I promise. I only tipped the boys into the water. The girl stayed dry," I tease, smiling innocently. He laughs and I emphasize, "Don't worry, I was on my best behavior."

"That's what I'm afraid of," he grumbles, grinning. "But seriously, thanks for helping out." I nod my head in acknowledgment. "Remember when we used to do that to T?"

I smile at the memory. "Yeah, then she would always offer to help us get Jason because it was the only way we weren't ganging up on her." We both laugh and I begin to relax. "I should probably warn your future wife," I tease.

He grins, claiming, "She already knows what she's in for. Besides, it's too late for her anyway." My lips twitch up and my eyebrows rise in question. He just shrugs and replies honestly, "There's no way I'm ever letting her go."

I slowly exhale and give my brother a small smile. "I really am happy for you, Christian. You deserve it. You both do," I admit.

He nods with a somber look on his face. I can tell he's remembering all the tough times Bree has been through, as well as living without her. He looks up, determined to change the subject. "So, are you ready to tell me more about this girl that has you all twisted up?"

I close my eyes and sigh in resignation. "She's just different. I don't even know if I can explain it, which is probably why I fucked up years ago. I didn't realize what I wanted or how I felt about her until it was too late. I figured we were too young, and it was all just meant to be fun. When I did figure it out, I came back here over one of my vacations, finally ready to say something to her. I looked all over for her, figuring she'd be home from college on break too. Unfortunately, when I found her, I didn't even have the chance to talk to her. Instead, I saw her accepting a proposal from a guy she always claimed was just her best friend. I watched as he put a ring on her finger. Then I walked away." I wince at the memory.

Christian takes a deep breath before he prods, "Engaged isn't married."

I nod in acknowledgement. "Yeah, but I wouldn't let go of my hurt ego long enough to do or say anything in time. I think they might even have kids now," I confess, remembering the car seat I saw in the back of her car when I ran into her at the market. "Besides, it was a long time ago," I add.

Christian looks away from me, trying to hide his cringe. "You sure you have the story straight, Matt? I know from experience things aren't always what they seem," he reminds me.

I paste on a fake smile. "Look at you, my *little* brother all grown up and giving me advice!" He chuckles and I heave a sigh, admitting, "I don't know."

"What's the alternative?" he prods imploringly. I pinch my lips shut tight with no response to that question because the alternative is something I've been trying not to think about for a long time. It's why I dated Natalie in the first place. It's why I didn't move closer to my family right after Theresa's accident. The alternative is not only depressing, but it feels like giving up and I'm still not ready for that. Even though I probably should be.

Christian opens his mouth to say something else, but I interrupt him when my phone goes off with a text and I notice the time. "Shit!" I exclaim jumping up. "Whatever you were about to say will have to wait. I have an appointment to go see an apartment rental tonight."

"You're moving already?" he prompts, surprised.

"I can't live here with mom and dad for too long. I love 'em, but I'm used to being on my own. I need to get my own place for my own sanity," I confess.

He nods in understanding. "I get it. How is there anything decent available at the beginning of the summer, though? Usually everything in this area is long gone by now with all the tourists. Where are you looking?"

"I'm looking at a place between here and town. The ad said it was an old barn that was refurbished into an apartment," I inform him as I pull my shoes back on. "When I talked to the woman on the phone she said they weren't sure they would have it done in time for a summer rental, so they just put the ad up. Fortunately, it works for me."

"It actually sounds pretty sweet," he proclaims, nodding.

"Yeah, I hope so because everything else I saw was too far away or too much. I'll find out in a few. But I definitely don't want to be late, or I won't have a chance to rent it at all." I grab my keys, phone and wallet as I head for the door. "I'll see you tomorrow night for your bachelor party."

He grins. "Yes you will! Bree and I may be around later too, though. Mom wanted to talk to Bree about some last minute wedding stuff. Let me know how it goes with the apartment!"

I wave over my shoulder to acknowledge him and stride out the door. I jog down the stairs and call to my parents talking in the kitchen. "I've got some errands to run. I'll be back in a couple hours," I vaguely inform them. I barely hear the beginning of a response before I'm out the front door and climbing into my truck thankful for something else to focus on.

In less than fifteen minutes, I'm pulling into a long dirt driveway. I park in front of what I assume used to be a barn, but it's painted a dark tan with dark evergreen trim. Hopping out of my truck, I assess the huge barn doors on the front, but I assume the apartment entrance must be on another side. Following a dirt path, I walk around the side of the building to find a front door painted in bright yellow. I knock on the door, and it's almost instantly pulled open by a pretty older dark-haired woman. "Hi! You must be Matt," she announces, grinning.

"Yes, Ma'am," I respond politely.

"Just call me Penny. Come on in and take a look around," she offers sweetly. I follow her inside and I'm instantly blown away by the enormity of the place. It's almost completely open, yet it unexpectedly looks and feels like a home. The floors have thick wood planks stained a light, natural color. The walls have slightly more narrow planks, painted a whitewash. Off to my right is the kitchen. It has cabinets painted a sage green with a granite countertop speckled with white, black and gray. All the appliances are a simple white, just like the deep farm sink. "You'd of course need to furnish it," she states, gesturing towards the large empty space I assume is the living room.

"Back there on the other side of the kitchen is a small bathroom and a small room you could use as an office. Then there are two bedrooms and another bathroom up in the loft area," she informs me, gesturing towards the stairs in the back directly across from the front door.

"Mind if I take a look?" I prod.

She nods and I make my way upstairs. At the top of the stairs, there's a small landing overlooking the rest of the apartment. I easily find the two bedrooms, the one on the left slightly bigger than the other. I'm assuming it's due to the bathroom between the two rooms. It seems to take up the space behind only one room and it's the only room with white tiles covering the floor. I shake my head, not wanting to ask about the cost of the rent again, afraid she'll change the price on me. It really is too good to be true. "What do you think?" she inquires expectantly.

"I'll take it," I inform her. "When can I move in?"

She grins. "The lease starts June first. We just have a few more things we want to finish up before we hand over the keys."

"Perfect!" I exclaim. We make our way back downstairs and discuss the details, including obtaining a copy of the lease to review before I sign it. "Thank you again," I reiterate as I leave. Making my way back to my truck, I feel slightly relieved. If this didn't work, I might've had to wait until the end of the summer to find a decent place around here and that would've made for a long few months.

I reach for my phone to text my brothers and sister. "I'm going to need your help moving again after the wedding."

My phone pings several times in a row almost instantly making me chuckle.

"WTF? You just got here!" Jason's text sounds almost like an accusation. "Thought you were going to stick around and help us out?"

"You can't leave!" Theresa pleads.

"Congrats! Can't wait to see it!" Christian replies.

"I'm not leaving. Renting my own place close by," I respond.

"How come Christian knew, and I didn't?" Theresa questions. I can't help but chuckle at her instant reaction.

"You couldn't have done this before so we don't have to move you twice?" Jason prods.

"Because I'm the cool one!" Christian teases Theresa. "And what are you talking about, Jason? You were late and didn't help with anything. Like always, I did all the work."

I chuckle again at my family's responses, but ignore them all. "Anyone have any furniture they want to donate to my new place?"

"Sara may have some stuff for the living room. I'll check with her," Jason comments.

"I have a few things from my place in Portland," Christian responds.

"I don't think I have anything. Sorry," Theresa answers. "Jason, doesn't Sara need her stuff for her place?"

"Meet at the house?" Jason asks without answering.

"On my way," I reply, sick of texting.

I drop my phone down in a cup holder, ignoring the rest of the texts coming through. I take one last appreciative look at my new place before I back out of the driveway. "Now I have to tell Mom I'm moving out already," I grumble.

Chapter 8

Sadie

"Mommy you look boo-tee-ful!" Holden tells me in his sweet little voice with wide eyes and a huge smile.

I unbuckle him from his car seat, returning his smile as I pick him up. I hug him tightly to my chest and adoringly reply, "Thank you, buddy." He quickly wiggles out of my arms and runs for the front door. Reaching into the car, I pull out his overnight bag along with his stuffed lion, one thing he never seems to sleep without.

The front door opens, revealing my mother-in-law standing in the doorway with a huge smile on her face for my son. "Grandma!" he squeals as he hugs her legs.

She runs her hand through his blonde hair and pats him on the back lovingly. "Hi, sweetheart. Are you ready for our sleepover?"

"So ready!" he exclaims.

"Is that my little man?" my father-in-law calls from down the hall.

Holden sprints inside and yells excitedly, "It's me, Grandpa! I'm here!"

I hand my mother-in-law Holden's bag. She takes it and then looks me up and down. "You're going to a bachelorette party?" she questions disapprovingly.

I fidget uncomfortably, tugging at the hem of my pale blue sundress. It has spaghetti straps and comes down slightly between my breasts. It falls loosely below my waist, but now I wonder if it's a little too short the way she's assessing me. "Um, it's not a normal one. Her fiancé will be there with his brothers and friends, too. They just wanted to relax with everyone before the wedding," I explain lamely.

She purses her lips and sighs. "Well, I get an extra night with my grandson out of it. We're going to take him to the café in town for breakfast, then we'll bring him home afterwards," she informs me.

"Thank you." I nod and smile stiffly in appreciation. "Holden, can Mommy have a hug goodbye?" I call down the hall to him. I hear his little feet running towards me, just before he rounds the corner and jumps into my arms. I breathe in his little boy scent as I hug him tightly. "I love you, Holden. Be a good boy and I'll see you in the morning. Okay?"

"Okay," he agrees, grinning. "I love you, Mommy." Then he quickly wiggles out of my arms again and sprints back down the hall.

"We'll see you tomorrow," my mother-in-law states sternly. "Be safe," she adds quietly just before she shuts the door in my face, so I'm not able to get another word out.

I heave a sigh and turn back towards my car to head to Bree's apartment. She wants all of us girls to leave together from there, so no one needs to worry about driving. I don't know if I would've even considered going tonight if it were any other way, but I don't have to worry about that with Bree.

When I pull up to Bree's apartment, I grab my purse and overnight bag before I slowly get out of the car. I never go out like this. I don't think I could be more nervous than I am right now. My hands are shaking, my heart is pounding, and I'm struggling to control my breathing. I guess part of it is probably because I don't know any of Bree's family or friends, not even her fiancé.

I work with Bree at the gift shop in town. She was the first person who was truly nice to me. She started there not too long after Micah's accident. She didn't grow up here and maybe that's part of the reason it was easy for her to ignore all the rumors, but what matters to me is she was a friend to me when I needed one the most. At least Emma will be here tonight, too. She works at the gift shop with Bree and me as well. She's from here like me, but she's a few years younger than me and never knew Micah. None of us hang out much outside of work, besides going out to lunch once in a while, but I've always enjoyed being around both Bree and Emma. I don't have very many people I can call my friends anymore, so I cherish the friends I have.

When I reach her door, I hesitantly knock. Standing anxiously, I look around, but no one comes to the door. Knocking a little harder, I wait. The door is soon flung open and a pretty blonde girl about the same size as me stands in front of me. "Um, I'm looking for Bree," I tell her nervously.

She raises her eyebrows and gives me a huge smile. "Hi, I'm Amy, Bree's roommate and best friend."

Returning her smile, I introduce myself, "Hi, I'm Sadie. I work with Bree at the gift shop."

She nods in understanding. "Come on in. Everyone is already here. We were just waiting for you. The car should be here any minute to pick us up," she informs me.

I nod and follow her up the stairs right into their kitchen. The kitchen has an off-white tile floor with white walls and yellow-gold appliances. The counters are a mustard yellow Formica and black walnut cabinets. A small square pine table and chairs sits in the center with what I assume is the living room just beyond the table. Bree sits with her back to me on an old brown couch surrounded by a small group of beautiful giggling girls I don't know, except for Emma. Emma glances up and smiles genuinely when she sees me. "Hi!"

I breathe a sigh of relief with her greeting and try to get rid of my nervous energy. "Hi, Emma. Hi Bree," I add.

Bree spins around and jumps up when she sees me. She walks over to me and gives me a quick hug before pulling me by the arm to the other side of the couch. "Okay everyone, this is Sadie. She works with Emma and me at the gift shop," she elaborates.

The girls all wave and smile. "Hi, Sadie."

"This is Liz, Sara, Theresa and you already met Amy." Bree points out each girl as she introduces them. "I'll wait until you meet all the guys to tell you who they're with. I'm sure it's confusing enough," she adds, grinning.

Nodding my head, I try not to stare as the girl with blonde hair and startling familiar green eyes steps up to me with a kind smile. I reflexively gasp but shake my head to clear it when she gives me a funny look. "I'm Theresa," she repeats, "the groom's sister."

"I'm sorry, you just remind me of someone," I explain. "I've actually never met Christian. He's never stopped in when I was working with Bree at the shop," I enlighten her. Holden has the majority of my time outside of work. "But it's nice to meet you," I add, "all of you."

"The limo is here!" Amy announces gleefully and everyone stands to leave.

"Um, Bree?" I question. She turns towards me and waits for me to continue. "Where should I put my bag?"

"Oh, you can just set it inside my room. It's the one over there," she instructs, pointing to the wall with only one door.

"Thanks," I murmur and walk over to set my bag down. Bree waits for me, making us the last two down the stairs and out the door.

I climb into the limo and take the last spot on the long bench along the side next to Sara with Bree sitting facing forward next to Amy. "I love your shoes," Amy gushes.

I glance down at my silver strappy sandals and smile appreciatively. "Thanks. They're actually more comfortable than they look, so I'm hoping they'll be good for dancing."

"Do you have a boyfriend?" Amy probes without preamble. Bree instantly elbows her in the gut. She knows about Micah, and she knows I have a son. "What?" Amy asks, confused. "It's an innocent question. I'm hoping I'm not the only single one tonight," she explains.

"It's okay, Bree," I reassure her, talking over the lump in my throat. "I don't have a boyfriend," I tell Amy stiffly. I take a deep breath, continuing, "But I do have a little man in my life. I have an almost four-year-old son."

Amy's eyes widen in shock, and I hear a choked sound from somewhere in the car I ignore. "Oh," she responds.

"He's a gorgeous little boy," Bree adds. "I've seen pictures." I smile at her appreciatively.

Amy swiftly pulls herself together and smiles. "I guess I'm not the only single girl tonight then!"

"I'm single too if it matters," Emma tosses out sarcastically. Amy grins politely at her in response.

I relax back into my seat and listen to the surrounding chatter. We pull into the parking lot at the end of the block and the driver directs us, pointing between the buildings down a wide brick walkway. "51 Wharf is right down there. I have to let you out here. I can't drive down there. I'll pick you up here at the end of the night as well."

A chorus of, "Thank you," surrounds me as we all begin climbing out of the limo.

Theresa looks at me and states with a touch of amusement in her voice, "I know I don't have to worry about the others, but my brother Matt better not hit on you." Her words cause me to freeze. My eyes widen in shock. I stop breathing and I'm afraid to move. Theresa takes in my terrified appearance and attempts to comfort me. "I was just joking. I just know he won't hit on Amy and you're really pretty. Plus, Bree told us how sweet you are. I don't want to scare you. He's a good guy. I was only teasing," she adds almost desperately when I still don't respond.

I open and close my mouth like a fish, trying to get the words out when I know from the bottom of my soul I already know the truth. I could see it the first moment I saw her, but I didn't believe it could be true. I finally rasp, "I think I know why you remind me of someone."

"You know my brother!" she cries with wide eyes.

"I think so," I confirm, nodding my head awkwardly, knowing it's the truth.

"You have a strange look on your face. I hope he's nice to you!" she exclaims.

I laugh humorlessly and attempt to paste a smile on my face, although I'm sure it doesn't look too genuine. "If it's the same Matt, yeah, we met a few years back, but we haven't hung out in a while," I tell her honestly, without really divulging anything.

Her curious eyes along with Bree's remain on me. "Matt is a pretty common name…" Theresa trails off.

"I know, but I'm sure there aren't a lot who have your hair and almost identical eyes and look so much like you. You reminded me of him the moment I saw you," I admit nervously. Theresa and Bree continue to assess me as I attempt to reassure them both. "It's fine. It will be good to see him," I insist, but even I know I sound like I'm lying.

This is Bree's night. There's no way I'm going to ruin it with a breakdown about Matt. I can do this. I can be civil. Isn't that what we said we'd do when we ran into each other the other day?

I shove myself out of the car and join the other girls, standing tall in attempt to force a feeling of confidence. Theresa and Bree exit the car last. I ignore the odd looks on their faces as I follow the other girls up to a brick building with dark green awnings. We walk through a wood and glass paneled door and I'm immediately engulfed by the beat of the music. I glance towards the dance floor, knowing it's just beginning to fill up, with a large DJ booth off to the side. I notice the brick walls inside as well, some painted and some natural, but I love the look of both.

Taking a deep breath, I listen as Amy tells a gorgeous, tall woman with dark hair and eyes that we're with the Emory group in one of the VIP sections. "Emory," I repeat, mumbling to myself. "Matt Emory," I whisper as I turn. My eyes lock with the man himself, making my heart skip a beat. "Hi," I squeak.

I watch as he pales slightly, even in this dim lighting, and his Adam's apple bobs up and down as he swallows hard. "What are you doing here?" he gasps in shock.

I open my mouth to answer when both Bree and Theresa are suddenly at my side. "Hi, Matt! Look who we brought with us," Theresa gushes happily. "We just realized you two already know each other. How about that?" she adds sarcastically, looking back and forth curiously between us.

"Yeah," he croaks. "Hi, Sadie," he rasps, his sexy voice rumbling through me causing goosebumps to pop up on my arms. "You look beautiful."

I blush and glance away, mumbling, "Thanks."

Theresa giggles making Matt narrow his eyes on her. She smiles and gives him a hug he returns. "I'm going to go find Jax," she informs us, cheerfully waving over her shoulder as she goes.

"Sadie and I work together at the gift shop," Bree enlightens him.

"I thought you didn't work there anymore?" he prods.

"I do sometimes and either way, Sadie has been a great friend," she emphasizes. Matt responds with a sigh. "When did you two meet?" she asks curiously.

Matt shrugs his shoulders, staring at me, remaining silent. "About five years ago," I answer.

A guy that looks a lot like Matt, but a little taller, with a bit darker hair, and bright blue eyes, walks up to us and wraps his arms around Bree. "Hi, Bree." He smiles placing a kiss on her cheek. She turns and grins up at him lovingly. She pushes up on her toes and briefly presses her lips to his.

Turning back towards me, she introduces us, "Christian, this is Sadie."

He grins and keeping one hand on Bree, reaches out with the other to shake mine. "Hi, Sadie. It's great to finally meet you. Bree has told me so much about you."

"It's good to finally meet you too. I was starting to wonder if you were real," I joke still sounding slightly stiff.

Bree reveals with a knowing grin, "It seems Matt and Sadie have actually known each other for quite a while. Small world," she mumbles.

I hold back my groan and attempt a smile while Christian's gaze floats back and forth between the two of us filled with curiosity. Eventually, he chuckles and slaps his brother on the back. He points towards the back corner of the room and lets us know, "We're back over there." Then he turns in that direction, taking Bree with him.

I take a step to follow Christian and Bree when Matt wraps his fingers firmly around my upper arm stopping me. My body instantly heats from his touch, and I slowly turn to face him. When I meet his gaze, his green eyes are sparking with anger, taking me aback. "Why are you here?" he prods accusingly.

I feel a stabbing pain in my chest with the intensity of his anger. Taking a deep breath, I push my shoulders back and look up at him with a confidence I don't feel. "Bree is my friend. I didn't know you were going to be here until about five minutes ago. It wouldn't have changed my decision though because I'm here for Bree," I remind him. His eyes turn soft. "But I didn't know he was your brother," I admit.

He nods stiffly and lightens his grip on my arm, but still doesn't let go. He stares at a spot just over my head when he asks, sounding slightly bitter, "Where's Micah?"

I gasp, my heart clenching for a different reason. "You know about him?"

He laughs humorlessly and informs me, "I know you married him."

I hold my breath feeling the pain of both Matt's accusation and missing Micah and all we went through. I may have married him, but it was a mistake and now he's gone. I jerk my arm away and stalk towards the bathrooms, holding back my tears. I need a few minutes to pull myself together before I make my way over to everyone else. Otherwise, I may not make it through a night of small talk and dancing with a couple friends, Matt, and a group of strangers.

Chapter 9

Matt

I swear someone is playing a sick joke on me. Sadie keeps appearing everywhere and now I find out her and Bree, my future sister-in-law, are good friends? There's being civil and there's just plain being tortured and that's exactly what's happening to me right now. Although the look on her face when I asked her about Micah was off, but then again, it's not like I can ask her about her marriage. I have no right to ask her about anything personal.

Clenching my jaw, I stare after her as she runs off to the bathroom. I don't know if I should go after her or if I should go back to our section. I debate for only a few minutes before I reluctantly turn and head to the back corner. Going after her will only cause my brothers and sister to ask more questions. I'm already prepared for them to give me enough shit as it is; I don't need to add to it.

I approach the VIP area, which is slightly raised from the rest of the room. Climbing the two steps up, I saunter towards a huge, rounded leather booth that appears like it will seat all of us with a small table in the middle. A security guard puts his arm up to stop me from going any further just as Christian calls out, "It's okay. He's with us." The guard drops his arm and Christian shrugs, explaining, "He comes with the table." I shake my head and he grins in response. I'm sure he wanted to make everything perfect for Bree, but security seems a little much to me.

Jason immediately changes the subject asking me, "How do you know Sadie? Theresa and Bree were just telling us you've known her for quite a long time," he adds with a smirk.

My jaw twitches with tension and struggle not to show my annoyance. Shrugging like it's no big deal, I slowly take a deep breath to attempt to slow my pounding heartbeat. "I met her along with a shitload of other people down at the swimming hole one summer. She's a cool girl and I hung out with her and her friends a few times," I inform them trying to keep my tone nonchalant.

I can feel Christian's eyes burning into the side of my head, but I refuse to look in his direction. He reads me too well and knows too much. Jason just raises his eyebrows in question. "Her and her friends, huh?"

I nod. "Yeah, a group of guys and girls she hung out with at the time. She's the same age as Christian," I add then grind my teeth in frustration for volunteering extra information.

Jason opens his mouth to say something else when I notice Sara elbow him in the gut. I grin over at her in appreciation. Then, I feel Sadie fidgeting nervously behind me. I step back and wave my arm in front of me for her to go first when I notice the security guard attempting to discreetly check out her ass. Stepping up behind her, I narrow my eyes at the guy, his eyes instantly drifting away. She slides into the booth, and I slip in right behind her, draping my arm over the back. She looks up at me in surprise, her blue eyes almost shockingly bright in contrast to her dark hair.

I clear my throat. "Are you okay?"

She opens her mouth and then closes it again, before nodding her head in response. The girls order a bottle of champagne and Jax orders a Jack and Coke. Raising my hand, I quickly double that order for me. "Another one of those please?"

I stop listening after that, putting all my effort into not staring at Sadie so much or at least not so noticeably. I don't want her running from me again, but I can't help it. Is it possible she's even more beautiful than the last time I saw her?

"So, what are you doing now that you're living here, Matt?" Amy questions, pulling my eyes away from Sadie.

"I'm working with my brothers. I started putting together a marketing plan, including some of T's ideas. They also have me doing a little bit of field work," I inform her.

"Is that what you've been doing since you graduated Baylor? Marketing?" Sadie asks curiously.

"Yeah, I worked for a firm down there until recently," I answer taking advantage of being able to look directly at her.

"Why did you leave?" she inquires.

"My family," I answer with the half-truth I tell everyone. I watch a cloud pass over her face with my words. My eyes scrunch together in confusion. I open my mouth to ask her what's wrong but pause as both of my brothers begin chuckling.

My eyes snap over to them. Christian's eyes dance with amusement while Jason mumbles, "Yeah, that's why." This time Theresa has my back and glares at them. I give her a small smile in appreciation just as our waitress sets drinks down in front of us before she pours champagne for the girls.

When she walks away Theresa holds her glass up. "We need to toast to Christian and Bree!" Everyone grabs their glasses and holds them up. "We'll save the serious ones for next week. Tonight is for fun. "Here's to you, here's to me, here's to my brother Christian and Bree. Here's to sharing a lifetime of love and kisses and making Bree your Misses." A combination of groans and laughter fill the table as we all drink to the toast. "What? You guys have something better?" she challenges. Smirking, I open my mouth to make a toast. Theresa instantly stops me. "Anyone except for Matt have something better?"

"Hey!" I chuckle feigning insult. Everyone joins in the laughter before they move on to their own conversations.

I finish my drink and set it down before I turn back towards Sadie. "What have you been doing since graduation?"

She blushes and looks down at her hands gripping her glass so tight I'm afraid she'll break the stem of the champagne glass. I reach out and gently cover her hand with mine in support. She jumps slightly and snaps her attention to me wide-eyed, but I don't budge. "Um, I didn't finish yet. I only made it through the first semester before I came home," she confesses shocking me. "I've been doing classes mostly on-line when I can, but..." she trails off and tries to pull away from me again, but I don't let her.

"That's okay, you know," I insist. "Things happen," I proclaim while wondering if Micah was her reason for leaving school. "At least you're still trying. A lot of people don't even do that," I remind her.

She releases a relieved breath and offers me a small smile. "Thanks Matt." I nod my head and grin, loving the feel of her appreciation, even if it's miniscule.

"Who wants to dance with me?" Theresa asks making my heart skip a beat. I haven't seen her dance since before her accident. I look over at her, grateful for the huge smile covering her face. "I'll get Jax out there soon," she grins flirtatiously at him, "but I'm ready to dance now."

Bree and Sara quickly jump up knowing what she's been through, followed by Liz. They're able to get past everyone without us having to stand with so much space between the large booth and small table. "You don't want to dance?" I ask Sadie. She scrunches her nose up, unsure of what to do. "Or maybe you're trying to decide which is the lesser of two evils, dancing or me," I tease.

She giggles then answers. "I don't know if I want to dance," pausing, she shrugs, "Or talk to you." I laugh hard at her honesty.

"Sadie," Amy prompts grabbing her attention away from me. "Did you bring pictures of your son?" she asks making Sadie blush instantly.

I stiffen and remove my arm from the back of the booth. I lean forward on my elbows just as another drink is set down in front of me. Tipping it back, I immediately drink half. Looking up at our waitress, I request, "Can I have another one of these when you have the chance?"

"Absolutely." She grins flirtatiously and I automatically smile back.

"Um, I didn't really bring anything with me tonight," she stammers. "You know, trying to travel light and all."

"What about your phone? You must have some pictures of him on your phone," Amy suggests.

"Um, yeah, but, um…" she stutters uncomfortably.

I can't take anyone giving her a hard time and she's obviously uncomfortable with Amy's prodding. Turning towards Sadie, I insist, "You're dancing with me."

Her eyes widen in surprise, but she allows me to grab her left hand and weave my fingers through hers as I tug her towards the dance floor. I can't help but notice the absence of a wedding ring as I'm holding her hand making my heart skip a beat. I should feel the cold hard metal, but I feel nothing but her smooth skin.

Just as we reach the dance floor the song changes to, 'Thinking Out Loud' by Ed Sheeran. Spinning around, I swiftly pull her into my arms. My entire body heats with having her so close while my heart pounds faster with each breath I take filled with the scent of her. I'm beginning to love the feel of her way too much. I need to separate myself from her. The best way I know to do that is to ask about Micah.

"Where's your ring?" I ask awkwardly.

Her eyes widen in mild surprise. "How did you know?" she questions instead of answering me. I shrug because it doesn't matter how I know, it just matters that I do. I continue to stare at her and wait for a real answer. I need to know. Eventually, she sighs and smiles sadly. She swallows hard and looks at me, obviously fighting tears just before she says the last thing I expect to hear leave her lips. "Micah died in a car accident about two and a half years ago."

Gasping in shock, I mumble, "I'm so sorry." I admit I was hoping she wasn't married anymore, but I didn't wish for this. My heart aches with the pain she feels, with everything she must have gone through. I wince when I think of her little boy. I can't help but feel bad for him even though I don't know the kid and for her now a single mom. "I didn't know. I'm so sorry, Sadie."

She grimaces and nods her head but continues to move with my body to the music. I feel like a complete asshole. We dance the rest of the song in silence as I struggle with what to say to her. When the song ends, I reluctantly release her, my whole body instantly going cold. Slowly, I follow her back to the table questioning how I can at least make tonight better for her.

Christian steps into my path, stopping me. He looks me in the eye and asks simply, "It's *her*, isn't it?" I cringe and look over his shoulder, watching as she sits back down. He sighs. "That's what I thought. I see it in your eyes."

"So, what Christian? What do you want me to say?" I question defensively.

He shakes his head. "Nothing. I just want you to think about her first with whatever you decide to do. From what Bree has told me about her, she's been through enough," he warns me.

I flinch but nod my head because I know he's right. "I know. I didn't realize," I pause to take in a much-needed deep breath, "but I know now."

He nods and smiles sadly at me. He glances over my shoulder and his grin turns more genuine. "I'm going to go dance with my future wife," he informs me moving to take a step around me.

"Christian?" He halts and raises his eyebrows at me in question. "I know you well enough to know you're going to share who Sadie is to me with Bree, but can we just keep it between the three of us for now?"

He chuckles and nods. "Sure, Matt." He pats me on the back and steps up behind Bree, immediately wrapping one arm around her waist.

I saunter back towards the table, finding the booth empty except for Sadie fidgeting nervously. I want to stay close to her, so even with more than enough room to spread out I cautiously sit next to her. Her body instantly tenses as I settle in beside her and drape my arm around the back of the booth where she sits. She begins to move away, and I drop my hand around her shoulder to stop her and hold her there as my heart begins beating erratically. "Please stay here," I beg. "I feel like you're always running away from me. I just want to talk Sadie. You and I used to be friends. I'd really like to get to know you again," I plead.

She looks up at me apprehensively. "I don't know if that's a good idea Matt."

"Why not?" I prod feeling desperate. "I'm sorry I was an asshole before. Just give me a chance. I just want to be friends again."

"I don't really have time for friends," she admits. Blushing deeply, she turns away from me.

I take my free hand and gently tug her chin until she's looking at me. "Your son," I tell her, "I get it." Tears well in her eyes and I attempt to swallow the lump forming in my throat. "I still want to be friends. I still want to get to know you again." I wipe away a tear that escapes down her cheek with my thumb. "I thought you were married. I thought it would be better if I stayed away," I confess trying to make her understand what I was thinking.

She shakes her head. "I still don't know if it's a good idea, Matt."

I grit my teeth in frustration and suggest, "How about we do a trial run then?" She scrunches up her face adorably in confusion making me chuckle. "My brother and Bree are getting married next week. The trial begins now and ends when the wedding is over. If you decide at the end of the night we can't be friends, then we can be civil when we run into each other. Otherwise, we get to be friends again." I grin, satisfied. "Please, Sadie. Just friends, for now," I mumble the last part and she laughs at me making my heart skip a beat. I fucking love her smile.

"Okay," she concedes. "We'll see how it goes this week." I breathe a sigh of relief eliciting a laugh from her lips. "I really don't have any time though," she emphasizes.

"That's okay, I'll figure it out," I insist just as Jason and Sara flop down on the other side of the booth.

"Did you see Theresa dancing? She looks so fucking happy," he gushes.

I relax back in my seat and smile as I glance out towards my sister on the dance floor. "Yeah, she does, and she deserves every second of it."

Chapter 10

Sadie

I flop down on the couch next to Emma. Glancing at me, she quietly asks, "So what's going on with you and Matt?"

Unfortunately, I realize she wasn't quiet enough for only me to hear as Bree adds, "Yeah, it looked like you two were getting pretty cozy." She grins at me leaning over the back of the couch on the other side of me.

I sigh and suppress my grin. "We're just friends. I haven't seen him in a really long time, so we were catching up," I tell them casually. Although it's the truth, I can feel that there's more between us, but for my own sanity I can't go there. My priority is Holden.

"What happened between you two before anyway?" Theresa prods innocently. Although, I know her question is anything but innocent.

Blushing, I answer defensively, "Nothing!"

She laughs. "Okay, you can say that all you want, but your blush just gave you away." I pinch my lips together annoyed that everyone can read me so well. "And besides," she adds, "I know my brother and I've honestly never seen him so attentive to anyone, let alone someone as sweet as you. His eyes followed you everywhere you went!"

I blush an even deeper shade of red at the same time my heart skips a beat from her words. I gulp and continue to deny what I'm feeling, "Although that's really sweet Theresa, there's nothing going on with me and your brother."

She raises her eyebrows in challenge. "And nothing ever has?"

I redden and look away fidgeting nervously. "Um…"

"I knew it!" She spins around and screeches excitedly.

I shake my head in denial. "We just hung out a few times nearly five years ago. It's no big deal. I almost didn't even recognize him," I lie.

"Yeah, he has changed," Theresa concedes looking melancholy. "He still looks the same though, only bigger."

"And his tattoo looks so hot on those arms," Amy adds dreamily.

My body heats thinking about his armband tattoo because Amy's right, but I also hate that she was checking him out, even though I have no right to be jealous. "Sadie thinks so too," Bree comments, noticing my reaction.

"Hey," I feebly attempt to argue, "I didn't say that."

She shrugs. "You didn't have to." Everyone laughs at my expense, but I join in admitting it's true with just a look.

"But there's nothing going on with us," I continue to protest.

"He didn't hug me like he did you when he said goodbye!" Theresa argues.

"I should hope not," Sara adds with a smirk. "After all, you are his sister!" Everyone bursts out laughing at Sara's exaggeration.

Theresa scrunches up her nose in disgust. "Ew, gross!" The look on her face makes us all laugh even harder. I enjoy the feel of some of my tension leaving my body as we all continue to laugh so hard my stomach begins to hurt.

When we all finally calm down, I take a breath to relax. Then I remind them, "I have a wonderful little man who is my priority and will continue to be for the rest of my life." I take a deep breath attempting to rid myself of the ache in my chest as I add my painful reality. "It doesn't matter if I have any interest in Matt or not. I have school, work and Holden. Plus, I have to figure out a plan for us for our future. He's the most important man in my life. For better or worse,

I don't have time to date Matt or anyone else right now. As for Matt," I pause, shrugging, "we have fun together. I'm honestly glad we're friends again," I claim trying to keep the sadness out of my voice.

"It's okay to date again Sadie," Emma reminds me. "Micah wouldn't want you to spend the rest of your life alone."

I wipe away a couple unwanted tears from my cheeks. "I know," I whisper, barely able to get the words out while I continue to fight my tears. Theresa, Bree and Emma give me a look of sympathy, but it feels more like pity to me, and I absolutely hate it. I glance down at my lap, not wanting to see that look from anyone else, especially from girls I just met and barely know like Theresa. It's hard enough to see that look from friends I admit to myself. It's moments like this I would give almost anything to be home peeking in on a sleeping Holden instead of here. I remind myself again I'm here for Bree. She deserves a happy ending after everything she's been through.

"Is Matt Young coming to the wedding next weekend?" Amy inquires changing the subject and turning her attention to Bree. I breathe a sigh of relief having the focus on a different Matt and tune out the conversation when Bree nods her head and Amy continues animatedly.

I gratefully accept the bottle of water Liz places in front of me. "Thanks," I mumble, smiling. I keep sipping at the water until I feel it's acceptable to tell them I'm going to sleep. "Where am I sleeping?" I ask. "I'm exhausted and I have to be home for Holden in a few hours."

"Christian brought over a couple air mattresses and blew them up so all of us could stay in one place. You and Emma can have those, and Theresa and I will sleep in my bed. Sara and Liz are going to pull out the couch and sleep on there. Is that okay?" Bree prompts.

"Of course, it's perfect," I reply. "Thank you, Bree. I hope you had fun tonight."

She nods in confirmation and grins. "I did. Thank you, guys. I think I needed tonight after all my finals. Christian insisted on tonight and I'm really glad he did. I almost forgot how to relax," she jokes.

"That's what Christian said!" Theresa giggles causing everyone else to join in again.

Their laughter makes for a perfect escape for me, and I stand, stretching my legs as I step around the couch. I slip into Bree's room and notice the two twin bed air mattresses perpendicular on the floor both at the bottom and far side of her bed. She already has them both covered in cranberry blankets and a pillow making me smile at her genuine kindness. I know I'm lucky to have friends like her. I just can't believe she's about to become Matt's sister-in-law.

Sighing, I quickly get myself ready for bed. Digging through my duffel, I find what I need. I pull on light blue floral pajama pants and a light blue matching tank top. I slip past the girls and across the hall to brush my teeth and wash my face, reluctantly waving, "Goodnight," on my way back to Bree's room.

I settle myself on the air mattress on the far side of the room, so I'm out of the way and I can plug my phone in for an alarm just in case I sleep too well without Holden waking me up. Just when I close my eyes, my cell phone goes off, but when I glance at the screen, I don't recognize the number. I open up the text and my heart flips at the words, "I hope it's okay I asked Christian to get your number from Bree."

I attempt to swallow the growing lump in my throat and ask the question I already know the answer to, "Who is this?"

"Matt Emory…I needed a way to get in touch with you. Is that okay?" he repeats. When I don't respond right away, he adds, "If it's not, I'll just pretend I don't have it."

I smile to myself as I type, "Stalker."

The dots begin dancing and I grip my phone, impatiently waiting for his response. "I try not to be with most girls, but you make it impossible not to be."

I roll my eyes at his exaggerated sweetness. "If you say so." I know he's just being himself, but sometimes it's hard for me to believe it's how he feels. "It's okay that you have my number," I proclaim and feel an overwhelming sense of relief as soon as I do.

"So, since I'm allowed to have your number, does that mean you'll answer a question for me?"

Biting my bottom lip nervously, I reply simply, "It depends."

"Christian told me your last name is Rossi. Is that Micah's name?"

I close my eyes hating how much that question hurts. Forcing them back open, I answer, "Yes, I couldn't go back to having my parents' last name." I can't explain to him my reasons, but he deserves some kind of honest answer from me.

"I want to ask you so much..." he informs me, "but I won't YET," he emphasizes. "Will you go to dinner with me tomorrow?" he proposes.

"I can't. Holden will be home," I inform him. He should understand now why we just wouldn't work.

"I could take both of you to dinner," he offers.

A gasp escapes my lips in shock. His suggestion comes completely unexpected. I feel like I'm going to throw up when I answer instinctively, "No!" I shove my phone away from me, curling up on my side, wanting to protect myself.

Focusing, I attempt to slow down my accelerated breathing and heartbeat. I can't do this. I shouldn't be talking to Matt. At least not without telling him everything about my past, but when the hell am I supposed to do that? His brother is getting married this week. He should focus on his family right now, not me.

My cell phone rings, startling me. I jump and fall off the side of the air mattress. "At least it's already on the floor," I grumble to myself as I try to untangle myself from the blanket and silence my phone.

I accidentally hit answer instead and begin to panic. My thumb unseeing searches for the button to hang up when I hear Matt's desperate plea, "Please don't hang up on me!" Holding my breath, I slowly move the phone to my ear, drawn in by the sound of his voice. "Sadie, please just listen to me for a minute," he begs.

I don't answer, but I don't hang up either. His sigh of relief echoes through the line at that realization while I wait quietly for him to continue.

"Sadie," he breathes my name, "I understand you not wanting me to meet your son. I was just trying to spend some time with you, but I get it's different involving him and I'm not about to push you into anything, especially something with him." He rambles, but I still can't even force myself to respond to him. "If you don't have any time to see me, I'm okay with just talking on the phone or texting, but please don't completely push me away. I want to get to really know you this time. Maybe the phone will be the perfect way for us to do that," he suggests.

Forcing out my breath, I'm finally able to speak and answer him, but even I'm shocked at the words that leave my mouth. "Okay, Matt. I'd like that."

He sighs and mumbles, "Thank fuck."

"What?" I ask giggling.

"Nothing," he claims, but I hear the grin in his voice, and it relaxes me. "You know you are going to have to actually see me next weekend at the wedding though, right?" he teases.

"I'll suffer through it for Bree," I joke making him laugh. The sound sends chills throughout my whole body, and I smile to myself.

"See? That's one of the reasons we were always so good together. You can dish it out as much as you can take it. There's not many girls that can handle me," he pushes. I cringe unexpectedly at the thought of him with other girls, but of course he was with other girls. We were never even really a couple. Then there's the fact that I haven't seen him in about four and a half years.

I did always like that we could tease each other and laugh together too, but I need to close my eyes and get some sleep. Hopefully I can process everything that happened tonight and figure out what to do. "Um, Matt," I begin hesitantly.

"Oh no, I'm getting the brush off already," he groans.

I apologize in response, "I'm sorry, but I really have to get some sleep. I have to be home for my son in a few hours."

"Excuses, excuses," he mumbles, teasing.

I chuckle even though he's right. I am using Holden as my excuse, but I need time to think. "Very funny, but I still have to go. I promise I'll eventually answer if you text me though," I tell him, my voice laced with humor.

He chuckles softly. "Okay. Get some rest. I'm really glad I moved here," he adds making me almost dizzy with his words. "Goodnight, Sadie."

"Goodnight, Matt," I whisper, barely able to get out the words.

Chapter 11

Sadie

I hang up my phone and curl up in my bed, ready to go to sleep after Holden had me running all day. I'm exhausted from not getting enough sleep the last couple nights, but it's not just from Bree's bachelorette party two days ago. Last night I stayed up late talking to Matt after Holden went to sleep. Now I can't seem to get him out of my head. I just hung up with him again, saying goodbye when I started falling asleep mid-sentence.

Heaving a sigh, I relax into my pillow in complete exhaustion.

4 Years and 10 Months Ago...

Sitting at the bonfire, I force myself to keep my back to the pathway everyone enters from. If I face the trail, my eyes will be drawn to it all night until he shows up...if he shows up. I grimace, hating the thought of not seeing him tonight. I keep nervously glancing from the dancing orange, yellow and blue flames to the dark rippling water of the swimming hole, the wind letting nothing stay still. Staring at the flames, I feel like there's anxiousness all around me, not just in me tonight. It's almost like the entire world is anticipating some kind of change. It feels more like an early fall night than the end of summer. The wind keeps me a little further back from the fire than I'd like, but my nerves assist in keeping me warm, so I guess they have some benefit.

I sigh as Micah flops down next to me, nudging me with his shoulder. As I turn my head towards him, his lips quirk up at the corners in a lazy smile. Reaching up, he tucks my hair behind my ear making his grin grow. "There she is. You've been hiding." He waits for a minute for my explanation, but I only offer him a shrug, a slight admission. I remain quiet causing him to groan like he just lost his best friend, but he's not at all surprised. "You're waiting for him to show up," he states.

"Yeah," I squeak out, even though I know he doesn't need my confirmation to know it's true.

He reaches for a stick and uses it to draw mindlessly in the sand while he talks. "Sadie, are you sure you know what you're doing?"

"Sadie? You never call me that," I mumble, ignoring his question.

He smiles sadly, not taking his eyes off of his drawings in the sand. Sighing, he continues without acknowledging my comment. "I know he's been around for a couple months, and he's been hanging out with all of us, but none of us really know anything about this guy. Besides the fact that he's here visiting family and he's leaving to go back to school in Texas in a few days. You'll probably never see the guy again when he leaves. Is that really what you want?" he questions pleadingly.

I shake my head, but not in answer to his question. I don't want Matt to leave. My heart pounds anxiously at the thought of never seeing him again. But he wouldn't give me any of his time if I didn't agree to forget about him after he's gone. He said it would be easier if we just lost each other's phone numbers. He said he wouldn't be back, so it was the only way he could be involved with me. I know he's probably right knowing we'll be in different parts of the country for at least the next four years. Plus, if I can't do it for Micah, how could I even think of doing it for someone who's practically a stranger?

Unfortunately, that fact doesn't make my stupid heart see sense.

"Sade," Micah states as he grips my shoulders and turns me towards him, forcing me to look at him. "Sade, I love you," he whispers with so much emotion tears spring to my eyes and a lump forms in my throat. His hands slide from my shoulders to behind my head, cradling my face between his hands as he looks into my eyes. "Are you sure this is what you want?" he repeats desperately.

I don't think I can give him the answer he's looking for making my chest ache. He stiffens slightly as his gaze flits to over my shoulder. My heartbeat speeds up feeling him behind me giving me the confidence I need to answer Micah. "I'm sure, Micah," I insist.

I watch as pain fleetingly passes through his eyes, but he quickly masks it as he pulls me towards him. He kisses me on the forehead, longer than necessary. As he tears his lips away, he wraps his arms around me, placing his lips next to my ear. "I'll be here for you when you need me," he whispers. He places another kiss next to my ear.

"Thank you, Micah," I rasp, my emotions overwhelming me. I kiss his cheek and pull myself out of his arms.

Clearing his throat, he steps back plastering a huge grin on his face. "Hey, Matt. Be careful with my girl," he adds warning him with a firm slap on the back. He saunters over to the other side of the fire and sits next to Clarissa, instantly dropping his arm around her shoulders.

I nervously glance up at Matt with a small smile. "Hi." He's wearing worn blue jeans and a black U2 concert t-shirt fitted nicely across his broad chest making my breath hitch at the sight.

He looks down at me nervously shuffling his bare feet in the sand. "Hi, Sadie." He grimaces before he drops down beside me reluctantly, making sure our bodies don't touch. "Listen, we need to talk," he stammers. My heart instantly drops like a lead weight to the pit of my stomach the moment those dreaded words leave his lips. "I've had fun hanging out with you this summer," he begins.

"Oh, no," I whimper feeling his rejection coming.

He winces at my reaction, but continues, anyway. "I'm leaving in a few days and after tonight, I'm honestly, not sure I'll get a chance to see you again before I go. Then, after I'm gone, I don't think we'll ever see each other again. I don't want you to ever regret anything between us, so I think we should just keep things light tonight," he suggests.

I look away from him feeling overwhelmed with disappointment. I've gotten myself all worked up preparing for a night with Matt. The way he kisses me sets my whole body on fire. We've fooled around and he's driven me over the edge, but he's been careful to stop before we go too far. I want him. I've never felt that way about anyone, but I want him. I want to lose my virginity to him. I don't care that I'll never see him again. I want him while I can still have him even if it's only for tonight.

Even though I know it's wrong, it feels right.

Tears begin forming in my eyes and I fight with myself to hold them back. Focusing on my breathing, I berate myself, feeling stupid. What teenage girl has sex with a guy who promises nothing?

In fact, he said after tonight I would never see him again. But I can't help the way I feel. My whole body vibrates when he's around. It's like we're meant to be together, even if it's only this one time. I can't let my time with him slip away without the memories, the thought of not even having that devastating me.

Wiping my tears away, I turn back towards him with determination. He leans away from me, appearing even more apprehensive. I tip my chin up in defiance as I insist, "I'll regret it if we're never together."

He tilts his head, unsure. "Sadie…" he mumbles my name.

I pinch my lips shut, trying not to get frustrated or show any hesitation. I don't want to give him more of a reason to walk away. Taking a deep breath, I stand up and reach for his hand. He takes it reluctantly, shocking my body with heat from head to toe as he stands to follow me. "Let's just go for a ride," I suggest. "We can go find a quiet place to just talk."

"I don't know if that's a good idea," he warns me drawing a smile from me.

"I think it's a great idea," I claim grinning mischievously. "If nothing happens, that's okay. Let's just spend some time together tonight without pressure. No regrets," I repeat his words.

Watching his face, I wait for him to give in and follow me, praying he does. I breathe a sigh of relief as he nods his head. "Okay, Sadie."

I turn away from him, so he doesn't see the huge smile instantly covering my face. He chuckles as I begin climbing the path towards where all our cars and trucks line the street. I glance back at him and prod, "What?"

He raises his eyebrows and states with a grin, "You're skipping."

I laugh as I turn to look for his truck. He tugs me towards his dark red Chevy Silverado and opens the door for me. Just as I take a step up, he lifts me and plants me inside his truck. He shuts the door and jogs around to the other side to climb in. "I know a place not too far where we can look at the stars and have some privacy."

He nods his head in agreement. "Okay, tell me where to go." I direct him through the dark, hilly roads further away from town until we reach a dirt road turn off into a cornfield. It's one of my parents' fields, but I don't need to tell him that. The property is huge, and no one is ever out here at night. He puts his truck in park and looks around him seeing nothing but corn. "Are you sure this is okay?"

I nod in response, but don't explain any further. "Do you have any blankets? We can sit in the back and look at the stars," I suggest.

"Sure," he agrees as he reaches behind my seat and comes out holding a red and black plaid blanket. "It won't be too comfortable back there though."

I shrug and push my door open, quickly jumping out of the truck. I slam the door and walk to the back of his truck to meet him. He lowers the tailgate and lifts me up, setting me back down on the end before I even have a chance to try to climb in. My eyes widen as I watch him push himself up, his arms rippling in the process as he sits next to me, causing my breath to hitch.

He looks down at me, his eyes turning a darker green with each second that passes. Matt gently places his hand on my chin, tipping my face up to meet his. He comes in so close to me I can feel his warm breath on my face and the taste of his minty breath mixes with mine. My chest heaves up and down in anticipation of his kiss, but when I push towards him, he pulls back just enough so our lips barely brush in the softest caress.

I unconsciously whimper needing to feel his lips on mine. He chuckles softly just before he presses his lips to mine. I sigh in relief as our mouths move together. We move impossibly close to one another, my whole body instantly heated with desire. His tongue slides across my lips and into my mouth, searching, tasting and tangling with my own. My hands twist into his t-shirt, desperately pulling him closer, needing more, wanting everything from him.

He pulls away and we both gasp for breath. "Sadie, we don't have to do anything. If all I get to do is hold you and kiss you, that's okay," he tells me sincerely. My heart warms with his words and confirms for me that I want him to be my first. He knows I've fooled around, but never had sex. He's been so good about it, but I want this memory with him.

I want him!

"Matt, I want you. I want it to be you! It needs to be tonight," I tell him with more confidence than I feel. "I'm nervous, but I know what I want and that's you," I insist.

His eyes turn even darker green as he whispers my name, "Sadie." He kisses me again, laying me back as he goes. "I'll take care of you," he whispers between kisses. "I'll go slow, and you can tell me to stop anytime," he reminds me as he leaves a trail of kisses down my neck.

"I don't want you to stop," I whimper. He pushes my shirt up and trails kisses over my belly. I push myself up and quickly tug my shirt over my head before I move to take his off as well.

He chuckles, helping me by pulling it off with one hand and tossing it to the side. My mouth drops open in appreciation as I ogle his ridged chest and abs. "Slow down, Sadie. I want to look at you." His deep voice rumbles through my whole body giving me goosebumps and making my nipples hard. A groan from deep in his throat tells me he notices. He lightly runs his hands over my covered breasts making me gasp.

Seconds later, he wraps one arm around me and pulls me close to him, kissing me deeply. I feel dizzy, tingly and warm, but mostly completely consumed by him and out of control. Both of our hands are suddenly everywhere, searching for more. He flicks the back of my bra, unhooking it and I instantly feel the cold air on my breasts.

"You are so fucking beautiful," he tells me breathily. His mouth goes to my breast, his tongue sneaking out and licking my nipple as his hand plays with the other one. He switches and does the same to the other side, eliciting a breathy moan from my lips. I arch my back into him, my body begging to get closer.

He brings his mouth back to mine, kissing me deeply. I can feel him through his jeans pressing against me making me push my hips against him wanting to feel more. He slides slightly away from me so he can slip his hand between us, *while keeping our lips fused together. His hand glides up between my legs and under my skirt. He rubs me gently over my panties, but it's not enough. I need more. I reach for the button on his jeans and his hands are quickly there to pull them down and kick them off. "Can I take these off?" he asks.*

I don't know exactly what he wants to take off, but I nod anyway. I don't care about any clothes at this point. I feel both my skirt and my underwear disappear down my legs. "Shit," he whispers just before his fingers touch my sex and he buries his head in my neck. My whimper nearly echoes in the empty field. He barely begins rubbing me and pushes his fingers inside when I gasp, holding onto him for dear life while my body pulses around his fingers.

My body begins to relax as I catch my breath. Slowly, I open my eyes finding Matt staring down at me with a sexy smile. His fingers lightly caressing from my hip, over my belly, around the side of my breast to my arm making me shiver. "Wow," he breathes before he begins kissing me again.

I want to see what he feels like. Reaching out, I lightly trace my fingers over his thick length as I curve my body into his. "Sadie," he warns sounding pained.

Laughing, I reiterate, "I want to, Matt." I push his Calvin Klein boxers down and off his legs. With my heart pounding, I again lightly trace my fingers over him on the way back up making him groan and bringing a smile to my face.

He kisses me and pushes my hands away from him, holding them above my head. Gasping, he looks into my eyes, his own green eyes wild. "Are you sure?"

"Yes," I answer with conviction and without hesitation.

As he releases my hands, he holds himself up, hovering over me. My hands skim down his back and lightly over his firm ass. He leans down and kisses me as he rubs

~ 103 ~

against me at my entrance. "I'll go in fast and then stop until you're okay," he informs me and waits for my acknowledgement.

"Okay." I nod my head and hold on tightly to his shoulders. He slides in just a little making me gasp at the large intrusion.

"Are you okay?" repeats. I just nod my head again, not able to speak. Bracing himself over me, he quickly pushes all the way in with one thrust. I cry out as a sharp pain hits me and a tear runs down my cheek. He doesn't move, but begins kissing my tears away whispering, "It's okay. I have you Sadie."

My heart soars with his words and I take a couple deep breaths to try to relax. "I'm okay," I whisper, panting. "Keep going." He looks into my eyes for confirmation and soon begins moving inside me. The pain slowly subsides, and everything slowly starts to feel better. Taking a deep breath, I'm able to relax again. Then finally, it starts to feel good as he moves methodically in and out of me, kissing me, both of us sweaty and gasping for breath.

Suddenly, he pulls out and lies on top of me with a groan. "Shit!" I can feel warm liquid covering my stomach between us and I cling to him as he finishes. He pulls back and looks at me, appearing panicked.

"What's wrong?" I ask.

"I forgot a condom. I'm so sorry. That's why I pulled away. I didn't even make you come," he complains.

I smile somewhat sadly up at him. "It's okay, Matt. I did before and I didn't expect to this time since it was my first time. It took a bit before it actually felt good you know." He grimaces at my comment. "I'm still glad you were my first," I add honestly.

He grins stiffly, still looking nervous, "But I forgot a condom. I pulled out, but I'm so sorry. You'd think I'd remember something like that after having it practically beaten into me by health teachers and my father. I haven't been with anyone else since I've been here and I've been tested since, but what if you get pregnant?" he rambles desperately.

I rub his arm, trying to calm his nerves and mine. "Matt it's okay. I'm not going to get pregnant," I insist.

"How do you know?" he asks. "Are you on birth control?"

I sigh knowing we should've had this conversation first like you're always taught in health class or by parents who care. That's not my parents, but I still know better. "Matt, I can't get pregnant," I confess quietly staring at his chest. I can't look at him while I say this. "I found out about six months ago that I have polycystic ovarian syndrome. Basically, it means I have these small cysts on my ovaries that make it almost impossible for me to get pregnant."

"You said almost impossible," he probes.

I squirm and nod uncomfortably. "Yeah, but I didn't think about it either and you pulled out..." I trail off, uncomfortable with this whole conversation.

He sighs heavily. "Sadie, look at me." I do hesitantly. "I know I said it would be easier if you lost my number, but if you need anything first..." he trails off. I nod my head and look away again. He sighs and grabs a roll of paper towels he has sitting in the back of his truck and cleans both of us off. I pull on my clothes afraid to look at him, but I'm more embarrassed about our conversation than what just happened between us. I can't help but think that isn't normal, but I can't help it. It felt good being in his arms; it felt right. I just wish it didn't have to end for us.

When we're both dressed, he sits further back in the truck and gestures for me to come sit by him. He wraps his arm around me, and I lean my head against his chest. I look up at the stars, overwhelmed by the brightness in the sky tonight.

"There are so many stars," he whispers my thoughts. "I really am going to miss you, Sadie."

"I'll miss you too. I wish things could be different," I admit. He doesn't reply.

Instead, he pulls me close, and I sit quietly in his embrace until he has to take me home.

Present Day...

I wake up with a gasp, completely startled by the vivid memories of my dreams. I take a couple deep breaths to calm myself down and push Matt out of my head. Just as I catch my breath, I hear Holden calling for me, "Mommy!" I push myself off my bed and stride down the hall to see the most important person in my life, my little boy.

"Good morning, my little man." I grin as I wrap my arms around him and pull him out of his bed. He wraps his little hands around my neck and his legs around my waist, resting his head on my shoulder.

"Good morning, Mommy," he mumbles sweetly. I close my eyes and breathe in his sweet scent. This is definitely my favorite part of the day.

Chapter 12

Sadie

I'm thankful I worked early today so I was able to spend the rest of the day with my little man. We decided to make it a day all about Mommy and Holden. In other words, we did things Holden loves to do together. We went to the park, had macaroni and cheese with applesauce for dinner and ended the night with Disney's Cars movie and popcorn. He's obsessed with all cars, trucks and tractors. I guess it will make his birthday easy in a few weeks.

Tucking a half-sleeping Holden into his bed, I whisper, "I love you Holden."

The groggy response I get from my little man makes me smile. "Vroom-vroom," he rumbles making car noises. "That means I love you too Mommy." I grin wider, my heart clenching as I suppress my giggle while placing a kiss on his cheek. I give him one more squeeze before his arms drop to the bed in exhaustion. I can't help but think I know how he feels as I smile down at him. My heart is so full of love every time I just look at him.

I tiptoe out of his room and quietly pull his door shut before I glide out to the kitchen to clean up. Just as I begin picking up, my cell phone rings and I reach for it without even looking at the caller-ID, already craving any distraction from cleaning.

"Hello," I answer.

"Sadie," his voice rumbles through the line sending chills down my spine.

I gulp with both excitement and nerves at the sound of his voice. "Hi, Matt," I reply feeling breathless.

"You answered again." I giggle in response. "You said if I texted you, you would eventually answer, but I haven't heard from you all day and I've been texting all day," he teases.

I giggle again and exaggerate my reply, "I did say eventually." He chuckles and I add more seriously, "I just put Holden to sleep. We had a busy day."

"I was just kidding," he tells me somewhat defensively.

"I know, it's okay," I let him know. "You should probably know, though, I don't always check my phone when I'm with Holden. I don't really get a lot of phone calls, at least not anything that can't wait when he's with me."

"Well, I guess you'll have to change that now since I'm calling," he jokes. I laugh and he insists, "Seriously, Sadie." I shake my head at him in amusement, even though he can't see me.

"So, what did you guys do tonight?" he asks casually.

"Watched Cars, played with cars and pretended to be a car." I grin thinking of Holden.

Matt laughs. "Sounds like me when I was a kid."

My heart plummets to the floor, my stomach starts to churn making me nauseous and I feel myself turning ghostly pale. "Um, Matt," I squeak nervously. "I um…I…"

He interrupts me, "I'm sorry. I know you're not ready to talk about him. Are you working tomorrow?" he asks changing the subject.

I sigh in relief because he's right. I'm not ready to talk about Holden yet. "Yeah, I'm opening tomorrow and have to be in at eight am," I inform him.

"Do you get a lunch break?"

"Yeah, I guess about noon. Why?" I question naively.

"I can meet you at the store and take you out to lunch," he tells me instead of asking.

"You will huh?" I prod the amusement back in my voice.

"Yup," he insists. "It's a lunch date."

I laugh. "Hey, I didn't agree to that."

"Well, everyone's gotta' eat, so I'll help you out with that tomorrow. We can catch up more then," he adds.

I smile to myself as I agree, "Okay. I'll see you tomorrow then, but I'll meet you in front of the store."

"Wait," he protests.

"What?"

"You're blowing me off already?" he asks dramatically.

I laugh. "I have to clean up and then get ready for tomorrow," I enlighten him. "Plus, I've been up late talking to some guy the last couple nights and little boys get up really early and so do their moms," I remind him. I need to make sure he understands Holden is always my priority.

"I'm sure you're exhausted. Sorry," he apologizes.

"It's okay, I enjoy talking to you," I admit softly.

He sighs, "Me too Sadie, me too. Okay. I'll see you tomorrow, Sadie," he relents.

"Goodbye, Matt."

"Goodnight, Sadie."

I click end on my phone and connect Pandora to the speaker in my kitchen before I drop it on the table. I grab a rag and some dish soap and start washing our dishes from dinner. I have no idea what to do. I want to get to know Matt again, or maybe even get to know him for the first time in a way. Last time we had such a strong physical attraction and we never really talked about anything real. I guess that's what it means to keep it casual, besides the fact that I made some really stupid decisions. I laugh humorlessly at myself, grimacing at some of the choices I made then.

The first notes of 'Last Name' by Carrie Underwood play and I burst out laughing at the irony. "What else am I gonna' do?" I mumble. I sing along as I clean, making sure I'm not too loud, not wanting to wake my son.

When I'm done, I peek in on Holden one more time before I make my way to my own room. Opening the closet, I pull out Holden's baby album and climb onto my bed. I begin looking through his pictures and I can't help but remember how scared I was when I found out I was pregnant. I don't know what I would've done without Micah. I swallow down the pain erupting in my chest every time I think of him and whimper, "I miss you."

4 Years and 9 Months Ago...

I stare wide-eyed at the stick in my hand. My hands are shaking and I'm barely able to breathe. "It's positive," I murmur feeling completely panicked. My heartbeat speeds up as I concentrate on breathing in and out.

A pounding on the bathroom door makes me jump and remember Micah's on the other side of the door waiting for me. "Sade, open up! You've been in there forever. You have to be done by now. Please, open up!" he pleads through the door.

I stiffly walk to the door and lift my hand to the knob to unlock it, feeling like it's physically the hardest thing I've ever had to do. As soon as the lock audibly clicks, the door swings open, nearly hitting me with its force.

"Sade?" Micah questions. I don't say anything. I'm too numb and at the same time feeling too much. I just hold the stick up for him to see for himself. "Fuck," he mumbles. I feel him physically shake himself just before his arms wrap tightly around me. "It will be okay, Sadie, we'll get through this. I promise. We'll be fine. We'll get through this together," he emphasizes.

I burst into tears and fall into his chest. My feet are suddenly off the ground and I'm in his arms. He carries me to my bed and lays me down gently. He climbs on my bed behind me and curls his body into mine. He wraps his arms protectively around me and holds me tightly while I sob uncontrollably. He whispers quietly in my ear, "I'll take care of you Sade. Everything will be okay." He kisses me on the forehead and continues to soothe me until I'm able to stop crying.

When I'm finally able to calm down, I grab a Kleenex and wipe my tears away. Then I slowly roll over to face him. "I'm sorry," I gasp. He shakes his head like he's telling me not to worry. "I'm really scared Micah," I whimper.

His eyes look sad when he replies, "I know, but I'm here for you Sade. I'll always be here for you." I nod my head knowing it's true and wipe at my eyes again. "What do you want to do?" he asks me, sounding nervous.

I shrug. "I need to have this baby, Micah. I didn't think I would ever be able to have children. You know that."

He nods his head sorrowfully. "Yeah."

"My parents are going to kill me!" I whine.

"Don't worry about them. You can't worry about them, Sade, not this time," he emphasizes. I sigh and nod reluctantly in agreement. Although, it is easier said than done, Micah's right. My parents have always cared more about their plans for me than my own dreams. When I step off their path even a little bit they freak out or practically act like they don't even know me. I'm positive it won't go well when I talk to them. It's the only thing I'm sure about.

Micah takes a deep breath and asks cautiously, "Are you going to try to get in touch with him? To tell him?"

I nod feeling both anxious and terrified at what could happen when I find him. "I have to. He should know, but I have no idea how to find him. I don't even know his last name." I laugh humorlessly and sigh trying to figure out where to begin. "It would help if I didn't already stupidly delete his phone number."

He nods again and holds me while we both remain quiet thinking. Just when I think I'm about to fall asleep from complete emotional exhaustion, he whispers in my ear, "No *matter what happens, I'll be here for you. If you find him, I'm here. If you don't find him, I'm here."*

"Thank you, Micah," I reply feeling overwhelmed.

"I always told you I would marry you one day," he reiterates, grinning. "It just may happen sooner now than later," he adds pushing my hair out of my face.

"Micah." I shake my head not understanding how he could be serious right now. "You don't want to marry me, especially now."

He smiles softly, proclaiming, "I've always wanted to marry you, especially now."

I sigh and curl up against him again, needing the comfort. We can talk about this more later, after the shock of me being pregnant wears off. He's the last person I want to argue with when he's not only my best friend, but also my only support right now.

Present Day...

"I have to tell him, and I have to tell him soon. I'm just not sure how," I wince feeling my heart clench at my reality. I'm terrified to tell Matt the truth. Yes, I can admit to myself I'm still attracted to him. "What girl wouldn't be?" I murmur laughing. I wish I could date him without worrying what will happen with Holden. Every time he's near me my whole body feels like it's on fire. I feel jittery, excited and happy. I want to get closer to him and know everything about him, but it's not that simple.

I sigh in resignation, knowing I need to think about Holden. He's the most important thing, not how Matt makes me feel. But what if I tell him about Holden and he breaks his heart. I couldn't take it. Holden deserves to have a father who will do anything for him. I know I can't choose who his father is, but I still want the best for him. Matt seems like a good guy, especially now that I know he'll soon be Bree's brother-in-law. She's always talked very highly of

Christian's entire family. I trust her. I don't think she could be wrong about this.

My heart on the other hand, I sometimes wonder about, but I believe I can trust her judgment. I also don't know how he'll react. He has every right to be upset with me. I should've kept his number until I knew like he asked, even though he was also the one who told me to lose his number in the first place.

Now, he's missed nearly four years of his son's life. He could truly hate me for it. I honestly wouldn't blame him if he did.

Walking down the hall, I toss the dirty rags into the laundry basket with a heavy sigh. I know I have to tell him, but maybe I can wait until after the wedding. If I tell him now, I could ruin Bree and Christian's big day. It's already been so long, a few more days couldn't hurt, I reason with myself. That way I won't ruin the wedding for anyone, and I can use his trial period to talk to him more and keep getting to know him better. Then, I'll have a clearer idea of how to handle the situation with him. After the wedding I'll tell him about Holden. I'll tell him he has a son.

I cringe at the thought, terrified of what will happen in that moment. I may accept my decision to wait until next week, but I truly don't know if it's the right one. I probably should have told him the day I ran into him at the store I admit with a grimace, but I was shocked to see him again. Heaving another sigh, I turn towards my bathroom to jump in the shower. I need to wash up and hopefully fall into a dreamless sleep tonight.

Chapter 13

Matt

It's surreal standing in my brother's room at my parents' house with my brothers and sister all dressed up for Christian's wedding. We're wearing gray suits with light blue ties that match the bridesmaids' dresses, while Christian's tie is white to match Bree. "Whoever thought our baby brother would be the first of all of us to get married?" Jason asks with humor lacing his voice.

"I did," Christian declares smirking. "Why would anyone want to marry your sorry asses?" he jokes. "Except for T of course," he adds grinning at our sister.

"Of course," she murmurs with a smile and a roll of her eyes as she tugs at her long shimmery blue fitted dress with spaghetti straps.

"Stop T, you look beautiful," I whisper. She smiles gratefully at me and drops her hands to her sides. I hate that she's so self-conscious now, but at least Jax has certainly helped her with that. She's definitely more confident than she was right after her accident.

"Well, at least I did find her," Jason adds under his breath chuckling.

"You have to get Sara to actually agree to marry you though," I taunt.

Jason grins secretively and looks down at his shoes. "Yeah…"

"No fucking way," I grumble.

Christian spins around and looks at me then over at Jason avoiding eye contact with any of us. He never avoids eye contact with us. "You proposed to Sara?" Christian asks, his voice cracking.

Jason shifts from foot to foot and looks up at Christian. "Today is your day little brother," he replies not answering him.

Theresa squeals in excitement and leaps towards Jason. She wraps her arms around him and cries, "Congratulations!"

"That doesn't mean you get to keep shit like this from us!" Christian declares. "We should still know when you're engaged. Nothing will interfere with today. I've waited long enough to make Bree my wife. But you're supposed to tell us big shit like this!" Christian pauses and looks at Theresa just releasing her hold on Jason then over at me still standing in shock. "Wait, did you know?" he questions glaring at me.

I shake my head, muttering. "No clue. When did you propose?"

Jason's lips twitch up and he admits, "Sunday night." He shrugs, "I was going to wait until after your wedding, but since we had a little extra time this week with the wedding and her finishing school, I didn't want to wait."

"Do Mom and Dad know?" Christian asks raising his eyebrows.

Jason rubs the back of his neck nervously. "Um, yeah. We told them earlier this week," he confesses. Christian crosses his arms over his chest and glares at Jason making us all laugh. "Like I'm going to get in trouble by telling *anyone* before Mom," Jason adds chuckling.

We all laugh even harder giving me the warm familiar feeling of being home again. This time though, I feel like something might be missing, but I'm not sure what it might be.

Christian strides over to Jason and gives him a quick hug with a hard pat on the back. "Congratulations big brother."

I step over to him and do the same. "Congratulations."

"Thanks," he murmurs. He clears his throat and jokes, "Now we just have to find you a good woman."

I shake my head, grumbling, "Nah, I'm good." He chuckles while Christian and Theresa both give me a knowing look, filled with a slight warning. I'm sure Sadie will be here today, and they don't want me to cause any problems.

"You seemed pretty friendly with that Sadie girl at the bachelor party last week," Jason comments with a sly grin, obviously searching for a reaction from me.

Luckily, I'm saved from responding when there's a knock at the door. It flings open revealing our parents on the other side. "Are you ready?" my mom prompts.

"Yes, Mom," we all mumble.

She strides over to Christian with a huge smile on her face. She looks absolutely beautiful in a sleeveless long mint green dress with an ivory sheer overlay. Her blonde hair is looped up with loose curls, similar to Theresa's. My dad steps up behind her placing his hand on her waist while he waits for her to talk to Christian. She places her hand on his cheek and smiles up at him, adoringly.

"You look so handsome," she gushes.

"Thanks, Mom," I respond, needing to joke a little bit. She turns and smiles wide at me, knowing I'm not really fishing for compliments.

Then, she turns back to my brother, obviously trying to reign in her emotions. "I'm so proud of you Christian," she proclaims with tears in her eyes. "Keep being the man I know you can be for Bree, for you," she emphasizes. "I'm so happy for you two," she adds her voice cracking. Then she wraps her arms tightly around his broad chest. "I love you."

"I love you too, Mom," Christian whispers into her hair as he hugs her back.

"I can't believe all my boys are bigger than me now." She laughs and pats him on the chest as she steps away dabbing at her eyes. "No phones during the ceremony," she warns, narrowing her eyes at each of us one by one. We all put our hands up, letting her know we wouldn't even think of it.

She shakes her head and turns towards Theresa with a grin. "Come on, Theresa," she urges reaching her hand out for T. Theresa immediately follows, clasping onto Mom's hand. "It's time for us to join Bree."

Theresa suddenly lets go of Mom and slips away from her. She steps up to Christian, wrapping her arms around him, his arms instantly embracing her. "I know you don't need it, but good luck anyway. I love you."

"I love you too, T," he emphasizes. We never used to say I love you to each other as much as we do now, but after Theresa's accident things changed. Now we don't want to miss the opportunity.

Theresa joins Mom again and they walk out, pulling the door shut behind them. My dad pats Christian firmly on the back and moves his hand up to his shoulder where he tightens his fingers until Christian looks him in the eyes. "Are you ready, son?"

"I've been ready since the day I met her dad," he replies honestly. My chest tightens and I have to look away from all of them for a moment.

When I turn back, Dad is grinning at Christian. He releases a slow breath. "Alright then. Keep making us proud, Christian." He pulls Christian in for a hug and pats him on the back again. I swear I see tears in my brother's eyes, but they're gone before he looks back up and I have a chance to confirm it.

Christian clears his throat before I hear him say, "Thanks, Dad."

"You boys better get out there to start seating people. I saw a few people arriving already," our father instructs.

"Christian and I will be there in a few minutes. We'll meet you up at the altar," he adds grinning.

I step up to give Christian a quick hug and firm pat on the back before we leave. "I'm really happy for you bro."

He smiles. "Thanks, Matt."

Jason steps up to do the same. "It's going to be a great day. Don't mess up," he jokes attempting to lighten the mood.

Christian chuckles and I add, "Just say, I do, and you'll be good."

"Assholes," he mumbles quietly. "Ouch," he complains as Dad flicks the back of his head making us laugh. He obviously wasn't quiet enough. He rubs the back of his head laughing and Dad just shakes his head with a small smile.

I follow Jason out the door, pulling it shut behind me. We walk down the stairs and immediately head outside to the backyard, which I admit doesn't look anything like our backyard right now. I squint into the sun and immediately pull out my gold aviator sunglasses to put them on while I can. I'm sure one of my parents will tell me to take them off soon enough.

"We're lucky it's such a beautiful day today," Jason comments.

"Yeah, since everything will be outside, I can't imagine what it would be like with rain," I add. Christian and Bree wanted the ceremony and the reception to all be right here on the lake.

They met on this lake, and they also say they fell in love here. Bree spent a lot of time here while she was growing up as well. She spent many summers here with her grandmother whom she lost suddenly a few years ago. She took it hard, but she says being here on the lake helps her feel closer to her grandmother and even her mom whom she lost to leukemia not long before her grandmother died. She says it's the one place that's always truly felt like home, which is something I understand. For me home has been where my family lives, not really an actual place. But I can see how a place like this could become home, especially with family here.

Towards the bottom of the lake, off to the right, rows of about sixty white wooden folding chairs are set up, separated by an aisle marked by two large planters overflowing with white roses and hydrangeas and accented with light blue hydrangeas and greenery. White flower petals are sprinkled down the makeshift aisle with a large wooden arch standing at the end of the aisle decorated with ivy along with the same white and blue flowers.

Then, just beyond the arch, where they'll say their vows, lies nothing but the incredible view of the lake.

To the left of where everything is set for the ceremony, but directly behind my parents' house, there's a large white tent set up with tables, chairs and everything else needed for the reception. Several people in black and white continue milling about under the tent, working hard to set-up in time.

Jason and I saunter down the hill preparing for our part. "Does it matter where we seat people?"

He shrugs. "I don't think so. As long as we put mom and dad in front on the same side as Christian and Bree's dad will sit on her side in the front."

"I guess Sara and Jax should sit behind mom and dad," I suggest and Jason nods in agreement.

"It's small enough that everyone is basically family or close friends. Liz will probably want to sit with Sara instead of on Bree's side by herself. Hopefully, none of the other seats matter," he mumbles, shrugging again.

Jason's smile grows the moment we spot Sara. He steps up to her and tilts his head down, giving her a chaste, but firm kiss in front of me making her blush.

I grin mischievously down at her and step up close. "Sara, you're breaking my heart," I proclaim. Her eyes scrunch together in confusion. "First Bree, now you," I mutter, my lips quirking up in a smile as I pull her into my arms. "Congratulations," I whisper in her ear.

She giggles and hugs me in return. "Thank you," she whispers. I step back and she turns towards the girl she was talking to. "You remember Liz? Blake's girlfriend?"

"And my little sister," Jax declares as he steps up wrapping his arm around Liz's neck. He smirks and kisses her on the top of the head. She laughs and gently pushes him away.

I nod in confirmation. "I do. How are you, Liz? Both of you look beautiful," I praise.

"Thank you," they say in unison.

"Alright, enough flirting with my girl and Liz," Jason jokes. Although I'm sure he's partly serious. "We need to seat some people. Where's Blake?"

We turn to look around just as he steps up next to us and places a kiss on the corner of Liz's mouth. He grins. "I had to wait outside Bree's door for her to be dressed before I could get in to talk to her. Hope you guys weren't waiting for me long."

I chuckle. "Better we wait then you barge in on Bree. None of us need Christian pissed off today," I tease.

Christian's best friend and old roommate Joe joins us to help us seat everyone as they come. When everyone is nearly seated, I turn to find Joe escorting Emma and Sadie together, one girl on each arm and my heart stops in my chest. I stand in the middle of the aisle frozen for a minute and stare.

Sadie looks absolutely gorgeous. Her dark hair is all pulled up off her neck, but a few strands have already escaped and are blowing lightly across her face. Her blue gray eyes look soft with her dark violet dress that clings to her body in all the right places. It has spaghetti straps and fits her curves so perfectly I can barely breathe. Her already tan skin appears velvety soft. I want to gently trail my fingers up her arm and run my lips along her shoulder to find all the sensitive spots on her neck.

I'm jostled by Jason from behind, making him chuckle. "Are you alright, Matt?" he prods with a knowing smirk.

I clear my throat and shake my head to pull myself out of my drifting thoughts. "I'm good," I declare.

He laughs louder, but I ignore him and approach Sadie instead. Her eyes widen when she sees me approaching her making me smile. "Let me help you out, Joe," I offer my eyes never leaving Sadie. He may respond, but I don't hear anything. I'm not paying attention to anything but the woman in front of me. I take her arm and loop it through mine following behind Joe. "You look incredibly beautiful, Sadie," I tell her honestly.

"Thank you," she murmurs blushing slightly. Her eyes quickly look me over causing my smile to grow with her perusal. "You clean up pretty good yourself," she admits shyly.

When I realize Emma is already sitting down, I know I have to let her go, but I do so hesitantly. I kiss the back of her hand gently before I release her. I smile genuinely before I have to force myself to turn away.

After that, my eyes constantly drift to Sadie every time I walk down the aisle making the time fly by. It feels like only a few minutes have passed when Christian and Dad join us. My dad sits in the front row, and I stand next to Christian at the end of the arch with Joe behind me, leaving a spot for Jason between us while he escorts Mom down the aisle.

Blake stands opposite us on Bree's side as her man of honor and we all wait for the girls to come down the aisle. Theresa and Bree's friend Amy are her other bridesmaids. I step up behind Christian and whisper, "You got this."

He turns and smiles at me with a confident nod. Then, we both turn, my eyes drifting to Sadie as she watches Amy before Theresa comes up the aisle.

When everyone stands to see the bride enter, my view of Sadie is temporarily blocked, and I attempt to focus my attention back to my brother and his girl. I glance down the aisle at Bree standing alongside her dad looking incredibly proud. Even I admit she looks absolutely stunning.

I peer over at my brother and the look on his face makes me smile. His mouth is slightly open, and his eyes are wide, as he stands completely stunned by her beauty. He closes his mouth and swallows hard. A look of such extreme love, respect and admiration consumes his features. I can't describe it as anything other than pure happiness. I've never seen Christian look like that, but he sure as hell deserves it.

They both do.

Chapter 14

Sadie

Matt looks so good my mouth is watering. I know I shouldn't be focused on him, but I can't help it. I've never seen him in a suit before. My eyes are completely drawn to him. His chest appears so broad in that jacket. His eyes seem lighter with the gray or maybe it's the sun. He appears so relaxed and happy making me sigh with content as I watch him. The way he smiles at Christian and Bree, I can tell he's truly happy for his brother. Although I can admit to myself it feels a bit strange that they're family and so close when Bree is one of my only friends now, along with Emma of course.

I attempt to pull my attention away from Matt and focus on Bree and her wedding. "Bree and Christian are lucky it's such a beautiful day. I wonder what they would've done if it had rained," I comment.

"I'm not sure, but it is a perfect day, so they don't have to worry about that and neither do we." Emma grins. "Did you see that the bridesmaids' dresses match the guys' ties?" she whispers in my ear. Then she gestures towards the bridal party standing at the man-made altar with the deep blue lake and light blue sky as their background. I nod, and she praises, "I love it."

"It's all so incredibly beautiful," I murmur admiring the picturesque wooden arches full of blue and white flowers and greenery, similar to the flowers in the bridesmaids' bouquets. A plain white satin ribbon wraps around the bridesmaids' bouquets, keeping them looking simple, but elegant, just like their dresses. Just beyond, the lake lightly ripples from a calm breeze.

Bree's white satin dress is simple, but beautiful, just like her. It's sleeveless but comes down from her shoulders in a slight v between her breasts. It shimmers at her waist with thick beadwork, almost like a belt and two open-ended intertwined hearts at her navel. It flows gently down to her feet with similar beadwork all along the bottom hem, but it flows more like waves curling up and down with the intertwined hearts at the top of each small wave. The back of the dress is mostly open to her waist with the two shoulder straps connected with thin straps at the top and two shimmering intertwined hearts holding it together at the nape of her neck.

She has her chestnut brown hair pinned up elegantly with a beautiful heart comb in loose curls with a few loose strands falling around her face. "Bree looks utterly gorgeous," I whisper to Emma. She nods and smiles with admiration of her own.

I happily watch my friend marry the man of her dreams, although I struggle to keep my eyes on them and away from Matt. The way the two of them look at each other sometimes makes me feel like I'm intruding on their moment, but it's one of the most incredibly striking things I've ever seen. I can't help but wish for a love like that for myself someday.

I did love Micah and I know he loved me. In fact, I still love him and probably always will, but what we shared was never anything like I'm seeing in front of me between Bree and Christian. It's obvious they have the kind of love you see in movies, the kind of love you read about in books and fairy tales, the kind of love I've only dreamed of and never experienced. I've always wondered if it really exists but looking at them, I know it does. Unfortunately, it might not be for everyone. I sigh refusing to feel sorry for myself today. I have Holden and that's already more than I thought I'd ever have.

They keep the ceremony short, repeating the standard wedding vows with a shaky, but confident voice. "I now pronounce you husband and wife," the priest declares. "You may kiss your bride."

Bree looks up at Christian with a timid smile. His grin is huge as he breathes an exaggerated sigh of relief. "Finally!"

We all burst out laughing as he quickly wraps her in his arms and presses his lips to hers. He leans her back slightly, so she has to cling to him to stay on her feet as his lips move smoothly over hers. Thunderous clapping and whistling fill the air and when Christian finally pulls away and sets Bree on her feet, both of them have the biggest smiles I've ever seen on their faces. He kisses her again as he entwines his fingers with hers. They turn towards all of us completely glowing with happiness.

"I'm pleased to announce for the very first time, Mr. and Mrs. Christian James Emory," the priest proclaims. We all stand and clap loudly. Emma puts her fingers in her mouth and whistles making me laugh as we watch them glide down the grassy aisle covered in white flower petals.

Matt strides by with Blake, winking at me on the way. Just his small look causes butterflies to take over my stomach and my heart to pound erratically. The rest of the wedding party, first Jason and Amy, then Joe and Theresa immediately follow them. "That was so beautiful," Emma gushes. I nod and she grins playfully. "Now let's go party."

I laugh and follow all the other guests across the Emory's lawn to a large white open tent. "I like that everything is so close, easy travel," I joke.

"You got that right," she adds and links her arm through mine. "Let's get a drink. I'm sure they'll be doing pictures for a little while," she adds, "And you can't stare at him the whole time." My eyes widen in shock making her giggle. "Well, it's not like you're exactly subtle Sadie," she teases. "But he sure is hot as hell and easy to look at!"

Blushing, I laugh along with her because we both know she's right. "Okay," I agree, "Let's go get a drink. I need to try to relax before I look at him again." She giggles as we try to take everything in as we walk.

The outside of the tent is outlined in white lights that will sparkle as the sun sets. As soon as we step underneath, I look all around me. There's a bar set up behind all the tables. I count only eight tables of eight all covered with white with a pale shimmery blue overlay. In the center of each table is a wide, but low vase full of white roses, blue and white hydrangeas and surrounding greens, just like the girls' bouquets. An icy blue candle sits in the middle of the bouquet adding to the ambiance.

On the other side of the tent is the area I assume is the dance floor with white lights hanging down like stars over that whole section and a DJ on the side opposite the tables. Eric Clapton begins playing softly through the speakers relaxing me as I continue to take in my surroundings. "Wow," I breathe.

Emma grins and tugs on me again. "Come on, I need a drink," she reminds me.

I laugh at her persistence and follow her towards the small bar. "Do you think we have assigned seats?" I ask as we step behind a few other guests in line.

Emma nods towards a table off to the side. "It looks like it."

"How about you grab me a glass of champagne and I'll go see where we're sitting," I suggest.

"Sure," she murmurs, nodding in agreement.

I stride over to the tables to find our names. I spot both my name and Emma's quickly. Skimming through the rest of the names, I search to see who's seated at our table. I'm surprised to find Blake and his girlfriend Liz, as well as Amy and Joe at our table since they're all in the wedding party except for Liz. We're also sitting with Dean whom we met last week and a Matt Young. I grab our tags and spin around to find Emma with our drinks. "Thank you." I smile as I take a glass before telling her what I discovered.

"Really?" she asks surprised. "We're sitting with Joe?"

Laughing at her response, I raise my eyebrows in question. "I guess I'm not the only one with a little crush in someone here tonight. Interested?"

She shrugs and smirks at me, dragging out her answer, "Maybe."

I link my arm through hers. "Come on. Let's put our purses down." We walk over to find a spot at the table and a couple minutes later the table is full of people. "I guess you guys are done with pictures?" I ask Joe who immediately sits on the other side of Emma.

He nods and smiles flirtatiously at her. "Hi, Emma." I guess the attraction is mutual. I smile, happy for her, but begin wondering how I can occupy my own time tonight.

I turn to find Dean standing behind me with another glass of champagne in his hand. "I noticed you were almost empty, and I thought I'd help you out," he offers holding it out to me with a smile. "Sadie, right?"

I nod and swallow the last bit of liquid in the glass I'm still holding and set it on the table. "Thank you, Dean," I tell him and take the glass from him.

He grins. "You remembered." He slips into the chair next to where I was sitting just a moment ago. I sigh and sit down next to him.

As everyone takes his or her seats at our table, I realize they all seem to be paired up in some way. The other Matt is sitting next to Blake talking to him, but Amy is already hanging all over him. Then with Emma and Joe seeming interested in one another, that leaves me with Dean. He seems nice and all, but I'm just not interested. I grin knowing what turns most men off. "So, we didn't get much of a chance to talk last week. Would you like to see a picture of my son? He'll be four in a few weeks."

His eyes go wide, his eyebrows nearly hitting his hairline. "Oh, I didn't think you were married with the way you were dancing with Matt last week and all."

I blush at the same time my heart clenches thinking of Micah. "Um, I'm not married anymore," I mumble not able to look him in the eyes.

"Oh, I'm sorry," he offers awkwardly. Then his grin grows teasing and he suggests, "You can always use me to get back at him or get over him if you'd like." My eyes grow wide with shock before I burst out laughing, not able to hold back. I shake my head and he shrugs, smirking at me. "Well, it was worth a shot. Right?"

I laugh even harder and proclaim while trying to catch my breath, "You're actually pretty funny, Dean."

"Thanks," he states, grinning appreciatively.

"What the hell is going on?" Matt's deep voice grumbles from just over my shoulder sending shivers down my spine.

Dean's grin actually grows the moment he sees Matt. He wraps his arm around my shoulders pulling me towards him causing me to stumble into his chest. "Sadie and I were just having a good time. We were talking about what we could do to have some fun together later," he claims, a mischievous twinkle in his eyes.

He winks at me making me chuckle. I can hear the playfulness in his voice, which makes me pretty sure he's messing with Matt, but I don't really know him very well. When I look up at Matt though, his steely gaze intently flashing from Dean to his arm around me causes me to freeze. My heart pounds and my breath catches in my throat at the blatant fire in his eyes.

Is he jealous?

When I'm finally able to breathe again, I know I have to break through this tension and help calm him down. "We…we were just talking," I stammer.

Matt crosses his arms across his broad chest with his fists clenched and continues to glare at Dean. Taking a deep breath, I pull myself together and cautiously slip out from underneath Dean's arm. He chuckles, clearly amused. "I'm going to get another drink. I'll see you in a few minutes at our table, Sadie," he emphasizes and winks at me again before he walks away.

"Stay away from him," he demands. "He's a player," Matt announces surprising me.

My eyebrows scrunch together in confusion. "So?"

Hurt flashes across Matt's face and he moves to step past me. "I guess I was wrong about things between us if you're into him."

"Matt wait," I insist as I reach for his arm. I gasp at the feel of his corded muscles under his suit. Pausing, I clear my throat and continue to defend myself, "I mean so because there's *nothing* going on between Dean and me."

He glances over at me sheepishly. "Really?"

I nod emphatically. "Of course, really."

He sighs and drops his arms. "Sorry, Sadie. I guess I didn't realize how jealous I could be until I saw you talking to Dean."

I smile, my stomach doing a flip. "No big deal. I'm good at scaring guys off. I just tell them about Holden and they go running."

He cringes and whispers my name with a shake of his head, "Sadie."

His grimace actually warms my heart. There couldn't be a more perfect reaction coming from him. "Thank you," I whisper appreciatively.

He pinches his lips together and prods, "Why in the hell are you thanking me?" I shrug and look down at my feet nervously. He sighs and reaches for my hand giving it a gentle squeeze. "I'd stay here right now if I could, but it looks like my mom wants me," he declares nodding behind me. I glance over my shoulder at his mom waving him over and then focus my attention back up at him. The corners of his mouth twitch up and he asks sweetly, "but promise you'll dance with me after dinner?"

My stomach twists in anticipation. I nod feeling jittery as I barely whisper, "I'd love to." He pulls my hand to his mouth and brushes his lips lightly over my knuckles causing goosebumps to cover my flesh. Matt's eyes move up my arm along with the goose bumps making him chuckle. My whole body instantly heats with awareness just before he releases my hand. Biting my lip, I watch as he turns and walks away towards his parents.

Chapter 15

Matt

I glance over at Sadie longingly. If I don't get away from my family and over by her soon, I think I might hit someone. I hate the way Dean keeps looking at her. I don't care if he's Christian's friend. He obviously wants her, and I'm stuck making sure I talk to relatives that haven't seen me in so long they probably wouldn't recognize me if I passed them on the street. I grit my teeth and clench my fists, struggling to hold back my groan as I glare at Dean who holds his hand out for Sadie and pulls her towards the dance floor. I don't want him anywhere near her, even though I know I have no right to feel that way or do anything about it. That doesn't mean I want to sit and watch her dance so closely with someone else.

"Matthew," my father states in a slightly harsh tone making me flinch. When I hear that tone, I know I've been in my head too long and I've either ignored him or done something I shouldn't have done. Tearing my eyes away from my own personal disaster on the dance floor, I focus on the one in front of me. "Your Uncle is talking to you," he informs me with a look that intimidated the hell out of me as a kid.

I still greatly respect him, but I chose to go to school in Texas to become my own man. I'm not about to revert to stressing or getting into trouble because I'm not like my brothers, especially Dad's golden child, Jason. Of course, Christian and I are the only ones that see it that way. Jason thinks Dad is hardest on him because he's the oldest. Jason and I get along great, especially now that we're older and no longer living at home, but he's like our father in so many ways. I can't compete with that, so I never bother trying.

I clear my throat and look my uncle in the eyes. "Sorry, I guess something has me a little distracted tonight," I admit truthfully keeping my tone light.

He smirks. "I can see that. She's very pretty. Maybe I should let you go cut in, instead of standing here pretending to be more interested in what us old men have to say," he jokes nodding towards the dance floor.

Quickly, I take advantage of his offer before he changes his mind or someone can stop me, "Thanks Uncle Bob. I think I'll do that." Shaking his hand, I pat him on the back with a huge grin. I can feel my dad watching me, but his look has turned more curious now than anything. I've never brought a girl home like Jason and Christian, not even in high school. My parents have never even seen me with a girl I was interested in, although they know I date. I realize eagerly pursuing a girl in front of my whole family is bound to bring out questions, but for the first time I really don't give a fuck. I have to get her out of Dean's arms now before I do something stupid.

As I approach, I notice his hands on her waist, inching towards her ass. She probably doesn't even realize what he's doing. Her hands are on his shoulders and he's talking and smiling down at her flirtatiously. I watch as she tips her head back and laughs, taking my breath away. I pause for a moment, lost in her beauty as her whole face lights up. Dean inches closer to her, pushing me to move rapidly to my destination. I stop only inches from her and watch as goosebumps break out on her arms as both of them look over at me.

"Can I help you," Dean questions smirking.

My jaw twitches in annoyance, but I focus my eyes on Sadie's blue-grey ones that appear to practically glow in this light. "May I cut in?"

"Matt…um…yeah," she stammers adorably, making my lips twitch in amusement.

Dean sighs with resignation and grins down at Sadie. "Thank you for dancing with me beautiful," he proclaims before kissing the back of her hand.

She blushes and nods her head in acknowledgement as she steps away. It's surreal to me how shy she seems. She was never really shy with me before. In fact, she was the one who pushed our relationship along. As Dean releases her and walks away with a nod in my direction, she hesitantly turns towards me.

I don't waste a moment of time with her. Swiftly, I wrap one arm around her waist to pull her close. With my other arm, I reach for her hand and clasp ours together, holding her hand to my chest right over my heart. She stares at my chest as we sway and spin to the end of "It's Your Love" by Tim McGraw and Faith Hill.

When the song ends, the DJ interrupts the music, "Can I please have everyone's attention?" He pauses waiting for the crowd to quiet. "Could I please get the bride and groom to come out on the dance floor? It's time for your first dance as husband and wife."

Sadie begins to slip away from me, but I keep hold of her hand, pulling her to stand directly in front of me. "Not so fast," I request firmly. I keep hold of her hand wrapping my arm around her and resting both our hands on her hip. "That dance didn't count. It wasn't even a whole song," I claim grinning. "I'm not letting you go anywhere."

She glances up at me nervously and I search her eyes like I might be able to see what she's thinking. "Okay," she whispers.

"When I asked Christian and Bree what song they wanted to play for their first dance they had trouble agreeing." The DJ laughs along with a few others. "Now of course Christian agreed to do whatever Bree wanted after only a few minutes, but then Bree went a completely different direction to find a compromise." Everyone laughs again and Bree just shrugs her shoulders grinning happily at Christian. "So, for their first dance here's 'Making Memories of Us' by Keith Urban." We all clap as Christian pulls Bree into his arms with a laugh and a chaste kiss.

I watch my brother for a moment with his girl when I hear Sadie mumble with reverence, "They're so happy."

A smile tugs at my lips until I tilt my head down and stare at her, watching her expression. My gut clenches painfully with the emotions I watch cross her face. She seems to be happy and sad, content then lost, confident yet terrified. I hate that she could be thinking of Micah as she stands here with me watching my brother, but I detest even more the thought of her with so much agony inside. I can't help but wonder if what I'm seeing is real. Reaching up, I caress her cheek lightly with my finger startling her. She turns her attention to me and visibly shakes herself to pull herself together. "Are you okay Sadie?" I whisper, my chest clenching with concern.

I watch as she takes a slow controlled breath. Then she glances at me and forces a smile. "I'm great! This wedding is so beautiful. I'm having a fabulous time."

I grimace, hating that she's lying to me, but I can't force her to talk to me when she just came back into my life. I pinch my lips shut tight and wait for the song to end. When it does the DJ requests that the wedding party join the bride and groom on the dance floor as the first notes of "Who You Love" by Katy Perry and John Mayer blasts through the speakers. I smirk at the song choice. This could be fitting for all of us in a way.

Without saying a word, I tug Sadie along with me and spin her around to face me. "I'm not in the wedding party Matt," she states the obvious looking around uncomfortably.

I nod and smirk. "I know, but who am I gonna' dance with Blake? I'm sure he's much happier with Sara," I tease.

She looks flustered and focuses on my chest with a sigh. Glancing up at me, she reluctantly agrees, "Okay."

I remove my hand from her side so I can tilt her chin up and look into her eyes. "What happened to the confident girl I used to know?" I ask perplexed.

She grimaces, shaking her head. "She's gone. Too much has happened. I'm just not the same girl anymore," she insists sounding defeated.

My heart clenches at the sound of her pain. I shake my head in denial. "Impossible. I still see her in there. You keep showing me glimpses of her. I know she's in there," I emphasize.

"Everything is different Matt. I'm different. I have my son and..." she trails off, not ready to talk about him quite yet. I understand why, but I hope she'll talk to me about him soon. "I don't think that girl is ever coming back," she admits trying to tear her gaze from mine, but I won't let her.

I sigh sadly as I trail my finger up and back down the side of her cheek. I can't help but search for her behind her eyes, behind her pain. I just know she's in there, but I have no idea how to help her find her way back. I tuck a lock of her loose silky dark hair behind her ear. I lock my green eyes on her blue-grey ones with renewed determination. "Then I'll get to know this girl in front of me, whomever she's now become," I inform her softly.

She whimpers at my confession causing my heart to beat erratically. She swallows hard and I watch as her Adam's apple bobs up and down. Her eyes fill with uncertainty as she opens her mouth and whispers my name, "Matt."

I don't want her to make excuses about us being together and I can't wait any longer. Tipping my head down, I interrupt her, crashing my mouth into hers, needing to taste her lips. The shock that travels through me reiterates why I couldn't wait another second to feel her soft full lips on mine. She gasps at first in surprise before she groans into my kiss, pressing into me. I cradle her face in my hand, still holding the other one to my heart, as everything around us seems to slip away. My tongue slips along the seam of her lips and she easily lets me in.

An elbow jabs into my side suddenly interrupting us. I flinch and pull away with a painful groan. Theresa smiles innocently. "Don't forget Mom is watching you, Romeo." Her boyfriend Jax chuckles at her words.

Sighing, I regretfully break away from Sadie. "Thanks, T," I whisper not taking my eyes off a now blushing Sadie. Theresa laughs as Jax spins her away from us on the dance floor just before the song ends.

A fast song follows, prompting me to tug Sadie along with me to the side of the dance floor still gripping her hand tightly. "Can I have my hand back?" she asks.

"No," I quickly reply, my lips twitching in amusement. "You may walk away if I let go," I tease.

She rolls her eyes, but I notice the small smile playing on her lips. "Maybe you should go talk to your mom or something," she suggests turning an even deeper shade of red.

I laugh and tell her, "You're funny. You don't want to kiss me in front of my mom and the rest of my family?" I taunt with a huge grin.

Her eyes go wide, and she turns so red, she appears like she might burst making me laugh even harder. "Umm..." she stammers.

Saved again by the DJ, he announces the father-daughter dance. Bree joins her dad, linking her arm through his with tears in her eyes and a wobbly smile on her face. Her dad pulls her close, with watery eyes himself as they dance to "Stealing Cinderella" by Chuck Wicks.

Christian walks over and stands next to me. "She's missing her mom and grandma so much right now. I wish there was something I could do for her," he utters painfully as he watches her with her dad.

"You already do Christian," I remind him. He glances at me and nods appreciatively before his eyes return to Bree and he watches her for the rest of the dance.

"Matt, I have to use the restroom," Sadie complains. I sigh but smile down at her as I reluctantly let her go.

I make my way back to our table and toss my jacket over the back of my chair. As soon as I turn around, my mom is standing in front of me smiling. "Matthew, are you going to introduce me to your friend when she comes back?"

I chuckle and shake my head. "I knew I should've followed her to the bathroom," I joke. She gives me a look, arching her eyebrows in challenge and making me laugh a little harder. "I'm kidding, Mom." I pause before adding, "I don't think this is really a meet the family thing."

"We're at your brother's wedding, Matthew!" she reminds me.

I nod and release an exasperated sigh. "Mom, I just caught up with her again. I haven't seen her, well, we haven't hung out anyway in nearly five years before two weeks ago. Please give me a break," I plead.

She grimaces and reluctantly nods. Before she has a chance to ask anything else, my aunt and a couple of my cousins approach us with hugs and congratulations. I don't really understand why I'm getting any congratulatory hugs, but I'm not about to ask and bring more attention to me.

We soon eat dinner and Christian and Bree cut the cake with me barely getting a glimpse of Sadie. I'm constantly being pulled in the opposite direction and I fucking hate it. The night is starting to feel like it will never end.

Christian approaches me, and my eyes widen, knowing why he's coming for me. "Let's go," he urges.

"I'm good," I grumble, narrowing my eyes at him.

He laughs, throwing his arm around my shoulders as he drags me out to the dance floor. "You're my brother, my best man and you're single. You have to be out there when I throw the garter," he demands.

"Are you sure you're not just trying to embarrass me?" I ask seriously and he grins mischievously. Groaning, I reluctantly oblige him as I stand alongside Joe, Dean, a few of my cousins and a couple of Bree and Christian's friends I don't really know. Christian spins around and tosses the garter, it nearly falling right into my hands. "I swear this was a set-up," I mutter. I paste on a smile, spinning it around my finger in mock celebration. I just hope Sadie will come out to try to catch the bouquet so I can dance with her again.

I spot her on the dance floor with her friend Emma, Amy and a few of my cousins awaiting Bree to throw her bouquet. "If one of our cousins catches it, you can kiss my ass on that dance," I threaten Christian making him laugh.

"It could be worse," he teases. "Amy could catch it." Our mouths drop open when in the next moment, Bree's bouquet lands in Amy's hands and it's no longer a joke. "I'm sorry brother," he adds regretfully and slaps me on the back, "but you have to dance with her."

Groaning, I drop my head mumbling, "You owe me."

Reluctantly, I stride towards Amy and offer her my hand as the first notes of "Today" by Brad Paisley flow through the speakers. She grins broadly at me as she takes it, putting one hand on my chest. She's small like Sadie and can't seem to rest her hands comfortably on my shoulders. "Bree said you're staying here now," she begins.

I nod. "Yup." She runs her hand lightly over my chest in appreciation. I hold back my grimace knowing she once dated Christian. I still wonder how Christian and Bree got through it all, but looking at them now, I'm so thankful they did.

"How did you like living in Texas? I heard it's beautiful," she asks curiously.

I nod in agreement. "It was fine, but I'm here now," I answer casually. I begin searching the area for Sadie, but I don't see her anywhere.

Amy pulls away and I stop and look down at her. "Listen, I know you don't really want to dance with me and since you're Christian's brother, I get it, but would it really kill you to not be an ass while you do?"

I cringe. "I'm sorry, Amy. I was just looking for someone and I don't see her anywhere. Let's finish the dance."

She nods and steps towards me again. "I think she went to the bathroom," she tells me. My eyes draw together in confusion, and she gives me a look like what she's telling me is obvious. "I assume you're looking for Sadie. I saw her walk out of the tent. She must be going to the bathroom or something."

I force a smile. "Thanks."

"Don't worry, one brother was more than enough for me," she jokes trying to lighten the mood. I chuckle and finally give her a genuine smile. She relaxes and adds, "Besides, I'm interested in a different Matt."

I glance around the perimeter to find a slightly familiar guy glaring at me making me laugh. I tip my head towards him. "The happy guy over there?"

She looks over my shoulder and giggles. "That's him." We break apart at the end of the song. "Thanks, Matt."

I nod my head in acknowledgement and turn to go find Sadie. Eventually, I find her sitting on my front porch with Emma helping me relax. "I've been looking everywhere for you," I call out.

Both their heads snap over to me in surprise and Emma immediately excuses herself. "I'm just going to find Joe to say goodbye." She waves and slips away.

"You guys are leaving?" I ask, almost overwhelmed with disappointment. I didn't have enough time with her.

Sadie nods. "Yeah, I have to pick up Holden first thing in the morning."

I nod my head slowly in understanding before I sit down next to her. "I want more time," I declare.

She glances at me and by the look in her eyes I start to prepare my rebuttal, knowing she'll refuse. "Okay, we can go to lunch or dinner this week," she agrees.

My eyes widen as I grin in surprise. I tilt her chin up towards me and lightly press my lips to hers. Closing my eyes, I deepen the kiss, moving my mouth effortlessly over hers. My tongue gently pushes through her parted lips, seeking out her tongue and tangling them together. She tastes like champagne and sugar, probably the cake I muse wanting more. She whimpers but pulls away making me groan in protest.

I whisper her name sounding desperate, "Sadie."

Emma comes around the corner just as a car pulls up. "My brother is here," Emma calls. "Are you ready, Sadie?"

"Coming," she yells back. She turns to me. "I'll text you, but I think I can do dinner on Wednesday if you're free."

"I'm free," I insist. I'll make sure I am. "I want lunch one day while you're working too," I add with a grin.

Her smile appears a little sad. "We'll see."

My stomach twists as I watch her go. I want more.

Chapter 16

Sadie

As I lie in bed staring at the ceiling, I keep thinking about last night, waiting until I can go pick up Holden. The wedding really was beautiful, but it also brought back so many memories. It's not like I had a wedding that was anything like that, but...I sigh heavily, telling myself I have no right to feel sorry for myself. If I would ever get married again, I wouldn't even want a big wedding. I don't even have anyone to invite.

I close my eyes as I remember the painful fallout of getting pregnant just as I started college. First, my parents kicking me out of the house and refusing to pay for college. Then I had to quit school and find a job. Of course, I'll never forget the day Micah and I got married just before the baby came. We bought a small cape near his parents. He made so many promises and I believed him. That's when Micah and I began drifting apart, only increasing my guilt for pulling him into my mess. I wanted to love him whole-heartedly, but every time either of us looked at Holden, we were both reminded of his biological father hurting us both. Micah was great with Holden, but he wanted a child of his own and I was never able to give that to him, weighing us down.

My phone dings with a text interrupting my thoughts. I sit up on the side of my bed and reach for it. My heart flutters at the sight of Matt's name. "Good morning. I had a great time with you last night and can't wait to see you again. Is tomorrow good for lunch?" he prods.

"I can do lunch tomorrow. I'll text you from work to let you know what time I can take my lunch break. Ok?" I reply.

"Perfect!" he answers.

Sighing, I push myself off my bed to get ready. I quickly shower and brush my teeth as I think about the way Matt kissed me last night. His kisses set my whole body on fire. I tingle everywhere, my heart pounding like it will beat out of my chest as I gasp for breath. I hate to compare, but I can't help it; I don't remember Micah ever making me feel that way when he kissed me.

I pull on a pair of black shorts and an ivory t-shirt with a black lace pattern across the front. Pulling my hair up into a loose ponytail, I grab my keys for the short drive over to Micah's parents' house.

This week, I have to tell Matt the truth. I only hope he doesn't hate me for everything he missed. But before I tell him, I need to let Micah's parents know Holden's biological father is in town and I'm going to tell him the truth. His parents have always been wonderful and treated me like family, but I have no idea how they're going to take this. They always treated Holden like their own grandson and never really asked any questions, but I don't have Micah by my side anymore. This time everything feels so different and I'm not afraid to admit I'm scared.

I park my car in the driveway and step out, slamming the door behind me. Pausing, I take a deep breath and walk slowly towards the house thinking about how to tell them. As I near the front door, my hands begin trembling and my knees wobble. I take a slow, deep breath trying to calm my nerves as I ring the doorbell.

The door opens revealing Micah's mom wiping her hands on her white frilly apron with a wide smile. "Sadie, you're here. I'm just about ready with brunch. Come on in." She turns and walks back to the kitchen before I say a word.

Anxiously, I take a step into the house and shut the door behind me. Just as it clicks, I hear little feet pounding the ground louder and louder as they get closer. "Mommy!" Holden screams and charges right for me.

Relief flows through me as I kneel down and put out my arms with a huge smile on my face. I brace myself in anticipation of him launching himself at me. "Good morning my little man," I whisper adoringly into his ear as I hug him tightly.

"I missed you, Mommy," he informs me sweetly.

"I missed you too, Holden. How was your sleepover with grandma and grandpa?" I ask as he pulls away from me.

"It was so much fun! Gamma made sghetti and meatballs for dinner and we played with the trucks and 'dozer in the sandbox! We ate ice cream and watched mine and grandpa's fav-wit movie!" I hold back my giggle at his animated excitement, smiling and nodding in encouragement. He continues, raising his hands as high as he can reach, "Grandpa helped me build the tallest tower ever with Legos, but I did most of it all by myself," he announces proudly puffing out his chest. "Come see!" he exclaims as he grabs my hand and tugs me towards the family room, which doubles as their playroom.

In the room sits a large sage and tan thin striped couch, a tan recliner and an entertainment center with a large sixty-inch television. Then to the left underneath a large window sits a train table currently covered in rainbow-colored Legos. On each side of the table sits shelves. One set of shelves is filled with kids' books and movies, while the other is filled with red, blue, yellow and green bins full of toys. They really do spoil him and I'm constantly reminded how lucky he is to have them in his life. Honestly, how lucky we both are.

Kneeling down next to Holden in front of the table, I exclaim, "Wow! That tower is bigger than you!" I turn to him my eyes wide. "How did you put the ones on top?"

His face turns serious as he answers, "I had to reach really, really high and be super careful." He pauses before admitting, "Grandpa did help me a little bit."

I nod my head and tell him sincerely, "It's really amazing Holden. You did such a great job."

He grins proudly. "Thanks, Mommy." He looks past me and proclaims, "Look, Mommy's here and I showed her the tower we made."

Turning, I find Micah's dad smiling at Holden. "You did all the hard work." Holden grins, enjoying the praise. "Brunch is ready. Are you two hungry?"

"Yeah!" Holden jumps up and takes off running for the kitchen.

I follow behind and join Holden at the table. "Thank you for having me," I tell them as soon as I sit down.

Micah's mom ignores my thanks like she always does. She once told me family doesn't need to say thank you, but that is one of the manners my mother instilled in me that I still believe is important. Instead, she watches Holden stuff blueberry pancakes into his mouth as she asks me, "How was your friend's wedding?"

I smile sadly and answer, "It was really beautiful. It was at his parents' house on the lake. It's obvious they're really happy together." She nods her head and pinches her lips tightly together. I feel a wave of sadness wash over me knowing she's thinking of Micah. Clearing my throat, I attempt to change the subject, "Thank you for watching Holden. It sounds like you guys had a lot of fun."

Holden nods vigorously and tries to talk through his mouth full of eggs and blueberry pancakes. "We did Mommy," he mumbles around his food.

I fight to hold back my smile as I remind him, "Don't talk with your mouth full." He instantly focuses his attention back to the food in front of him.

The rest of the meal remains painfully quiet, except for the clanging of the dishes and silverware causing my anxiety to increase. Holden soon finishes and requests, "Can I go play with the trucks before we go home?"

Gulping, I nod my head knowing this is the perfect opportunity to be able to speak with them without his little ears in the room. "Wash your hands first," I remind him. I watch as he climbs up on a stool to wash his hands, then quickly jumps down and runs towards the playroom.

"No running in the house, Holden," Grandma warns.

"Sorry Gamma," he calls.

"He's such a good boy," she offers softly. I smile stiffly in response. Narrowing her eyes she prods, "Is everything alright, Sadie?"

My mouth falls open, but I can't make a sound. I close my mouth and take a deep breath, releasing it slowly before I try again. I grip my coffee cup tightly and barely glance at Micah's parents as I try to find the right words. "Um, everything is okay, but I have something to tell you."

She tenses and her eyes go wide as she asks, "What is it?" At the same time Micah's dad remains incredibly still, watching my every move.

A lump forms in my throat and I attempt to swallow it down. My stomach begins churning and I answer my voice shaky. "Um, I ran into someone a few times recently," I stammer.

"Are you dating someone?" she asks sounding surprised, but not upset.

Clearing my throat, I shake my head and murmur, "No."

"What could it be, then?" she questions quietly, but she seems to be asking herself more than she's asking me.

I take another deep breath and force myself to spit it out. "Holden's biological father is back in town, and I need to tell him he has a son."

My statement is met with a gasp and a loud clang of a coffee cup dropping to the table. "He can't take him away from us. He's *our* grandson!" Micah's mom exclaims.

My own mouth drops open in surprise. "He wouldn't, he can't!"

"How do you know? You didn't even know him well enough to find him before his son was born!" she yells.

I cringe, but she's right. "I won't let him," I insist.

"What if he tries to take Holden away from you?" Micah's dad probes, finally speaking up.

I gasp, feeling sick at the thought of anyone trying to take him away from me. I shake my head vehemently. "No, that won't happen. He wouldn't take him away from the only life he's ever known, away from his mother."

"How do you know? What do you know about him," he pushes.

I swallow hard and answer with a shaky voice. "He's a good man. He has a college degree and works in marketing mostly. He's helping his brothers with their business here. He has a big family and they all live close by here. His last name is Emory. My friend Bree married his brother yesterday," I blurt out as quickly as I can.

"I've heard that name," he mumbles then pinches his lips together in frustration. "He doesn't know yet?"

I shake my head. "I didn't want to ruin his brother's wedding with such a big shock. He knows I have a son, but he assumes he's Micah's."

Micah's mom twists a towel nervously in her hands while his dad gets a look of determination on his face as he adds emphatically, "We want to meet him. He needs to know he's *our* grandson."

Taking a shaky breath, I nod in agreement as Holden bounds into the room. "Mommy, can I have some more juice? I'm thirsty."

I nod. "Of course. Why don't we put it in a Sippy-cup and take it with us though. We should get home," I tell him pasting a smile on my face. "Why don't you help grandpa get your things," I suggest.

Stiffly, I walk to the refrigerator and fill a cup with juice, twisting the top on tight. I turn back towards the table, glancing at Micah's mom still sitting in her chair nervously twisting the towel. I step up to her and put my hand on her shoulder. She looks up at me, her eyes filled with worry. "I promise, he won't take Holden away. He's a good man," I reiterate, my voice cracking.

She nods her head and takes a deep breath before she whispers, "I know it will all work out. Maybe Micah sent him to us so Holden could have a dad again."

My heart squeezes painfully, a huge weight pressing on my chest. Tears spring to my eyes and I can't do anything to stop them. I wrap my arms around her and hug her tightly, not able to even speak. She gently hugs me back like she's my mother as tears slip out of both of our eyes.

Holden sneaks up behind me and taps me on my leg. "I'm ready, Mommy."

I rush to wipe away the tears as Micah's mom does the same. I turn to grin at him. "Okay, let's go home. Say goodbye to Grandma and Grandpa," I remind him.

He gives them both a hug and cheerfully tells them, "I love you! See you on Wednesday!"

They walk us to the door and Micah's mom whispers in my ear, "Please let us know what's happening." I nod and we all wave goodbye.

Holden climbs into the back of the car, setting his backpack next to him on the seat. He helps me buckle him into his car seat before I slide in the front behind the wheel. I start the car and try to shake off the mixed emotions running through me on the ride home. "What are we gonna' do today, Mommy?" Holden inquires.

"What would you like to do?" I ask and push everything out of my head, focusing on my little boy.

Chapter 17

Matt

I shove a stack of sweatshirts into one of the empty boxes littering my floor, already sick of packing. "You're lucky you didn't completely unpack so you don't have to do all of it over again," my mom mumbles casually from the doorway.

I glance over at her and can't help but notice the look of melancholy on her face. I take a step towards her with my hands resting low on my hips and remind her, "Mom, I'm getting a place close by this time. I'm not really moving away."

She sighs softly and steps into my room. "I know, but you've been gone so long. Your brothers stayed pretty close, and Theresa at least stayed in driving distance even if it was a long drive before she moved back. You were so far away," she emphasizes, her voice hitching. "I was so excited when you said you were moving here. I just got you back and you're already moving out," she adds honestly.

Holding back my groan, I sit at the end of my bed feeling slightly guilty. My mom sits on the chair by the desk, and I ask her with a slight smirk, "Are you sure you're not just emotional because Christian got married this weekend?"

She laughs and shrugs in response. "Maybe, but we have missed you."

I nod in understanding. "I know Mom and I'm staying close this time. I promise." She tilts her head to the side studying me. My stomach twists and I arch my eyebrows in question. "What?"

"Are you sure it doesn't have anything to do with Bree's friend from the wedding? You seemed to know her a lot better than you suggested," she blushes as she teases me.

I grimace, forcing myself to maintain eye-contact. "You're right. I met her the summer you guys first bought this place and I was home from college on summer break. I hung out with her and a bunch of her friends that summer. I guess you could even say I dated her," I admit. "But," I emphasize, giving her a pointed look, "I haven't seen her in a very long time until the last couple weeks."

"Are you going to see her again?" she probes, suddenly over-eager.

I cross my arms over my chest defensively. "Yeah, we were friends then and I hope we'll be friends again." She gives me a doubtful look, but I ignore it. "A lot has changed in that time, Mom. She was married and she has a son," I inform her.

"She's married?" she gasps with wide eyes.

I shake my head sadly. Even though I'm happy she's single, I never wanted Micah to die. "Her husband died in a car accident a couple years ago."

My mom gasps as her hand flies to her mouth in shock. "Oh, the poor girl." I nod in agreement. My heart clenches as we both remain quiet for a few moments lost in thought. I hate all the pain she's gone through.

"Matt, be careful with her."

My eyes flit back to her as my eyebrows draw together in confusion. She's *my* mom. Shouldn't she be worried about me?

Pursing her lips, she quickly explains, "She's a single mom who's obviously been through a lot already. She has a little boy to worry about. She doesn't need you..." she pauses, pursing her lips. Squaring her shoulders, she starts again, "It's just I've never seen you with a girl, even though I've heard about some of the girls you've dated over the years Matthew," she cringes, briefly glancing away. "You have to be careful with her because it's not just her you have to think about."

"I know Mom," I insist with a shake of my head.

My insides churn with anxiety, prompting my need to lighten the mood again. "So, since you saw me kiss a girl, you think I'm dating her?" My mom's mouth drops open and her eyes widen, her horrified expression making me laugh loudly. "I'm kidding, Mom. I do want to get to know her again. I'll even admit I want to date her." She shakes her head in annoyance with me making me chuckle. "In fact, I'm taking her to lunch in a little bit. I should head into town," I inform her glancing at the clock.

She breathes a sigh of relief and grins at me. "Where are you going?"

"I'm just taking her to the café. It's her lunch hour. She's not ready for me to meet her son, so for now we'll try lunch hours and times he has someone else watching him. I don't really know yet. I'll have to ask her," I admit.

She nods and smiles, satisfied. "Sounds like you're doing okay."

"Gee, thanks Mom," I reply sarcastically making her laugh. I push myself up off my bed and she stands as well stepping towards me.

She stops right in front of me and looks up at me, her face softening. "I am very proud of you, Matthew. Your Dad and I both are," she softly proclaims grinning.

"Thanks Mom." She wraps her arms around me, and I hug her back, grateful to be back where my family lives. I know how lucky I am to have them in my life like this and I want to be better about taking them for granted. Stepping away from her, I mumble, "I gotta' go. I'll see you later."

"Bye, have fun!" she calls as I walk out of the room and down the stairs.

I snag my keys out of the kitchen before I'm out the front door and in my truck. Pulling out, a smile tugs at the corners of my lips. I admit I'm anxious to see her again. I know this is just a lunch date, but I wonder if she'll let me kiss her again. Damn, I love the feel of her lips on mine.

Mom's right though, I need to be careful. I want to get to know her again, but that will take time. Hopefully I'll be able to tell if what we share is more than just pure lust and wanting her again or if there's much more like I believe. Then again, maybe I built her up in my head years ago and she's not my one. Maybe I built a standard for women that no one would ever be able to meet based on the girl I thought I'd never see again. I laugh humorlessly and mumble under my breath, "When did I become such a girl?"

Honestly, I guess I'm just ready to grow up. I want a relationship and that's something I've never wanted before. As for Sadie, there's just something about her that gets me excited about a relationship again. I want to experience all of that with her.

As I pull into town, I find a parking spot right on Main Street. I'm surprised with the summer tourist traffic beginning to pick up, but I'll take it. Jumping out of my truck, I walk down the sidewalk until I reach the door to the gift shop and step inside. Slowing my pace, I take in my surroundings finding wooden hand painted signs, a small section of Maine made pottery, a small section of decorative Maine lighthouses and boats of Maine, decorative hand-blown vases and dishes, candles, a section with nautical decorations and an area for small gifts and jewelry.

I step up to the counter smiling at a petite, older woman with gray hair piled on top of her head. Turning away from the register, she asks, "Can I help you?"

"I'm actually looking for Sadie. Is she here?"

She grins giddily, announcing, "She is! She just went to get her purse to leave for her lunch break." Just then Sadie steps out from the back room and spots me.

"Hi, Sadie." I smile at her as I take her in. She's wearing a loose navy eyelet skirt that falls to her knees with a white button-down sleeveless shirt and matching flip-flops.

My heart beats erratically as I swiftly reel in my dirty thoughts. Clearing my throat I prompt, "Are you ready?"

She nods her head, barely squeaking out her answer, "Yup." Spinning back to the woman she informs her, "We're just going to lunch down the street. I'll be back soon."

"No rush! It's good to see you taking a real lunch!" she insists. She waves energetically as we walk out the door.

The moment we're outside I reach for Sadie's hand. Her eyes snap to mine in surprise, but she doesn't pull away, sending tingles up my arm. "That's a great store," I tell her ignoring the urge to press my lips to hers.

She looks up at me in confusion. "You've never been there? But Bree has worked there for so long." I laugh and shrug. "Wow!" she exclaims surprised.

We reach the café and I pull the door open for her. "Thank you."

The café seems pretty busy. It reminds me of an old-fashioned diner with the white counter, lined with silver edges, and silver and red stools along the whole length of the counter. Square tables and chairs with the same look are found throughout the middle of the room with similar booths lined up on the outside along the windows. It's seat-yourself and thankfully I spot a booth in the back. I stride right over to it with her in tow.

"This, okay?" I prod as we step up to the table.

"Sure." She nods as she sits down across from me.

"Why don't we figure out what we're going to eat so I can focus on you," I suggest, offering her a crooked grin.

Her cheeks turn pink as she reaches for a menu. "Okay."

We both order turkey clubs with fries, mine with a Coke and hers with Lemonade. As soon as the waitress steps away, she clasps her hands in her lap and glances over at me with an odd look on her face I can't quite figure out. "Are you okay?" I ask not quite sure that's the question I should be asking.

She smiles tightly. "I'm good. Just tired," she explains, but I'm honestly not sure if that's what it really is.

Feeling the need to change the subject, I tell her sincerely, "You look beautiful."

She blushes lightly, her rosy cheeks quickening my heartbeat. "Thank you."

Picking up her napkin in front of her, she begins fidgeting, soon adding the silverware. I hate that she's uncomfortable, especially with me, so I try to lighten the mood. Clearing my throat, I smirk, prompting, "So, I've been warned not to be such a bad influence on you. Am I really that bad?"

She glances up from the napkin with a wide smile. "Really?" she questions with utter disbelief.

I nod my head. "Yup." Watching her closely, I shrug. "I mean I was only caught streaking twice, the other two times the principal wasn't even around!" I exclaim feigning exasperation.

She laughs out loud and this time she appears completely relaxed as she comments, "You did not do that!"

Grinning, I nod my head. "I did. I lost a bet to Christian back in high school. I was more mortified over losing to my little brother than getting caught streaking." She laughs even louder making my heart clench, loving her reaction. "My parents weren't happy with either of us. Christian was only grounded for a week, though, and I got two because, and I quote, 'I was stupid enough to go along with it'."

"Oh my gosh, your poor parents," she emphasizes. My eyes widen and my hand falls to my chest, pretending to be hurt. "It sounds like you and Christian really gave them a hard time."

I shrug, nonchalant, knowing it's the truth. Christian and I would both tend to push the limits, but especially me. "I think my mother referred to it as middle child syndrome," I claim. I grin, enjoying the sparkle back in Sadie's eyes.

The waitress interrupts our conversation as she sets both our drinks and our food down in front of us all at once. "Can I get you anything else?" she prods sweetly.

"No, thank you," I respond without looking up at her. I glance across the table at Sadie, reiterating, "We better eat before you have to get back to work."

She nods in agreement and takes a sip of her lemonade. "So, what was living in Texas like?" she inquires directing the conversation.

I keep the chitchat away from Natalie wanting to keep it light. There's no point in talking about my ex, but I let Sadie keep the focus of the conversation on me, since something obviously has her on edge that she doesn't want to talk about. I continue making jokes and we fall into an easy banter. We finish all too soon and I pay the bill, following her outside to escort her back to work.

We stroll hand in hand in comfortable silence but reach her store much too soon. Halting my movement, I stop her with a gentle tug of my hand before she has a chance to reach for the door. I ask, "So you said you were free Wednesday night for dinner?" She nods appearing slightly nervous again. "Can I ask where your son will be?"

"He'll be with Micah's parents," she admits, her eyes drifting away from me. "They watch him on Wednesday nights and every other weekend. Sometimes they'll help out when I'm at work too, but he usually goes to an in-home day care with four other kids while I'm working."

"What about school? You said you've been taking classes?"

"I do everything I can on-line and during the regular school year I've been trying to take a class during the day. Is that okay?" she asks sounding slightly defensive.

I put my hands up and my voice turns soft as I tell her, "I think it's amazing what you're doing. I'm sure it's really hard to do it all."

She sighs and looks down at her feet. "I'm sorry, Matt. I've just had to defend my actions for so long..."

"Don't be sorry. I think you've become so incredibly strong with everything you've been through. I admire you," I confess. Her look turns doubtful prompting me to insist, "I do."

Gently, I tilt her face up towards mine. Tipping my head down, I whisper over her lips, "I've been dying to do this again since you left me on Saturday." I close the distance and softly place my lips over hers. My hearts speeds up and my body starts to tingle as we both relax into the kiss with a quiet moan. I move my lips slowly with hers, struggling not to push it any further. I flick out my tongue and run it along the seam of her lips to taste her before I reluctantly pull away, reminding myself where I am.

I look into her eyes, trying to see what's in her head and her heart as we both catch our breaths. "I was just curious about school, and I wanted to make sure I still had a date for Wednesday night," I tell her playfully, the corners of my lips twitching up in amusement.

She nods in acknowledgement, smiling up at me and making me want to pull her closer and not let her go back to work. "I'll see you Wednesday night at six," she responds. "I'll meet you at the clam bar, the one we ate at together before," she adds blushing deeply. I nod remembering the first time I took her out. "There's no live music Wednesday, but it should be good."

"Definitely," I murmur. Leaning in for one last chaste, lingering kiss, I reluctantly pull back, whispering, "I'll be there. See you then, Sadie."

She waves. "Thank you. Bye, Matt." Then she turns and slips inside the store, disappearing from my sight, my heart already clenching from the loss.

Chapter 18

Sadie

Sitting down at the table, I begin fidgeting nervously while I wait for Matt. He's texted me several times in the last two days, but I know tonight is the night I have to tell him the truth and I'm terrified he'll hate me. It feels like everything is going so well between us. The first time we were together there was so much I didn't know. I feel like this is my chance to fix that and find out everything about him. Well, maybe not everything, but I would love to know it all.

Grimacing, I sigh, annoyed with myself. He probably won't even talk to me after he finds out about Holden. My heart flips painfully at the thought. I close my eyes and take a deep breath mumbling to myself, "I need to make this right."

I glance at my phone flinching as 6:12 p.m. flashes on my screen. My anxiety increases knowing he's late. Slowly, I scan the area looking for him, but no luck. Heaving a sigh, I turn to stare out at the rapid water flowing over the rocks and turn my gaze towards the boats sitting tranquilly in the marina behind the clam bar. Maybe some of the calm will rub off on me. I don't want to seem too anxious when he arrives…if he arrives.

Looking down at my lap, I find a napkin torn to shreds. Shaking my hands, I realize that's probably impossible. I laugh at myself knowing there probably isn't anything that will make me appear calm tonight. This feels so much different than lunch Wednesday and I was nervous for that date, but then again tonight is different. I sigh and pick up the pieces of the shredded napkin off my lap and begin placing them in a pile on the table.

"I don't think we should feed the seagulls paper scraps," Matt jokes nodding at the mess I made as he steps up behind me. He runs his finger lightly over my shoulder as he steps around me.

Chills shoot through me at his delicate touch. I jump slightly and feel myself blush. I attempt to gulp down my growing nerves and keep the mood light. "I was bored waiting for my date." I make a show of looking around. "He's really late. It doesn't look like he's going to show up if you want to join me," I tease and shrug like it's no big deal. I force a smile, attempting to make myself relax.

He smirks, his green eyes sparkling as they slowly rake over me from my head to my toes. I'm wearing a faded blue jean mini skirt made to appear worn even though this is only the second time I've worn it. I have a shimmery aqua blue off the shoulder top that ruffles and hangs down a couple inches layer after layer all the way around. My matching sandals have a one-inch heel and wrap around my ankles with a silver buckle across the top.

He's dressed in chocolate brown cargo shorts and a dark, emerald green polo golf shirt with a couple buttons unhooked at the top and brown OluKai flip-flops. If it's possible, I think he looks sexier than when he wore the suit at the wedding. His green eyes lift back up to meet mine, appearing a darker green.

How could they change so fast?

He gulps and whispers something inaudibly. My eyebrows scrunch together in confusion, but he seems to shake it off before grinning at me. "Well, he's an idiot, but I'd love to join you. You look amazing, Sadie," he tells me with such sincerity I blush a deeper shade of red.

"Thank you," I murmur as he sits in the chair across from me. I watch the way he's looking at me causing my heart to hammer, feeling like it's about to beat out of my chest. If I didn't know better, I'd believe he's about to climb over the small table just to get closer to me and kiss me. I love the way he looks at me. I release a shaky breath, terrified he won't look at me like that ever again after tonight. I realize our relationship is sort of new, but I can also admit to myself that I've never gotten over him. How can I when I see him every time I look into my son's identical green eyes?

"Sorry I'm late. Traffic was horrendous," he proclaims. His lips twitch up in amusement making me laugh. He grins, "Actually, I was just finishing something up with my brother, Jason. He's needed a little extra help this week with Christian gone on his honeymoon with Bree."

I nod in understanding. "Have you heard from them?"

He smirks, stating, "Just to hear they made it." He shrugs, elaborating, "They're actually coming back late tomorrow night so he can be here for the weekend. They're swamped this weekend, so that's the best they could do for a honeymoon right now. He said that will give him a reason to get away with her for a few days over the winter anyway."

"How do you like working with your brothers?" I want to know as much as I can about him while he's still talking to me. We have all night for me to tell him and I admit I'm also trying to work up the nerve to get the words out.

He shrugs, mumbling, "It's fine. I like that I'm not stuck in an office so much. I figure once Christian's back and I'm settled, I'll help them with research on more locations, activities and even partnership opportunities on top of the marketing. It will be fun always doing a little something different, but I like that I'll be able to help out in the field not only when they need me, but also when I need to get away from the walls closing in on me from doing too much paperwork."

I smile, enjoying listening to him. He gets so animated talking about it. "You look happy."

Giving me a crooked smile, he nods in agreement. "Yeah, this was a good move for me." I nod in understanding, at the same time, grateful to hear him say that. I hope that means he'll be sticking around, especially for Holden's sake. He opens his mouth when a tall, thin, brunette waitress who appears to be young enough to still be in high school steps up to take our order.

"Could we have a bucket of clams for us to start and an Oxbow Farmhouse Pale Ale?" Matt requests.

"Of course," she murmurs, turning to me with a polite smile.

"I'll just have a Diet Coke for now," I mumble, my nerves too crazy to even think about having a drink with my dinner.

The waitress nods in acknowledgement and turns back towards the kitchen, walking away.

I look up and meet Matt's eyes, butterflies instantly consuming my insides. He tilts his head to the side. "Can I ask how much school you have left before you do your student teaching? That is if you're still planning on being a teacher," he adds, not wanting to offend me.

I swallow hard and nod my head. "Yeah. I like the idea of being on a similar schedule as Holden, but I still have probably two years before student teaching at the rate I've been going, although I'll try to do it faster. I took a semester off after I found out I was pregnant. Then, it was just easier to be home with him the first year. I started going back part time before Micah died, but…" I flinch and quickly move on. "I've been doing what I can. I don't really have much help, just Micah's family," I admit.

He pinches his lips tightly together and narrows his eyes. "What about your family?" he probes causing my stomach to twist into knots.

The waitress picks that moment to step up to our table and set our drinks in front of us. I offer her a tight smile before she walks away. I reach for the cup, taking a large sip through the straw. I grip the cup tightly and stare at it, afraid to look him in the eyes as I bluntly spit out the sad truth, "They don't have time for me or Holden."

He reaches across the table and pries one of my hands away from my glass, clasping it in his. He gives my hand a squeeze in support. I don't look up, prompting him to squeeze again. Forcing myself to move, I hesitantly meet his gaze and find nothing but empathy and a bit of anger for me causing my heart to skip a beat.

"I'm so sorry Sadie," he whispers honestly.

I take in a shaky breath as I hold his stare for a moment a rush of emotions washing over me. I finally tear my eyes away and whimper, "Thank you, but it's okay. They're the ones missing out." Although it's true, even I can hear the pain in my voice, and I hate it. I take a few more calming breaths before I dare to lift my eyes again.

He's watching me with something I can't decipher, but his look gives me chills, instantly spreading goosebumps over my whole body. "I think every moment I spend with you, I'm blown away by you a little more. It's pretty amazing what you've been through, what you've done and who you are now. I think you're incredible, and I imagine your little boy is just like that too," he adds making my stomach tie churn. "If your family doesn't see that, it's definitely their loss, not yours or your son's. I know it's easier said than done, but remember that," he emphasizes still holding tightly to my hand.

I gasp as a couple tears fall without my consent. "Thank you," I whisper.

"Sadie, please don't cry. We're supposed to have fun tonight," he encourages as he wipes my tears away with the pad of his thumb. He grins sheepishly, proclaiming, "I'm like the worst date ever for making you cry in the first hour!" I huff a laugh causing him to relax as he chuckles along with me. He shakes his head, muttering, "I didn't know about your family, I'm sorry. I'll try to keep the conversation light. I promise."

I smile halfheartedly back at him knowing I can't keep the same promise, but I can at least wait until after dinner. The waitress steps up to our table again and Matt releases my hand so she can put the food in front of us. She sets a huge bucket of clams down with a bowl of lemon wedges and sauce as well as a basket of bread on the table between us. She lifts off the empty bucket from underneath for us to toss the empty shells. "Anything else?" she questions looking slightly distracted.

"No, thank you," I instantly reply.

I blush, glancing over at Matt hoping he didn't need anything. He chuckles and repeats, "No, thank you."

"I'm used to answering for Holden and me," I shrug my explanation. He grins as we both dig into the clams.

Throughout the rest of dinner, we successfully keep the conversation light. We talk about favorite things and places we want to go or things we want to do. I offer him small pieces of Holden knowing tonight I have to share everything with him.

When the table is cleared, Matt props his elbows on the table and leans forward, clasping his hands together. My breath hitches as my eyes are automatically drawn to his biceps with the movement. "Thank you for coming tonight," he tells me sweetly.

I cringe hoping he'll still be thankful in a moment. I take a deep breath and slowly let it out before I force myself to meet his eyes. I feel the helplessness and sadness begin to consume my insides. My stomach ties itself in knots and I can feel my whole body shaking from the inside out.

"Matt," I squeak, "I need to tell you something."

His eyebrows draw together in confusion and concern as he assesses me. "Sadie, are you okay?"

Ignoring his question, I focus on breathing steady and getting the words out. I lick my dry lips, my mouth feeling suddenly parched and I drink down the last of my Diet Coke before I try again. "Um, I have something very important to tell you," I admit feeling like I'm about to throw up. Matt's eyes search mine full of worry. Exhaling a shaky breath, I finally blurt out, "It's about my son..." His eyebrows draw together in trepidation as I open my mouth, steeling myself to tell him the truth.

"Matt!" a female voice calls from across the deck. Both of our heads swivel towards the sound spotting his sister Theresa with her boyfriend Jax following behind her. She stops at our table and grins broadly. "What are you doing here?"

"Eating," he offers her the obvious answer. "What are you doing here? I thought you were back in Portland."

She smirks. "We were, now we're here." Then, she brings her eyes to me, her smile growing wide and genuine as she says my name, "Sadie!" She bends down, wrapping her arms around me, giving me a hug. "It's so good to see you here with my brother!"

I smile shakily, still feeling my extreme anxiety from being on the verge of telling Matt the truth. "Hi, Theresa. It's good to see you too," I offer lamely. "Hi, Jax," I murmur as he peers down at us over her shoulder.

He steps up behind Theresa and rests his hand gently on her waist before he greets both of us, "Hey, guys."

"Hey, Jax," Matt states. Then he leans back and crosses his arms in front of his chest. "What are you doing out T? Aren't you supposed to work tomorrow morning?"

She shakes her head at her brother feigning annoyance, "Yes, Dad!" Jax chuckles and tightens his grip on her. She explains, "With Jax still working at the bar, it's easier for us to go out during the week, so we came to see Mom and Dad then stayed for our date, but don't worry we won't stay out too late."

Matt groans dramatically, complaining, "I don't need to hear about your sex life either."

She blushes and glares at him while Jax chuckles, unsuccessfully hiding his laughter behind his fist. "We weren't talking about that!" she argues, attempting to defend herself.

He shakes his head and adds, "I've seen enough from you two to last me a lifetime."

"You've only ever seen us kissing! You act like you've walked in on us having sex!" she accuses and then blushes realizing people are watching her. She hits her brother in the arm twice. "Move you jerk. Let me sit down," she pleads.

He chuckles but jumps up and pulls the empty table and chairs next to us with Jax's help before he sits down next to me. He lays his arm over the back of my chair grinning. "You know you missed me, T."

She sighs, narrowing her eyes at him. "I did and that's probably why I'm letting you get away with this."

He nods at Jax. "Well, if I didn't like Jax, I'd hit him for touching you."

Jax smirks as Theresa defends him, "Thanks, but you'd probably hurt your hand if you tried."

Jax shakes his head chuckling and turns to me. "They're entertaining, aren't they?" I nod my head in acknowledgment and he adds, "I think I know their script by heart now. I've learned to just stay out of it." Theresa leans over and kisses him on the corner of his mouth. She grins up at him with a shrug making him laugh and lean back into her for a chaste kiss on the lips.

Matt jokes gesturing to his sister, "See what I mean?" I giggle in response. "So, I guess you're joining us for a drink? We already ate."

"Sounds good, so did we," Jax adds with a mischievous grin as he looks at Theresa.

Matt leans in towards my ear and asks, "We'll talk later tonight?" I gulp and nod my head in agreement. I might as well enjoy all the time I can with him.

The rest of the night flies by as we talk with Theresa and Jax. Before I know it, they've left, and Matt is standing with me at my car door. He looks down at me, his eyes appearing dark green with only the light of the streetlamps, causing me to melt in his arms. "Sorry my sister and Jax crashed our date."

"It's okay," I barely squeak out.

He shakes his head and whispers, "Next time, I want you all to myself." My heart pounds so hard I think it will burst out of my chest as his words wash over me. He leans towards me and lightly brushes his lips over mine, eliciting a soft whimper from me. In the next moment, he crushes his mouth against mine and we move together with increased need, my body heating instantly.

He pushes closer making me gasp at the feel of him against my stomach as he pushes his tongue through my lips searching for mine. I moan into his mouth, loving the taste and feel of him, tangling our tongues together. Our kiss deepens as he presses against me, my body pinned between him and my car. Every part of me feels like it's on fire and I can't get enough of him. My hands rest on his hard chest between us, sending more tingles through my fingertips. A loud whistle startles us both, shaking us out of our stupor as he pulls away, both of us gasping for air.

"Damn," he mumbles under his breath.

I glance down at my hands and unwind them from his shirt making him chuckle. He looks down at me adoringly causing my insides to flutter. I love it and I can't help but want more. My heart beats erratically in response to him. After catching my breath, I lean into him and sigh feeling content. I murmur in agreement, "Yeah."

He chuckles again and brushes my hair out of my eyes, tucking a couple loose strands behind my ear as his eyes roam over my face. I do the same, taking in as much of him as I can. He sighs and leans forward again, softly pressing our lips together. My insides vibrate as he keeps the kiss so gentle and caring that I think my heart is melting like butter and will soon lie helplessly at his feet.

He pulls back from my lips but remains close. His face turns serious as he reminds me, "You were about to tell me something when Jax and T interrupted us, something about your son."

I shake my head, too shaken up from making out with him to attempt to get those words out. "I'll tell you next time I see you," I rasp.

He cocks his head to the side, seeming uncertain. "Are you sure? I want to hear everything about him. I love that you want to share him with me."

I reflexively flinch at his words feeling the weight of my guilt. "Matt, I…I…"

He shakes his head and caresses the side of face with his thumb trying to reassure me, "Sadie, I'm not trying to do anything except get to know more of you. I want you to share your son with me when you're ready."

Blood begins rushing in my ears and my hands start to shake. I have to get out of here before I throw up on him. "I have to go Matt," I whimper without explanation.

"Are you okay?" he repeats his voice full of concern. Gulping, I nod my head, now on autopilot. He gives me a chaste kiss before he insists, "I'm following you home to make sure you get home okay." I don't bother arguing. As we get to my car, I let him open my door. I slip in behind the wheel and start my car feeling slightly numb.

I park my car, not really remembering the drive. Matt tugs my door open, reaching me before I move to get out. Offering his hand, he pulls me out, maintaining his hold as he walks me to my door, but I stiffen, knowing I can't let him come in yet. There are pictures of Holden everywhere, making it obvious who his daddy really is. He brushes his lips over mine, his eyes full of worry. "I'll call you in the morning. I want to see you again."

I nod my head, knowing I will see him and next time I need to tell him no matter what. If Theresa and Jax hadn't shown up when they did, he would've already known, but my body is starting to shut down after holding it all in. I definitely need more strength to confess everything to him. I don't want him to see me like this. "Thank you, Matt," I whisper. "I really had fun. Tonight really meant a lot to me," I proclaim sincerely, my voice cracking. Maybe one day he'll truly understand how much.

I squeeze through my front door and lean back against it waiting with bated breath until I hear his truck pull away. Pushing off the door, I trudge woodenly to my room. Without much thought, I get ready for bed on autopilot before I collapse onto the mattress.

My hand falls to my chest, my heart aching with loneliness and guilt, knowing I can never completely fix it. I really wish things could be different because being with him tonight felt so right. I would give almost anything for us to all be a family, but I know I'm being ridiculous. There's no way he'll want me after he knows the truth. He may be the father of my child, but I'm not all that important. Besides, because of me, he doesn't even know his own son.

Rolling over on my side, I curl up in a ball, allowing my pain to encompass me. Holding on tight, I let myself sob into my pillow until I fall asleep.

Chapter 19

Matt

I'm so fucking confused. I really want to see Sadie. She hasn't exactly been ignoring me, but she hasn't been welcoming either. I thought we had a great time on our dates earlier this week, but since I left her on her doorstep Wednesday night, it feels like she's pulled away from me. It's not like she's completely shut me out, she has answered my calls and responded to my texts, but it feels like she's been brushing me off.

It's Saturday of Memorial Day Weekend and she still says she can't see me until tomorrow. I've never felt this anxious before. It's killing me trying to figure out what's going on in her head. She was about to tell me something when T showed up, maybe it has something to do with that, but how am I supposed to find out when I haven't really had a chance to talk to her about it yet.

I drag the last kayak I was using with the groups today up to the small office my brothers just rented near the lake for their business. It's really nothing more than a storage shed and bathroom, but it's easier to have some of the equipment up here. They also leased a small office and storage unit in Portland next door to Jason's apartment for their business as well. The landlords for his apartment own the building and love having him as a tenant. They offered him a great deal on the property, and he immediately jumped on it. It's great for the business, but I can't seem to keep my focus on work and toss the oar into the shed, showing my frustration.

"Easy there," Jason urges as he steps up behind me. "I think after this weekend we'll send you out to do some research, so you don't take anymore shit out on our kayaks." He arches his eyebrows in challenge.

I run my hand through my hair and glare at him. "Screw you!"

His eyes flash before they calm and he prods, "Relax, Matt. I'm sure you're not pissed because all your tours are by kayak this weekend. So, what the hell is wrong with you?"

I sigh and grumble, "Sorry."

"It doesn't happen to be that Sadie girl that has you all stressed out?" he prods casually. I grunt in response and he continues, "She's always pretty busy from what Bree said."

I heave a sigh knowing he's right. But then again, I've never had a girl do this to me before. It was either blatantly obvious we were done, like with Natalie or I was done with them and told them. When it comes to women, I tend to be a little direct and I've never had a girl get to me like Sadie does and it's pushing me over the edge. I groan in annoyance knowing that's why I feel so lost. If it was anyone else, I'd probably stop trying, but with her I can't even force myself to stop thinking about her. Hopefully it's just her son that has her distracted. That could be it, I've never dated anyone with a kid before, I remind myself.

Jason steps up to me and lightly smacks me on the back, gripping my shoulder in support. "You're done for today. Why don't you go for a run or something?" he suggests. "Maybe that will help you get your head on straight. It's just strange when you're so serious and only respond with animal noises and threats," he teases smirking.

I chuckle humorlessly knowing he's right. I'm definitely not acting like myself. "Thanks, Jason," I mutter, turning for the exit before he changes his mind. I stride out to my truck grabbing my gym bag and come back inside. Making my way to the bathroom, I quickly change into red net shorts and a gray t-shirt. I tie my running shoes and grab my iPod before I walk out the door ignoring the strange looks I'm still getting from my brother.

I turn on a running playlist currently consisting of mostly 2000's rock bands like Linkin Park, Green Day, Muse and Foo Fighters. After I left Texas, I wanted the opposite of country. I take off in a fast jog, needing to get rid of some of this tension immediately.

I head away from Main Street towards the lake knowing I'll pass the schools and a couple parks on the way. I stare straight ahead attempting to keep my focus on running and away from Sadie, but that proves to be harder than expected. U2's Beautiful Day echoes in my ears, making it impossible. Agitated, I pull my headphones out and stuff them in my armband with my iPod even though I love that song. Swiftly, I pick up my pace, listening to the sounds of my feet hitting the pavement, the wind whistling through the trees, birds chirping and a few cars rumbling as they pass.

Without any music to keep me distracted, my mind drifts back to Sadie without my consent. I completely get lost in her, thinking about when we're close. I love kissing her, I can barely hold myself back when I do. The way she responds to my kisses has me wondering what it would be like to be with her again. We've obviously both changed a lot since I saw her last, but I feel like I know her better than I ever did before. I'm confident that will make a difference for both of us in bed.

I shake my head trying to refocus on what I have to do before my move later this week. Unfortunately, that doesn't last when I come upon a park with kids playing and parents milling about. I move to jog around the perimeter of the park when I spot someone who looks exactly like Sadie, veering towards her instead. As I get closer, I realize it's definitely her. I smile to myself as I take in her frayed jean shorts making her tan legs look sexy as hell along with her purple Luke Bryan "Play It Again" concert t-shirt.

Just before I approach, she turns as if she senses someone watching her and immediately spots me. Grinning, I offer her a small wave. I watch as her face transforms to shock followed by fear causing me to feel like she just punched me in the chest. My head cocks to the side and my eyes narrow in confusion at her reaction.

Just then, I hear a little boy's voice call for her as he runs full force towards Sadie, "Mommy! Mommy! They have a digger! Come see!" he demands tugging on Sadie's hand. His bright green eyes, identical to mine are filled with excitement.

My heart completely stops along with my feet. I stand frozen in place taking in the most incredible site I've ever seen. The little boy tugging at Sadie's hand doesn't look anything like Micah. He looks exactly like me with his wavy blonde curls, bright green eyes and even his huge Emory smile. He has Sadie's tan skin and full lips, but I can already tell he's just like me.

I gasp for breath as my heart begins to beat again and I swear it's pounding so hard it's trying to claw its way out of my chest. My eyes widen and find hers. I see the regret, the pain and the guilt she holds there making me flinch. I shake my head feeling like she has no right.

I watch stiffly as she leans down and whispers something to him. My eyes go back to him and remain there, drawn to him like nothing I've ever felt before. But I can't look at her. How could she keep him from me?

He nods vigorously and turns to sprint for the small yellow digger. I watch as he immediately begins to use the claws to dig up sand in the super-size sandbox and dump it, making a huge pile.

"He's mine," I mumble in shock. I feel Sadie moving, but I refuse to look at her right now. "I have a son," I say out loud, the words feeling foreign and painful on my tongue.

"Yes," she rasps, now standing right in front of me.

"Were you ever planning on telling me?" I ask feeling so betrayed. I clench my fists tightly at my sides as I struggle to keep my chest from caving in on me. When I don't hear her answer, I turn on her, feeling all my anger bubbling up inside of me. "Were you ever going to tell me?" I repeat deathly quiet, demanding an answer.

"Yes," she nods as tears roll down her cheeks. "I looked for you after you left, but I didn't know how to find you."

I huff out a laugh of disbelief. "You had my fucking phone number, Sadie! I told you to keep it until you knew. Hell, you told me you didn't think you could get pregnant!" I spit through my teeth knowing I can't raise my voice here. "Was that a lie too?"

"No! I didn't think I could," she cries, trying to defend herself. "I deleted your number like you wanted me to because I thought I couldn't get pregnant. Then Micah tried to help me find you, but I didn't even know your last name, Matt. I didn't know anything *real* about you!"

I laugh humorlessly and shake my head. "I'm sure Micah tried really fucking hard to find me," I reply sarcastically.

"He did help me, Matt," she insists. Pausing, she glances over at Holden before looking back at me. "Can we not do this right now? Not with Holden here," she pleads. "He doesn't need to see me fighting with a stranger," she claims.

I cringe at her words. My head drops to my chest feeling like my whole body is absorbing the pain. I whisper my son's name, "Holden." Closing my eyes, I attempt to control my breathing.

"His middle name is Matthew," she informs me.

My stomach ties itself into even tighter knots. His middle name is Matthew after me. "How old is he?" I rasp barely able to process what's happening, but I'm suddenly starved for information about him. I need to know more, but I don't know where to begin.

"He'll be four in two weeks. His birthday is June 12th," she enlightens me. "I've been trying to tell you, Matt. I was about to tell you the other night when your sister and Jax showed up."

I shake my head feeling completely overwhelmed. I'm lightheaded and confused. I feel like I'm standing in someone else's shoes watching their life unfold right in front of me and I don't know which way to turn. I look down at my trembling hands and clench them back into fists. "Maybe," I pause, "but you didn't," I remind her harshly. I knew she wanted to say something the other night, but she let everything else get in the way of telling me about my son. *Nothing* should have gotten in the way of that information! I growl, "Either way I fucking know now."

Her voice sounds so small as she whispers, "I'm sorry, Matt. I thought I'd never see you again."

I finally turn my head and glare at her with a sick bundle of knots in my gut. "We need to talk Sadie," I demand coldly.

Her voice comes out shaky as she responds, "I know. Micah's parents have Holden tomorrow while I work. I can meet you after work like we planned."

I shake my head in refusal. "No." Taking a step towards her, I glare down at her. "I'll wait until tomorrow, so I have time to process this, but you've already made me wait too fucking long. You can call in sick tomorrow. Drop Holden off and I'll be at your house at 9 a.m.," I inform her, leaving no room for argument.

"But...but I wasn't supposed to drop Holden off until 9:30 a.m. I was supposed to start work at ten tomorrow," she tells me.

I shrug because it doesn't matter to me what she does. She can figure it out. I'm not waiting longer than tomorrow morning to get my answers. "I'll be at your house at 9 a.m.

tomorrow," I repeat my eyes hard. I step past her not waiting to hear anything else from her.

I stride to the edge of the park and crouch down to watch Holden play. His face scrunches up appearing as if he's making noises as he moves the arms of the digger, just like I used to do when I was a kid. My heart clenches, my hand falling to my chest as I watch him play.

It's only a few minutes later when Sadie walks over to him. She takes him by the hand, and he frowns, reluctantly following as they walk over to their car. He climbs in the back seat by himself and into his car seat. She buckles him in before she sits in the front and starts the car. I continue watching, staring after them long after her Volkswagen has completely disappeared from my sight.

"Shit," I mumble. I take another deep breath and stand, shaking out my hands and legs. My whole body is clenched so tightly I don't think I'll ever be able to relax. I don't think anything will help me right now, not even this. I spin on my heel and start running back towards town to get my truck. "I need a drink," I grumble under my breath.

Just as I approach the lot, Jason steps outside. When he looks at me, I turn away and stride towards the front of my truck. "How come you look even more stressed out than you did before you left for your run?" he questions, his eyebrows drawing down in puzzlement.

I turn and glare at him. I'm not ready to tell him anything. I don't even know what I would say. "Stay out of it," I demand.

His eyes narrow on me and instead of arguing he asks, "Are you going home?"

I grunt, "To shower." I really wish I were already in my own place. The last thing I want to do is deal with my parents right now.

"Want me to call T?" he prods.

Theresa and I are close and usually we all talk to her when we want a girl's perspective, but there's no way I'm talking to her about this yet. "Fuck no," I answer firmly.

He crosses his arms and sighs as I climb into my truck and slam the door. I pull out and glance in my rearview mirror seeing him still staring after me looking confused. I don't blame him, but I need some time to process what just happened with Sadie and *my* son. Heaving a sigh, I feel my whole body begin to deflate.

I can't believe I have a son!

Chapter 20

Matt

On the drive home, I stare at the road feeling numb. I try to sneak in quietly, hoping to go unnoticed. I quickly shower and change. I'm almost home free when I reach for my wallet and keys, but a knock at my door stops me cold. "Fuck," I grumble.

Trudging to the door, I throw it open to find Christian standing on the other side with his arms crossed over his chest. "What do you want?" I prod attempting to smirk at him. When he takes a step in without saying anything, I shake my head in disbelief. "Jason sent you?"

Instead of answering, he questions, "What's going on?"

I heave sigh, relenting, knowing I would probably go looking for Christian later when I was ready to talk. "I'm going for some drinks. Want to be my designated driver?" I ask, so I don't have to worry about getting home later.

He nods, continuing to assess me. "Sure."

"Great. Can I stay at your place then? I can't come back here tonight," I tell him grimacing. I still don't like walking into my parents' house drunk and I'm almost positive that's where my night is headed.

"Yeah, I'll text Bree, but she won't care, and the spare room is all set." He shrugs like it's no big deal.

"Thanks," I mumble before turning to quickly grab clean clothes and a toothbrush for tomorrow. I follow him down the stairs and towards the front door with my bag slung over my shoulder.

"Where are you boys headed?" Dad asks as he steps out of the kitchen.

"We're going to grab dinner and a beer with some friends tonight. Then Matt is going to stay over at my place. I have some things I want to go over with him," Christian declares.

Although, I know what he's saying is true, I'm sure Dad thinks he's referring to the business. I nod in agreement, thankful it's not Mom stopping us. She can read all of us like a book. She would definitely know something's wrong with me and I'm not talking to her about this yet.

"Okay, I know Mom wants all of you here tomorrow night for dinner," he reminds us. We nod our heads in agreement. He waves. "I'll see you boys tomorrow."

While Christian drives, I stare out the window, clenching and unclenching my hands over and over again. I feel him eyeing me out of the corner of his eyes as I stew in silence. Christian pulls up to a small bar out in the middle of nowhere and parks his truck. As we step out onto the gravel parking lot, I look around, glancing at the burnt-out neon sign claiming Rita's to be the name of the place.

We step through a thick wooden door and into a dimly lit musty room. "This place must've been here forever," I grumble.

Christian smirks. "Figured you needed somewhere you wouldn't run into anyone you know."

I groan in annoyance and shrug my shoulders as I step up to an old wooden bar to find carvings of names and dates covering most of it. "Can I get two pints of whatever's on tap?" I ask the woman behind the bar. Noticing her red frizzy hair, I glance at her, guessing she's older than our mom by the looks of it. Pursing her lips, she looks both of us over, her eyes filled with curiosity. Finally, she nods and swiftly fills two pints with summer ale and sets them in front of me without a word. "Can I have a shot of whiskey too?" Quickly, she pours and hands me the shot. Without hesitation, I throw it down my throat enjoying the slow burn down to my chest. I drop the glass on the bar along with a twenty-dollar bill and pick up the beers. Turning towards my brother, I follow him to a table in the back corner.

I sit down at the table and slide one beer across to Christian before taking in my surroundings. It's definitely a place for the locals. At each end of the bar sits an old man in fishing pants and a flannel shirt. Both men appear skinny with gray hair and beards. They have their heads hung low and beers in their hands while they both eye the bartender whom I assume is Rita. Instead of pictures on the walls, various signs of long-standing local beers are scattered throughout.

"So, are you going to say anything or am I going to have to guess what's going on with you?" Christian probes, pulling me away from my perusal. I turn my eyes on him, finding his arms crossed and his head cocked to the side assessing me through narrowed eyes. "Jason told me you didn't want to talk to T, so I figure it must be really serious."

I nod slowly and laugh humorlessly. "You could say that." I run my hand over my face and through my hair in frustration. Shaking my head, I mutter, "I don't even know where to begin, Christian. Everything is so fucked up," I tell him honestly before chugging my beer. I slam it down on the table and move to stand. "I need another one first."

"Take mine," he offers sliding the one I bought for him across the table. I know he doesn't really drink anymore, but sometimes he'll nurse a beer while he sits with me.

I lower myself back to my seat and grumble, "Thanks." I keep rolling the same words around in my head over and over again, but I have no idea how it will sound coming out. "I have a son," I finally blurt out.

Swiftly, I move my eyes to my brother to watch his reaction. His hands drop to the table with a thump, his mouth sitting slightly agape, and his eyes widen to the size of saucers. "What?" he gasps in shock.

I huff and point across the table at him. "That was the same reaction I had before everything else shoved its way over me like a steamroller."

"How?" I give him a cocky smirk and he rolls his eyes like Bree always does. "I mean you said *son*, so who is he? Who's his mom? Natalie?" he questions.

I shake my head, feeling like everything with Natalie happened a lifetime ago. "No. Sadie," I inform him.

His eyes draw together in confusion, and he repeats his earlier question, "What?"

I sigh heavily and give him a brief explanation, "You already know we hung out years ago. Like I already told you, back then we decided to keep our relationship casual. She got pregnant and claims she couldn't find me after she found out. Her son is *mine*," I emphasize.

He leans back in his chair, obviously stunned by my news. I drink my beer in silence and walk to the bar to grab two more, again sliding one across the table towards him. This time he grabs it and takes a sip. "She *just* told you?" he questions flabbergasted.

I smirk and respond sarcastically, "No, that's the *funny* part. I went for a run and saw her at a park. When I walked up to talk to her, my mini clone ran up to her calling her Mommy. He's obviously mine when Micah and Sadie look so much alike. He had my blond hair, my green eyes, and my smile. We had a big ol' family reunion right there in the park."

He eyes me skeptically and I give him a fake laugh. "Matt," he warns knowing I'm close to losing it. But can he really blame me?

I shake my head in disbelief. "I find out I have a son by running into him at the park? That's bullshit Christian! I've missed out on nearly four years of his life because of her! He started out his life with a different dad because of her! He doesn't know me because of her!" I tell him feeling my anger building up again inside me.

He leans forward, quietly demanding, "Relax, Matt!" I fall back into my chair with my beer in my hand. "I know you need time to wrap your head around this, hell, even I need time with this one, but you really need to think about this. From what you told me, I'm not surprised she couldn't find you. You even boycott social media," he reminds me. I cringe, hating his words. "Did you talk to him?" he prods cautiously.

I shake my head feeling an overwhelming amount of disappointment. "No. I was too pissed. I kind of hope he didn't notice me," I admit, cringing. "He looks amazing though Christian," I proclaim with obvious awe in my voice.

"Did you get a picture?" he prompts hopeful.

I shake my head and sigh, "Nah, I didn't even think of it. Plus, people would probably try to have me arrested if they saw some strange guy trying to take pictures of kids at a park from far away," I attempt a joke, but wince at my horrendous humor. I groan, "What the fuck am I going to do?"

"Get to know him," he states confidently.

I raise my eyebrows. "Obviously, but what am I going to do about Sadie?" His eyes drop to his beer, and I add, "I feel like she lied to me. I feel like she completely betrayed me. I feel like she punched me in the chest and stomped all over me. Even if she couldn't find me then, why did she wait so long to tell me now?" I question painfully.

He sighs. "I don't know Matt, but I do think you need to talk to her. These are questions only she can answer. You need to ask her," he emphasizes. "I remember feeling the same way with Bree at one point and if I would've gone to talk to her and asked her my questions, everything could've been so different for us," he admits.

I nod even though I don't completely agree. This is different than what happened with Bree and him. He stands and points to the restrooms. I chug the rest of my beer and stand to grab another one. I step up to the bar between two girls who appear to be here together. First, I turn towards the tall leggy brunette and run my eyes down her legs poking out of navy shorts along with a lacy white tank top. Then I turn my head toward a petite redhead with white shorts and a black tank exposing her midriff along with a lot of cleavage. The redhead leans towards me with a flirty grin as the bartender approaches us. In a last-second decision, I look to them hoping one of these two girls can help me forget about Sadie and her lies. "Can I have three shots of whiskey and another pint of beer?"

She lines up the shots first and I place one in front of each girl. The brunette eyes it with disgust and I shrug my shoulders before I toss mine down. I take hers and hold it up to her friend. She takes it and toasts me, bringing a smile to my face. I toss the second shot down and watch her wince as hers goes down making my grin grow. I lean my ass on a stool behind me and let my hand rest on her hip. "What are you up to tonight?"

"Just hanging out with my friend," she states. She smiles linking her finger through my belt loop. "Thank you for the shot," she states appreciatively.

I nod and tug her closer to me. "Why don't you come sit with me," I suggest. She smiles and nods in agreement. I reach for my beer and stumble slightly as I push off the bar stool and saunter back to the table. As I sit, I pull the redhead down on my lap making her giggle just as my brother returns.

"What the fuck are you doing, Matt?" he asks in annoyance.

"Trying to forget," I mumble.

"This isn't the way to do it," he insists, narrowing his eyes on me.

I look at him doubtfully. "And you would know."

"Actually, yeah, I would, dumbass. That's one of the reasons I almost lost Bree," he reminds me making me flinch.

I attempt to ignore him and instead kiss the surprised girl in my lap, but all I see is Sadie. A hard smack on the side of my head pulls me away from her. "Ow," I wince and glare at my brother.

"I'm not going to let you fuck up," he declares earning a glare from the girl in my lap. He grinds his jaw and looks at her apologetically. "I'm sorry. I meant no offense; this has nothing to do with you." She arches her eyebrows in doubt, but Christian ignores her, refocusing his attention on me. "Okay, take Sadie out of this equation for a minute," he suggests. "What about the fact that you now have to be a good role model for your son?"

My entire body sags in defeat. I groan and look down at the girl with regret. "I'm sorry, but maybe we'll run into each other when I'm in a better place." She frowns and shakes her head in exasperation before shoving off my lap and stomping away dramatically back towards her friend still sitting at the bar.

"I think it's time we head back to my place," he advises.

"I'm not that kind of guy," I joke. I wince as he makes contact with the back of my head this time. "Ow! What was that for?" I complain.

He shakes his head, "Even your jokes are bad tonight. Just please stop," he begs making me chuckle.

Standing, I follow him out to his truck, dropping my head against the window. I stare out the window at blackness, not able to decipher anything outside the beam of the truck's headlights. It's not long before we pull into Christian's dirt driveway, and he shuts off the car.

Reaching out, I grasp his arm to stop him. "I'm scared, Christian," I admit quietly. "I go from trying to figure out how I'm feeling about Sadie to finding out I'm a dad. Now I need to jump right into it, and I have no idea how to do it. I've already missed so much," I emphasize again.

"We're all here for you Matt," he reminds me.

I nod at him appreciatively. "I know. Thank you."

He nods and then the corners of his lips twitch, "Besides, sooner or later you'll have to tell Mom and Dad. We both know Mom will be all over this," he states grinning.

"After she kicks my ass," I add grimacing.

He chuckles, but doesn't comment, probably knowing I'm right. He glances towards his house, "Come on. Let's go inside before Bree decides to come out here to find out what's going on." I groan and push myself out of his truck to follow him inside. I need to get some sleep before I deal with Sadie tomorrow morning.

Chapter 21

Sadie

I continue pacing my small living room glancing nervously from the clock in the kitchen to the front door to my phone, constantly checking for missed calls or texts making myself dizzy. Thankfully, I was able to drop Holden off with Micah's parents at 8:45 this morning, so I could get back here at nine, but Matt's late. It's just after 9:30 and he still hasn't shown up. I'm not sure if I should text him to make sure he's still coming, but the last thing I want to do is annoy him after what happened yesterday. I can't believe that's the way he found out. I should've told him sooner.

Admittedly, I think Bree's wedding was just my excuse to put off telling him a little bit longer, afraid of how he'd react.

I jump at the loud knock on my door, even though I'm expecting it. I turn to stare at it with wide eyes, like he might burst right through it. A second knock soon follows, startling me again and I stride towards the door, pulling it open.

"Did you look out the window to check if it was me?" he snaps at me taking me by surprise. My eyebrows draw together as I stare at him in confusion. "How did you know it was me? Or do you open the door for anyone?"

My mouth drops open in disbelief. Is he joking? I snap my mouth shut and glare at him refusing to answer. "You're late!"

He sighs, steps inside and shuts the door behind him. His eyes look red. He runs a tired hand over his face and through his hair before dropping his arms to his sides. "I wanted to make sure you had time to drop Holden off. I didn't want him here for this," he tells me sounding more than just exhausted.

I narrow my eyes and grit my teeth in annoyance. He could've told me, so I didn't have to go crazy reorganizing everyone's schedule, but I keep my mouth shut, figuring now's not the time to say anything about it.

I watch him move around my living room taking everything in. I look around the room, trying to see things through his eyes. My eyes graze over our worn brown leather couch and chairs, the scratched up white coffee table and entertainment center with a small TV sitting on top, the baskets of toys in the corner and a soft rug in the middle. I know it's not much, but it works for us. I grimace wondering what he's thinking.

He stops at every picture of Holden as he wanders quietly around the room. My gut twists itself in knots as an overwhelming sense of guilt washes over me. I take a deep breath in attempt to shake off my anxiety and prepare myself for the questions I know are about to come at me. "Can I get you something to drink?" I ask softly.

He turns towards me but continues to stare at the picture of Holden in his hand. "Um, yeah, sure, coffee, water, both," he mumbles distractedly.

My body aches watching him. I sigh and turn towards the kitchen. Reaching up for a glass, I quickly fill it with water and set it down on the counter as I try to settle my shaky hands. When I think I have myself under control, I reach for two coffee mugs out of the cabinet and pour from the pot I made while I waited for him to arrive.

"How do you like your coffee?" I call out to him.

"Black is fine," he answers.

I grab his coffee and water, concentrating on not spilling as I bring it out to him and set it on the coffee table before spinning on my heel to go back for mine. I add cream and sugar to my coffee and cradle it in both hands before trudging back out to the living room.

My breath catches in my throat at the sight of Matt sitting on the couch with his elbows resting on his knees and his head in his hands. The coffee and water are right in front of him next to a picture of Holden from his third birthday. My heart clenches and tears spring to my eyes. I hurt for him, hating myself even more.

"Are you okay?" I prompt, my voice cracking.

His head snaps up to mine and he answers honestly, "Not really."

"I'm sorry, Matt. I really am," I insist my entire body aching with guilt and nerves of what's to come.

He nods stiffly, his Adam's apple bobbing up and down as he gulps down a lump in his throat. I watch his body tense as he grumbles, "I get that you're sorry." His jaw twitches and his eyes narrow on me before he reminds me, "That doesn't help me get back four years of my son's life."

I gasp and look away clutching at my chest for a breath, but he's right. It's my fault. I have no right to even try arguing.

"You told me you didn't think you could get pregnant, but I asked you to keep my number until you knew for sure, Sadie," he accuses.

I set my coffee cup down on the table as tears begin streaming down my face. I ramble attempting to force out my explanation, "I know, Matt." I shake my head, overwhelmed with pain. "I really didn't think I could get pregnant, and you pulled out when you remembered you didn't have a condom. I thought it was impossible. I've never regretted anything so much in my life than I did when I deleted your number."

He flinches as an unwanted grunt leaves his lips at the reminder of our conversation so long ago.

"Micah and I talked to everyone who met you that summer to see if we could find you. We looked all over social media. I tried everything I could think of, but I couldn't find you. I kept hoping you would come back, but you never did. I finally had to focus on him and just hope you'd come find us some day. He's my little miracle."

Reaching for a box of Kleenex, I pull one out and dry my face the best I can, but my tears continue to flow. I take a deep shaky breath and then I hear him whisper, "I did."

"What?" I ask, my eyebrows drawing down in confusion.

"I did come back, Sadie," he informs me, staring into my eyes. "Several times," he insists.

My mouth drops open in surprise. "What?"

"The first time I came back for you. I saw Micah propose to you," he reveals wincing.

I gasp painfully as my hand falls to my chest as if I can stop my heart from falling out of my chest.

"After that, I stopped looking for you when I came to visit my family. In fact, I did everything I could to stay away from places I thought I might run into you," he admits.

My tears fall even harder, and I begin sobbing as I struggle to catch my breath. Everything should've been so different. "I'm so sorry," I whimper. "That's not what I wanted. I'm so sorry," I repeat over and over again.

I feel Matt scoot closer to me on the couch. With a heavy sigh, he gathers me in his arms and encloses me in his warmth. He rubs my back in circles and brushes my hair away from my face whispering, "It's going to be okay, Sadie. It's alright." I lean closer to him, burying my face in his chest and soaking his shirt, but I need his comfort and I'm grateful right now he's giving it to me. As my sobs eventually subside, he leans his head back. "Are you okay?"

I hiccup, then smirk, repeating his words, "Not really." Before I hiccup again.

He chuckles humorlessly. "Well, we're both kind of fucked up then. I'm hung-over as hell and really don't have the energy to argue with you right now and you're..." he trails off, briefly glancing away.

I hiccup and scrunch up my nose in disgust. "No explanation needed for me. I'm a mess and that's just fine." He nods rigidly and remains quiet as he releases me. He falls against the back of the couch, dropping his hands to his lap and stares at the picture in front of him. I lean back and pull my feet up with me, protectively wrapping my arms around my knees and holding on tight.

After a few quiet minutes he turns towards me and inquires, "What's his full name?"

I swallow the lump in my throat and inform him, "Holden Matthew Rossi." He flinches the moment I speak. "I didn't know your last name, but I wanted to make sure he had a part of you," I explain hesitantly with a shrug.

"But why Micah's last name?" he questions, hurt evident in his voice.

Taking a deep breath, I attempt to steady myself. I knew I'd have to tell him about my past, but that doesn't make it easy. I stare at his thick muscled legs, not able to look him in the eyes with what I'm about to reveal. "I already told you my parents didn't have time for us, but what I didn't tell you is they disowned me when I refused to have an abortion. They said I was an embarrassment, and I was ruining my life as well as theirs. They kicked me out of the house and stopped paying for school. I had to drop out of college and come home, but I no longer had a home to come home to. I didn't even have a job at the time. If it wasn't for Micah, I don't know what I would've done," I confess.

"We would have been homeless, no food, no health insurance."

Pausing, I again gulp down the lump in my throat feeling the pain and betrayal of it all over again. "We got married before Holden was born. Micah was my best friend, and he was all I had," I cry. "He was good to Holden and me," I add quietly.

He runs his fingers through his hair and tugs on the ends in obvious frustration, but I have no idea what he's thinking. I'm afraid to say something, but I'm also afraid not to say anything. He lifts his head and opens his mouth, but quickly snaps it shut again and looks away. I go over everything I said in my head, wondering what I should say next when he puts me out of my misery, finally asking hoarsely, "Why didn't you tell me sooner?"

I hug myself tighter and look down at my knees, ashamed. Releasing a shaky breath, I answer, "At first, I was completely shocked to see you again. I was scared. I kept trying to tell you and the words just wouldn't come out," I admit. Pausing, I take a deep breath and force myself to continue, "Then I thought I should wait until after your brother's wedding. I was afraid I would ruin it for everyone, and Bree has always been so nice to me. I didn't want to ruin her wedding. Although now I think maybe it was just an excuse to put it off a little longer." I cringe with my admission.

I peek up at him just as he flinches and I swiftly look away, continuing, "I started to tell you the other night, but I lost my nerve after your sister left. I promised myself I would tell you when I saw you this weekend, but then you saw us at the park, and it was too late." I shake my head and shrug, "I just kept trying to find the right time, but I know there's really no right time when it comes to something like this. I just…I just…I just didn't want you to hate me, or even Holden," I stammer over the lump in my throat as more tears fall.

"Fuck," he rumbles and sighs in resignation. "I don't hate you, Sadie. And I could never hate my own son!" he exclaims vehemently. "I'm not going to lie, I am pissed at you and that's putting it mildly, but I'm trying to understand all of this. Give me time to process everything. I think right now I need to focus on Holden. I can't even think about a relationship with you or anyone else at the moment, so please don't ask," he confesses looking hurt and lost all because of me. "I have so much time to make up for and I don't even know where to begin. I want to get to know my son," he painfully whispers his wish.

I reach for another Kleenex and wipe my face feeling my heart breaking inside my chest. My body aches and I'm not sure what to do. Taking a deep breath, I nod stiffly agreeing with Matt, "Okay." I can at least concur with whatever he wants or needs from me with our son, as long as it's good for Holden.

He drops his shoulders as he stares adoringly down at the picture of Holden sitting on the coffee table in front of him. With his emotion apparent, he rasps, "Does he know about me?"

I whimper slightly as I answer, "He knows he has a daddy who lives far away. He knows he looks like his Daddy. He has a picture in his room that I had taken of you that summer. I told him his Daddy loves him and he would come if he knew where to find him, but that's it. He's too young to understand anything else."

"Micah was okay with that?" he probes skeptically.

I shrug. "He had to be, it's the truth. But even as small as Holden was when Micah died, he was also dad to him," I admit.

He cringes and I hate myself for it, but he should know Micah loved Holden. He gets a faraway look in his eyes, but then shakes his head slightly before he focuses on me. "Can you tell me about him?"

I nod releasing a slow breath along with some of my tension. Talking about Holden is the easy part. I reach for my coffee cup to take a sip of my now cold coffee. I stare straight ahead and think about my little miracle as I speak. "He's a good boy, Matt. He's happy. He loves to play with anything that moves," I laugh thinking about how his face lights up when he plays with his toys. "He loves his cars, trucks, trains, tractors, planes," I list, laughing again, "like I said, anything that moves. Even his favorite movies are Disney's Cars or Disney's Planes. He'll run around outside

~ 189 ~

imitating the different sounds of the motors. He recently started playing with Legos. He mostly likes to build big towers with them until they start to lean to the side. Would you like to see his room?"

"Yes, I'd love to," he declares, his green eyes sparkling. He offers me a small smile as he stands. He holds his hand out towards me and I take it. His warm touch sends chills up my arm as he pulls me to my feet. "After you," he gestures in front of him.

I take a shaky step past him and stumble to Holden's room at the end of the hallway, right next to mine. I push his door open and step back for Matt to go in front of me. He takes a step into the room and halts. I watch as he turns in a circle taking in Holden's room. His room definitely portrays Holden, painted a light green with his bed pushed up against the largest wall. It's low to the ground with a safari comforter and a Lightning McQueen decorative pillow. His stuffed lion sits on top of the pillows, always close. He has a green toy box in the corner and a bookshelf on the far wall near it with a blue jean beanbag chair in between. A small dresser sits on the wall opposite his bookshelf and toy box, right next to his closet filled with little boy clothes.

"Shit," Matt mumbles.

My eyes focus back on Matt standing in the middle of Holden's room with his shoulders hunched and his head dropped down in his hands. He's obviously hurting, and I want to comfort him, but I'm probably the last person he wants near him for anything. I wouldn't blame him. I'm the one who did this to him.

"Are you okay?" I ask cautiously.

He takes a deep breath as his head drops back. He groans in frustration at the ceiling. His head moves slowly as he runs his hands through his hair on its way down, gripping the ends tightly just before letting it go and glaring at me making me wince.

"When can I meet my son?" he rasps without answering my question. I clench my own fists completely terrified for what happens next.

Chapter 22

Matt

I'm doing everything I can to keep my patience, but I don't know if I can wait any longer. I'm about to lose my mind. I need to see him.

I stare at the gift sitting by the front door in a green gift bag. When I asked if I could bring something for Holden, Sadie agreed, but asked me not to overdo it. I have no idea what she meant by that, but hopefully the matchbox sized Disney Cars set I bought him along with a plush John Deere tractor with the creepy cartoon eyes and smile works because there's no way I'm walking in to meet my son without a present for him in my hands.

I drove around slightly clueless on what to get an almost four-year-old, but then I thought about what she said about him loving anything that moves as well as Disney's Cars and Planes. I've never seen those movies, but I've seen the advertisements. I decided to go to the toy store and wander around to find something. When I hadn't heard from Sadie yet, I went to the John Deere tractor store. I used to love going there with my dad and brothers, roaming the huge aisle just for kids. I want to bring him back there, I bet he'd love it.

Sighing irritably, I run my hand through my hair again. I reach for my phone, checking the time. "It's almost 4:30," I mumble, groaning to myself in annoyance. She said she needs to tell him I'm here first and I get that, but...I need this to start now. I don't think I've ever felt so anxious about anything in my life. She promised me dinner tonight with them as long as he seems okay after she tells him. I flip through the photo books she gave me looking through as I impatiently wait for her call.

I glance at my phone again and grimace at the missed calls from my mom, but I can't talk to her right now. Knowing her, she'll know something is going on if I call her back and she never even checks her texts.

Continuing to scroll, I notice a few texts I've left unanswered from Christian. "If you don't tell me what's up, I'm coming to find you…wherever you might be!"

I huff in irritation, but take a deep breath to calm my nerves, knowing he's only trying to watch out for me. "I'm fine. I talked to Sadie. I'm heading over to talk to her again. Can you tell Mom I'm busy with work or something today and I'll talk to her in the morning? I can't deal with that yet," I plead.

"I'll cover for you," he responds, causing me to breathe a sigh of relief.

"Thanks. I'll call you tomorrow." I need him to give me a little more time. I need to meet him first.

"You sure you're okay?" he prods.

Grimacing at the screen, I quickly reply, "Yes, Mom!"

"Ok smartass," he answers. "Tomorrow," he reiterates as if letting me know he means it more like a demand. Even though he's my younger brother, I'm grateful we all watch out for one another.

I'm about to text him again with a flippant comeback, but it disappears from the tip of my tongue as my phone buzzes with a message from Sadie. "He's waiting for you."

My hand falls to my chest as my heart stops, and an instant ache consumes me starting with my heart. I concentrate on breathing in and out slowly and attempt to swallow the lump in my throat as well as relax my trembling hands clenched into fists, but it's not working. I close my eyes and focus on ridding myself of the tingling ache.

Why the fuck won't it go away? Those words say so much. I shake my head and force myself to place one foot in front of the other and walk out the door to my truck, grabbing the gift for Holden on my way out.

I drive to her house on autopilot with my body ironically both achy and numb. It takes everything in me to concentrate on the curvy road in front of me, especially with my mind going non-stop. I can't stop thinking of all the possible reactions he might have of me, good, bad and indifferent. But I honestly don't know how to respond to a single one of them.

Exhaling a shaky sigh, I drop my head against the steering wheel as soon as I pull into the driveway. I take a deep breath and lift my heavy head, glancing up at her house. Just the sight of it sends my nerves into overdrive.

The tan curtains in the front window rustle back and forth just before I see a small blond head pop up. He presses his face to the window and his eyes go wide the moment he spots me, taking my breath away. He quickly slips away from the glass as the curtains fall back into place, covering the window.

Taking another deep breath, I force myself to move and step out of my truck. I don't want to leave him waiting now that he knows I'm here. As I stride woodenly towards the door, I try to force myself to relax, but I think that might be impossible right now. I don't think I've ever been truly frightened of anything in my life, but I'm definitely terrified to walk in that door and meet my little boy; the thought again taking my breath from me.

Halfway up the path, my head snaps up to the sound of the front door opening and closing. Holding my breath, I look up to find Sadie standing in front of me. She has her arms crossed tightly in front of her pushing her chest up and reflexively drawing my eyes there. I clear my throat and force myself to meet her steely gaze. "Hi," I rasp.

"Before you walk through that door, there's something important you need to understand," she tells me without preamble. I nod my head and wait to hear what she has to say. She straightens, standing a little taller just before she speaks. "You can't *ever* walk away after this Matt, not from him. I won't let you," she threatens me, making my lips twitch into a full grin. That's the strong girl I remember.

I take a step closer to her without veering my gaze from hers. Staring into her eyes, I open my eyes to her attempting to let her see inside of me. I need to show her how serious I am. "He's my son, too. I'm not going anywhere."

She gulps hard and I watch her Adam's apple bob up and down as she studies me intently. She finally gives me a stiff nod in acceptance. "Okay." She spins on her heel without another word, and I quickly follow as she strides back towards her house. I take one more quick breath trying to prepare myself a little bit more as I walk through the door, but nothing could ever prepare me to see this little boy now that I know he's mine.

With his head down, Holden dives behind Sadie's legs and wraps his arms around them as soon as she walks through the door. A smile tugs at the corners of my lips and I tilt my head down towards him desperately trying to get a better look, but all I can see is a little boy with blonde waves like mine.

"Hi, Holden," I rasp, overwhelmed with emotion. Bright green eyes peer at me with an enormous amount of curiosity through Sadie's legs and I can't help but chuckle at the sight.

Sadie twists her body around the best she can attempting to pull him around in front of her. "Come say hello, Holden," she encourages softly.

He glances up at her nervously before he scrunches his eyebrows together in determination and takes a step in front of her. He crosses his arms over his chest and looks up at me. I crouch down in front of him so I can look at him and he can look at me a little bit closer. There's definitely no doubt in my mind that he's mine. He appears to be a perfect mix of Sadie and me. He has my hair and eyes, but Sadie's tan Italian skin. I wonder if it's soft like hers. He's wearing red net shorts with a gray Nike t-shirt and no shoes or socks. I watch his perfect little toes wiggling before I look back up at his face.

He narrows his eyes and moves closer so he's only about three inches from my nose. He stares at me as I hold my breath waiting anxiously for some kind of reaction from him or even just a simple greeting. Tilting his head to the side, he finally cautiously inquires, "Are you my Daddy?"

I gasp feeling my heart beat erratically in my chest with his question coming from that tiny little voice. I answer him with obvious emotion, my voice cracking, "Yeah, Holden, I am."

He reaches his tiny little hands up towards me and softly touches my face eliciting a soft gasp from me. I remain as still as possible as he starts by placing his palms on my cheeks and pinching gently. He squeezes my nose before giving it a solid tug. I have no idea what he's doing, but I let him do whatever he needs with my hands hanging at my sides, twitching as I hold myself back from pulling him to me.

Reaching up, he wiggles my ears before he moves his hands to my blonde wavy hair that looks just like his and pulls that as well. When he's done poking and prodding me, he takes a step back and tilts his head to the side as he looks at me quizzically one more time. A small smile slowly grows on his face, and I can't help but think that looks familiar to me too.

Suddenly, Holden jumps up and down with a shout startling me, "Woo-hoo! He found us, Mommy! He's real! Daddy found us!" He throws himself into my arms. I catch him wrapping my arms tightly around his little body holding back my own whimper. His small arms wrap around my neck and I can't hold back my tears for another second. I feel completely overwhelmed. None of this seems real.

How do I already love this little boy so much it hurts, yet I just found out he's mine?

He tears himself away from me as quickly as he threw himself into my arms and I reluctantly let him go. He runs down the hall calling over his shoulder to me, "I have something to show you! Stay there!"

I wipe at my face before I dare look up. Taking a deep breath, I place my hands on my knees and stand, glancing briefly at Sadie, noticing she's wiping her own tears away. I take a step towards her wanting to say something, but even I'm not sure what's about to leave my mouth.

"Sadie," I rasp her name, but neither of us have the chance to find out what I was going to say because we're interrupted by the sound of Holden's little feet charging back towards us again.

"Look!" he exclaims proudly holding up the picture of me in the black wooden frame from his bedroom. I'm wearing black board shorts with the bottom of one leg a dark green and a matching dark green t-shirt standing in front of the swimming hole where I first met Sadie. "I have this picture of you in my room. Mommy told me you didn't know where to find us, but I knew you would find us," he informs me, making me choke up again. I nod and smile down at him, too emotional to even speak. "Wanna' see my room?" he asks, his voice full of excitement.

Clearing my throat, I reply with a huge grin, "I'd love to." I want to see anything and everything he wants to show me.

"Is that okay, Mommy?" he prods looking up at Sadie while he bounces on his toes impatiently waiting for her answer.

She nods her head. "I think that's a great idea, Holden. You can bring him to see your room and show him your things. If it's okay with you little man, I'll go finish up dinner while you do that," Sadie barely squeaks out.

"Okay," he agrees, barely able to contain his elation already looking down the hall towards his room.

Sadie clears her throat before adding with a forced smile, "Go ahead, Holden. I'll call you both when dinner is ready."

"Okay," Holden yells and runs towards his room. "Come on, Daddy! Come on! I have so much to show you!"

I turn towards Sadie and barely grate out, "Thank you."

She nods her head and I see a few more tears fall before she spins on her heel and strides rapidly towards the kitchen. I watch for a moment before I shake my head to pull myself out of my stupor.

"I'm coming, Holden," I call after him. "You're just too fast for me," I tease knowing the lump in my throat won't be going anywhere anytime soon.

Holden pops out of his room and stops in front of me, placing his small hand in mine. He leans forward and tugs on my hand, guiding me. He mumbles, "I'll help. I don't want you to get lost again, Daddy."

My heart stutters and I have a quick intake of breath at his words. I close my eyes for a moment, letting him guide me to his room as a few more tears fall. Taking another deep breath, I force my eyes to open and struggle to maintain my balance as I step into his little world.

The rest of the night passes by in a blur. He shows me his toys, which consists mostly of cars, trucks, tractors and planes. We build a Lego tower together. We read a book about Monster Trucks, twice. Sadie made pasta for dinner, one of Holden's favorite foods and he didn't stop talking the whole time, even trying to speak around his food before being gently scolded.

He told me about his pre-school, his teacher and his friends. He showed me all his movies and made me promise to watch one with him next time. He asked me to read him "Goodnight Moon" and "Goodnight Maine" before he wanted both Sadie and me to tuck him into bed.

Before he closes his eyes, his gaze turns wary as he looks up at me and asks innocently, "Will I get to see you in the morning?"

I try to control my voice before I answer him, but my attempts were futile. My voice cracks as I emphasize, "I don't know if I'll see you in the morning, but I promise I'll see you tomorrow."

My answer must be good enough for him because he nods his head and smiles with tired eyes. He wraps his arms around my neck and whispers, "Goodnight, Daddy. I'm so glad you found us."

"Me too, Holden," I whimper, "Me too. Goodnight, buddy."

Reluctantly, I step out of the room and stride immediately for the couch. I drop down on the end with my elbows on my knees and my head in my hands, letting my emotions go. I sit for a few minutes, letting my tears fall freely. It feels foreign to me, but I don't know how to handle any of this.

I feel her the moment she steps into the room, but it feels like hours before I hear her whisper, "I'm so sorry, Matt."

Forcing myself to lift my head up, I look into her eyes. It's obvious her pain and regret matches mine, but right now I don't seem to care. I force myself to keep my voice quiet, so we don't wake him, but I feel my anger vibrating through every part of me. "I missed out on so fucking much, Sadie! How could you do this to me? How could you do this to him? All you had to do was hold on to my fucking number until you knew, but I guess I didn't matter enough to even do that?"

She shakes her head, tears streaming down her face. "No, Matt, that's not true!" she denies desperately.

"It's almost like he thinks we were playing an elaborate game of hide and seek!" I add exasperated, ignoring her comment. "I want," I begin, but shake my head and start over. "No, I *need* to see him every single day. I don't know how we're going to do all of this, but we need to figure it out fast."

She nods her head in agreement, refusing to look at me.

"I'm going to tell my family. They will want to meet him right away." She nods again but doesn't say anything. I sigh and run my hand over my face and through my hair feeling indescribably lost.

"I have to go," I grumble pushing myself to stand. When I reach the door, I turn to look at her again and I'm completely overwhelmed by the haunted expression on her face. I take a deep breath and attempt to shake off whatever I'm feeling, not able to define it.

I have the strongest urge to tell her at least something good. I can't leave when she looks so devastated. "He's amazing Sadie," I proclaim with admiration and awe clear in my voice. "He's an incredible kid," I emphasize, feeling like my words are not even close to enough. "You've been doing a great job with him," I add because it's the truth.

Her head snaps up as her eyes widen with surprise, but I don't give her a chance to respond. I stalk out the door and get in my truck, driving away without looking back once. If I do, I'm afraid I won't give her a choice and I'll move in, permanently.

Chapter 23

Sadie

The past couple days, being able to watch Matt with Holden has been the most amazing thing I've ever seen. I'm so screwed. Everything about him makes my heart beat faster, but he only talks to me about Holden now. It seems like he doesn't even want to look at me. I realize it hasn't been very long since he found out the truth but knowing about our son has changed everything between us. There no longer is an us when it comes to Matt and me. Saying that fact breaks my heart is honestly an understatement. Don't get me wrong; I'm thrilled he came back. No matter what, I always wanted Holden to have him. I just didn't know how to make it happen. Matt's focus is on Holden, exactly where it should be I remind myself again.

Unfortunately, every time I see Matt or even just think about him, I want him more and more. He's so good with Holden. I love listening to the two of them talking. Half of their conversations are complete nonsense. He couldn't be more perfect. With the way I'm feeling, I know I'm falling in love with him, but I attempt to shove those feelings away. I know he'll never feel the same way about me. Why would he? I probably deserve it after what I did to him and for what happened with Micah too. It is my fault everything turned out this way and I hate myself for it. I cringe and try to shake away my negative thoughts.

Holden calls my name, "Mommy!" interrupting my thoughts.

I peek my head into his room to find him standing in his underwear pulling all his clothes out of his drawers and tossing them on the ground. "Holden, what are you doing?" I prod, bewildered. Crouching down next to him, I begin picking up his discarded clothes. "You didn't' like what you were wearing?"

"I want to wear shorts like Daddy's, but I can't find any," he explains still digging through his dresser.

A lump forms in my throat and I take a deep breath in through my nose and blow it out slowly through my mouth in an attempt to control my breathing, so my tears don't fall. Tears have been way too common with me the last few days. "You have a pair of tan cargo shorts down here little man," I rasp and quickly pull them out. Matt always seems to be in either cargo shorts or board shorts. I wonder what he wears when it gets cold.

"Yay!" he cheers as he grabs them from me, again pulling me out of my thoughts. He sits on the floor and tugs his shorts on. Then he stands, walking over to me with one arm in an army green shirt. "Can you help me put this on?"

I smile at him. "Of course." I pull the shirt over his head and kiss his nose when his head pops through. I button up his pants for him and remind him, "If you have to go to the bathroom, don't forget to ask for help with the button on your shorts. You're not used to these."

"Okay, Mommy," he agrees, grinning proudly at me. "I will."

"Are you almost ready to go to grandma and grandpa's house?" I question.

I want to get over there before Matt shows up. He agreed to come meet Micah's parents today for lunch. I'm nervous, wondering what it will be like. We all realize they aren't Holden's real grandparents, but they are the only ones he has ever known.

My parents have never made any effort and I obviously didn't know whom Matt's parents were until recently. I know they're afraid of losing Holden now that Matt's here and Micah's gone. I'm hoping this meeting will help ease their worry. But it doesn't help my anxiety that we're already running a little late.

"Can I bring the new cars Daddy gave me to show them?" he prompts instead of answering.

I sigh and nod my head. "Okay." He grabs the special case he put the cars in and runs towards the front door. "I think you forgot your shoes," I call after him.

He turns and laughs. "No, I didn't, Mommy. I don't want to wear shoes," he informs me like it's the most obvious explanation in the world.

I struggle to hold back my own smile as I respond. "You have to at least wear shoes over there. You can take them off when you get to grandma and grandpa's house. You have Crocs by the front door."

He scrunches his face up adorably, but obeys anyway, immediately sliding the navy-blue Crocs onto his feet. I open the front door and we walk out to the car. I quickly buckle him into his car seat and climb in behind the wheel.

As we drive the short distance to Micah's parents' house, my nerves begin to take over my stomach, feeling like a swarm of angry bees has taken over my insides. Anytime my mind starts to wander to the possibilities of what might happen today, I try to pull my focus to Holden's car sounds from the back seat as he pretends to drive along with me.

We pull into the driveway, and I breathe a sigh of relief when I don't see any sign of Matt yet. I climb out of the car and help Holden out of his seat. He sprints for the front door carrying his case of cars. The door opens before he reaches it and I watch as Micah's Mom immediately scoops him up into a hug. By the time I reach the door he's wiggling away from her and running down the hall announcing his arrival, "Grandpa, Grandpa, I'm here!"

We both laugh, but her smile instantly fades as her eyes land on something behind me. I turn and watch as Matt parks his truck at the curb and steps out. He's wearing a grey V-neck t-shirt that wraps perfectly around his sculpted arms and chest with dark green cargo shorts and flip-flops. I grin at the sight of him.

He glances towards us and our eyes meet. The corner of his mouth twitches up as he approaches us with a small bouquet of daisies in one hand. "Hi," he greets me before his eyes move beyond me. He clears his throat, introducing himself, "Hi, Mrs. Rossi. I'm Matt Emory. It's nice to meet you."

He offers her his hand to shake, and I can't help but notice tears form in her eyes. She brushes them away with one hand, while she shakes his hand with the other. "It's nice to meet you, Matt and please, call me, Bee. It's short for Bianca."

He grins and offers her the flowers, "Well then, Bee, I brought these for you."

She smiles appreciatively. "Thank you. Please come in, come in," she insists. I step inside with Matt right behind me.

Little feet come running down the hall. "Grandma!" Holden yells, but he stops and changes direction as soon as he spots Matt. "Daddy!" He sprints towards Matt and throws his arms around his legs. "You're here!"

"Hey, Holden. How are you doing today?" he asks hugging him back the best he can without moving him from around his legs.

"I'm dressed just like you," he announces proudly.

Matt chuckles softly. "I see that. You look great!"

Holden' grins up at him. "Come on, I have so much to show you!" he exclaims with pure excitement.

Matt smiles down at him, but I interrupt before he can say anything, "How about we introduce him to Grandpa first?" I suggest.

He nods in agreement as he loosens his hold on Matt's legs. "Okay." Without letting his hands fall to his sides, he reaches for Matt's hand and without turning around, he begins tugging on him wanting Matt to follow. He bumps into Micah's dad just as he steps up behind him making us all giggle. Holden reaches for his grandpa's hand and stands between them proudly, "Grandpa, this is my Daddy. Then he looks at Matt and repeats the gesture, "Daddy, this is my Grandpa."

I hear a gasp next to me and without looking, know Micah's mom is as choked up as I am. Matt reaches with the hand not holding onto Holden and offers, "I'm Matt Emory. It's nice to meet you, Mr. Rossi."

"You can call me Marco," he replies. He clears his throat and steps away, obviously choked with emotion. "Why don't we go into the family room to talk before we eat lunch," he suggests.

We all follow without a word, Holden obliviously happy.

As soon as we walk in the room, I notice Matt's eyes moving around the space taking in pictures of Micah, Holden and even one of the three of us when Holden was born. I watch his Adam's apple bob up and down as he swallows hard.

He lowers himself stiffly across from Marco into a gold armchair, while I sit hesitantly with Bee on the gold and tan floral couch. Now that we're all in the same room, I have no idea what to say. As the silence continues, my breaths become quicker, and I open my mouth trying to come up with something to say.

Holden breaks the silence as he steps in front of Matt with a picture frame in his tiny hands. He holds it up to him with a small smile. "This is my other Daddy. Mommy says he watches over me from heaven now." Glancing over, I realize it's a picture of Micah holding Holden on his first birthday, both of them smiling brightly.

With Holden's words and the sight of the picture, all of us feel the sudden weight of air in the room. I feel like the ceiling and walls are closing in on me. Feeling the pressure, I hold my breath, waiting for anyone to react.

My eyes drift to Matt and I watch as a range of emotions pass swiftly over his face. Suddenly, he clears his throat and rasps, "I've met him before. We were sort of friends one summer before you were born," he enlightens him.

"Really?" Holden asks as his eyes go wide and a huge grin lights up his face. Matt just nods his head in confirmation, unable to speak. I want to know what he's feeling. I can only imagine he's angry and hurt hearing his son say those words and to see Micah holding him as his dad at a time when Matt didn't know he existed. I cringe at the thought, the weight on my chest becoming crushing.

"Do you have to go potty?" Matt asks him suddenly.

I glance at my son, seeing him dancing around, pulling at his shorts. I quickly blurt out, "He can't undo the button."

"Can I help you with that?" Matt asks. Holden nods vigorously. Matt quickly undoes his button and Holden takes off in a sprint for the bathroom.

As soon as the bathroom door slams shut, Bee stands and blurts out, "You can't take our grandson away from us. He's all we have left. I know he's not...but he is...he is to us," she pleads desperately, stumbling over her words.

Matt shakes his head as his face turns to stone before he speaks, addressing them both. "I obviously don't know you and you don't know me, but I would never do that to Holden," he states firmly. Pausing, he takes a deep breath, attempting to get his emotions under control. "He obviously loves you. In his eyes, you're his grandparents. I would never deprive him of having someone he loves in his life," he emphasizes.

I gasp at his words, feeling like he just took a knife and stabbed me in my chest because I understand his implication. That's exactly what I did to him. I deprived him of nearly four years of his son's life. He can never get that time back. I took that away from him. I may not have done it intentionally, but that's exactly what I did. I don't know if he'll ever forgive me, or even if I deserve his forgiveness in the first place, but my heart nearly overflows with regret.

"You won't?" Marco questions.

"I promise." Matt adds in a hoarse whisper, "I know what it feels like." I flinch and quickly turn away, not able to look at any of them as unwanted tears roll down my cheeks.

I feel Bee move off the couch and listen as she moves across the room. She whimpers, "Thank you." I wipe my tears and slowly turn back towards them to see her hugging Matt as he pats her back uncomfortably.

Marco looks him in the eyes and repeats the emotional sentiment, "Thank you." He opens his mouth to say something else, but then closes it and gently tugs Bee away from Matt.

She smiles up at him in embarrassment as Holden charges his way back towards us. I quickly wipe at my cheeks again to rid myself of my tears, but not quickly enough. Holden steps up to me and asks, "Mommy, why are you crying? Are you okay?"

"I'm great my little man," I reply with a forced smile. "I'm just happy we're all together," I declare. He scrunches his nose and eyes like he's not quite sure about my answer, but then he shrugs and hugs me tightly. His hug gives me breath again. I whisper into his hair, "I love you so much, Holden." I kiss the top of his head just before he wiggles out of my embrace.

"Love you too, Mommy!" Then, he spins around and calls over his shoulder, "Come on everybody, I wanna' show you my tower!"

I take a deep breath and push to my feet. Instantly, I feel dizzy, swaying on my feet and hold myself completely still for a moment, trying to regain my balance. Suddenly Matt's in front of me, a hand on my elbow and his eyebrows furrowed in concern. "Are you okay?"

I nod my head, not able to speak. His eyes swiftly roam over me, assessing me. I watch him as a range of emotions pass over his face. His jaw twitches and he gives me a stiff nod in acceptance before releasing my arm. I promptly feel the loss of his touch as I watch him walk down the hall towards the sound of Holden's voice, wondering how we'll get through this.

Chapter 24

Matt

I sit down at my parents' large rectangular wooden kitchen table cupping a large mug of coffee in my hands and stare out at the lake. I'm supposed to be moving into my new place today, but first I need to tell mom and dad about Holden. I sigh and drop my head wondering how they'll react. Unfortunately, the longer I put it off, the more pissed off they'll be at me. I should understand that better than anyone I think bitterly.

"Good morning," Mom declares in an almost singsong voice as she steps into the room.

I lift my head and force a smile in greeting knowing she's coming right for me. "Morning, Mom." She kisses the top of my head like she has every morning I'm home since I was a little kid.

"Morning, Matt. Moving day again today?" Dad prompts as he steps into the kitchen right behind my mom going right for the coffee.

I groan quietly. "Yeah. I'm all packed up. I guess it's good I didn't really unpack everything. Plus, I don't have too far to go," I remind them.

"Although you're always welcome to stay here, I'm so happy you'll be close." Mom grins. "Would you like some breakfast? Dad is going to make some eggs and bacon, plus I made some blueberry muffins this morning."

"Thanks." I jump at her offer as she pulls out a platter of muffins she had hidden on top of the refrigerator. I grab a plate and a couple muffins to eat while I patiently wait for both of my parents to join me at the table.

After my dad finishes cooking the eggs, he sits at one end and my mom sits down between us. Like always, she says, "No point in sitting so far away from each other when we're not sitting at a full table."

"What time are your brothers going to be here to help you?" Dad inquires. I look up to answer him, but no sound comes out. I shrug and take another sip of my coffee. His eyebrows draw together in concern as he gently prods, "Are you alright, Matt?"

I set my coffee cup down and close my eyes. I slowly release the breath I didn't know I was holding before I open them back up. I look back and forth between both of my parents nervously, my palms beginning to sweat. Instead of answering his question, I inform them, "I actually have something I have to tell you."

Mom slowly sets down her mug as Dad cautiously places his fork back on his plate, folding his hands in front of him. "What's going on?" he probes through narrowed eyes.

I heave a sigh knowing it's time to tell them the truth. I focus on my mom, trying to stay calm. "I have a son," I state, my voice cracking.

She gasps and her hand falls to her chest, covering her heart. "What?" she asks as I watch her face go deathly pale making my stomach churn. I take a quick glance at my dad, noticing his fists are clenched so tightly together his knuckles have turned white.

I grind my jaw and take a deep breath, ready to repeat myself. I tell them again with a little more confidence, "I have a son."

"This girl, Natalie? Who we've never even met?" my mom asks appearing stricken.

I shake my head in contradiction. Natalie feels like a distant memory at this point. "No. It happened before her. He's going to be four in a couple weeks." Dad's eyes narrow as tears begin to fall down Mom's cheeks making me realize I need to talk much faster to explain everything, but it's not easy. "I didn't know. If I would've…" I trail off not ready for the conversation to go in that direction with them quite yet. "I didn't know about him. I just found out a few days ago," I inform them.

"How?" Mom asks her voice trembling. "How did you find out after all this time?" she clarifies.

I shake my head attempting to clear the fog with everything still feeling like a dream to me. "I was running and ran into them in the park. The guy I thought was the father," I begin, "I knew him." I shake my head again. "Her little boy looks exactly like I did when I was that age," I emphasize. I attempt to gulp down the growing nerves in my throat before I emphasize, "I just *knew* as soon as I saw him."

"I don't understand! Did she try to keep him from you? Was she cheating on her boyfriend or something with you? Did she not want him to know?" Mom probes, her voice slowly rising with each question. She looks absolutely terrified of my answers. I don't blame her considering these circumstances, but the insinuation still hurts. I wouldn't want to be that guy either.

I shake my head and rasp, "No. We went out a few times, hung out most of the summer, but we were exclusive while I was here, but casual. She was going to be leaving for college and I was going back to Texas, so that's all it could be. I left before she even knew she was pregnant. She had no idea how to get in touch with me." I don't need to give them more details than that. It will already be awkward enough. The last thing I need to do is make the situation worse.

"What's his name?" Dad asks.

"Holden Matthew Rossi," I proclaim as I watch them carefully.

Mom's eyes narrow. "Why does that name sound familiar? Rossi?" she ponders.

Suddenly she gasps just as I open my mouth to tell them. "Sadie," I whisper her name as both of their eyes widen in surprise. "Bree's friend," I croak.

"Isn't she the girl who lost her husband a couple years ago?" Dad questions, but I think it's more of a reminder than anything.

I nod my head. "Yeah."

"How do you know this little boy wasn't his?" he pushes.

I could feel myself getting hot, my whole body tensing with anger at the simple question. I knew it was coming, but I still don't like it. I grit my teeth and try to speak without taking it out on them, "Micah was Italian, like Sadie. He looked like Sadie. Holden has my blonde hair and my green eyes. He looks just like me," I insist vehemently.

Dad nods and looks out the window towards the lake, his face blank. I want to know what he's thinking, but in a way I don't. I don't need to hear him tell me why I messed up. I'm already paying for my mistake in spades.

"I'll still get a DNA test. I need it so I can be added to his birth certificate. I want my rights as his father. But I *know* he's mine," I reiterate.

"When can we meet him?" Mom asks softly.

I shrug. "I don't know. I'll have to talk to Sadie. Maybe this weekend," I suggest. "Now that Jason and Christian have some help, they may be able to come. I could try for Sunday?"

Mom nods in agreement. "Sunday would be good. We've already missed four years, I don't want to miss anymore," she speaks the same thoughts that have been eating at me, making me cringe. Her hand falls to my shoulder with a heavy sigh. "I'm sorry, Matthew."

Dad focuses back on me and for the first time I notice unshed tears in his eyes as well, causing my chest to clench. "Please, tell her we want to meet him soon."

Overwhelmed by all the emotion in the room, I nod. "Okay," I whisper hoarsely.

"Do either of your brothers know? Or Theresa?" Dad prods.

I grimace. "Christian knows, so probably Bree, but that's it. The last couple days I just tried to spend some time with him and get to know him. I want him comfortable with me." I sigh and run my hand through my hair in frustration. "I honestly have just been trying to wrap my own head around it."

Both my parents nod in acknowledgement. Suddenly, mom's eyes widen as she turns to me with hope. "Do you have a picture?"

Nodding, I reach for my phone. I swiftly pull up a picture of Holden grinning and hand it over to my mom. She gasps and her hand covers her mouth in shock. She stares at the picture as she lets more tears slide down her cheeks. Dad stands and leans over her shoulder to see the photo, wrapping one arm around her in support.

"He looks just like you," she states in awe. "He has the Emory smile," she grins proudly. "He's absolutely beautiful, Matthew." I nod in agreement.

"Wow," Dad murmurs in astonishment at a loss for words.

We all sit in the kitchen looking from the picture of Holden and out to the lake, attempting to process the whole conversation.

Christian calling from the foyer startles all of us out of our thoughts, "Good morning! Did you make breakfast, Mom?"

He steps into the kitchen with Bree at his side. "I thought once you were married mom wouldn't need to stock the kitchen for you," I tease needing to lighten the mood. Bree blushes and I add, "I'm kidding, Bree."

"I came here to help you. I can leave if you want," Christian offers staring at me. I just laugh without responding. I know he'll stay to help.

"I always want all of you here," Mom mumbles. She turns to Christian and Bree announcing tearfully, "I'm a grandmother."

Christian and Bree's eyes both shift right to me. "You told them?" Christian asks. I just shrug since the answer is obvious. "Does anyone else know?"

"Not yet, but I'm still waiting on my lecture," I admit.

Dad's eyes narrow and Mom sighs, wiping away a few more tears. "We're not going to lecture you Matt. A few years ago, we probably would've, but you're an adult. The worst part about this is that we've all missed so much with him that we can't get back," Dad declares shocking me.

Mom leans over and hugs me tightly. "I agree with your father." She leans back and looks into my eyes, apologizing again as if it's her fault, "I'm so sorry, Matthew." She hugs me again and whispers, "I can't believe I'm a grandma!"

Mom releases me and I turn towards Bree as she asks, "Are you doing okay, Matt?"

I huff a humorless laugh and shrug. "Honestly, I don't know. Everything about this is surreal. I feel like I'm either looking into the future or in someone else's shoes or something. I don't know. It sure as hell doesn't feel like my life!" I admit.

"You're going to be an amazing dad," Mom whimpers. My heart lodges itself in my throat and I have to close my eyes to regain my composure. I can't believe I'm someone's dad.

I glance over at Bree needing to know something from her. I don't really know how to ask this, but I feel compelled to. It's something I know will eat at my soul if I keep my mouth shut. "Bree, you're friends with her," I begin hesitantly.

She nods appearing wary. "Yeah."

"Have you ever met Holden before? Or even Micah? Did you know Holden wasn't his son?" I ask her, holding my breath as I await her response.

She shakes her head. "I met Holden once when we first started working together. Micah's mom had to meet

Sadie at the store to pick him up that day, but she mostly just showed me pictures of him. I didn't know her before Micah died. I never met him or even saw a picture of him. I just assumed that Holden looked like his dad and I assumed his dad was Micah. I'm so sorry, Matt," she apologizes her eyes full of regret on my behalf.

I nod in understanding. "Okay. Thanks Bree," I rasp. She nods and steps over to me giving me a hug. I exhale heavily and lean into her, grateful for the support.

"Find your own wife to cuddle," Christian teases.

I grin mischievously and pull her even closer to me. "I think she realizes she married the wrong brother. She definitely likes me better," I joke. Bree giggles in my ear before swatting at me playfully. I chuckle at Christian's glare and duck, dodging the flying strawberry headed right for my head.

"Hey, no more flying fruit," dad admonishes.

"Want to see a picture?" I ask Christian.

He grins and steps over to me, looking at the picture on my phone. "Wow, he looks just like you, only much better looking."

Bree rolls her eyes as she peers over his shoulder to see and visibly flinches. "Don't," I insist knowing exactly what she's thinking.

She glances at me, full of remorse. "Now that I know, I see it so clearly," she confesses.

I shake my head. "Don't do that. You never had any idea I knew Sadie until recently. There's no way you could've realized Holden was my son," I insist. She nods her head in agreement, although I can still tell she feels bad about it. Christian sees it too and instantly moves closer to her. He kisses her on the forehead and wraps his arms around her in support.

"Aren't we too young to be grandparents?" dad asks attempting to change the direction of the conversation.

"What did you just say?" Jason prompts with wide eyes as he steps into the room with Sara.

I grimace and tell them, "I can't do this again right now. Someone else has to tell him. I'm going to start putting boxes in my truck to bring over to my new place," I add just before I walk out of the room. I have to get this done so I can go over to Sadie's house to see Holden later tonight. I don't want to miss a minute of time with him.

Chapter 25

Sadie

Holden and I are meeting Matt's family today. I'm scared it will be too much for us, but mostly too much for him. Matt said we would take the day slow, whatever that means. We're meeting his parents first. Then, later the rest of his family including Bree will be coming over for a barbecue.

I know I've met everyone already and I'm friends with Bree, but this will be different. This time they'll be seeing me as Holden's mom, their nephew's mom or their grandson's mom. I'm also the one who kept Holden away from them for the past four years. I'm the reason they missed so much. It may have been unknowingly, but it still happened and it's my fault. When it comes to Holden, I have so many regrets.

Every day I feel like they eat at me more and more.

Matt said he'd pick us up right after lunch. I'm struggling to keep myself calm while we wait. I'm sick to my stomach, but I don't want Holden to know how I feel. Fortunately, he's been so preoccupied with everything Matt that I don't matter much right now because he's usually way too observant for a four-year-old boy when it comes to me. He has his face pressed to the front window, impatiently waiting to see Matt's truck.

I take one last look in the mirror to make sure I look okay. I'm hoping I look nice for them. Honestly, I want to look like a good mom, but what does that even look like? I'm wearing an aqua skirt and a white button-up tank top with white flip-flops.

Holden slaps the window with the palms of his hands startling me. He pushes himself away from the window and shouts excitedly, "He's here!" I place my hand on my chest to calm my heart, which seems to be pounding even harder. "Come on, Mommy! Come on!" Holden prompts pulling at my arm.

I take a deep breath and allow him to drag me towards the front door. We reach it just as the doorbell chimes. I place my hand on the cold metal knob and turn it slowly with Holden bouncing on his feet next to me. I tug the door open, and my breath catches in my throat at the sight. Matt stands in front of me in blue and white board shorts and a blue fitted Under Armour t-shirt with a heart-melting grin for our son.

"Hey, Holden!" He crouches down on one knee and puts his arms out to Holden. He jumps towards him and throws his arms around him in a tight hug.

"Hi, Daddy!" He smiles up at him.

"Are you guys ready?" he prompts as he stands. I nod my head, not able to get the words out. Matt appraises me for a moment, his eyes quickly roaming over me. He pinches his lips together and runs his hand through his blonde waves. I watch as he takes a deep controlled breath before continuing, "Okay, then, let's go."

I really want to know what he's thinking, but I definitely don't dare ask. Instead, I reach for my bag, but he takes it from me as soon as it touches my fingertips. I offer him a stiff smile to say thank you. I lock the front door and follow him out to his truck.

Suddenly, I stop in my tracks. "Wait! I have to get Holden's car seat."

Matt shakes his head. "No, you don't. I bought one of my own for my truck. I want to be able to drive my son around safely without having to move that thing all the time," he informs me.

My heart flips at his thoughtfulness, but I also feel like he's taking a piece of Holden away from me and I hate it. I have no right to feel that way. "That was a good idea, Matt. Thank you," I state, forcing the words out of my mouth.

We climb into the truck, and I stare out the window in silence listening to the two of them chatter about trucks. As soon as we pull into his parents' long dirt drive, Holden stops talking mid-sentence. A beautiful white farmhouse sits in front of us with a wraparound front porch and a huge garage separate from the house.

The house is surrounded by green trees, which appear to be mostly some form of pine with a few others scattered in between. The trees all lead down a hill to the beautiful blue of the lake, with a dock right at the edge. It looks like there's a boat tied to the dock and a few kayaks as well. It's an incredible sight with the sun glistening off the water down below.

"This is it," Matt mumbles.

I glance back at Holden to find his eyes wide with nerves and fear. Focusing on him, I give him the biggest smile I can muster. "Come on Little Man. This will be fun," I encourage.

He nods and begins fumbling with his seatbelt. Matt hops out of the truck to help him and I slowly climb out, moving around to the other side of the truck. Matt reaches for Holden's hand, but before he can grab it, Holden wraps himself around my leg, trying to hide behind me. I notice Matt wince from the rejection, and it makes my heart ache. He swiftly shakes it off and attempts to comfort him with words instead.

"Everyone is really happy you're here Holden. They can't wait to meet you. Plus, there's so much for us to do. We'll have fun, okay?"

Holden looks up at Matt from under his long eyelashes and nods his head still clinging to me. Matt pinches his lips together and grinds his jaw, gesturing for me to go in front of him. I take two steps and face-plant from the Holden-size extra appendage. I lean down and pick him up with a small sigh. He wraps his arms around me and buries his face in my neck, which ironically helps me relax. Having him close may be his safe place, but in a way, it's mine as well. I place one hand underneath him and the other on his back as we walk up the wooden steps to the front door.

"You're okay," I whisper in Holden's ear, but he doesn't react.

Matt pushes the door open for me and I step inside a large foyer. He walks in right behind me, and I gasp at the sudden feel of his body heat, goosebumps spreading rapidly over my body. His hand gently touches my elbow and guides me a little further inside. My breathing picks up and I cling a little tighter to our son in my arms.

"Mom, Dad," he calls, "we're here."

His hand falls to the small of my back and he guides me further into the house to a large open living room with wood floors and huge wooden beams. A stone fireplace sits at the center of the room and the wall facing the lake is covered in windows from floor to ceiling. I can't help but be amazed at the view.

"Hello," he yells again.

I hear a door slam from the side of the house followed by a man's voice, "Matt?"

"In here, Dad," he answers. He drops his hand from my back, my body instantly going cold with the loss of his touch.

I watch the entryway to my left in the direction the voice came from until both Matt's parents step into view. Matt's mom instantly gets teary, and she covers her mouth with her hand as they cautiously walk towards us, his hand on her back just as Matt's had been on mine.

"Is this the handsome man I've heard so much about?" she asks straining to keep her voice from shaking.

Holden squeezes me tighter, not even daring to peek. Matt clears his throat, but I still hear a crack as he announces proudly, "Mom, Dad, this is my son, Holden."

I take in a shaky breath as Matt's dad greets him softly with his gruff voice, "Hey, Holden, your dad's been telling me so much about you. It's really great to meet you."

Holden moves his head slightly to the side trying to peer over at them without being seen making me chuckle quietly. "Hey, little man," I attempt to encourage him. "Can you say hi to your grandma and grandpa? They're very excited to meet you."

He moves his head just slightly and whispers, "Hi."

"Are you hungry?" his mom questions. "I just made some chocolate chip cookies and I need a taste tester to see if they're any good."

"Hey, I thought that was my job," Matt argues the corners of his lips twitching up.

"Maybe, Holden would like to share that job with you?" she suggests with a welcoming smile.

Holden turns completely towards her still holding on to me tightly. He grins and questions, "Is there 'nuf for both of us to have the job?"

She breathes a sigh of relief, her grin covering her whole face and lighting up her green eyes just like Matt's and our son's. "Absolutely! The kitchen is this way," she states gesturing to where they just came from. Holden wiggles out of my arms and runs in that direction, allowing me to relax as well.

"He's beautiful. He looks just like you Matthew," she whimpers proudly before hurrying after him.

Matt nods and looks towards his dad for a reaction. His dad glances at me before focusing back on Matt. "It's like looking at you when you were that age," he proclaims his voice cracking. He clears his throat and pats Matt on the back. "Excuse me, I need to get to know my grandson." He walks away without another word.

I continue to watch Matt as an array of emotions pass over his face. "Are you okay?" I ask him hesitantly.

He turns to me staring intently into my eyes. Butterflies take flight in my stomach instantly and I hold my breath waiting for what he might say. Eventually he opens his mouth, but only answers with, "Yeah." He squares his shoulders and urges, "Come on, let's go have some cookies before Holden eats them all. I'm pretty sure my mom will let him have anything he wants." He turns and strides towards the kitchen, leaving me no other choice but to follow.

Hesitantly, I sit down at their long rectangular kitchen table. I remain quiet and watch Holden with the three of them. He sits on his knees on the chair across from me with cookies and milk sitting in front of him. He munches on the cookies with Matt sitting next to him doing the same. "This is how you get more," he whispers to Holden. "Mom, I don't know if these are good enough. We may have to test another one of your cookies."

Holden giggles. "Yeah, Grandma. We have to test 'nother one."

Her smile grows and she swiftly flicks away a tear as she laughs. "Is that so?" Matt nods seriously and Holden attempts to follow his lead. "Well, I think I could spare one more for my boys." She places one more cookie in front of each of them.

Holden whispers loudly, "It worked!" making us all laugh.

"How about after you're done with your cookies, we go out to the garage?" his dad suggests. "I have some big machines you can sit on and some smaller ones with remote controls."

Holden's eyes light up making me laugh. "I think you just made his day."

The rest of the afternoon I sit back, watch and listen to Holden interact with Matt and his family. After the first five minutes, Holden was in his comfort zone. He acted like he'd known them forever. This is how it should have been from the beginning.

Even when Matt's siblings came in, Holden seemed to eat up all the attention. Bree and Christian came in first and then, Matt's sister Theresa came in with her boyfriend, Jax, followed by his brother Jason with his girlfriend, Sara. It's overwhelming to see all of them together, but they're family. They're all Holden's family. He's always had Micah's parents and me, but he should have a big family like this to love him. He does have that now, but he could've always had this with Matt's family, and I hate myself for it.

"I'm a horrible mother," I mumble under my breath.

"No, you're not," Bree argues, startling me. She sits down beside me at the picnic table in the backyard. "You're a good mom, Sadie," she insists.

I grimace my stomach feeling like it's full of rocks. "But I kept all this from him."

"Not on purpose," she reminds me. "You didn't' know. I'm sure you look back now and think about all the things you wish you could change, things you would do differently. We all do, but you have to move forward with the choices you made. Regrets will rot your insides if you let them. I know that better than anyone," she admits as a touch of sadness passes through her eyes. She gulps and continues, "But if I didn't force myself to look at what I had in front of me, I could've lost everything."

I shake my head and insist, "It's not like that for me."

She shrugs and glances over at Matt who is swinging Holden up in the air. "Maybe it's more like that than either of you are ready to admit right now."

Heaving a sigh, I look down at my hands, wanting this conversation to be over. I crave the quiet again so I can watch from the sidelines where I belong. I mumble, "Thanks Bree."

"Anytime," she murmurs as she stands. She pats my shoulder in support before she walks back over to Christian.

I know she was hinting at Matt and I being a couple, but I think my chance with him disappeared the day he found out about Holden. I betrayed him. I may fall a little bit more in love with him every day I spend time with him or every moment I watch him with Holden, but he'll never love me. That's just not possible.

I don't deserve it.

Chills cover my body even though the sun's shining and it's warm for the beginning of June in Maine. I wrap my arms around myself, craving the warmth and comfort. Taking a slow breath, I remind myself this isn't my family. This is Matt's family. This is Holden's family. Holden is my son, but to everyone else, I'm just an outsider. I inhale a shaky breath and wipe away the lone tear I let escape.

I'm glad I'm at least able to give him this now, although we all wish it had been sooner.

Chapter 26

Sadie

I walk out of Holden's room after tucking him in and quietly pull the door closed behind me. Then I pause outside his door, taking a calming breath, before I nervously make my way back to my living room. As I step into the room, I spot Matt sitting in one of the armchairs looking torn. I want to know what he's thinking, but I'm terrified of his answer. I cautiously sit on the edge of the couch near him my whole body filled with tension.

"He's going to be sound asleep in seconds. He had a lot of fun with your family today. He obviously loved meeting them," I proclaim keeping my eyes on the ground.

He sighs in irritation and ignores my comment. "He should've had that sooner. He should've had the big family dinners and parties. We all should've been there for his first birthday, especially me," he emphasizes, his face scrunching up in frustration.

I wince at the truth. "I know. I'm so sorry, Matt. I know it doesn't really help, but I am sorry. I can't even explain how bad I feel," I rasp. "I would do anything to go back in time and change everything!"

He nods his head and sighs again, dropping his head into his hands in defeat. After two agonizingly long minutes of silence, he lifts his head and looks at me, his eyes so full of hurt. I gasp, feeling his pain seer right through me like a punch to my heart. "He's amazing, Sadie. He's such an incredible kid, but I feel like I had nothing to do with it. But he's my fucking son!" he exclaims emotionally. "I should've been there for everything!"

Tingles prick at me like needles from the inside, tearing me up from the inside, out. They spread like wildfire from my heart to every piece of me, making my body ache with his pain. I don't bother to wipe away my tears as I speak my truth, "You did though, Matt. He's you and not just his looks. He moves like you, he's left-handed like you. I know he's going to be strong like you. I swear he has your personality in so many ways because he tries to be funny, and he uses his charm to his advantage. He's also a complete flirt with any girl he talks to without even trying. I think we're going to see things from him every single day that remind us how much he's like you. I don't even see me in him at all sometimes and I've always…" I trail off as pain crosses his features.

"What?" he rasps.

I speak much quieter when I continue. "He's one of the reasons I thought of you every single day and not just because he's yours. He's so much like you that every day I would see what we both lost when we lost you."

He flinches again at my admission. I watch as he takes a deep breath and visibly shakes it off before returning his focus to me. "You really think he's like me?" he questions, seeming surprised.

I nod and smile. "I know he is Matt."

He nods in acceptance. "I want him to have a big family, cousins, brothers and sisters, like I do," he admits making it my turn to flinch.

"I'd love for him to have that too. Micah and I tried to give him a sibling, we just weren't able to," I confess. Agony crosses his face again with my admission, but this time I don't understand it. He pushed away from me the moment he found out about Holden, almost like we never had a chance to be together. I remind myself that I'm not what he wants.

"Maybe you can give that to him some day," I whisper, my heart lodging itself in my throat. Turning away from him, I wipe away my tears. I don't want him to see how much the thought of him with another family, his family, hurts so much.

I feel his body slide in next to me on the couch, but with my tears now falling rapidly, I keep my head turned away. "Sadie," he whispers, as his warm breath brushes my cheek making me whimper. "Please, look at me."

I close my eyes and attempt to pull myself together when I feel his fingers on my chin, gently guiding me towards him. Gasping, I turn and slowly open my eyes as I attempt to wipe my tears away. I find myself staring into his deep green eyes as he searches for something in mine. I wince, feeling my whole body wanting to curve in to protect my heart from pain, but I know better now. The pain never leaves and giving Matt what he needs is what's important in this moment.

"I'm so sorry, Matt," I repeat. "I know it doesn't help, but I just can't stop saying it. I am so, so sorry. I want you both to have everything," I add struggling to breathe. I hold my hand to my chest and gently rub, trying to make the constant ache go away.

"Did you know that I never really had a girlfriend until I met you?" he questions unexpectedly changing direction. I cringe and try to look away, but he holds firm, attempting to hold me in place.

"I wasn't your girlfriend," I whisper not meeting his eyes.

He laughs humorlessly. "No, no you weren't, but you should've been." My eyes widen in surprise and snap up to his. He repeats himself as my eyes meet his, "You should've been, Sadie." My heart pounds harder with his words, my chest aching for a different reason, for hope. "You were the first girl I wanted more from, but I held myself back. Between Micah and going to college in different parts of the country, I was convinced we would never work." He shrugs. "I made rules for us trying to protect myself."

"Micah?" I repeat confused.

"I'm not blind, Sadie. I knew he was in love with you and you two had history," he informs me with a nonchalant shrug. I glance away again feeling overwhelmed with guilt that I never knew that. I truly believed we were just friends. "I was just the guy visiting from out of town," he whispers hoarsely.

I look at him and shake my head vehemently. "You were never just the guy visiting, Matt, not to me," I insist.

He shrugs. "It doesn't matter. When I realized what I was losing after I walked away from you, I knew I had to find you. I wanted to really get to know you. I came back here the first chance I could, and I found you accepting a proposal from Micah." I flinch and open my mouth to respond, but he stops me with a shake of his head. "It doesn't matter anymore what the situation was. I saw what I saw, but honestly, my ego took a hit. I decided I didn't want that kind of future anymore. Well, that's not true. I did, but if I couldn't have it with you," he shrugs and lets me gather my own conclusions.

I gasp in disbelief. There's no way he wanted a future with me then.

"I tried to have a serious relationship to forget about you. I forced it, but I was a horrible boyfriend because I honestly didn't care. I didn't cheat on her or anything, but I dated Natalie for over two years, and she never met my family. I never wanted her to. When I walked in on her cheating on me, I barely flinched. I resigned and moved close to my family." He shrugs like it's no big deal.

"She cheated on you?" I repeat in shock.

He waves it off again, "Yeah, but it was no big deal to me. But seeing you engaged to Micah was a stab to my chest. Seeing a car seat in the back of your car and thinking the two of you had kids felt like you ran me over with your car. I know we were only hanging out for a couple months, but you worked your way inside my heart back then and I couldn't get rid of you no matter what I did. I never forgot about you,

Sadie. You were my biggest regret. The girl I never should've let go. The only girl I have ever pictured having a family with," he admits.

I gasp, my heart hammering inside my ribcage, stunned by his admission. "What?" I murmur inaudibly.

"Then, what do you know, we have a son," he mutters sounding exasperated. "I take part of the blame for us because I set the rules." I shake my head because it's not his fault at all. He doesn't deserve any blame. He sighs ignoring me and concedes, "I should've never let you go."

My heart leaps from my chest. He wants me. I gasp feeling overwhelmed. Without thought, I lean into him, pressing my lips to his, needing to be close to him. My body vibrates with need for him, but I quickly pull back, unsure if this is what he wants. Even after his confession, I'm still unsure. He wanted me then, but now he's just trying to understand how we got to this point, how he lost so much with his son.

Why would he feel the same way about me that I feel about him after everything that happened?

"Sorry," I mumble blushing, feeling like I'm suddenly on fire.

"I'm not," he declares. My eyes widen as he grabs the back of my neck and pulls me to him, smashing his lips to mine. He moves his mouth over mine in perfect rhythm. I lean into him with a moan, spurring him on, my whole body heated with desire for him. He pushes his tongue into my mouth, tasting, sucking and licking, consuming me until I'm completely lost in him.

He slowly lowers me back on the couch without removing his lips from mine. I push his shirt up and let my hands wander up his hard chest. Our lips part, so I can pull his shirt over his head, but then we crash our mouths together desperately. I continue to let my hands roam his body, trailing my fingers over his broad shoulders and down his ridged back, feeling every muscle.

His hand slides slowly down from behind my neck, over my collarbone and down my side, softly caressing the side of my breast on the way, before continuing down until he reaches my hip. Then his hand slides towards my back and moves down until he gently cups my ass and pulls me closer to him. His hips roll into me, and I groan at the feel of him pressing against me.

He pulls back and leans on one arm, letting his eyes rove over my body. His eyes fill with heat mirroring my own desire. He begins kissing a trail along my neck, leaving goosebumps everywhere his lips touch. His hand moves to my waist, sliding underneath my shirt. His thumb caresses back and forth and my body arches into him wanting more.

"Please," I whimper not wanting this moment to ever end. It feels like I'm dreaming but if I am I don't ever want to wake up.

His hand slides up at my request, trailing over my ribs and hesitating slightly before he skims his palm over my breast, my nipples hardening with barely a touch through the fabric. He reaches back with one hand, unhooking my bra with a flick of his wrist. He pushes my shirt and bra up until my breasts are exposed to the cold air. He quickly covers one with his hand and the other with his mouth. My body instinctually arches towards him as his tongue circles my nipple and then he grazes it with his teeth making me groan with need.

He abandons my breasts and moves back up my body until his mouth finds mine, kissing me with so much fervor I feel like my whole body might combust. His hand moves down to my hip and slowly slides down my leg and up under my skirt, both of us too frantic to bother to take the time to remove more clothing. His finger slides into my underwear and his first touch is almost too much, letting me know it won't take much to set me off. I don't think I've ever felt like this.

My body is wired with desire. He runs his fingers lightly over my folds and I moan into his mouth, my own fingers clinging to his back. He pushes one finger inside of me and then two as his palm rubs me at the same time. It takes merely seconds when all my surroundings disappear and I feel nothing, but Matt, my insides clenching around his fingers over and over again.

He pulls away swiftly and my body instantly feels cold as I begin to register the sights and sounds around me. Matt's standing up next to the couch pulling his shirt back on mumbling incoherently to himself.

Holden calls for me sounding fearful from down the hall. "Mommy," he yells.

"Are you going to go check on him, or should I? He might not be ready for me yet," he reminds me, "but you also need to pull yourself together fast, Sadie." He sounds pissed causing a lump to form in my throat.

I push myself off the couch and readjust my clothes feeling like I just got caught fooling around with my boyfriend by my parents. But I'm not a teenager and I'm not his girlfriend, besides the fact that my parents don't even care. I stumble clumsily to Holden's room as I push my tears away "I'm here little man. Are you okay?" I prompt shakily as I sit on the side of his bed.

"I had a bad dream, Mommy," he cries.

"It's just a dream, Holden, I'm here," I remind him rubbing soothing circles on his back. "Do you want to tell me what it was about?" I prod but he doesn't answer. He huddles close to me and holds on tightly as I continue to rub his back. After only a few minutes, he quiets. I look down to see him fast asleep in my lap. I smile down at him and gently move him back over to his pillow. Carefully, I pull the covers up to his neck and place a kiss on the top of his head. "I love you, my little man," I whisper. Then, I stand and sneak back out his bedroom door hoping I don't wake him.

Cautiously tiptoeing back to the living room, I'm more apprehensive than before. My stomach turns and I feel myself blush just before I step into the room. My eyes skim over the couch and chairs, but I find them empty. I find Matt standing by the front door with his arms crossed over his chest, appearing closed off. I gulp down my nerves and lift my eyes up to him, trying to seem more confident than I am.

"Is he okay?" he inquires. I nod my head and wait for him to continue. He grimaces. "I'm sorry, Sadie." He shakes his head, grumbling, "That was a mistake. I shouldn't have done that, I'm sorry."

It feels as if everything begins closing in on me as my heart breaks with his words. I wrap my arms around myself protectively. I should've known it was too good to be true. I open my mouth to respond, but devastated all over again, I remain mute.

"We can't, I mean I can't do this," he stammers. "I'm sorry," he whispers as he turns and walks out the door without another word leaving an ache in my chest.

I don't bother suppressing my tears. I'll give myself one night to cry again over him. After tonight though, I can't. He's Holden's dad and I can't ever let my feelings for Matt get in the way of that, not again.

I lie on the couch on my side and curl up in a ball, letting my sobs quietly wrack my body.

Chapter 27

Matt

I sit at my kitchen table with my head in my hands, feeling like I'm stuck living someone else's life. I force myself to lift my head and pick up the laboratory papers in front of me one more time. I stare at the numbers confirming what I already knew in both my head and my heart.

Holden is mine. He is my son.

A pounding on my front door startles me out of my stupor, but I remain frozen. My brothers will be sure to let me know if it's them and I'm definitely not in the mood to see anyone else. "We're coming in Matt," Christian announces after knocking again.

"It's open," I yell.

The door slides open and Christian walks through with a bag of food from the bakery, followed by Jason holding a tray of coffee. "Thanks for letting us in," Christian greets me as he flops down across from me at my farmhouse style rectangular plank kitchen table. He begins taking food out of the bag in his hand.

"Don't you ever stay in Portland anymore?" I grumble to Jason. To Christian I add, "And you could be home with your wife."

"We brought breakfast," Jason offers ignoring me. He sets down the coffee before he turns and walks to one of the kitchen cabinets. He pulls out three plates, bringing them back to the table with him. He hands one to each of us and sits down on the closest end between Christian and me. I eye both of them warily even though I know they came here to talk business, but I can't even open my mouth and force any words out. I'm still processing these papers even though they're exactly what I expected.

They both glance at what I'm holding, and Jason raises his eyebrows in question. "Is that what I think it is?" Instead of answering I hand him the papers. He takes them and quickly scans them over before handing them to Christian to do the same. "This is what you believed…" he begins.

"How are you?" Christian asks simply, his eyes narrowed on me as he takes a bite out of a blueberry muffin.

I huff a laugh at his question. It's crazy to me how well Christian knows me, but then again, we are the same in so many ways. "I'm about to lose my mind," I rasp honestly. "I have no idea what the fuck I'm supposed to do now!" I state with a shake of my head. I run my hand through my hair, and then drop both hands to the table with a groan.

"Understandable," Jason mumbles while Christian just nods slowly, like he's taking my every movement in and processing it.

Sighing again, I shake my head. "Honestly, this is all so surreal," I proclaim gesturing towards the papers. "I kissed her last night," I blurt out feeling my body heat with just the thought of her mouth on mine. My heart pounds erratically with the memory of the way her body reacted to me. "I mean I really kissed her like I've been wanting to do for so fucking long."

"Matt," Jason begins, his tone sounding like a warning. I turn to glare at him, and his mouth snaps shut as he waits for me to continue.

"I wouldn't have stopped when I did, but Holden woke up with a nightmare. I flipped out and took off after he fell back asleep. I told her it was a mistake, but how do I know if it was?" I ask not really wanting an answer, so I keep my eyes glued to the table in front of me instead.

"He's my son. I've known I'm a father for all of a week. What if Sadie and I try and it doesn't work? Who

~ 234 ~

knows, maybe I always idealized her and she's not what I always remembered or imagined or maybe I'm not what she wants. What happens to Holden then? I can't lose him before I even have the chance to really be his dad."

"Sadie won't take him away from you. She's not that kind of girl," Christian insists, trying to be my voice of reason.

I grimace and state the fact that hurts me the most, "She already did once. Maybe she didn't do it intentionally, but she did. I lost the first four years of my son's life, while she married another guy who had the chance to be his dad when he came into this world." I pause and attempt to swallow the growing lump in my throat. "I would've been there no matter what if I would've known," I remind them my voice cracking. Honestly, I don't know if I can let that go.

We all sit quietly for a few minutes, contemplating my words. Jason breaks the silence in an attempt to get me to move into action instead of feeling sorry for myself. "Well, none of us can change the past. You can be there for him now. We all can. We need to figure out what you do now that you have the DNA results," he reminds me reasonably.

"I want him to have my name," I state, and both of my brothers nod in agreement. "I'll need to be put officially on his birth certificate before I can do that."

"Why aren't you on the birth certificate? I thought she said she always knew you were Holden's father," Christian questions.

I shrug and reply sarcastically, "Apparently you have to be present to sign the papers and show your ID for official documents like birth certificates. Besides the fact that she didn't even have my last name at the time."

"What about custody?" Jason questions cautiously.

Christian shakes his head. "Can't you just talk to Sadie about that?"

I shake my head and concede, "Jason's right. That's one of the reasons I keep going back to what to do about how I feel about Sadie. If we figure out the logistics for Holden now, I believe we could share custody. If I act on my feelings for Sadie and it doesn't work out between us…" I trail off feeling an intense ache in my chest at the thought of losing both of them and run my hand through my hair in frustration. "What if…What if she tries to take him away from me? I may be his father, but he just met me," I stammer.

Christian shakes his head refusing to believe that would happen to me. "I don't think she would do that to him. She wants what's best for Holden and you're his father. You being in his life is what's best for him," he emphasizes.

I shrug feeling completely helpless. "I don't know if I can take that chance. What I want doesn't matter. I should stay away from Sadie for Holden. I can't lose him," I proclaim vehemently. "I guess I have to talk to a lawyer now that I have this," I mumble gesturing towards the laboratory papers. "Who do you guys suggest? Who do you use for business?" I inquire trying to turn the conversation away from the emotional crap.

Jason offers, "We use Smith and Wyles in town. Besides being local, they were recommended to us from some other businesses."

Christian shrugs. "They've worked out well enough, although we haven't used them too much as of yet," he mumbles, grinning mischievously.

Jason grimaces. "Hopefully, we'll just need them for standard practices."

Christian chuckles at Jason's reaction. We all knew that would get a rise out of him and I join in the laughter. "Alright, I'm done talking about this for now. I can't think about it anymore. I'll deal with it later. Let's eat."

"Who says we brought food for you?" Christian smirks.

"You did." I grin and grab a pastry. Jason hands me a coffee and I immediately take a sip. I sigh and force myself to relax. "Let's go over the marketing plan before my new bosses decide to fire me." I smirk eliciting a laugh from both of them. "I know you didn't come here to listen to my crap."

"No, but unless we want to get our asses kicked by mom, you know you're not getting fired," Christian teases.

I shrug and grin at him. "What's your point?"

We all laugh, and I grab my laptop and a folder I have for the business so we can all hopefully turn our attention to work. We successfully stay focused for a couple hours and it's not long before both of my brothers stand to leave. "This is great work, Matt. Thank you." He grins appreciatively.

I nod my head, grateful for the acknowledgement. "Thanks."

"I'm headed back to Portland to pick up Sara for a late lunch. Let me know if you need anything," Jason offers sincerely. I nod my head in agreement before he walks out the door with a wave.

Christian stays back and waits until Jason is gone before he turns to me, both his face and demeanor serious. "Listen Matt, I understand what's holding you back with Sadie. Holden is the most important thing right now and he should be," he begins. He takes a deep breath and asks, "But what if there's a chance you could give him more? What if you could give Holden everything?"

I visibly flinch and look away. Christian grips me by the shoulder, forcing my attention on him. "I've been watching you since you've been here and with Sadie. I saw you hope for the first time. When it comes to women, I've never seen that in you, but I do with her. I know what that looks like," he reminds me. "Now that you have Holden, you're happy, but you're also completely lost. If how you feel about Sadie is what I think it is, you can't give up on her," he insists, giving my shoulder a squeeze. "I know what it's like to be without that when you've found it. It changes you and not for the better."

I shake my head, grumbling, "I don't know, Christian."

He stops me, "Don't give up on her. She never wanted her son to be without a father. She won't try to take him away from you. Give her a chance with you Matt, not just as Holden's mom, but as the girl I know you've compared every other one you've met or dated since you met her. I know that's what you do whether you want to or not. I know what that's like, and it doesn't ever stop. Sadie is the same girl you regretted letting go last week before you knew about Holden. Give her a chance with you. Just think about it," he demands. "You will regret it if you don't. I know you will, and I don't want you to have any more regrets," he pleads with me.

"Maybe," I mumble, nodding slowly.

With a shrug, he adds, "I just want to see you happy, Matt." When I don't say anything, he asks, "What about this, could you imagine your life without Sadie? And is that picture of your future what you want?"

I run my hand through my hair in frustration. I'm so confused, and I can't figure it out with Christian standing here pushing me. My situation with Sadie is not the same as his with Bree. I paste on a smirk attempting to end this conversation. "Wow, Bree has really turned my little brother into a feelings guy, huh?"

He rolls his eyes and chuckles. I'm sure he knows exactly what I'm doing, but he lets it go at the same time making a point. He shrugs. "What do I care? I finally got my girl."

I grimace, feeling my heart clench tightly in my chest from his comment. I don't know if I'll ever have the girl. "Thanks for breakfast," I mutter as I shove him out the door making him laugh. "Bye," I add as I push the door shut on him.

I lean back against the door with a groan and listen as his truck pulls away. "What the fuck am I going to do?" I grumble to myself.

Christian may be right, but what if he's not? Do I take a chance with Sadie? She's all I've thought about since moving here. When I found out she was single again, I can't even describe the intense relief I felt. Or should I hold myself back from her and just focus on Holden? No matter what I do, I'm not losing him. I groan feeling like I'm losing control of my life.

My cell phone begins ringing, still sitting on the kitchen table. I slowly push myself up off the wall with a heavy sigh and saunter towards it, not in a hurry to talk to anyone. By the time I reach it, my phone stops ringing. Picking it up, I find Sadie's name in missed calls. I hesitate for a moment, not ready to hear her voice. I click on her name to text her instead, but I notice the bouncing dots indicating she's writing and wait for her message. "I'm done with work for the day. I'm taking Holden to the park at three if you want to join us."

I immediately text her back, hoping to get some control over our situation. "I'll be at your place at 2:30. I'll drive."

I grip my phone tightly, hoping she doesn't argue with me. Her response comes through, a simple, "Ok."

I breathe a sigh of relief and turn to grab some lunch before I get ready to take my family to the park. I stumble over my feet and stop in my tracks. "My family," I mumble. "I have my own family," I repeat. I shake my head in disbelief, again feeling the shock of how surreal my life has become. Now, I just have to decide what to do, I groan.

Chapter 28

Sadie

As soon as we pull into the parking lot at the park, Holden lets out an excited squeal. Matt parks and quickly steps out of his truck. He moves to help Holden out of his car seat before I even have a chance to grab my phone and stuff my wallet under the seat. "Are you ready to go play buddy?" he asks animatedly.

"Yeah!" he exclaims kicking his feet to run before he's even on the ground. Matt laughs sending shivers down my spine as he sets him down gently.

Matt chases after him, not even trying to catch him as Holden laughs hysterically, while I slowly lag behind, watching them play. I smile sadly, feeling like I'm an outsider. The thought makes me grimace knowing how ridiculous I'm being about it. I know I'm not being fair to even have thoughts like that especially with Matt. Sighing, I trudge towards a bench in the middle of the park and flop onto it with an irritated huff, annoyed with myself. I need to just enjoy watching them together. In reality, I'm jealous of Matt with our son and I hate myself for it.

I sit back and watch as Holden shows Matt the digger. He struggles to move some sand, so Matt moves behind him and has him place his small hands over his larger ones so they can do it together. The smile that lights up Holden's face is priceless. The way that Matt melts with our little boy's look has my heart melting a little more at the sight. Matt is already such a great dad making my heart lurch. I drop my head and stare at the ground while I try to pull myself together, pushing my tears back.

I lift my head just as Holden jumps up and runs over to the slide where another group of kids are playing. Matt follows happily and nods his head in greeting to the other moms or babysitters. Of course he's the only man in a group of admiring women I think bitterly. Nothing is sexier than a man who not only looks like Matt, but he's also a doting father.

I stand stiffly, feeling my jealousy overwhelm me as he talks to the women. I realize I have no right, but that doesn't stop my heart from listening. My stomach nervously flutters as I cautiously walk over to Matt. I stand next to him, inhaling his musky scent to calm my anxiety. I swallow the lump in my throat and hesitantly get his attention by purposely placing my hand gently on his arm.

"Hey," I rasp with a shy smile.

He turns towards me and raises his eyebrows in question. As soon as he meets my tentative gaze, he smirks down at me like he truly sees me, making me blush in response. "What's up, Sade?" he prods softly.

I grimace, knowing the only time he ever called me that was when Micah was around. I don't know his reasons, but to me it shows his familiarity with me to everyone else and I like it way more than I should. I need to come up with a reason I came over here and I need to come up with something fast.

Clearing my throat, I toss out the first thing that comes to my mind. "I was thinking we could all grab some dinner after this," I suggest as I feel the heat of the glares from around me.

Matt nods, a lazy grin covering his face. "I can agree to that, but only if Mommy plays tag with us first." I smile and slowly drop my hand from his arm as I breathe a sigh of relief. I'm grateful he's humoring me and playing along instead of calling me out on my obvious jealousy.

"Okay," I quickly agree.

He spins on his heel and picks up Holden as he barrels down the slide. He lifts him into the air and then plants his little feet on the ground announcing, "Run Holden, Mommy's it."

Holden giggles and runs away from me yelling, "Mommy can't catch me!"

I run after my little man and soon I'm joining in their laughter. Eventually, I tag Holden and Matt slows so Holden can tag him. He opens his arms wide and swiftly picks up Holden with one arm and grabs me with the other wrapping all of us together. Holden wiggles away laughing and I move to step out of his hold, but I only succeed in coming face to face with Matt. He's so close I can feel his warm breath on my cheek, his breath becoming more rapid by the second. My heartbeat picks up and the world around me slips away as I stare into his deep green eyes.

He pinches his lips together and turns his head, letting me slip from his arms. I hold back my whimper at the loss of his touch. "How about we play follow the leader Holden?" he suggests as he turns towards our son.

I find a nearby bench before my shaky legs collapse beneath me. "I think I'll just watch this time," I inform them, although I don't think either of them are paying attention to me anymore.

After another half hour I give Holden the five-minute warning with complaints from both of them, "Do we have to?" Holden pouts. I give him a look, letting him know not to argue with me and he scrunches up his face in distaste, but turns and takes off for one last run over the bridges and down the big slide.

The rest of the afternoon and evening pass quickly and it feels like only minutes have gone by when Holden begs Matt to tuck him in. I give Holden a hug and kiss goodnight and then leave Matt to read him a bedtime story. "Goodnight, my little man. I love you!"

"I love you too, Mommy," he replies tiredly, rubbing his eyes.

I wander to the kitchen, looking for something to keep myself busy until Matt reappears. I move to the sink and glare at the dirty dishes from dinner but pick one up anyway since it has to be done. As I rinse the dishes and put them in the dishwasher, my mind drifts to Matt like always lately. I can't help but think how, besides all our complications, today felt normal. My heart skips a beat as I admit to myself that today we felt like a family. I close my eyes and sigh in resignation. I know that's the furthest thing from reality, but my stupid heart can't help but dream.

It's obvious how incredible Matt is for Holden. He's an amazing dad, but I don't need to be in his life for him to be that way. I release a shaky breath and open my eyes to put the last of the dishes in the dishwasher. I just don't understand why it hurts so much. Matt was never mine to begin with, even though I've wanted him to be.

I close the dishwasher and turn off the faucet, quickly drying my hands on a towel lying over the sink. Reaching for the silver teakettle on the stove, I fill it with water hoping tea will help calm me. I reach for two mugs just as the water comes to a whistling boil.

The hairs on the back of my neck stand at attention as I not only hear, but feel Matt enter the room. I glance over at him, and he leans back against the counter, crossing his arms over his hard chest. His armband tattoo peeks out from under his t-shirt, and I snap my mouth shut at the beautiful sight as heat spreads throughout my whole body. I've never had the urge to actually lick someone until now, causing me to blush deeply. I turn my focus back towards the mugs and rasp, "Would you like some tea?"

"I'll just have some water," he whispers hoarsely. I nod my head and pour myself a cup of tea and him some water before bringing both cups to the kitchen table and setting them down. I sit down bringing my feet up on my chair. Cradling my tea in both hands, I take a small sip before I dare to glance over at him. When I do, I grimace at the serious look covering his face.

He sighs as he sits down across from me. He reaches for the water and leans back in his chair. "I got the papers from the lab today," he informs me.

I nod slowly, feeling my anxiety grow with the direction of this conversation. I clear my throat, acknowledging, "Yeah, I got mine too. It didn't matter though, I already knew."

He winces and looks towards the hallway, where Holden lies sleeping. "I want to get his name changed Sadie. He should have *my* name." I nod in agreement because he's right. "He should've always had my name," he adds softly making me flinch, but I keep my lips pinched shut. "Now that I have the lab papers, I can submit for the change on his birth certificate, but it will go a lot faster if I have your signature. I'd like to change his last name at the same time," he admits.

"Okay, Matt," I squeak out. "We're going to have to talk to Holden about it though. It might take some getting used to for him."

Matt's face scrunches up in obvious pain, but he nods in understanding. "Yeah, I know. He'll probably have a lot of questions, but it's better to do it now than later because this is definitely not something I will ever change my mind on."

"You're right," I agree. I let the sadness of that reality wash over me and hold myself a little tighter.

We sit in uncomfortable silence, sipping our drinks for a few minutes, both I'm sure thinking about Holden. He sets down his cup abruptly with a loud thud breaking the stillness. "I should go," he announces and begins to push himself up from the table.

"Wait!" I exclaim suddenly feeling panicked. I don't want him to leave, but I refuse to think about my reasons. "Holden's birthday is in two weeks." He clumsily drops back into the chair, a stunned look on his face. "I'm going to have a birthday party for him here. I just invited Micah's parents and a couple friends from Holden's day care and pre-school. I would love it, I mean Holden would love it if you and your family were here," I tell him sincerely. When I don't hear a response, I look a little closer at him and realize his body is full of tension and he's attempting to calm down before he responds to me. My body stiffens in anticipation of the words he's about to throw my way, but I know they'll be deserved.

"Of course, I'll fucking be at my own son's fourth birthday party! I wouldn't miss it for anything! I would've been at every other one and his birth if I had known. There's no way in hell I'm missing anything else for Holden!" he chokes out.

I cringe and hate myself a little more if that's even possible. "Matt," I begin sounding desperate, "I know that; I do. I'm so sorry."

He interrupts me by putting his hand up and shaking his head in warning. "I don't want to hear it again, Sadie. I know you're fucking sorry!" he exclaims in exasperation glaring at me. He gulps and asks me with agony so evident my heart feels like it's breaking into a million pieces inside my chest, "Do you have any idea what it's like to know I've missed the first four years of my own son's life? I'm not that guy! I would've been there no matter what happened between us. But you wouldn't know that because you never gave me that chance," he accuses. "You never should've gotten rid of my number until you knew!" he rants, struggling with keeping his voice quiet. I can no longer stop the tears as he voices one of the biggest regrets of my life.

I feel like a weight is crushing my chest making it hard to breathe. He's right and I hate myself for it. I let the tears fall down my cheeks as pain completely consumes me. His words are true, and I've always realized it, but knowing it doesn't make hearing them leave his mouth hurt any less. "You're right, but I can't change it. I wish I could! I'll regret it for the rest of my life along with so many other things when it comes to you, but I can't change it. I'm so sorry Matt," I whimper.

He shakes his head again in disgust. "That's what I keep hearing over and over again, Sadie. You're sorry and I get that you mean it. Like you said though, it doesn't change a fucking thing," he replies bitterly. He grunts and runs his fingers through his hair in frustration. I watch as his jaw twitches with anger as I wipe my tears away. "I need some space from you, Sadie. I want Holden tomorrow while you go to work. I need some father-son time," he emphasizes. "I'll bring him home before bedtime," he informs me, leaving no room for argument.

Gasping for breath, I realize this isn't a request and my fear of being alone feels a little more real. Although, I know Matt deserves not only this, but so much more and I do the only thing I can and nod in agreement. "Okay," I rasp.

He turns stiffly and walks towards my front door without a backwards glance. "I'll see you at eight tomorrow morning," he proclaims just before he strides outside and pulls the door shut tightly behind him.

I move robotically towards the door to lock up behind him. I drop my forehead against the front door in agony. "I am so sorry, Matt," I cry no longer bothering to wipe my tears away. "What am I going to do, Micah?" I question the empty room, desperate for answers. "I wish I could talk to you. I don't know how to fix this," I complain, pain searing my heart.

Chapter 29

Matt

I've kept my distance from Sadie, hoping a little space from her would help keep my thoughts straight. It's the only thing I've been able to do to keep my focus on Holden. I want to get to know every part of him. I want him to know me. I want him to be completely safe and comfortable with me. I want him to get to know my family, who are his family and the family he should've known as his all along. I grimace as the familiar ache in my chest throbs painfully.

I told Jason and Christian I didn't want to do any tours or field work for now unless they really need my help. I want to be able to spend as much time as I can with Holden, and I can do that better if I work from home. I've been focusing on their marketing, which is something I can easily do from here with my laptop and my cell phone.

My brothers understand as much as they can and are of course fine with it. I realize how fortunate I am that I'm able to take the time I need with my son and I'm incredibly thankful for it. I work when Holden takes a break to rest and watch TV. I also work at night after I drop him off at his house with his mom, but I haven't been staying like I would when I first found out.

"Sadie," I whisper her name as I exhale, trying to release the constant ache in my chest when I think of her, which is all the time I admit to myself irritably. She has been letting me spend a lot of time with Holden, allowing me to take him when she's working and even other times as well. I hate that I wonder what she's doing when she's not at work and he's with me, but I can't help it. I don't know how to get her out of my head, but at the same time, I'm still so pissed at her I don't know how to get over it. I want to move past it, but even if I'm able to, what happens then? I sigh in frustration and run my hand through my hair, trying to shake it off for now.

I pull into Christian's driveway to pick up Bree. She's coming with me to help me find a birthday present for my son. I want him to have a perfect birthday since I missed his first three, but I have no idea where to begin. Since Christian is working today and Bree wants to shop for him as well, she offered to help me out. I of course instantly jumped on her offer.

As soon as I put my truck in park, she's pulling the passenger door open and hopping up next to me. I chuckle. "In a hurry, Bree?"

She grins broadly and shrugs nonchalantly. "Hi, Matt! I'm just excited to go shopping for my first nephew!"

I flinch and avert my gaze as my heart flips uncomfortably at her words. A startling and overpowering moment of sadness consumes me. I force myself out of my head and offer her an awkward smile.

I croak, "Yeah."

Her face falls at my reaction. "Oh my gosh, I'm sorry, Matt." She shakes her head. "I didn't think…" she trails off with a grimace.

I shake my head and try to brush it off like it's no big deal. "It's okay, Bree. I'm fine."

Taking a deep breath, I force myself to relax. I smile genuinely this time because she's right in a way, too. I have my chance to shop for my son now and I want to appreciate every moment I have that has to do with him. Without another word, I put my truck in reverse and quickly back out of her driveway.

When we're on the road headed towards the outlets, I notice Bree fidgeting nervously. I open my mouth to ask what's on her mind when she whispers cautiously, "I'm really sorry, Matt." I shake my head and open my mouth again to tell her not to worry when she interrupts me, "No, Matt," she says more sternly. "I mean I'm sorry I didn't know. We only got together on a girls' night or for lunch or dinner around work. I had only met him that one time. I did see pictures often enough though and I feel like I should've known." I shake my head, but she continues to ramble her apology, "Maybe if she would've met Christian since you definitely look like brothers. Of course I talked about him all the time, but..." she trails off and brushes a few tears off her cheeks with the back of her hands.

I glance quickly over at her and find her eyes full of regret. I sigh and look back at the road in front of me, trying to pull my thoughts together. Eventually I'm able to mumble what I know to be true. "Bree, there's nothing you could've done. You only see me in Holden now because you know he's mine," I begin.

"But he looks so much like you..." she argues attempting to interrupt me.

Ignoring her comment, I continue to talk right over her just as she did me, "Even if she met Christian, she probably wouldn't have been able to connect the dots. It's something that seems simple when you already know everything about the situation, but in reality, she probably wouldn't have figured it out. I don't think anyone could've."

I take a deep breath to calm my anxiety with a sudden urge to talk to someone about everything. With my eyes on the road in front of me, I continue to talk, "The fact is Sadie and I both should've done so many things different. Micah too for that matter, but I feel like shit saying anything negative against the guy when he's not alive to defend himself," I add with a wince.

"Sadie and I were the ones that treated our relationship as casual. I could've called to check up on her, especially with what I knew when I left, but honestly, I was too scared," I admit. "Then I had a chance to talk to her when

I came back the first time, but instead of talking to her I let my wounded ego send me running the minute I saw her with Micah. Yeah, she never should've gotten rid of my number, but I was the asshole who told her to do exactly that," I confess feeling my gut clench painfully. "I always told her our relationship had a deadline and asked her to stick with it." Clenching my jaw, I feel my anger at myself grow by the second.

"Matt, you can't keep going back to what you could've done," Bree reminds me. "It won't help anything or anyone."

Maybe, but I continue to ignore her comments anyway. "Now because of my stupidity, she had to raise our son without me for the first four years of his life and honestly, she did a fan-fucking-tastic job. He's an absolutely incredible kid," I announce with an odd sense of pride.

"Then, during that time, she also lost her best friend who was actually there for her, unlike me. I'm just the asshole that got her pregnant and then abandoned them," I grumble hating myself more and more with each word that comes out of my mouth. "It's my fault I wasn't here for my son," I rasp as the truth of my words assaults me full force.

I readjust my grip on the steering wheel, holding on so tight my knuckles turn white. I clench my jaw and try to blink back the tears beginning to well in my eyes as I attempt to see the road clearly. "It's not your fault, Matt." I give a slight shake of my head, not able to speak. "You didn't know. We all know you would've been here if you knew about Holden. I know you believe that too," she whispers trying to comfort me.

She's right, but I worked so hard to push Sadie out of my head that I didn't follow-up with her like I knew I should've back then. I keep blaming Sadie for losing those years with Holden, but it's my fault. All I can do is pray the two of them can forgive me one day, even though I'll probably never forgive myself for losing so much time with him and honestly Sadie too.

"You have to look forward and stop berating yourself for the past," she encourages. "Trust me, I know what I'm talking about," she emphasizes.

"You sound like my brother," I mutter grimacing.

A smile tugs at her lips as she adds, "Focus on your future, Holden's future, and even Sadie's." I glance at her out of the corner of my eye as she sighs in frustration. "You all deserve to be happy," she whispers with her hand over her heart.

I grimace, disgusted with myself. I don't deserve to be happy. Sadie and Holden do, and I will do anything to make them happy, but I caused this mess. I can't believe it's taken me this long to see it. It's time I make up for my mistakes.

Bree tries to talk to me again, but I stare at the road in front of me, not even processing her words. She eventually sighs and gives up, knowing it's a short ride to the toy store. As soon as I park my truck and reach for the door handle, she stops me with a gentle hand to my arm. "Matt, I just want you to know that Sadie really is a good person and a really good mom. She made a mistake and like you said, you both made some mistakes." She gulps hard. "Sooner or later, you're going to have to not only forgive Sadie, but also forgive yourself. You're going to have to let everything go, if not for yourself or for Sadie, do it for your son."

I stare at her for a moment absorbing her words. She's right to a point. I know I need to start by letting Sadie know I'm sorry for blaming her for everything. The sadness that radiates off her kills me and I'm sure a lot of her sadness is my fault. It's time to change that. I also need her to know I'm sorry for not being there and I need that to change like it has already started to. I need to be there for her and for him no matter what.

They're my family now, and I'm not about to lose them, either of them, I admit to myself. More than anything I need to make sure Holden knows I'm not going anywhere. Now that I have him, I'm never letting him go and he needs to know it without a single doubt in his beautiful little head. As for me, I don't know if I'll ever be able to forgive myself. I took away so much from them just by not being here.

I nod my head stiffly in agreement, but instead of responding to her plea, I make a joke, desperately needing to lighten the mood. I glance down at her hand still resting gently on my forearm and let the corners of my mouth turn up into a smirk. "You know, Bree, I'm going to have to tell my brother you had your hands all over me in my truck. I don't think he's going to like that too much," I tease. She rolls her eyes in response, immediately dropping her hand. "I know I'm the best looking Emory by far, but you decided to marry my brother instead of run away with me." I grin.

"Of course, you would turn it into a joke," she giggles.

I shrug carelessly. "Your loss."

She shakes her head at me like she's annoyed with me, but a small smile plays on her lips defying her actions. "You're crazy," she grumbles as she reaches for her small black purse and slides towards her door to get out of the truck.

Although I'm grateful she's letting it go for now, I stop her. "Bree?" Her head turns towards me with raised eyebrows as her hand remains on the door. "Thank you," I tell her sincerely, my voice cracking as I keep my eyes focused on her.

"You're welcome," she whispers as she grins shyly at the recognition.

"My brother did really well marrying you," I taunt. She laughs and I playfully add, "I don't know if I can say the same for you, though."

She rolls her eyes dramatically and grins. "I can."

I clap my hands once loudly, needing out of the moment. I chuckle as Bree jumps slightly from the sound. "Let's go shopping for my boy," I announce boisterously. Grabbing my keys and wallet, I jump out of my truck.

Slowing my pace, I let Bree catch up before I stride towards the entrance of the toy store. "So, what do you want to look at first?" she prompts as we step through the sliding doors.

I grin, claiming, "Everything."

She laughs. "You can't buy him everything."

I shrug chuckling. "That's what Sadie said, but with the size of our family, we're going to spoil the hell out of my little boy!" I smile broadly as we begin to take in our colorful surroundings. "And I honestly can't wait to do exactly that," I admit.

Chapter 30

Sadie

My nerves are a wreck as I wait for everyone to get here for Holden's birthday party. If I'm honest, I'm mostly nervous awaiting Matt and his family. I hope they're okay with everything. I grimace, looking around at all the Cars decorations. My parents would hate everything about this party, but they don't have a say in Holden's life I remind myself and square my shoulders. This is perfect for my little man and that's all that matters.

"Mommy, Mommy! Daddy's here!" Holden yells excitedly. He jumps down from his perch on the chair looking out the front window and runs to the front door. He tries to open the door, but grunts in frustration when he can't open the child safety lock making me chuckle.

"I'm coming, Holden." I smile as I walk up behind him and unlock the door. I pull the door open, and Holden runs as fast as he can out to Matt's truck. Matt picks him up and spins him around in a hug the moment he reaches him, and a lump instantly forms in my throat. Matt meets my eyes as he holds our son and my breath hitches at the emotion I see in him, even from this distance. I hold his gaze for a moment until my chest begins to ache so badly, I drop my head in defeat. I took so many other moments like this away from both of them and that knowledge crushes me.

Suddenly, Matt's voice is close. "Hey, Sadie," he rumbles sending goosebumps up my arms. I look up and try to smile as he sets Holden down with a grin so beautiful, I can't even open my mouth to reply to his greeting. He leans down and kisses me sweetly on my cheek making me gasp.

He lets his lips linger longer than a normal hello causing a whimper to pass through my lips. My heart instantly starts pounding furiously in my chest. I watch with wide eyes waiting to see what he'll do next. He slowly pulls back and smirks down at me. He has to know what he's doing to me by suddenly flirting with me again after being so cold towards me since he found out about Holden. I search his face for answers, but I don't get any. Instead, his grin grows even wider and his green eyes glint with mischief. He ignores the question in my eyes and innocently asks, "Do you need help with anything before everyone else gets here?"

"N…No…I…No," I stammer shaking my head. I look around in confusion, not able to process anything I'm seeing as I clumsily turn around in a circle.

He chuckles as his eyes hold me captive. I can't stop staring at him. I'm completely mesmerized by the sparkle in his bright green eyes. "Sadie!" he prompts smirking at me again.

"What?" I ask finally shaking myself out of my stupor. "Did you say something?" I prod feeling a little off-balance.

"I asked if you could help me grab a couple things out of my truck," he repeats, grinning. "I know you told me not to go overboard, but I had to get him something for each birthday I missed, not just today," he explains. He shrugs, trying to brush it off. Unfortunately, I know how much it hurts him that he's already missed three of his birthdays. I nod sadly following him to his truck, perplexed by his supposed turnaround with me.

He yanks the back door open, and I glance into the back seat. My mouth drops slightly open at the sight in front of me. There are several presents wrapped in dark blue wrapping paper with different sports balls covering it, as well as a few gift bags with pictures of Disney's Cars characters on them. "Matt," I begin at a loss for words.

He shrugs and offers me an apologetic smile, "I couldn't help myself. I promise, I'll let him know it's just because I missed his other birthdays, and he can't expect this in the future. I just needed to make up for what I missed," he explains pleading with me. My heart drops into my stomach at the gesture. "Forgive me," he pleads innocently.

"Okay, of course," I whisper trying to shove my tears back down before they fall. "I get it," I add nodding my head in understanding, while keeping my eyes averted. "I'm sorry," I squeak again.

"Sadie," he whispers softly causing my heart to skip a beat. I slowly lift my head to meet his eyes. "I'm the one who needs to be sorry," he whimpers his voice full of emotion. I search his face, looking for the meaning behind his words, my gut clenching painfully. "I am truly sorry," he emphasizes again almost agonizingly.

"Can I carry another one in?" Holden asks excitedly pushing himself between us.

"Yeah buddy!" Matt grins down at him and hands him another small gift.

"I can't believe this is all for me!" he exclaims running into the house with his arms tightly gripping a small shoe-sized wrapped box.

Matt brings his focus back to me as Holden runs in the house. He places his thumb and forefinger on my jaw and slowly runs it along the line of the bone sending shivers down my spine. I glance down at his lips and back to his eyes almost begging him to kiss me again. My breath picks up its pace and my whole body vibrates with need for him. He slowly leans towards me, his eyes filled with heat and right before I think our lips will touch, I notice movement out of the corner of my eye.

Matt and I both turn just as both Micah's parents and his parents park in front of my house. I sigh in resignation, and I swear I hear Matt do the same, but that could just be my hopeful imagination. Why would he suddenly want to kiss me again?

He places his hand softly on my lower back and whispers into my ear, "We will talk later." My breath hitches with the warmth of his breath on my neck. I nod, feeling lightheaded as I watch him stride towards his mom and dad. I shake my head to get my bearings and paste a smile on my face as I turn towards Micah's mom and dad to greet them.

In no time at all, my kitchen, living room and back yard are filled with family and friends who love Holden. Honestly, I couldn't be more grateful for every single one of them. Holden happily soaks up all the attention, but he's also not quite sure what to do with himself. He keeps going from playing a game with his friends, to chasing Matt, to spinning around with his new aunts and uncles, to hugs for Micah's parents, then back to his friends. I soak up every minute of his happiness.

I can't help but notice Matt's eyes remain mostly fixed on Holden, causing my heart to ache for him even more. The few times his eyes stray from our son, I find him staring at me with a look I can't describe, but a look that leaves me slightly unsettled. I sigh wistfully, wishing I could be in his arms, but I know that's a dangerous thought.

Matt stands by our small play set in the backyard with Holden as I get the picnic table ready for his birthday cake. A surge of jealousy envelops me the moment I spot Mary, one of the only other single moms I know striding confidently up to Matt with a flirtatious grin. She's absolutely gorgeous with naturally curly dark brown hair and curves any man would appreciate. She knows we're not together and my stomach flips with nerves at the sight of them talking. I freeze right where I'm standing as my gaze suddenly focuses solely on them.

He crosses his arms over his chest and smiles politely at her but continues watching Holden. She then places her hand on his bicep, and I watch as his muscles twitch at the contact. She leans in towards him whispering something to him and he throws his head back and laughs in response. I have a quick intake of breath. The sight of him laughing is one of the most beautiful things I've ever seen. I only wish I were a part of it.

"Sadie?" Bree prods, pulling me out of my trance. I release a breath I didn't know I was holding as I turn towards her, forcing a smile. She laughs. "Relax, he's not about to accept a date with someone else at Holden's birthday party."

My eyebrows scrunch together in confusion. "What?"

She smirks at me. "You two aren't fooling anyone." I open my mouth to deny anything between us, but she stops me with a shake of her head. "Talk to him, Sadie. He's just processing everything. You can't blame him for needing time."

I sigh in resignation and instead of responding, I change the subject. "Can you help me get the cake and ice cream?" I request, giving her a pleading smile.

"Of course." She grins and follows me inside to get the dessert and all the supplies.

After we sing Happy Birthday and we all have a piece of Holden's Cars cake, everyone begins to leave. "Thank you so much for coming," I repeat appreciatively for the last time to Mary and her son at my front door.

Holden hands his friend a small gift bag to take home just before he turns and runs away. "Bye. Thank you!"

She nods and glances over my shoulder, relief flooding her features just as I feel Matt step up behind me. I know it's him by his musky scent and the goosebumps that cover the back of my neck the moment he gets close to me.

"Matt, it was so nice finally meeting you."

He smiles down at her, responding politely, "It was nice meeting you, too."

I see in her eyes the courage his grin gives her to continue. "We'll have to get the boys together to play sometime. I could show you some of the places the boys like to go around here, and we could go to dinner afterwards," she suggests. "I know some great places for adults too," she adds flirtatiously.

My whole body stiffens, like if I stay still enough, I could completely disappear. My stomach churns and I think I might throw up, but I can't move. I don't want to be here listening to her ask Matt out. Why would she do this in front of me? I feel myself about to go into a full-blown panic attack.

Suddenly, Matt steps even closer to me. He places his hand on the small of my back, my skin burning where he touches me through my shirt. "We'd love to get the boys together," he states, giving her his panty-melting grin, "and I'd love any tips. I do believe Sadie can show me around though," he adds, tipping his head slightly towards me.

She blushes and hastily adds, "Oh, I'm sorry...I didn't know."

He glances down at me, the corners of his lips twitching up, daring me with his eyes to argue. When I don't say a word, he shrugs. "No big deal. I'm flattered."

She blushes a deeper shade of red and puts her arm around her son, gently pushing him out the door. "Bye, thank you!"

As soon as the door closes behind them, my breath rushes out of me, and I nervously turn to face him. "What's going on, Matt?" I ask shakily.

He smiles but doesn't answer me. Instead, he laces his fingers through mine, warming me from my fingertips as he turns towards the back yard. With a gentle tug of my hand he encourages, "Come on. Let's go clean up while Holden plays for a little while. We'll talk after he goes to bed."

I let him drag me outside and we both quietly begin picking up party decorations, dirty plates, cups and napkins. I'm so confused, but I don't even know where to begin. I guess it doesn't matter because we can't even really talk until we put Holden to sleep anyway and before that can happen, we still have to have dinner and Holden will want to open the rest of his presents. I sigh in frustration and drop into a seat at the picnic table.

"Are you okay?" Matt asks. I look up at him warily, trying to read him. He sighs and sits down across from me. "Thank you for today. You did a great job with his party," he praises.

I shrug. "It was no big deal. I always wish I could do more."

He shakes his head and reaches across the table to give my hand a reassuring squeeze. Lifting my head, I look into his eyes as he insists, "It was perfect."

I gulp and nod appreciatively. "Thank you."

"You've done a really good job with him, Sadie. You're a good Mom," he proclaims still holding my gaze.

"Mommy, Daddy, watch me! Watch me!" Holden yells. We both turn our heads towards our son just as he flies down his slide on his stomach. "I'm Superman!" he announces proudly.

We both laugh as he runs around to the ladder and climbs back up to the top again. He does the same thing and runs back towards the ladder. "One more time on the slide Holden, then it's time to go inside," I gently demand.

"Okay," he responds as he begins to climb.

One step short of the top platform, his little foot slips off the ladder and his face hits the platform hard with a loud crack. I jump up with a gasp as my heart stops. He seems to fall in slow motion as I scramble as fast as I possibly can to get to him. He hits the ground with a hard thud and for one incredibly long moment he's deathly quiet, the wind getting knocked out of him. His piercing scream finally hits my ears and although I'm thankful, I'm still terrified. I'm over to him in just a few short strides, but Matt is already kneeling down next to him as Holden screams in pain.

"Holden, buddy, are you okay?" Matt asks reaching for him.

Holden pushes himself up crying loudly. "Mommy!" Holden cries and my heart leaps as I reach for my boy, blood pouring from his chin like a faucet. "Mommy!" he cries again pushing Matt away and clamoring over to my lap.

I wrap him up in my arms, not caring about the blood coating both of us, not caring about anything except him. "It's okay little man, Mommy has you," I coo into his ear. I attempt to peek at his chin, but Holden clings tighter to me. "Matt, can you look at his face? I think it's his chin. He might need stitches," I instruct trying to remain calm while my insides have exploded with fear.

After a few agonizingly quiet seconds Matt agrees, "I think you're right. I'll get some clean towels to put on it while you get him in my truck to go to the hospital."

"I don't wanna' go to the hospital!" Holden screams and clings to me even tighter, terrified.

My heart breaks for my little man and I attempt to push my own anxiety away to calm him down. "It will be okay. The doctor has to fix your cut up this time, but I'll, I mean we'll be with you the whole time," I tell him holding him tightly.

Chapter 31

Matt

I unbuckle Holden from his car seat and reach to pick him up, but even in his groggy state he wants nothing to do with me. He unknowingly, yet painfully clenches my heart with his little hands when he pushes me away with a whine, "I want Mommy."

I gulp knowing the pain in my chest isn't going anywhere and step back. My voice cracks when I say her name, "Sadie, he wants you."

She nods at me, offering me a sympathetic smile as she walks around the truck and lifts him up out of his seat and wraps him up in her arms. "It's okay little man," she whispers in his ear lovingly. "Let's get you in your bed." He wraps his little arms around her neck and his legs at her waist, burying his face in her hair.

I feel so fucking helpless, just like I have for the last few hours while we sat at the hospital, but I still try to do whatever I can. "I've got the bags," I tell Sadie quietly.

I pick up the navy bag decorated with white daisies and hang it over my shoulder as I glance back in the truck to make sure I have everything he needs. I close the door behind her as she steps away from my truck with Holden in her arms and follow them up the walkway. "Where are your keys?"

"Side pocket of the bag you're holding," she answers while rocking our son. I find the keys and unlock her front door. I push it open and hold the screen door for her to walk through. I follow her inside before she has a chance to ask me to stay or leave. I'm not going anywhere. Slowly, I shut the front door behind me and set the bag down on the floor just to the side of the entryway.

Quietly, I walk down the hallway and peek into Holden's room finding Sadie already covering him up with his blankets and handing him a worn stuffed lion. "I love you my Little Man," she whispers and gives him a kiss on his forehead as she gently rubs the top of his head with obvious adoration.

"I love you too, Mommy," he whimpers. Sadie moves like she's about to get up when Holden stops her with his cry, "No! I don't want you to go."

She sighs softly, the sound of his cry utterly painful even to my ears. "It's okay, Holden. I'm right here," she whispers as she continues to caress his head softly. "I'll stay with you for a little while, but you have to get some sleep," she offers.

"Okay, Mommy," he mumbles through a yawn as he reaches for her with his free hand. She curls up next to him without even a glance in my direction making my heart clench even tighter.

I spin on my heel and stride back towards the living room. With a groan, I sit on the couch, placing my elbows on my knees and dropping my head into my hands as I let the events of today wash over me. I rub my hands down my face and back up into my hair, where I stop, letting my head hang in my hands feeling completely helpless, overwhelmed, and exhausted.

I don't understand how today started out so well and ended like this. I wanted to tell Sadie how I'm feeling and celebrate Holden's birthday with him together with our families. It was so much fun watching him today with his friends and my family, especially with Sadie. The relationship is so overwhelming I feel it everywhere.

When he slipped and hit his chin before falling off the ladder, I've never been so fucking scared in my life. I pull on my hair tightly at the memory. I shudder at the sound of silence as blood pumped in my ears. The way his little body moved so awkwardly as he tumbled to the ground and how it was impossible to get to him to stop it from happening had me trembling. My heart stopped at the same time I jumped up to get to him. The moment before he took a gasping breath and started to cry had my whole world crashing down around me.

I desperately wanted to help him, but he didn't want anything from me. I cringe at the way he turned away from me and pushed me away. He only wanted her, just Sadie. All the blood, I shake my head thinking I've never seen so much blood and it all came out of his little body. I felt so powerless, and I hated it.

The way Sadie took care of him without thinking of anything else was amazing. She was incredibly calm while I felt like I would lose it any second. I have to admit, her demeanor and even her off-key quiet singing to him probably helped soothe me as well. I just tried to concentrate on doing what I could to help her and watching his small chest moving up and down.

"You're still here," Sadie mumbles, startling me out of my thoughts. Lifting my head, I look up to find her freshly showered and changed into her pajamas. She stands in front of me making my mouth water in a sky-blue tank top with spaghetti straps and pale blue and yellow striped pajama shorts. I want to pull her to me and wrap her in my arms. "I thought you left," she murmurs, fidgeting with the hem of her tank top.

I run my fingers through my hair and drop my hands back down to my lap. With a shake of my head, I continue staring at her. "I can't leave," I declare.

Her eyebrows scrunch together in confusion. "What? Why? What's wrong?"

I laugh humorlessly because there are so many answers to those questions. Sighing heavily, I give her the easy answer first. "I can't leave Holden tonight," I admit.

"Seven stitches," I murmur. "I can't believe it was only seven stitches with all that blood. I've never been so scared Sadie," I confess, gulping down the lump in my throat.

She nods in understanding. "Every time he gets hurt, I feel myself panic."

"Really?" I question, arching my eyebrows with doubt. "It sure didn't seem like you were panicked."

She shrugs. "I don't want to scare him. But it hasn't gotten any easier that's for sure," she admits cringing.

"I know we were lucky he wasn't hurt worse, but when the doctor said those exact words to us," I shake my head in disbelief, "let's just say he was lucky I didn't punch him."

Sadie smiles softly. "That would've been interesting."

I chuckle at her choice of words. "Yeah," I mutter with a sigh.

I grimace, not liking the words that are about to come out of my mouth, but she needs to hear the truth. "Sadie, I hate that I felt so helpless tonight. It wasn't just because I couldn't fix his cut either," I emphasize. "It was because when I went to comfort my own son, he wanted nothing to do with me. He only wanted you and wouldn't have cared if I left. He didn't even want me to touch him," I flinch painfully. "I felt like an outsider watching the two of you. I wanted to just do something," I reiterate, exasperated. "I'm his dad, but he didn't want me. I get that you're his mom and lots of kids want their mom when they get hurt, but he also wanted you because you've always been there for him, and the fact is I haven't. It doesn't matter to him where I was before." I feel my cheeks getting wet from my tears I didn't realize were falling. Ignoring them, I look her in the eyes as I ask agonizingly, "Will he ever be able to depend on me like I really am his dad?"

She gasps and her hand flies up to cover her mouth in shock. She looks at me full of regret as she cautiously sits down on the couch next to me. "I'm so sorry, Matt. I'll do everything I can to fix this," she pleads as she hesitantly places her hand on my back.

I shake my head because I don't want her apologizing to me anymore. "Stop saying you're sorry! We both fucked up. I need to move past our mistakes and concentrate on now," I insist, staring intently at her and needing her to know I mean it. "I've done a lot of thinking these last couple weeks and Bree actually helped me straighten out my thoughts. I had so much I wanted to tell you tonight, but then today…" I trail off, shaking my head. "Do you mind if I sleep on the couch tonight?" I ask changing direction.

"Um, no. It's fine," she stammers.

"I need to be close to him," I explain. She nods in understanding. I lift my head and stare at her until she looks me in the eyes. "I need to be close to you," I admit, my chest tightening with my words.

Her eyes widen and her face goes pale. "Wh…what?" she stutters.

I gulp over the lump in my throat. "I wanted to talk to you tonight anyway, but with what happened with Holden, it may have delayed this conversation a couple hours, but seeing him get hurt only strengthened my resolve," I confess. She searches my face for answers I'm finally ready to give and pray she wants to hear what I have to say. "I can't stay away anymore, Sadie. I want it all. I want our son. I want you," I insist, holding her gaze.

She inhales quickly in surprise, appearing to stop breathing.

"Fuck it," I mumble and crash my mouth into hers. She gasps into my mouth in astonishment, shooting heat into my body. I move my mouth over hers, devouring her as she pushes back, kissing me just as passionately. I pull her into me, and she straddles my lap to get closer to me, causing me to groan as she rubs against me. I shove my tongue into her mouth, needing to taste her. Her tongue hungrily meets mine and they lick and twist playfully. I put my hands on her hips and attempt to pull her even closer, causing a whimper to fall from her lips as her core pushes up against mine.

I force myself to tear my lips away from hers, holding her tightly in my lap. I drop my forehead to hers as we both catch our breath, our chests rapidly rising and falling. "Sadie, I need you to understand what I want. I want you. I've always wanted you and not just for this," I insist squeezing her thighs. "We've always had fun together and now getting to know you again," I shake my head in wonder, "you're incredible. I admire how hard you're working to finish school and take care of Holden by yourself. I've been pushing you away because I was pissed about losing all that time with Holden, but it was my fault too. I was the fucking idiot who told you to lose my number. I was the idiot who walked away when I saw you with Micah. I always knew where to find you, but I never gave you a shot at finding me. It's my fault and I'm the one that has to live with those regrets for the rest of my life," I cringe as she shakes her head in denial.

"No!" She argues shaking her head.

"I am going to do everything I can to make it up to both of you." I tip my head forward and kiss her softly. I pull away with a groan.

"It's not your fault," she declares.

"It is," I insist, not wanting to talk about that anymore. "I want you to be mine Sadie and not because you're Holden's mom, but because I'm falling in love with you."

She gasps, her head falling away from mine so she can look me in the eyes. "You're falling in love with me?"

I nod and answer with a confident smile, "I am. You should've been mine a long time ago and I fucked that up. I've been messing it up again, not only because I want to focus on Holden, but also because I'm scared you don't want the same thing."

"I do want the same thing," she answers her voice filling with hope as she gives me the same.

"I'm scared something will change and I'll not only lose you, I'll also lose my son," I confess, my voice catching in my throat.

She shakes her head softly in denial as her tears begin mixing with mine. "Holden will always be yours. I will never take him away from you no matter what. I couldn't do that to either of you now that we finally have you in our lives again," she proclaims tearfully.

With emotion overwhelming me, I cradle her face in my hands and pull her lips back down to mine. I kiss her slowly, but deeply as I stare into her eyes. The moment our tongues tangle together, our eyes close as our breathing picks up. I let one hand curl behind her neck to keep her lips fused to mine as she clings to my shoulders. I allow my other hand to slowly drift down outlining the side of her breast until I reach her stomach. Then I let my fingers glide in over her belly and then up between her breasts. "Fuck," I moan realizing she's not wearing a bra. I lightly circle around her breast, slowly making my way in until I reach her nipple and lightly pinch her through her shirt.

She gasps and breaks away from my mouth, but I don't let her go as I continue to do the same on the other side. "Matt," she whimpers.

I cover her mouth with mine and let my fingers slowly drag down her center until I meet the waistband of her pajamas. Dragging my finger under the waistline, I whimper at the realization she's not wearing anything under these shorts. "You're killing me," I groan and let my hand fall to her thigh. I slowly massage my way up and under her shorts, until the tips of my fingers reach her folds. Softly, I caress the edges and her entire body shudders on my lap, causing me to become as hard as granite. I curl my finger into her and leave my thumb to circle the edges of her folds as I kiss her hard. She clings to me moving with my hand as I desperately search for her release in my hands. It feels like only seconds as her body begins pulsing around my hand and I hungrily swallow her soft moans in our kiss.

She pulls away to catch her breath and I let my hand slide out of her shorts. Looking at me, she gasps, "What just happened?"

I chuckle softly, loving her response. "Would you like me to explain it to you? Or I could demonstrate again," I offer, smirking.

The corners of her lips twitch up and she whispers, "Let's go to my room."

My eyebrows rise in question. "Are you sure?"

She looks at me as if I lost my mind making me laugh. "Shhh," she admonishes. "We don't want to wake Holden."

Closing my mouth, I grin down at her. I already feel like a huge weight has been lifted from my chest just by letting the past go and telling her how I really feel. I stand and readjust myself so I'm able to follow her down the hallway with my hand in hers. I know I'm doing the right thing for me being here with not only Holden, but also with Sadie. I believe this is where I'm meant to be.

I'm finally moving my life in the right direction.

Chapter 32

Sadie

I can't believe this is happening.

Today, I went from being nervous, to being happy watching Holden. To jealous of my friend, Mary when I had no right to be. To terrified for my son. To regretful. To hopeful. And finally, to feeling amazing and so in love.

I'm not about to tell him that yet and scare him off, but he did say he was falling in love with me. My heart flips as I repeat his words in my head. Words I never believed I'd hear from him, but always dreamed I would hear fall from his lips just the same, even when I thought I might never see him again. All of that makes this moment seem surreal.

Dragging him down the hall, I pull him into my room as he shuts the door behind him. He spins me to face him and steps into me. He tangles his hand in my hair and slowly backs me up towards my bed until I hit the mattress and my knees buckle, causing me to fall back with a soft bounce. His eyes rake over my body, and he leans down, placing soft kisses on my skin, igniting a fire inside me. He kisses my leg, my hip, and my belly, as his breath and mouth leave a heated trail in their wake.

He crawls his way up until he hovers just inches over me and meets my gaze. My heart pounds erratically in my chest as he stares intently into my eyes. "Is this too fast for you Sadie?"

I giggle, thinking of Holden. "We even have proof we've already had sex, Matt."

His lips twitch and he pushes my hair out of my face, tucking it behind my ear before he responds. "Yeah, but it's been almost five years since we've been together like that and this time, I want to make sure we do this whole relationship thing right."

"Relationship thing?" I smirk attempting to appear confident while my heart clenches tightly at this reality.

He grins. "I don't want to rush things. This time I need to do a much better job of taking care of you and taking care of us."

Butterflies flutter around inside my stomach as goosebumps cover my flesh. "The only thing those words accomplished Matt is making me want to be with you even more," I rasp knowing I've never wanted anyone more, not even him five years ago. I bite my lip and wait to see what he'll do next.

His beautiful smile makes it hard to breathe. He runs his thumb gently over my lips and follows it softly with a brush of his mouth. He kisses me along my jaw, until it meets my ear and sucks lightly into his mouth. His tongue sneaks out as he trails kisses down my neck making me whimper at his heated delicate touch.

I run my fingers into his soft blonde waves and pull him to me for a desperate kiss. My tongue traces his lips until he lets me in and allows our tongues to fight for control. My body reflexively curves into him when he suddenly pulls back.

He stares down at me with wide eyes. "Will we hear him if he needs us?"

I giggle, loving his unnecessary concern. "Don't worry. My house is small. We'll definitely hear him, but that also means we have to be quiet."

He relaxes and settles back into me with a grin. "This should be fun."

He kisses me again, softer this time. His hand slides under my tank top at my waist and he softly caresses me with his thumb. My hand moves to his waist, and I slide my hands under his t-shirt. My first touch of his hard smooth muscles causes a whimper to escape from my mouth.

I let my hands wander halfway up his back before I whine, "Take this off."

He chuckles and reaches for the bottom with one hand, swiftly pulling it over his head and tossing it to the floor. I reach for him, wanting to trace the lines of his muscles with my fingertips. He sucks in a quick breath at the contact, holding it for a moment. Suddenly he exhales quickly, clamping onto my hands and pinning them above my head as his mouth comes crashing down on mine. He licks, tastes and sucks my tongue, pushing our kiss deeper. His hard body presses up against my soft one as he swallows my groan. He releases one of my hands and pushes my shirt up to my chest, caressing with his thumb on the edge of my breast.

Without breaking our kiss, he prods, "Can I take this off?"

"Yeah," I answer breathily as I pull away from him.

He lets go of my other hand and pulls my tank top over my head. Leaning back, he lets his eyes roam over my body. I blush and move my hands to cover myself. "Don't." He stops me, gently pushing my hands away. "You're beautiful."

My nose scrunches up in distaste. "I don't feel very beautiful since I had Holden. I don't look anything like I did last time you saw me," I admit, afraid to meet his eyes.

"Sadie, look at me," he demands. I cautiously find his gaze, only seeing adoration. "You are more beautiful than the first time we were together. The reality of having you here like this in front of me is so much better than all the fantasies I've had of you since I met you," he grins mischievously.

My face turns tomato red again at his admission at the same time a shy smile covers my face. Deciding I'm ready, I reach down, tugging my shorts off and tossing them to the floor. I lay back down bare beneath him, running my lower lip through my teeth as I await his reaction.

His eyes widen with amazement. "Fuck," he mumbles. "Beautiful doesn't even begin to describe you."

He cups my breast and runs his thumb over my already hard nipple. His head comes down and he kisses my other breast, making me moan. Slowly, he licks his way to the top, sucking my nipple into his mouth. My breath becomes ragged as I struggle to hold back any unconscious sounds from the sensations he's causing to run through my body. He begins kissing his way down my belly and hovers just over my core. When I realize his intentions, I reach out, stopping him. "Matt, tonight I just need you." When he doesn't move, I tug lightly on his arm and beg so he knows I truly mean it, "Please."

He stands and without taking his now dark green eyes off me, drops his shorts and plain black Calvin Klein boxers at once. He reaches down and grabs something out of his shorts and drops them back to the ground with the growing pile of clothes. Slowly crawling over me, he moves to position himself over my core. Reaching up, he brushes my hair out of my face and continues to hold my stare. "Are you sure?" he asks causing me to feel an overwhelming sense of deja-vu.

Nodding, I pull him down to me and kiss him thoroughly in response. As he pulls away gasping for air I whisper, "Yes."

Bringing a wrapped condom up to his mouth, he tears it open with his teeth. He throws the wrapper to the side, and I watch as he easily rolls it on his thickness. He quickly positions himself right at my entrance and pauses. I lift one leg up and wrap it around his back to encourage him. In one swift move, he pushes himself all the way inside and I can't stop my gasp of both surprise and pleasure from leaving my lips.

He looks at me in awe as he murmurs, "I've wanted this with you for so long, Sadie, so fucking long." My heart hammers at my ribs like it's trying to claw its way out. He begins moving in and out of me achingly slow and my hips buck towards him attempting to get him to move faster. He chuckles softly. "Not this time. I want to feel you come around me."

Our mouths fuse together in a slow dance, matching the movement of our hips. My whole body feels like it's on fire as our kisses become more and more desperate. I finally pull my mouth away, my body desperate for air. He drops his forehead to mine and starts moving faster.

He holds me tight with one arm, while the other hand slides between us and rubs me gently in tiny circles just above where our bodies meet. Our breaths become faster and his thrusts harder. Just when I think I can't take anymore his mouth comes back to mine.

"Come on, Sadie," he whispers

His lips press to mine, and we breathe together, attempting to muffle each other's sounds as we push for more. My insides begin clenching around him and he pushes inside one, two more times as far as he can go, hitting a spot deep inside me.

He holds me tightly at the height of his own climax as I start to come down from mine. As he takes his hand out from between us, he pulls his mouth away from our kiss but stays close. He pulls me even tighter as he collapses partially on top of me, both of us completely sated as we try to catch our breath.

"Wow," I whisper as I exhale.

He grins and kisses me on the forehead, then on my nose before kissing me sweetly on my lips. "You're amazing." I smile shyly making him chuckle. He sighs and slowly pulls out of me as he places another kiss on my lips before he pushes himself off the bed. I immediately shiver inside and out with the loss. "I'm just going to clean up and I'll be right back," he informs me.

I breathe a sigh of relief and close my eyes to wait for him. I'm not able to wipe the smile from my face. I can't believe that just happened.

He groans when he returns. "Wish you could stay like that all the time. I smirk and open my eyes to look at him. He hovers over me with his boxers now on. "I brought a cloth to clean you up," he offers holding up a lilac washcloth. I reach for it, but he pulls it away, requesting, "Let me."

"Okay," I concede. Instantly, I drop my arms back to the bed, my limbs still feeling like jelly.

He gently wipes the warm cloth between my legs before he slides my shorts back on. He chuckles as he helps me pull on my tank top. "You're not much help, but I need you dressed."

I giggle, knowing he's right. "Why?"

He shakes his head grinning at me. "Two reasons. It's hard enough to keep my hands off you with your clothes on and because of Holden." I nod my agreement. With the things he just did to me, my brain is having trouble coming back to reality. "I just peaked in on him and he's sleeping peacefully," he informs me. Tilting his head down, he places a light kiss on my lips before he falls to my side. He rests his hand on my hip and faces me.

I roll over to face him and he smiles at me. "It's never been like that for me," I blurt out, without preamble, my face instantly blushing.

"Fuck, it's never been like that for me either, Sadie," he tells me staring at me intently.

"We need to clean up your mouth," I declare still blushing.

"Are you sure about that?" he jokes grinning mischievously. I smile back at him, blushing a deeper shade of red. Then he sighs and agrees, "You're right. I'm definitely going to try."

"Good," I mumble, nodding in agreement. I reach my hand to trace along the lines of his armband tattoo. "I love this. When did you get it?"

He shrugs. "This year. I got it when I lost a bet."

"Really?" I ask with wide eyes.

"Yeah, but I love it now that I have it," he admits watching my fingers trail over his skin.

"Me too," I concur. Glancing up at him, I lick my lips. I feel the urge to trace it with my tongue and so I do, eliciting a surprised gasp just before his lips find mine again.

Chapter 33

Sadie

It's been a week since Holden's birthday party, a week since Matt and I got together again and it's nothing like I could ever dream. It's been even better. He's been staying with us some nights, but he sneaks out before Holden wakes up, so he doesn't know he slept here. Then he comes back with breakfast for all of us.

Tonight, Holden is having a sleep over at Micah's parents. They haven't been able to spend as much time with him since Matt came into the picture and they miss him. With Holden gone, Matt asked me to come to his place because he wanted to make me dinner. At the end of dinner, I smile and declare, "I have to say, I'm impressed." I'm full from the delicious steak, baked potatoes and green beans.

He just laughs and shrugs it off like it's no big deal. "It's either this or boil a box of pasta and sauce out of a jar for the Italian girl. I figured I was better off with steak." I laugh along with him and give him a kiss in appreciation, which leads us to his bedroom. We've had to wait until Holden is sound asleep and stay quiet, so we definitely want to take advantage of our extra free time.

I lie cuddled up against Matt in his bed tracing the lines of his stomach muscles when his phone rings for the fifth time in the past hour. He groans in annoyance. I sigh and push up so I can look him in the eyes. "Why don't you just go ahead and answer it. Whoever is trying to get ahold of you is obviously quite persistent. Maybe it's important." After everything with Micah and of course with Holden not home, I tend to worry something might be wrong.

"It's not my family, so it's not important," he states trying to end our discussion. "I'll just turn my phone off," he offers.

I shake my head. "Don't do that. What if someone really does need to get in touch with you?" Heaving a sigh, I kiss him lightly on the mouth. He attempts to pull me closer, but I lean back and smirk at him. "Answer the call. You're going to have to sooner or later. I'll go clean myself up while you're on the phone," I suggest.

His jaw twitches as he stares at me. Then he kisses me hard and I reflexively moan into his mouth, immediately reacting to him. He abruptly pulls away with a groan, "Fine!" Then he snaps up his phone and storms away.

I'm not sure what the call is about or even who it is, but the way he just reacted has my stomach churning with anxiety. I push myself off the bed with a sigh and make my way to the bathroom. I glance at myself in the mirror and my eyes widen in surprise. My dark hair is such a mess, it actually appears full, making me giggle. My lips are swollen from Matt's kisses, my cheeks are flushed, and my blue-grey eyes are sparkling. I don't think I remember a time I looked this happy. I lament a touch of guilt beginning to gnaw at me for that thought because Holden does make me happy, but I guess I can admit, at least to myself, it's a different kind of happiness.

Micah flashes in my mind and I tear my gaze away from the mirror wondering if I have a right to feel this way. Taking a deep breath, I push those thoughts out of my head and focus on the reason I'm in here. I quickly clean myself up with a washcloth and brush my hair and my teeth. Then I pull on a pair of short yellow pajama shorts with tiny white flowers on them and a white tank top before finally making my way out of the bathroom, still no sign of Matt.

Exhaling slowly, I ponder what else I could do for him. Honestly, I wish I had some sexy lingerie to put on, but at least I know Matt likes me in this. Satisfied, I sit on his bed to wait for him to get off the phone. I don't want to go out there and have him think I'm trying to listen in on his conversation, although my curiosity is overwhelming.

Suddenly, I hear Matt's voice rise in anger making me flinch. Pulling my knees up tight to my chest, I protectively wrap my arms tightly around them resting my chin on top. I wrack my brain trying to figure out who could possibly make Matt that pissed, but as my mind begins drifting to really bad scenarios, I wonder if I want to know.

I have no idea how long I remain sitting in that position when he storms back into his room. He sets his phone down on the top of his dresser clenching his jaw. Halting his movements, he runs his hand over his face and back up through his hair, obviously irritated. He sighs and drops his hands to rest on his hips before he turns and lifts his head looking at me. The stressed look on his face has me hugging my legs even tighter. He bites his lip and takes a step toward me before he finally opens his mouth. "That was Natalie," he states gaging my reaction.

My eyes widen in surprise. "Your ex-girlfriend Natalie?"

He nods his head as I search his face for answers, not moving from my position on the bed. "She was so insistent because I've been ignoring her calls." My mouth drops open and he explains, "She started calling a few days ago, but I didn't care what she had to say. I only gave in and answered to tell her to stop calling." I feel like I'm going to throw up because he was on the phone a lot longer than it takes to tell someone to stop calling you. He sighs, "She booked a plane ticket to come see me, to talk. She said she would be here next weekend, but I told her I didn't want her here."

I'm shaking when I open my mouth to remind him of my awful betrayal, but something like that can never happen to him again. I won't allow it, even if it kills me in the process. "Matt, what if she's pregnant?" I barely squeak out my question.

He sighs and averts my gaze. "I asked her the same thing. I couldn't..." he shakes his head since we both know he's thinking he wouldn't take a chance of missing out on anything with a child of his. "Anyway, at first she didn't answer my question, she just kept insisting that she had to see me. When I told her she had no chance with me and that I'm back with my old girlfriend, she still pushed me. I finally told her we have a son and I'm staying here. That's when she finally admitted she thought if I saw her, I'd forgive her and take her back. She's not pregnant. She just thought if I questioned it, I would see her." He shakes his head in disbelief. "Telling her about Holden is what made her actually tell me the truth. If she's lying about being pregnant, I'll find out. I still talk to one of my friends down there who works with her. After that, my only response was to tell her to stay the fuck away from me."

"You're back with your old girlfriend?" I prompt, my heart skipping a beat.

"Out of everything I just said, that's your question?" he smirks. I just shrug and he relaxes a little bit as he steps closer to me until his knees hit the bed. He reaches his hand out for me. I loosen my hold around my legs and before I can fully stretch my arms and legs, Matt slides up next to me on the bed and softly kisses my cheek. "We may have called it a summer fling, but you were my girlfriend, I was the idiot who should've never walked away."

My heart jumps up in my throat and I throw myself in his lap and press my lips to his with fervor. I kiss him hard until he falls back on the bed making him chuckle. I grin down at him, proclaiming, "I was so stupid." He laughs louder in response. Sliding down his side, I lay on my arm facing him. "Are you okay?" I prod softly. I can't help but wonder what's going through his head after hearing from her, especially like that.

He rests his hand on my hip and stares at me thoughtfully. Eventually, he opens his mouth and sighs heavily. "Sadie, after hearing from Natalie, there's something I feel like I need to tell you. I don't know if now is the right time to talk about it, but..." Matt pauses, pinching his lips tightly together.

My heart drops like lead into my stomach and I can feel myself go pale, scared for what he's about to say. "Wh...what?" I ask shakily, my brain already imagining the worst.

Noticing my reaction, he instantly tries to calm me down. "No, no, I don't know what you're thinking, but it's nothing crazy. It's just something I need to say." I nod stiffly and attempt to swallow the lump in my throat, feeling like I'm barely breathing.

He pulls my hip a little closer to him and looks into my eyes with determination. "It's just that I hate to think about it, let alone admit it, but I'm truly grateful you had Micah." I flinch at Micah's name passing over his lips. "I'm just really sorry you had to lose him the way you did. I feel guilty that I'm happy he's not here to steal you away from me. I'm not glad he's really gone, I just want you to be mine," he confesses, his green orbs full of emotion.

My eyes well with tears, but I don't let them fall as I admit, "It wouldn't have mattered if Micah was still here. I'll always be yours, Matt," I rasp feeling unsettled with those words, although I know they're true.

He sighs and moves his hand to cup my cheek, adoringly. "You don't have to say that, Sadie. Fortunately, or unfortunately, that's a situation none of us will ever be in."

I nod my head as my tears escape. He wipes them away with his thumb and I whisper, "I know, but it's still true, although it makes me feel guilty. Even Micah knew the truth in those words."

With the loss of Micah and my guilt for loving Matt weighing heavily on my chest, he pulls me close to him, tucking me underneath his chin. "Oh Sadie, I'm so sorry I wasn't here for you," he whispers into my hair as I cry softly into his chest.

"My best friend is dead because of me," I mumble into his chest needing to tell someone.

He shakes his head and tries to pull back to look me in the eyes. "Sadie, that's not true. I may not have been there, but even I know that's not true." He rubs my back and squeezes me tightly as he realizes I won't look up, attempting to comfort me.

After a few minutes I'm finally able to calm down enough to speak. My heart is telling me I need to voice everything I've been holding back before we can really move forward, no matter how much it hurts. Hopefully after I tell him everything, he'll still want to move forward with me and not just our son.

"You already know some of this, but I need you to know it all, so please just let me talk," I plead. He nods his head in agreement and I breathe a nervous sigh of relief as I curl into him, needing his support.

"When I married Micah, I knew he was in love with me and he knew I loved him, but I was never *in love* with him. He believed I would eventually feel as strongly as he did and I was naïve enough to believe him. My parents had already disowned me," I scrunch my face up in bitter aggravation. "Micah wanted to help me with everything. He wanted to give me a home, insurance for me and the baby and himself to love both of us with everything he had. I couldn't even find you to tell you I was pregnant, and my best friend only wanted to love me," I whimper, hating myself. "I also reminded myself that even if I did find you, you had only wanted a casual summer fling, so it didn't matter what I felt for you."

He flinches and his arms tighten around me. He takes a deep breath preparing to interrupt me, "Sadie…"

I shake my head in his chest and keep going. "It got really hard Matt," I whimper painfully. "We both could see you every single time we even looked at Holden. How could you not?" I challenge, shrugging. "Other people could see it too and people started to talk. I was accused of cheating and called every name in the book. Everyone hated me and blamed me for trapping Micah with someone else's son. Micah denied it and continued to stand up for me, but I started pulling away from him wracked with guilt. I felt like I was ruining all our lives, Holden's included."

"My list of regrets is long, but most of all I couldn't stop thinking about you. I kept hoping one day you'd come back and find us, which just made me feel even guiltier. I became really depressed and withdrawn. Micah tried so hard to bring me back, but he began turning into someone else too and I know that's my fault too. I had to start forcing myself to go through the motions of daily life, including being Micah's wife because after everything he did for me, he deserved everything he ever wanted. I would have a few moments of happiness, but they were always because of Holden, but then there were times I even struggled with being his mom. I hated myself more and more every day," I cry.

"Fuck, Sadie! Did you have anyone you could talk to?" Matt probes painfully.

"Just Micah and I couldn't talk to him about you," I emphasize shaking my head.

"Shit," he grumbles and kisses the top of my head as he squeezes me and kisses me again.

"Not so tight," I grit out realizing his hold is only becoming tighter.

"Sorry," he mutters and loosens his hold placing another kiss on my head.

Sighing heavily, I shut my eyes, burying myself in his chest again. "The night he died, he wanted to go out on a date. I knew he had been drinking. That's why I drove us home." I pause, shaking my head at the memory, still wishing it was a nightmare. "But then Tim called probably less than an hour after we came home. I let him go because I was too busy feeling sorry for myself to use my head. He never made it to the bar to pick Tim up. I should've been the one to go or find someone who could."

"No, you can't blame yourself. It's not your fault," Matt insists vehemently.

"It is my fault. I was the one who married him even though I didn't love him like he deserved. If they didn't judge me already, they did as soon as they saw Holden. Micah was the saint, and I was the bitch. His friends said I wasn't worth it, but they tolerated me for him. If he had been with someone else, he could've been happy, and I know he'd still be alive. I just know it," I declare feeling Matt's head shaking in denial. "After he died, everyone said it should've been me, even my own parents," I whimper.

Matt gasps in shock and mumbles, "What the fuck?"

Ignoring his reaction I continue, "Micah's parents never did, but of course they'd rather have their son than me. They're just too good to say it out loud, although they never treated me differently. In fact, they really stepped up to help me with everything, especially Holden, after Micah died. I'd agree with everyone else, but Holden doesn't deserve it. He deserves to have his mom and his dad. He's been my reason for getting up in the morning. He's my reason for surviving. He's my miracle," I cry clinging to Matt as if he is my lifeline.

"Sadie?" Matt questions, his voice cracking. The distress I hear in him causes me to lift my head away from his chest just enough so I can peer at him from under my eyelashes. "That's not enough, I need you to really fucking look at me!" he demands.

I flinch and my breath catches in my throat at his intensity. Shakily, I pull myself back a little further. He grips my hips and slides me exactly where he wants me, looking him directly in his eyes. His jaw twitches in anger, causing me to fear what's about to come out of his mouth. "It's not your fault. Nothing about it is your fault. We all made some naïve choices back then, but not a single one of them caused Micah's death, except for Micah's choice to get behind the wheel and drive when he'd been drinking."

"But I could've stopped him," I argue.

He laughs humorlessly. "Maybe." My eyebrows draw together in confusion. "With everything you've told me, there's no way in hell Micah would've let you go pick up his friend. One thing I know about Micah is he was always protecting you in one way or another. He wouldn't dare leave you alone in a car with one of his supposed friends who hated you, especially when the guy was drunk." I scrunch up my face with doubt and he repeats with more force, "He wouldn't have let you go pick him up and someone had to stay with Holden."

I exhale harshly, thinking maybe he's right, but how do I know? "I miss my best friend," I confess, overwhelmed. "I feel guilty every day. Lately, I feel even worse now that you're back and even more now that we're together."

"He would want you to be happy!"

"I know he would want that," I concede quietly, "but if I would have found you from the start, you could've helped me and been there for Holden. I wouldn't have expected you to marry me or anything, but it could've changed everything for him. He might still be alive."

"Or it might've only changed who Micah was with at the time. He still would've been friends with Tim and probably still received the same phone call," he argues, attempting to make me see rationally. He obviously can tell I still have doubts and adds, "He would've never wanted you to carry so much burden from his death. Getting in that car to go pick up his friend was his choice. We can't go back and play the 'what if' game. We have to move forward and honor his memory. That's all you can do Sadie. I know you've been trying for Holden, but now you need to believe it for all of us. Micah's accident was not your fault!"

I nod and collapse into his chest. My heart feels overwhelmed with how strongly I feel for him, and I need to get it out before I regret not getting the chance. "I love you, Matt," I whisper clinging tightly to him. "I love you so much it hurts. I'm so thankful you found us."

After a pause, he whispers my name, "Sadie."

I shake my head, "Please don't say anything. Right now, I can't handle one way or the other how you feel about me. I just need you to know how I really feel. Right now, that's all I need."

"Okay," he reluctantly concedes.

I can't deal with him rejecting me right now and I don't want him to say he loves me because he feels bad for me either. All I can do is hope someday he'll feel the same way. I cringe knowing that's exactly what Micah longed for with me. I can't help but feel crushing sadness again at the thought, but this time it's tinged with hope because I know, no matter how Matt feels I want him to be happy, even if he's not with me. If he does find someone else someday, I'd get exactly what I deserved.

I take a deep breath and press my body as close to Matt as possible, craving his comfort, which for now he willingly gives me.

Chapter 34

Matt

I'm still processing everything Sadie said to me the other night. I don't understand how she can blame herself for what happened to Micah or how she believes she doesn't deserve to be happy. I realize she didn't say she doesn't deserve to be happy, but close enough. When she told me she loved me, I wanted to beat my chest like a caveman and claim her as mine, but she didn't want anything from me. I huff in frustration, I guess I'm supposed to be lucky she let me comfort her, but that's just bullshit.

"What's your problem?" Christian asks sounding irritated. Grinding my jaw, I spin towards him, ready to tell him off. He stands glaring at me with his arms crossed and eyebrows raised in question. He gestures to the water skis, kneeboards and other water sports equipment I'm digging roughly through making me wince. "Take it easy with our equipment!"

Sighing heavily, I drop the rope in my hand in defeat. "Sorry man." I run my fingers through my blonde waves in frustration. "I was just trying to organize some of the equipment," I claim.

He cocks his head to the side as his eyebrows rise to his hairline. "Seriously? That's your idea of organizing? You're lucky Jason lives in Portland and runs that end. If he were here, he'd kick your ass," he smirks.

I nod my head and mumble, "Yeah, I know." My vague response makes him look even more confused.

He takes a step towards me and asks again, "What's going on? Is it something to do with Holden?"

I shrug my shoulders. "Not exactly."

He nods in understanding. "Ah." As I turn to him with a question in my eyes, he chuckles and explains. "It's Sadie."

"Yup," I drag out the word, popping the p on the end.

Christian sits in one of the few chairs we have in this storage shed and stretches out his legs making himself comfortable. Then he smirks at me and shrugs. "I can wait all day, Bree's helping out at the gift shop today."

I shake my head in mock annoyance, my lips twitching up at the corners. "Don't you have work to do or something?"

He shrugs. "Nah, Jason and one of the new guys, Gary both had bookings this morning, but I don't have anything until tomorrow. I'm stuck with an overnight up in Camden with the other new kid. I have a group doing a few different sites and some bike trails up there and I'm bringing Cody up to train, so Jason and I don't always have to do the overnights. I need to grab some things from here for the trip, so you get to see my gorgeous face and I get to find out why you're throwing our equipment around like it's a bucket of balls."

I chuckle and apologize again, "Sorry. Are you going to do the bike trails at the Camden Snow Bowl?" I prod attempting to change the subject.

He grins and keeps his answer short, "Yup."

Sighing in resignation, I run my hand through my hair. I need to talk to someone about it and not only are Christian and I a lot alike, I admit, albeit reluctantly, but he also has an idea the kind of position I'm in with everything he went through with Bree. I stuff my hands in the pockets of my cargo shorts and cautiously look up at him. "I'm just trying to figure Sadie out," I tell him quietly.

He laughs. "Well, we both know that won't go very well." I narrow my eyes at him making him laugh even louder. "She'll only let you know what she's ready to tell you," he states confidently.

Resting my hands on my hips, I admit to my brother with confidence, "I'm completely in love with her, Christian."

His eyes snap up to mine, trying to read me. He only stares for a moment before nodding in understanding. "Took you long enough," he teases. My eyes widen and he chuckles. "Five years?" he questions smirking at me.

I grimace and drop my eyes towards the ground. He's right.

His face turns serious as he sighs, stepping towards me. "Look, it might feel like it's all happening too fast, but even before you saw her again, you couldn't stop thinking about her," he reminds me. "I caught you pining over her when you didn't even know about Holden," he jokes, his lips twitching in amusement. "You can't deny that."

Chuckling softly, I nod in agreement. "You're right, but that's not even what this is all about." Christian crosses his arms across his chest, obviously confused, but waits patiently for me to continue. I take a deep breath and release it slowly before I explain myself. "I know Bree has told you at least a little bit about Sadie's past, but without really divulging anything to you, she's been through a lot. The worst part is she blames herself for most of it too," I wince the moment I say the words out loud.

"Wait," he interrupts. "You don't mean she blames herself for her husband's accident?" he probes with disbelief.

I sigh and nod my head. "Yeah, but it wasn't her fault. I don't know how to convince her she needs to let go of all the guilt she's holding for everything with Micah, including his accident. She still feels guilty for me and even Holden," I admit sadly, "but that's probably more my fault with how I acted when I first found out about him."

"You were an asshole," Christian agrees smirking at me.

I huff a laugh, but don't deny it because it's true. "Well, I need to do the same thing I'm trying to get her to do."

"And what's that?" he questions, arching his eyebrow in challenge.

"Forgive myself and move on. Your wife really helped me out talking about it," I tease him.

He feigns hurt. "And I didn't? She probably told you the same thing I did." Nonchalant, I shrug and grin at him mischievously. "Figures," he grumbles.

I chuckle and follow it with another sigh. "I want to do the same thing for her. I know how I feel about her, and I wanted to tell her. When she told me she loved me," I sigh reverently, "I thought it was the perfect time to do the same, but she stopped me. I don't think she believes she deserves to be loved," I elaborate, remembering the torn look on her face. "She absolutely refused to listen to anything I had to say after she told me and practically begged me not to respond to her at all. I did what she asked, but..." I flinch, trailing off.

Christian's eyes widen in surprise. After a moment, he sighs and understanding covers his face. He's most likely remembering when Bree pushed him away, thinking it was the best thing to do for him. "You have to find a way to get her to listen to you and convince her she's wrong, Matt," he emphasizes. "Don't let her push you away."

"I agree," I nod, "although she's not exactly pushing me away, she's just not completely opening up to me. The thing is, I have no idea how to assure Sadie I'm in love with her and *want* to be with her solely because it's *her*. I don't want her to think I'm with her because of our son. I don't have any misplaced feelings of guilt or obligation. I just want to be with her. I don't want her to have any doubts about how I feel," I confess, trying to get him to understand where I'm coming from.

"I already know what your answer will be, but I have to ask anyway," he starts, preparing me for his question. I narrow my eyes as he intently stares at me. "Are you absolutely sure?"

Smiling, I breathe a sigh of relief at his question and chuckle. I nod my head and grin wider, answering him with conviction, "As sure as I am that Holden is my son."

Christian grins. "Then, you have to do something drastic."

"Like what?" I prod, annoyed with him for stating the obvious.

He shrugs and sarcastically suggests, "I don't know, marry her?"

I freeze as I let his words soak in. A slow smile spreads across my face. I turn towards my brother, declaring with excitement, "That's it!"

His eyes widen in shock. "Matt, I was kidding."

"I know," I tell him as I take a step towards him. I place both of my hands firmly on his shoulders. "No worries, Christian. This isn't on you. I know what I want."

"Um, you're going to talk to Mom, right?" he questions nervously.

I chuckle and give him a quick hug, patting him hard on the back twice. "Thank you, Christian!" I exclaim ignoring his question.

"Matt?" he probes as I pull away and turn towards the front door. "Matt!" he yells again as I jog out to my truck.

"Later, Christian," I call over my shoulder with a wave of my hand.

"What about the mess you made inside," he complains as he follows me outside.

"I'll finish it later. I promise," I claim, then pull my door open.

"Matthew," he admonishes making me laugh as I climb into my truck.

I pull the door shut and turn to wave to my brother. He glares and flips me off in return. I laugh heartily in response enjoying every second of annoying the shit out of him. I have a lot to do if I want this to work and I'm not going to waste my time appeasing Christian.

Now that I have my head straight, I know exactly what I want, and I already have an idea on what I can do to get us there. Veering towards my place, I head home to do some necessary research before I can follow through with my plan.

As soon as I pull into my driveway, I send Sadie a quick text, "My parents want Holden for another overnight."

"Okay, when?" she replies instantly.

I grin, satisfied with her response. "I'll get back to you."

"Ok…" she replies. I laugh because I know she's now confused why I already mentioned it if they didn't have an idea when, but that's only because they don't know yet.

Jumping out of my truck, I jog inside and grab my laptop, needing a bigger screen than my phone to see the information. I grab a water and plant myself on the couch. I open it up to search for info on marriage licenses and venues. I also need to do a little bit of research on rings to get an idea how it will affect my bank account before I head to the jewelry store. I'll tell my parents when I have a plan. I'll pray that Sadie will accept because for the first time I'm happy and excited about where this will take me, take us. I smile as I look down at my laptop and begin searching.

With a groan, I stop what I'm doing. I realize there's one other thing I need to do. I set my laptop to the side and reach for my phone, gripping it tightly in my hand. My hesitation makes me realize this is something I really need to do in person. I sigh and grab my wallet and my keys before turning and heading back towards my truck. It's only a few minutes later when I pull up outside the Rossi's house, thankful to see their car parked in the driveway so I can get this over with.

I hop out of my truck and stuff my hands in the pockets of my cargo shorts as I walk up to their front door. Taking a deep breath, I tentatively knock, quickly going over what I want to say. The door swings open and Bee stands in the doorway her eyes wide.

"Is Holden, okay?" she asks without a greeting, clearly panicked.

"Yes, yes!" I emphasize feeling guilty for showing up unexpectedly like this. "Holden is fine! I'm sorry to just show up. I didn't think." I wince.

She breathes a sigh of relief and I watch as her whole body relaxes. Quickly pulling herself together, she smiles. "Well then, would you like to come in?"

Nodding, I step inside. I clear my throat nervously. "I'd really like to talk to you and Mr. Rossi, I mean Marco, if that's okay?"

She nods appearing slightly perplexed. "Sure. Marco?" she calls down the hall. When he steps out of another room, my gut clenches with guilt again as his face pales. "He's assured me Holden is absolutely fine and he's just here to talk to us," she immediately informs him. Color instantly returns to his cheeks. "Would you like something to drink?" she offers, walking into the kitchen.

As I follow behind, I mumble, "Just some water would be great."

I sit down at the table with Marco as Bee gets three glasses and fills them with water before bringing them to the table. She sets them down and sits in the chair between Marco and me before she prods, "What can we do for you, Matt?"

I take a sip of the water and set it back down in front of me. Then, I clear my throat before I speak. "I don't know if this is the right way to handle this or not, but from what Sadie has told me, the two of you have been more like parents to her than her own. She loves you and Holden loves you. He couldn't ask for better grandparents. Sadie loved Micah very much and I know he loved her," I admit trying not to flinch. A sad smile of acknowledgement passes over both of their faces. "I saw it clearly when I first met both of them and I know he would want her to be happy," I ramble trying to get it all out.

"We agree with you, but what are you trying to say?" Bee probes, attempting to push me to my point.

"Well, I believe both Sadie and Holden consider you their only family now, so I thought I should come to you," I stammer nervously. "I'm in love with Sadie and I believe I have been since the day I met her. I'm going to ask her to marry me." I pause as they both gasp in shock. "It may seem fast to you, but not to me. I'm not exactly asking for your permission, but I thought you should know. I also want you to know I also consider you both Holden's and Sadie's family. I couldn't even begin to thank you for what you've done for them the past five years, for Sadie's whole life for that matter. I don't want you to be threatened by my presence. I don't want to take anything away from you. I just want them to be a part of my life."

"Are you sure you don't want to marry Sadie to be with your son? She won't take him from you," Marco declares.

I shake my head vehemently. "I came back for her five years ago. I only stayed away because I saw Micah propose to her and I watched her say yes. She entered my heart without me ever realizing it, then never left. I want to be with her. I believe I always have."

"Are you going to stay here?" Bee questions softly, her fear evident in the sound of her voice.

"I promise I'm not going anywhere," I insist, looking them both in the eyes. "My whole family lives close by," I inform them. They both nod their heads still appearing uncertain. Ironically or not, I feel the need to comfort them and really would like to have their acceptance in even a small way. "I just thought you should know my plan since we share a family. I hold nothing but respect for Micah and just as I know Sadie will never forget him, we won't let Holden either," I proclaim, my voice cracking with unexpected emotion.

I take a gulp of my water to attempt to clear my nerves. Marco gives me a stiff nod and Bee attempts a smile. "Thank you for coming to us," she states, her eyes glassy.

I nod my head and push my chair back to stand from the table. "I have some things to take care of but thank you for listening."

Bee quietly walks me to the door and waves as I leave. I climb in my truck with a sigh. I'm not naïve. I don't expect them to suddenly accept me and everything else that comes along with me being in Holden and Sadie's lives. I do know it's the right thing to do for all of us to try and hope they feel the same.

Chapter 35

Sadie

It's been nearly a month since I told Matt I loved him. He's been wonderful to say the least, but I still attempt to stop the conversation whenever he begins to tell me he loves me. I don't know why I keep trying to shut him up. I don't know if it's guilt or if hearing it will make me want to believe it's true and I'm afraid he'll change his mind. Either way, I know he's sick of me shutting the conversation down. I need to let things happen and move on. Or really do what Matt suggests and forgive myself. If he believes I deserve it, maybe he's right.

Matt just left to drive Holden over to Micah's parents. They're taking him to DEW Haven in Mount Vernon. It's a working farm except it houses exotic animals as well as wild and domestic ones. He was so excited. I almost wonder if he'll be able to sit still in his car seat for the hour drive.

Matt and I decided we're going to the swimming hole to relax. We haven't been back there together since he came back into my life. He thought it would be fun to hang out where we met.

I look in the mirror to give myself another quick look before I throw my cover-up on. I'm wearing an aqua blue tankini that's ruffled by my chest and stops just above my belly button. Even though Matt's seen me naked, I can't help but feel self-conscious since I had Holden, and I just can't bear to wear a bikini like most girls my age. I pull my hair up in a loose ponytail and pull a short navy-blue sundress on as my cover-up. Grimacing at my reflection, I walk away before

I decide to change again. I want to be ready when Matt gets back.

Reaching for my beach bag, I sling it over my shoulder. I begin to make my way to the kitchen to make some food for us for lunch when a loud knock has me changing direction and moving towards the front door. I pull the door open to a smiling Matt wearing green and blue board shorts and a plain dark gray t-shirt.

"Hi," I grin up at him.

He steps inside and wraps his arm around my waist, pulling me close to him so our bodies our flush. "Hi," he mumbles over my mouth just before his lips softly cover mine in a tender kiss. I groan as he pulls away all too quickly, making him chuckle. "Ready?" he prods grinning.

"I was just about to throw something together for lunch," I claim, pointing towards the kitchen.

"I already took care of it," he informs me.

"When?" I question, arching my eyebrows in surprise.

His eyes sparkle as he smiles, urging, "Let's go." He reaches for my hand and gives it a soft tug, pulling me along with him out the door.

I laugh as he grabs my bag from me and picks me up to place me in the passenger seat. "You're quite controlling today."

He laughs along with me as he closes my door. I watch as he jogs around the front of his truck and climbs in. He turns to me still laughing. "Not really, but I could be."

I roll my eyes at him only making him laugh harder as he starts his truck and backs out of the driveway. "You're in a great mood today," I observe, not bothering to hide my own smile.

"Why wouldn't I be? I have a beautiful girl next to me. We're going to spend the day relaxing together and our son is happy. Plus, I got to see both of you today," he adds making me flinch.

He notices my reaction and sighs with regret. "I'm sorry, Sadie. I didn't mean it like that," he insists. He reaches for my knee giving it a gentle squeeze, eliciting goosebumps across my skin. "I just meant that every day I get to wake up and see both of you is a great day in my book. I'm not looking back anymore, I'm only looking forward."

My heart clenches with both love and sadness with his words. I sigh as he parks alongside the road so we can make our way down the ramp to the swimming hole. "How do you do it?" I ask softly, barely getting the words out.

He pulls his keys out of the ignition and turns to face me. "Sadie, please look at me," he pleads. I hesitantly lift my head to look into his eyes. His hand comes up to caress my cheek as he stares into my eyes with determination. "I don't believe you intentionally set out to hurt me and I sure as hell never meant to hurt you."

"Of course not!" I exclaim.

He smiles gently. "Exactly. I'm done letting our mistakes take control of our future. We have an amazing son and you and I have always been explosive together." He pauses smirking at me. "Just forgive me and forgive yourself. Everything else will come together if you do. But you need to let it go."

I nod my head and proclaim, "If you can do it, I should be able to as well. As for you, you were forgiven the moment you came back," I confess.

He grins and gently presses his lips to mine. Sighing into his mouth, I slide my hands up into his hair. I tug him towards me, attempting to push our kiss deeper. He concedes for a moment before he falls back in his seat with a groan. "We just got here and you're already trying to fog up my windows," he jokes. "I know I'm hot, but let's try to make it out of the truck for a little while at least," he teases making me blush. He chuckles and moves closer to me again. "I love making you blush, but if I don't get out of this truck, we're going back to my place. It's closer." He gives me a chaste kiss before he quickly backs himself out of his truck.

He grabs my beach bag and a small cooler before he steps over to the trail. "I can carry something you know," I remind him, my lips twitching up in amusement.

He turns and smiles sheepishly. "I know, but this way I can be your knight in shining armor. I'll carry everything and you can even hang on to me as you walk down the trail, so you don't fall."

I glare at him, watching as he attempts not to laugh, but my giggle pops out first. "Yeah, I'm not the best of friends with my feet," I joke.

He laughs. "I don't mind. I love being able to catch you." Rolling my eyes, I shake my head with a smirk at the same time I step up behind him at the top of the trail. I place my hands on his shoulders, slightly corded from carrying the cooler and bite my tongue to hold back a moan. I follow him down and look up as we reach the bottom.

"Wow, I can't believe it's practically empty when it's already so hot!" I exclaim glancing around. There are only a few teenage girls lying on the sand and no one in the water.

He grins. "Works for me, although it is still early for most people." I shrug because I know it's true, but I haven't been a late sleeper since before I was pregnant. I follow him over to a sandy area away from the only other people here. He sets the cooler down and reaches inside my bag to grab a towel.

Shaking it out he offers, "For you."

"Thank you," I murmur and kiss him on the cheek before I sit down.

He grabs another towel and drops my tote bag on the sand. Shaking it out, he places it right next to mine before dropping down next to me. He places his elbows on his knees and asks, "Would you like me to do your sunscreen?"

I laugh, admitting, "I didn't think that was a good idea, so I did mine at home."

He pouts and grumbles, "You're no fun," causing me to laugh harder. "Do I at least get to see you in your bathing suit today?" I roll my eyes and pull off my cover-up, tossing it towards the bag. Then I lean back on my hands, feeling confident as Matt's heated gaze takes me in. "I was hoping it was white like last time." He smirks, wiggling his eyebrows suggestively, "But you look hot."

I blush as he leans over and lightly brushes his fingers along my navel before kissing me sweetly. Lifting my hand, I place it on his chest and push him away, but as soon as I do, my back crashes to the sand. I laugh. "Maybe this wasn't the best idea."

He grins and kisses me again. "It was a perfect idea." With a sigh, he leans back on his own towel and lies on his side, propping himself up on his elbow so he can look at me. My eyes are instantly drawn to his tattoo on his bulging bicep, and I bite my lip to keep from licking it. He laughs, as if reading my thoughts. "If you keep giving me looks like that, we really won't be here long. Time for a subject change."

"What do you want to talk about?" I prod.

"Would you be willing to move?" he questions, taking me by surprise.

My mouth drops open in shock. He said he was staying here. "Wh…what?"

He immediately begins to explain his question. "I just mean out of your house, to somewhere else in the area."

"Oh. I guess," I mumble as I try to gage how I feel about moving. "Why?"

He sighs and hesitates briefly before he admits, "I don't really want to live in the house you and Micah shared as husband and wife."

"Oh." My eyes widen in understanding.

He reaches for my hand with his free one and entwines them together. "I want to make our own home where the three of us can be happy together. That could be my place, or we could look for a house to buy."

"Together?" I squeak.

He chuckles. "There's nowhere else I'd rather be. I don't really care where we live as long as it's together." He winces. "I would just prefer it to be a place where we can make a fresh start, create our own memories."

I nod in understanding while at the same time my insides begin churning like a hurricane. "You want to live with me? Why?" I ask stupidly.

His head falls back as he bursts out laughing. "Seriously?" I blush and he sits up tugging on my arm, urging me to come closer to him.

"I just...I mean...Is it because of Holden?" I stammer as I sit facing him.

He shakes his head and moves to his knees, cradling my face in his hands. He sighs as he looks at me with so much love I feel it in every inch of my body, my heart clenching with joy. "Sadie, it's because of you," he whispers searching my face. "Of course, I don't want to be without my son, but I don't want to be without *you*," he emphasizes.

I open my mouth to interrupt him when he stops me with a shake of his head. "Not this time! You're going to sit right here with your mouth shut and listen," he demands.

My eyes widen in surprise, and I can't help but smirk as I sassily reply, "So bossy!"

He grins. "Yup!" He continues staring into my eyes and sighs with contentment before he speaks. "Sadie, when you literally fell into my arms here over five years ago, you took my breath away. You're absolutely stunning. Then the more we hung out, the more I realized you're so much more than beautiful. I knew I was in trouble because there's so much I liked about you. You're funny, smart, loyal, confident, sweet and kind. Plus, you like to put up with me," he teases making me giggle.

His face turns serious again as he continues, "When I went back to Baylor, losing you hit me hard. Then, when I thought I'd lost you forever, I did everything I could do forget about you, but you never left my mind or my heart," he admits, sincerity shining in his green gaze.

I gasp at the overwhelming feeling of love and whisper his name, "Matt."

"Now that I found you again, I *know* there's so much more to you. I admire you for so much; what you've endured with your parents, losing Micah and being a single mom, as well as still pushing through school when you don't have the time to do it. You're an incredible mom and I'm so grateful Holden is ours. You're dedicated and you work so hard to take care of him and make everything perfect for him. You have such a big heart. I know you would do anything for the ones you love. I can't even express how much it means to me that I'm one of those people," he states, a smile tugging at the corners of his lips.

"Matt," I rasp. Unwanted tears roll down my cheeks and he gently wipes them away with his thumbs.

"I can't let you stop me anymore. I *need* you to know how much you mean to me and how much I love you because I do love you, Sadie. I love you more than I think you'll ever realize," he emphasizes as I choke back a sob.

"Matt," I whimper, again, not able to get anything except his name to pass my lips.

He silences me with a soft kiss. He pulls back and licks his lips. He grins mumbling, "Mmm, salty."

I burst out laughing. "Hey."

I quiet instantly as he continues. "I love you, Sadie, and I want you to be mine forever. I want you to take my name, just like our son and become Mrs. Emory. Sadie, will you marry me?" he asks suddenly pulling out a princess cut diamond solitaire ring.

My hand flies to my mouth in shock. "Wh…what?" I stammer.

He grins wide. "You're going to make me ask again?" I laugh and he repeats himself before I can say a word, "Sadie will you make me the happiest man in the world and marry me?"

I throw myself into his arms and sob into his neck. "Do you mean it?" I question clinging to him.

His entire body shakes with his laughter. "Where's my confident girl?" he teases. "I have a ring here that confirms I definitely mean it!"

I blush and gulp down the lump in my throat. "Yes," I whisper.

"Yes?" he repeats as a question, still laughing.

I pull back to look him in the eyes as I happily answer again, "Yes!"

He sighs with relief as he slips the ring on my left ring finger. I don't even glance at it before pressing my lips to his. He chuckles and leans back on his towel, proclaiming, "Now I can relax." I laugh and he shrugs like it's no big deal. "I was going to propose after we ate, but I don't have the patience."

I giggle, declaring, "You're crazy!"

"Speaking of being crazy," he begins, and my eyebrows draw together in confusion.

"What?" I ask nervously.

He links his fingers with mine again and inquires, "Do you want a big wedding?"

I shake my head vehemently. "No, I don't want to do that again. Besides, I don't really have anyone I'd want to invite. Micah's parents are my only family and I think that would be kind of awkward," I admit sheepishly.

He breathes a sigh of relief. "Good, but don't worry about Micah's parents."

"What?" I ask, my eyebrows drawn down in confusion.

He shrugs, his only sign of nerves showing by his constant fidgeting with my fingers. "I talked to them. I would've asked your dad, but under the circumstances, I thought I should talk to them."

My eyes widen, taken aback. "That was really sweet." My heart stutters with his thoughtfulness.

"Anyway," he quickly changes the subject, "since we're not having a big wedding, wanna' get married next weekend?"

"What?" I gasp, my eyes widening in shock. "But that's so fast!"

"I think we've waited long enough. It has been over five long years. I already have it all planned out. I just need you to agree and then tomorrow morning we go to town hall and apply for a marriage license. All you would have to do this week is find a dress," he states simply.

"But…" I begin to argue.

Attempting to stop me from panicking, he squeezes my hand, waiting to speak until I meet his gaze. "Do you trust me?"

I snap my mouth closed and nod my head. "Of course," I answer with confidence.

He grins, urging, "Then, say yes!"

I hold my breath for a moment feeling slightly queasy. Then I nod my head. "Yes!" He leans up and presses his lips to mine hard before he drops back to his towel with a smile. "We have to talk to Holden!" I state anxiously.

He nods in agreement. "We can do that together tonight."

"Okay," I concur knowing Holden will be thrilled to have us all together. "I don't think I can relax. There's so much to do," I remind him.

He shakes his head laughing. "There's not. We can't get the marriage license until tomorrow and you can't look for a dress with me. Plus, I'm not letting you out of my sight today."

I smile. "What about my house? We have to find a realtor?"

He chuckles. "If it will make you feel better, we can leave after lunch."

"Okay," I concede. Smiling mischievously, I begin digging through the picnic basket.

He laughs and stands, sweeping me up in his arms before I can grab anything. I giggle and wrap my arms around his neck as he walks into the lake. He kisses me just before he lowers us both into the water with a broad smile.

"Time to cool off," he proclaims grinning.

Chapter 36

Matt

I quickly finish cleaning up the last of Holden's toys while he's still sleeping. I hope we can keep it clean enough until the realtor can take pictures of the house. My cell phone rings as I walk into the kitchen to grab a glass of water. Glancing at the screen, I grin at the sight of Sadie's name. "Hi beautiful! How's the dress shopping going?"

I can hear how flustered she is through the phone, just by hearing me calling her beautiful, which makes my smile grow even more. She better get used to it; she deserves to hear it every day. "Um, I...I think I found a dress," she answers quietly. "I love it and Bree says it looks good."

"She looks gorgeous, Matt," Bree calls from somewhere behind Sadie eliciting a laugh from me.

"That's great," I tell her honestly. "I personally don't care if you don't wear anything." I smirk at my comment even though she can't see me.

She huffs. "Anyway, we'll just be a little bit longer. I need to pick out shoes too. How's Holden?"

"Holden is still sleeping," I inform her.

"Wow, I can't believe it," she expresses. "He hasn't napped in forever."

"Well, he was exhausted from refusing to go to sleep last night," I remind her.

"I guess," she concedes. "Which reminds me, is the house ready for the realtor? I got all the papers signed this morning on our way here. She should be over in about twenty minutes to take pictures."

"Everything looks great, and we should be able to keep it that way for twenty minutes," I joke.

She laughs and I enjoy the carefree sound. "Thank you so much for helping me with this, Matt."

"You don't have to thank me, Sadie. That's what you do for people you love," I tell her honestly. "Besides, it helps get me much closer to my goal, which is to get both you and Holden completely moved in with me."

She giggles in response. "Thank you, anyway."

"If you're really appreciative, I'm sure you could find some way to show me how much it means to you."

I hear her smile even through her sigh, but she ignores my comment. "I have to go find some shoes now."

"I love you, Sadie," I declare wanting those to be the last words she hears from me every time she either hangs up or one of us walks out the door.

"I love you too," she whispers, her voice catching, just before she ends the call.

I set my phone down and fill a glass with water, immediately gulping half of it down. The doorbell rings and I glance at the time, mumbling to myself, "She's early," as I saunter towards the door.

I pull the door open to an older couple, I'm guessing in their late forties. "Can I help you?" I prod. As I narrow my eyes on the two people standing in front of me, I attempt to figure out why they look so familiar.

The man glares at me and yells accusingly, "Who the hell are you and what are you doing in my daughter's house?"

I gasp in surprise, but instantly swallow that down as my anger surfaces, easily reminded how they've treated Sadie and Holden too for that matter. I'll do everything I can to protect my family. I widen my stance blocking the doorway and cross my arms over my chest, glaring at both of them. "It's none of your business. You're not welcome here!"

Her mother suggests, "I think you need to clarify that with Sadie. Sadie?" she calls over my shoulder since I won't budge.

I partially close the door and stand in the doorway. "Stop calling for her, she's not here." I really don't want them to wake Holden. I know he'll be awake any minute, but he doesn't need to wake up to this.

She purses her lips like she doesn't believe me as she's trying to decide what to do. Then she huffs in annoyance and shrugs defiantly. "We'll wait. I want to meet my grandson and find out where she's moving."

"Oh, hell no!" I declare.

"What gives you the right?" her father probes.

I smirk, my blood beginning to boil. "Oh, I have every right. He's *my* son."

They both look at me with disgust and disbelief. Her mother dares to say, "His father abandoned Sadie before he was even born. That child is illegitimate."

I clench my fists and grind my jaw, struggling to maintain my temper. When I open my mouth to speak, my voice comes out deadly, "Stay away from my son and stay away from my wife!"

She may not be my wife yet, but they don't know that.

Her mother shakes her head with distaste. "She never could handle anything alone."

I glare down at her. "Sadie is one of the strongest women I know, no thanks to either of you. There's no reason for you to even be here. Get off the property."

"We're here because a friend of ours saw that her house was listed. I'm not letting my daughter move away and take my grandson with her without telling us where she's going," she declares as if she has every right.

I laugh humorlessly. "It's a good thing you have no say, then."

"Daddy," Holden calls from inside the house.

"It's time for you to leave," I tell them and walk inside. I close and lock the door behind me and rush down the hall towards my son. "I'm here buddy," I call as I step into his room.

He rubs his eyes with his small fists as he yawns. Then, he stretches his arms above his head and reaches for me. My heart flips at the gesture. "Is Mommy back?"

I pick him up in my arms and whisper, "No, buddy, not yet." He lays his head on my shoulder and I try to soak up his warmth and love to calm me down. I make my way out to the kitchen and quickly text Christian, "SOS!!!!"

He responds immediately, "What's wrong?"

"I need someone to take Holden. Sadie's parents just showed up." I glance out the window and grimace at their black Lincoln Navigator still parked in front of the house. "Doesn't look like they're leaving," I add, and press send.

I breathe a sigh of relief at his instant response, "On way."

I begin pacing back and forth down the hallway with Holden in my arms, not wanting to bring him too close to any windows. I don't even want them to see him, and I hope I'm right, thinking Sadie would want the same thing.

Holden soon begins to wiggle out of my arms, and I offer him some goldfish and water. "Can we go outside to play?" he asks, his energy beginning to return.

"No!" I exclaim and wince as he flinches at my reaction. I berate myself for taking my anxiety out on him. I crouch down to his eye level, softening my tone. "I'm sorry buddy, but I don't want you outside without me and we have to wait for the lady who's coming to take pictures of the house so she can do a good job selling it."

He nods in understanding, but I hate the defeated look that covers his face. "Why don't you go in your room and build me the biggest tower you can with your Legos. Uncle Christian is on the way over to see you. He loves big towers, too."

"Okay," he answers satisfied as he runs to his room.

A loud knock at the door causes me to freeze momentarily. I take a step towards the door to see who it is when Christian calls through the door, "Open up Matt, it's me."

I breathe a sigh of relief and pull the door open. Christian steps inside and I smile stiffly, "Thanks for coming." He looks at me like I've lost my mind. I sigh heavily. "Holden is in his room building a tower for you. I don't want him out here no matter what until I come get him," I instruct.

Christian nods. "I'll take care of him." He begins making his way to Holden's room and quickly disappears inside.

I continue to pace as I wait for the doorbell to ring and breathe a sigh of relief the moment it does. Cautiously, I move towards the door and peek out through the side window. I relax slightly as I see the realtor standing on the porch. Pulling the door open with a smile pasted on my face, I mumble, "Hello."

She smiles. "Hi, Mr. Emory. I'm just back to take the pictures."

I nod. "Yes, Sadie told me you were coming." I gesture inside. "Go right ahead."

"Thank you." She grins.

Patiently, I stand quietly and try to move out of the way while she takes pictures. I follow her to Holden's room. "Hey buddy, we just need to take a couple pictures of your room okay."

He smiles as he looks at the woman. "Make sure you get the tower in the picture. The new people will love it even though we're taking it with us."

We all laugh in response. "I bet they will, Holden," I tell him as my brother agrees.

I follow the woman as she finishes taking pictures of the house and breathe another sigh of relief when she leaves.

"I'll just take a few pictures from the outside and then I'll be gone."

"Thank you."

"Thank you," she replies as she leaves. I smile and shut the front door behind her.

"Now I need to get rid of them before Sadie gets home," I grumble to Christian.

"I texted Bree to tell her what's going on," he informs me.

I nod my head, hoping she'll know how to help Sadie with this one on her end. "Thanks," I murmur.

I glance out the window again just in time to see Sadie and Bree pull into the driveway in Sadie's Volkswagen. "They're here," I sigh, my stomach twisting into knots. "Christian?" I prod.

"I've got Holden. You go," he urges.

Nodding, I walk out without looking back. I immediately make my way over to Bree and Sadie, my whole body filled with concern. I stare down at Sadie who appears completely confused, like she's not sure what to do. "What are they doing here?" she asks not expecting an answer.

"I told them to leave. I don't think they believed anything I told them, so why would they listen?" I grumble sarcastically. Sadie grimaces but remains silent as her parents step out of their car again and begin striding up the walkway with confidence.

"Bree, can you help Christian keep Holden occupied?" I request. "I don't want him anywhere near them."

Sadie smiles stiffly at my comment and Bree nods her head in agreement. She gives Sadie a quick hug of encouragement before she heads inside. "I'm okay," Sadie tells me quietly. I nod and grip her hand tightly as we quickly approach her parents, hoping to get this over with.

Her mom glares down at our hands before asking, "It's true then? You're married to him?"

Sadie stutters for a second before she takes a deep breath, and a look of determination covers her face. "What are you doing here?"

"We came to see you. We came to see our grandson. We miss you," her mom attempts.

Sadie laughs humorlessly. "No, you don't and you're never seeing him. What? Has it been an acceptable amount of time that you think people have forgotten and will accept me again? Is that it?" she challenges.

Her mom gasps in shock as her dad admonishes her, "Don't talk to your mother that way."

She smirks, shaking her head. "She's not my mother. Mothers don't abandon their children."

"Fathers don't either?" she attempts to bait her.

Sadie shakes her head, "Don't you dare say a word about Matt when you know nothing about him or our son!"

"Sadie," she attempts.

"You need to leave. I don't want you here. You're trespassing," she proclaims and swiftly turns her back on them.

"If you come back, I'll report you to the police," I inform them. Turning quickly, I guide a trembling Sadie back into the house.

As soon as we shut the front door, I pull her into my arms and hold her tight. "It's okay," I attempt to reassure her. Then I quietly ask, "Are you okay?"

She laughs and shakes her head, wiping at her eyes. "I love you Matt."

With my lips twitching, I breathe a sigh of relief. "I love you too, Sadie." I kiss her softly on the lips and pull her back to my chest.

"Where did they even come from?" she questions not expecting an answer.

"They heard you were selling the house," I enlighten her.

She grimaces and replies sarcastically, "Of course they did." Heaving a sigh, she shakes it off, then smirks up at me. "So, we're already married, huh? I guess I missed the wedding."

I chuckle and offer her a shrug as my answer. "Come on, Holden wants to see you," I tell her, knowing she'll probably feel better after she has him in her arms.

Chapter 37

Sadie

The shock of seeing my parents the other day didn't last long with Matt at my side. Having his support as well as Bree's and Christian's was just what I needed to give me the confidence to close the door on them forever. I'm not going to let them get to me anymore. I have my own family and it's so much more than what I ever had as their daughter.

I fold back the white wooden shutters and look out the window of my room. A smile lights up my face at the sight of Camden Harbor, which leads out to Penobscot Bay. I exhale softly, feeling content. At the same time, today already feels surreal.

I still can't believe Matt and I are eloping. We're getting married today at the Norumbega in Camden, Maine. It's actually a historic stone castle and it's absolutely stunning. Matt arranged everything like he said he would. Including having Holden stay with his parents for the weekend. He figured it was the only way they wouldn't insist on coming along. Plus, we didn't want Holden here for our wedding night. Besides the fact I'd be afraid Holden would break something valuable. Although we do need witnesses, so since Christian had a group hiking at Camden Hills State Park yesterday, Matt asked Bree to come along as well. Then, he asked for the two of them to stay for the weekend and be our witnesses.

"Sadie?" Bree calls as she opens the door to our room.

"I'm in the library," I answer laughing. She steps in and grins at me. I shrug. "It's just kinda' fun to say."

She laughs along with me. Matt and I may not be doing everything about our wedding traditionally, but we did sleep separately last night. He stayed with Christian in the Warwick room where we'll stay tonight, while Bree and I stayed in the Library Suite.

Our room is a two-room suite, and the bedroom was the castle's original library, the scent of old books apparent. The room we slept in has a balcony around the inside of the whole room lined with shelves of books. It makes for very low ceilings on the outside of the room. It's one of the few times it's actually benefitted me to be short. Bree and I spent over an hour before we went to sleep last night looking through all the books that included many classics. I've only seen something like this in movies or read about it in books, but I love it.

The armchairs, curtains and even the lampshades are covered in the same white fabric decorated with Nantucket red flowers with greens and thick accent strips in the red similar to Matt's armband tattoo. At the bottom of the bed, there are steps up to the balcony library and off to the side of the room, a couple steps up to a narrow sitting room with a couch, a couple tables and chairs with a white, green and gold palm fabric. Both rooms have beautiful built-in bookshelves. We walk through the sitting room to reach our bathroom, where I've spent most of the morning getting ready.

"Matt and Christian are back in their room and are going to head out back in a little bit," Bree informs me.

"Did you see their room?" I ask curiously.

She laughs and shakes her head. Her eyes sparkle mischievously as she reminds me, "You'll see it tonight." I grimace starting to feel impatient for today to really begin. "I brought you some fruit to snack on so you're not too hungry until we get the chance to eat," she informs me as she sets a full plate of fruit down on a side table.

"Thank you," I murmur, smiling in appreciation.

We ate breakfast early before we started getting ready and I'm already kind of hungry even though we ate so much. I usually don't eat that much at breakfast, but the food was so good. Reaching for a few strawberries and blueberries, I pop them in my mouth, the sweet juices exploding on my tongue. "Mmm."

"Are you nervous?"

I barely think before I answer with a shrug, "Actually, no." She raises her eyebrows with surprise, and I continue my explanation. "When I married Micah, I had so many doubts. I was so confused, but I was naïve, and I didn't know what else to do. I also had to keep reminding myself he was my best friend."

I pause remembering Micah. "With Matt, even though it may seem fast, he's everything I always wanted but never thought I could have. Even when I was young and stupid, I had such a strong connection to him, I just didn't understand it. There's no way I'm ever letting go of that again."

Bree nods in understanding. "I get it. As you know, there were a couple years Christian and I spent apart." She winces at the memory. "I still hate thinking about it."

"Thank you for coming with us this weekend," I tell her sincerely. "I'm thankful to have you as my friend Bree." I don't think I've had such a wonderful, genuine friend since Micah.

Although, no one will ever replace him in my heart, I've missed that.

She takes a deep breath and steps up to me, embracing me tightly and I hug her back. She moves back and my arms drop to my sides as we both fight back tears. "I'm honored to be a part of this whole weekend with you and Matt. Honestly," she pauses, grinning, "Christian would've been upset if he had to miss it too. Although he'll never admit it."

We both laugh knowing it's true when I suddenly have an uneasy thought. "Do you think Jason and Theresa will be mad?" I ask nervously. I've already caused so many problems, I don't want this to be an issue.

She shrugs. "Jason will get over it. Christian and Matt are closer, plus he's a guy. Theresa may have a harder time, but it will all be directed at Matt, not you. Don't worry." I bite my lip, suddenly slightly anxious. "We should put our dresses on," she suggests.

I reach for my cell to glance at the time and nod in agreement. "You're right. We have to be down there soon."

Bree quickly slips on her dress before I even walk across the room. "Will you zip me up?" she requests turning her back to me. I pull up the short zipper and she spins around slowly for me. "What do you think?"

She's wearing a simple sleeveless pale yellow dress that hangs loosely around her curves. It has a scoop neck in front and also hangs low on her back. She has her chestnut brown hair pulled up in a loose ponytail, pinning some of it up and adding extra curls to the loose hair. "You look absolutely gorgeous Bree," I murmur honestly. "Please don't let Christian drag you away before today is over."

She blushes and laughs. "Don't worry, I won't let that happen. Thank you," she adds. Glancing at me, admiring her, she purses her lips. "I'm beginning to feel overdressed. It's your wedding. Get dressed," she demands offering me a huge smile.

Taking a deep breath, I take off my robe and glance one more time at the new ivory lacy bustier and panties I picked out for Matt hoping he'll like them. I run my fingers lightly over my silky white ivory dress before I step into it and pull it up. "Can you help zip me up, Bree?" I ask spinning around. I picked out a strapless dress since my breasts are big enough to hold it up. The material crisscrosses across my chest as if it were wrapped there. A small, jeweled wave pattern sits just above my waist as if it's holding it all together. It flows loosely around my hips and flows to the ground.

"Got it," Bree proclaims. "Turn around so I can see." I do as she says and her mouth drops open. "Wow! You look incredible! I can't believe we found that on the rack! That just doesn't happen."

I shrug. "Lucky, I guess."

"You definitely are. Just, wow," Bree repeats making me laugh. "You look absolutely stunning, Sadie. Matt is going to lose his mind when he sees you."

I grin, feeling my body heat. "That's what I'm hoping for." I step over to the mirror to take another look at my hair and make-up. My hair is pulled up like Bree's, but it looks completely different since my hair is so straight. I have a few strands already hanging down by my ears and I carefully move to fix it.

"Leave those," Bree suggests. "I'll just add a little curl and hairspray for you."

She quickly touches up my hair bringing a smile to my face as I look in the mirror again. "Thank you, Bree, again."

"You're welcome." She grins. "Ready?"

"Let me just grab my sandals." I slip on a pair of silver strappy sandals that match the buckle more than the dress, but I like it that way.

She grabs her wristlet for her room key and her phone. "Wait! I have to take your picture," she announces. "I can't believe I almost forgot! I'm such a terrible friend," she jokes, and I roll my eyes like she often does. She puts me how she wants me in front of the window and snaps a couple pictures. "Selfie," she declares. Holding the phone up above us, she squeezes into the frame with me as both of us laugh.

"At least I don't have to depend on you to take pictures for the next couple hours or we might not have any wedding pictures," I tease. I reach for her hand and give her a tug, "It's time to go Bree."

She laughs, nodding in agreement. "I'll text Christian to let him know we're on our way down."

"Okay." I smile.

We walk out the door and my stomach flips in anticipation and nervous energy. Everyone we pass by smiles and waves like they know me making me blush. Strangers begin taking pictures of me. I really don't understand it and I admit it makes me slightly uncomfortable. I loop my arm through Bree's to bring her closer to me for support, but I can tell she sort of feels the same way as me, so we cling to each other as we walk through the castle halls.

We make it downstairs, and I glance into the eating area with the piano, finding it's only occupied by an employee cleaning up, while to the left in the cigar room and bar, it's completely vacated. We walk to the back of the building through another small dining area and out onto the back walkway outside. As soon as we hit the fresh air, I notice a photographer standing off to the side taking our picture. We walk down onto the huge lush green grass with green trees lining the grounds down below and the bay just beyond. Beautiful gardens are spread out throughout the extravagant grounds, and I again feel this moment is surreal.

Eyes remain on me as we descend the slight slope down to the small gazebo. My heart continues to palpitate erratically as I concentrate on putting one foot in front of the other until my eyes finally find Matt. I breathe a sigh of relief at the sight of him, my smile becoming genuine. My heart begins to slow and my grip on Bree loosens. I step up to Matt standing with Christian and another man who appears to be a few years older than us with similar coloring to me. I assume he's the one who will perform the ceremony. Matt said he's a lawyer who Christian uses for their business, but he's actually officiated weddings a few times before. He promises it will all be legal, and I trust him.

Matt immediately reaches for both of my hands and smiles down at me with his green eyes sparkling brightly. "You look absolutely stunning, Sadie."

A smile lights up my face. "Thank you. So do you," I tell him, as I look him over. He's wearing a navy suit with a crisp white shirt and a blue and green striped tie. I have to admit I wondered if he'd wear a suit, but he definitely looks absolutely amazing in it. He's always in shorts. In fact, I haven't seen him in pants since his brother's wedding. He chuckles and I blush, realizing what I said. "I mean you look gorgeous," I amend with a playful shrug.

He grins. "Ready?" he prompts as he searches my eyes for the truth.

"So, ready!" I admit smiling happily. He chuckles and turns towards the man about to marry us without releasing either of my hands.

"You heard her," he grins proudly, "so let's get on with it."

Chapter 38

Matt

I've never seen anyone so breathtaking in all my life. I happily pull Sadie into my arms to dance with me. The way she smiles at me and throws her head back in laughter literally takes my breath away. As we sway back and forth to the piano music I mumble, "How did I get so lucky?"

She grins and responds, "I'm the lucky one." Then, she cocks her head to the side and asks thoughtfully, "How are we going to know what our wedding song is?"

My eyebrows draw together in confusion at her abrupt change in subject. "What?" I ask chuckling.

"There are no words and even if there were, is this a happy song or a sad one? Or is this a bunch of songs linked together?" She shrugs and continues rambling. "It doesn't really matter though because I have no idea what song he's playing."

I laugh, shaking my head in amusement. "Only you. But you're right it doesn't matter. This way we can pick our own song," I suggest. "Make it anything we want it to be, just like you and me."

"Good idea," she agrees softly.

Leaning down, I press my lips to hers, not able to wait another second without kissing her. I forget about everything around me and focus solely on her. I slide my hands delicately over her bare arms and shoulders, followed by her neck, until I'm cupping her face gently in my hands. Then I deepen our kiss, pushing my tongue inside her mouth to taste her. She whimpers and her hands fall to my chest. I groan quietly at her touch and pull away before I can't keep my hands off her.

"Kissing my wife, now that was a good idea," I rasp huskily.

She smiles, sighing wistfully. "I love hearing that."

"That kissing you was a good idea?" Not waiting for a response, I grin, mumbling, "It's always a good idea!" I kiss her chastely as she laughs.

"I mean hearing that I'm your wife. The fact that we're married is a reality. We're finally a family," she adds, appearing sheepish.

I caress her cheek with my thumb and agree as I look into her eyes, "We are." I drop my forehead to hers and prompt, "Are you ready to get out of here? I want to take you to our room."

"Okay," she replies sweetly and tips her head up to meet my lips in an all too brief kiss before she drops back on her heels.

I link my fingers through hers and walk over to my brother and Bree. "You guys can get out of here now." I smirk knowing my brother has been drooling over his wife all night. I'd say he's more anxious to get out of here tonight than me, but that's just not possible. "We're leaving," I announce.

"It's about time!" Christian grins and gets a playful tap to his stomach from Bree. He chuckles softly. "Congratulations, Matt. Thanks for including us today," he adds before giving me a hug with a hard pat on my back, which I return.

"Thank you for being here," I proclaim appreciatively.

He moves to Sadie and gently hugs her. "Congratulations, Sadie and welcome to the family."

The glow of her smile with his words is so wide and genuine I have to clear my throat to attempt to remove the growing lump. "Thank you," she whispers.

Bree hugs both of us as well and offers her own, "Congratulations."

We both reply with a simple, "Thank you."

I reach for my discarded jacket and tie before we head in opposite directions towards our rooms. Christian and Bree are taking the library suite tonight and I have everything ready for Sadie in our room, thanks to help from both Christian and Bree as well as the staff. We're staying in the penthouse suite, although Sadie doesn't know that yet.

As we get to our room, I open the door and then sweep her up in my arms, carrying her inside. I pull her body flush against mine as soon as we're over the threshold and kick the door shut behind me. Holding her to me, I kiss her with all the love and passion I can muster without attempting to take her right here on the floor. I pull away, both of us gasping for breath.

"Want to check out our room?" I rasp.

"I guess," she murmurs biting her bottom lip.

I groan and loosen my hold on her only to grasp her fingers and spin her around to take in her surroundings. She gasps at the view in front of her. We have a large sitting room with an amazing view of the bay, although right now we can only see the beautiful grounds lit up with complete darkness behind. There's a fire on in the fireplace with lit candles and small vases of red roses on every surface. On the coffee table sits a large bucket with a bottle of champagne along with two glasses and two plates, one filled with shortbread cookies and the other with chocolate covered strawberries. I stay close as she walks over to the table and picks up an envelope.

She flips it around so I can see it as she smiles looking giddy, "Mr. and Mrs. Emory." I grin and she adds adorably, "That's us."

Laughing, I nod my head. "Yeah, Sade."

She sets the envelope back on the table without opening it. Then she steps up to me and tilts her head back to look up at me. "I like it when you call me that," she confesses.

"Sade," I whisper.

My heartbeat speeds up just having her close. I slip one hand around her waist and the other up her arm until I'm cupping the back of her neck. I lean down as she pushes up on her tiptoes to meet my lips. My whole body instantly ignites with heat the moment our mouths fuse together. She clings to my shoulders as I push my way into her mouth needing every part of me deeper in her. I slide both hands to the back of her dress, searching for the zipper.

She laughs as I continue fumbling, breaking our kiss. "I think I'm going to have to turn around for you to find this one. It's buried under the material."

"Well get on with it then Mrs. Emory," I rasp huskily.

She giggles and spins around for me. I find her zipper and slowly tug it down, pressing my lips to the soft skin of her shoulders and neck. When the zipper is all the way down, I stand back to let her dress fall to the floor, puddling at her feet. My mouth drops open and I groan at the sight in front of me. She's standing in a lacy ivory bustier and a matching thong. Her already full curves are pushed up and nearly spilling out of the top. "Are you trying to kill me on our wedding night?" I rasp hoarsely.

She giggles in response. "Matt," she murmurs.

"Fuck," I mumble and step towards her, needing to put my hands on her. My hands grip her hips tightly and pull her to me as my mouth drops to her chest. I lick and kiss the tops of her breasts before finding her mouth again. I dip her back and lower her onto the couch as I plunge my tongue inside her mouth.

Her hands tangle into my hair as she fights to get closer. My hands begin desperately roaming her body, wanting to touch her everywhere. I curve one hand around her back and squeeze her ass towards me, while the other moves to her breast popping one of her nipples free.

I rip my mouth from hers, lightly sucking her breast into my mouth. She groans my name sounding desperate, "Matt," and setting me on fire. Her hands move to my shoulders and down my back as I circle her nipple with my tongue and flick it lightly. "Matt," she whimpers, "Your clothes need to be gone."

"Not yet," I grumble and stop her protest with another fervent kiss. I bring my hand from behind slowly around, lightly caressing the inside of her thigh. Then, I slide my fingers over her already wet and heated core. I easily move the tiny piece of fabric and cover her with my palm before my finger slips inside. She groans into my mouth at my touch. I push two fingers in, at the same time rubbing her with the heel of my hand as she begins moving along with me. As I begin moving my hand faster, her head falls away from our kiss with a groan.

I watch her with awe as her body curves into me, but then she suddenly shoves at my chest. "Matt, please stop," she rasps. I instantly freeze, my heart pounding as I wait for her to speak. When she catches her breath she tells me shyly, "I just want my first orgasm as Mrs. Emory to be with you inside me."

The air rushes out of my lungs as I rasp her name, "Sadie." I kiss her hard, feeling so much love and passion for this woman I'm not even sure how to let it all out. I break our kiss as she begins unbuttoning my shirt to help me. Reaching up, I finish and toss it to the ground. I quickly pull my undershirt off as well and her eyes widen as she takes in my bare chest.

She begins to unhook her bustier as she watches me strip, so I continue, unbuttoning my pants and kicking them off my feet. I pull my socks off just as the bustier falls to the ground and she sits in front of me in only her tiny thong. I gasp as she kicks that to the floor. I pull off my own boxers before I kneel in front of her gently kissing her lips, trying to slow myself down so this isn't all over in an instant.

With one hand, I reach for her fingers and entwine our hands together. I grab the blanket off the top of the couch with the other before tugging at her hand. "Come with me. We need more room." I grasp a condom out of a side table drawer I had put in there earlier and make my way over to the fireplace. Swiftly, I spread the blanket out right in front of it and guide her down on her back. I lie down next to her and lightly trail my fingers up the side of her body, intending to make this last when she feels my rigid length and I lose all my inhibitions. "I wanted to take it slow and cherish you, but you're making it so hard to do that."

"Then, don't. I want you now!" she insists. I kiss her fervently and when we stop, gasping for breath she reaches for the condom and tears it open. "Let me," she requests urging me to lean back for her. I hold my breath as she easily rolls on the condom. She looks up at me from under her long eyelashes with a satisfied smile, her blue-grey eyes sparkling like diamonds.

Forcing the air out of my lungs, I position myself at her entrance and hover just above her. "Are you ready for me, Mrs. Emory?" I smirk. "After this you're stuck with me forever," I remind her.

She grins, prompting me, "Hurry up, already!"

I chuckle with my heart full. Grinning, I take a deep breath, breathing her in. As I exhale, I slowly push into her, enjoying the sensation of feeling her around me. When I'm all the way in I pause and look down at her covered in sweat, never looking sexier than she does in this moment.

"Damn, you're beautiful," I rasp breathlessly.

I see the smile in her eyes as I start moving in and out. Her hips begin bucking into me, begging for more. I pick up the pace as her hands skim over the muscles in my back, burning a trail as she goes. She clings tighter to me as her breathing gets faster. I slide one hand between us, cupping her breast and running my thumb over her hard nipple.

She breaks our gaze, kissing me and groaning into my mouth. I move faster knowing she's close when her lips fall away from mine as her head drops back and her body arches towards me. Skimming my hand over her skin from her breast to where our bodies meet, as soon as I touch her folds, I feel her explode around me. I slide my hand away to pull her close, pushing in and out rapidly with the pulses of her climax, quickly following with my own. I cover her mouth and kiss her hard as she slowly comes down and everything goes white as I empty myself, coming hard.

With an exhausted, but satisfied groan, I collapse on top of her. Then, I slide my own sweaty body to the side, to release some of my weight off her, but rolling her with me to keep us together as long as possible. Eventually, I sigh and pull out of her with a soft, tender kiss.

"I love you, Sadie," I proclaim, needing to say the words.

She sighs happily and smiles at me. "I love you too, Matt."

I cradle her face in my hands and kiss her again. "How about we go clean up together in the bathtub before round two," I suggest.

"Sure," she grins. "We never did make it to see the rest of the room," she adds giggling as her face turns a beautiful shade of red.

I chuckle, claiming, "I had better things to do." Standing, I grab her hands pulling her up to me with a chaste kiss. I roll the condom off and knot it, tossing it in the garbage can.

We walk through the bedroom with a beautifully carved king-sized bed and more flowers and candles. I point outside as I keep moving towards the bathroom, acknowledging, "We have a balcony too. We can have breakfast there."

Inside the bathroom we find more lit candles sitting around an oversized tub with more roses on the counter of the double sink. I turn on the water and pour in some bubble bath and bath salts sitting on the side. Slowly turning Sadie around so she's facing the mirror with her back to me, I begin pulling pins out of her hair. She smiles at me through the mirror and helps me along, much quicker than I am.

By the time we're done with her hair, I'm able to turn off the water and step into the bathtub. I sit down and hold out my hand for Sadie to join me. She lowers herself in front of me and leans back into my chest, resting her head on my shoulder so she's able to look up at me. I wrap my arms around her middle, holding on tight.

"Relax with me for a little while," I request just wanting to enjoy having her in my arms.

After a few minutes of quiet she asks, "There's something I should've asked you before we got married." My eyebrows draw together in confusion knowing nothing would change my mind about wanting her exactly where she is now. She sighs and I kiss the side of her head in encouragement. "What about kids, Matt? Do you want more? You know about my…" she gulps hard and trails off, looking away from me.

I reach for her chin and pull it towards me until she meets my eyes. "I would love to have more kids with you, but I don't care as long as we're together. We already have an amazing son. If we can't have any more kids that's okay. If you want a bigger family and you want to try to adopt, we can do that too as long as we do it together."

She smiles and her whole body relaxes into me. "Really?" I nod my head in affirmation. Appearing overwhelmed, she whispers, "I love you, Matt."

My stomach flips and I grin. "I love you, Sade."

She giggles. "I love it when you call me that."

I chuckle and whisper her name again, "Sade." After a beat, I prompt, "So, does that mean we can try this next round without a condom?"

She blushes and questions, "But even though it's nearly impossible, what if we ended up with another miracle?"

"I'm all for miracles," I mumble and kiss her hard.

Epilogue

Sadie

Day after Christmas ~ 5 months later

"Sadie! It's so good to see you," Theresa proclaims as she embraces me.

I happily hug her back. "You too, Theresa, although we did just see you guys yesterday." I laugh. "Hi, Jax."

He chuckles at Theresa's antics, already knowing what she's doing. "Hi, Sadie."

"Where's your idiot *husband* hiding?" she questions loudly.

"I heard that!" Matt calls as he walks into the room smiling.

"Good! You were supposed to," she states grinning at him. "I gave you a break the last couple days because it was Christmas, but..." she trails off with a smirk.

Matt laughs and shakes his head, pulling Theresa in for a hug. "Good to see you too, T," he mumbles squeezing her tightly.

She huffs. "You deserve for me to give you a hard time. I thought I was your favorite, and I don't even get to go to your wedding!"

"You are my favorite sister," he tells her grinning mischievously. She rolls her eyes in response. "We weren't going to tell anyone, but mom and dad until it was over. Jason didn't know either, but we needed witnesses for it to be legal." He shrugs nonchalantly and turns to Jax. "Hey, Jax."

Jax nods his head. "Hi, Matt and everyone," he mumbles grinning as he gestures towards Matt and Theresa's parents who are talking with Bree's dad, as well as Jason and Sara as they enter the room.

Matt leans down and gives me a quick kiss, his green eyes still sparkling with humor. "Where's Holden?" I question as he pulls away.

He shrugs. "Christian said he wanted him for something special." I can't help but wonder what that could possibly be. He chuckles, claiming, "I have no idea either. He's in there with him and Bree and Blake and Liz are here too," he informs me.

"Are Holden's grandparents going to be here soon?" he questions. We've both been starting to call Marco and Bee Holden's grandparents instead of Micah's parents. We'll never forget who they really are, but we're also trying to move on and remembering Micah as my best friend, instead of the reminder that he was there for Holden and me when he was born, is a better way for us to do that together. I believe Micah would be okay with it too because all of us have remained a family.

"They should be here any minute." Since Christmas is so busy, Matt's family decided to have a big family dinner the day after Christmas at their house and invite everyone that's important to all of us. Bree's Dad is here, as well as her best friend Blake and his fiancée Liz, who is also Jax's sister and Sara's best friend.

Holden suddenly comes sprinting into the room and crashes into Matt's legs at full force yelling for me, "Mommy, Mommy, Mommy! Guess what? Guess what?" he asks excitedly bouncing on his toes.

We all burst out laughing while Matt picks Holden up to bring him closer. Now that he has the attention of the whole room with his excitement, Matt asks him, "What's up buddy?"

"I'm gonna' be a cousin!" he screams.

I hear several gasps of surprise echo all around the room. Everyone steps a little closer to us as I rasp, "What?"

Holden repeats himself proudly, "I'm gonna' be a cousin! Uncle Christian and Aunt Bree told me." He grins wide, full of pride.

Every head in the room snaps to the kitchen doorway Christian and Bree just stepped through hand in hand. They both smile and Bree blushes, nodding her head with tears in her eyes. Christian grins happily, reiterating, "We're having a baby."

Gasps and cheers of happiness follow as everyone rushes towards them to give their congratulations. I look back over to Holden, still patiently waiting for me to respond to him. "That's so great my little man! You're going to be such a great cousin," I tell him with a wide smile, my heart briefly clenching inside my chest.

Matt gives him a squeeze and agrees, "You will be the best!" I wrap my arms around both of them for barely a moment before Holden begins to wiggle his way out from between us. We laugh and let him go.

"I'm going to play with my new Legos! Uncle Jason said he would help me build," he informs us gleefully as he takes off in a sprint for the playroom on the other side of the open living room that used to be an office. "Come on, Uncle Jason," he yells animatedly.

"I'm coming," he calls as he follows after our son.

I sigh in contentment as I fall into Matt's chest and wrap my arms around his waist. "I'm sorry, he's just like me," he states in mock disappointment. I laugh and he adds with an exaggerated groan, "All that energy."

"You love it," I declare as I look up at him.

He nods in agreement, a huge smile covering his face as he gladly concedes, "Every single second of it." He leans down and kisses me gently on the lips, making them tingle.

"Come on, the crowd is parting," I prompt, tilting my head towards the other side of the room. "Let's go say congratulations to your brother and Bree," I suggest.

He offers me another genuine smile. "That's really great, huh? Holden will have a cousin," he murmurs with awe.

"Probably a lot of cousins before you know it. You do have a big family," I remind him, arching my eyebrows in challenge. He laughs as we step over to Christian and Bree. "Congratulations guys!" Matt exclaims as we take turns hugging Christian and Bree.

"We're so happy for you guys," I add.

"Thank you," Christian replies proudly. "Holden did awesome! He's so funny. That must be the Emory in him," he jokes.

We laugh as Bree admits with a heavy sigh, "I'm exhausted. I have to sit down. You can all join me if you like."

We follow her to the couches, and all sit down to relax. "How have you been feeling Bree?" I inquire, knowing what pregnancy can be like.

She grimaces. "Okay, I guess. I've been a little nauseous and tired, but," she shrugs, "not too bad, I guess."

I look at her with disbelief since she seems to be brushing off my worry. "Remember that I went through it already. If there's anything you want to talk about or ask or if you need anything, I'm here for you. I haven't really forgotten like they say you do."

She smiles genuinely, relief flashing in her eyes. "Thank you, I'll definitely take you up on that."

"Not right now though, right?" Matt jokes smirking. Christian laughs as Bree and I both roll our eyes at him. "What? I thought we were eating soon." He shrugs and I just shake my head in response.

"Are we all still going snowmobiling after dinner?" Christian prompts.

"Yeah, but I'm going to take Holden for an easy ride first. Then I'll leave him here with all the grandparents and bring Sadie to meet up with you guys," he reveals.

"Did you bring his helmet?" I prod. Matt bought him his own helmet for Christmas, promising he would take it easy with him, so I agreed, albeit reluctantly.

He nods his head just as Theresa and Jax sit down with all of us. Matt looks up at Theresa and smiles mischievously. We all know he's looking to cause trouble as he glances over towards Jax and asks, "So Jax, with all this big news around here the last few months, what are your plans? You know, since Jason's engaged, I eloped and Christian's having a baby," he reminds us. "Don't you think it's time for you to step up? Make my sister an honest woman?" he teases.

Theresa groans and crosses her arms glaring at her brother. Jax chuckles and shrugs, claiming, "I'm not one to step into the spotlight. We can wait until another day." Theresa laughs while her brothers and Bree join her. I've heard the story about how Jax sang to Theresa to help him win her back. He still maintains he'll never do it again.

Theresa jumps in to help him, obviously not wanting to wait any longer. She flips her left hand out towards all of us and smiles brightly. "But since you asked so nicely, this is my Christmas present." A round cut diamond ring with a small diamond chip on each side sits on her left ring finger. Bree and I both squeal in excitement, jumping up to hug her.

Christian grumbles his congratulations and gives Jax a warning glare causing Bree and me to burst out laughing. Then, he gives Jax a one-armed hug. "I'm kidding, as long as you take care of her."

Jax chuckles in response. "You know I will."

I elbow Matt in the gut as I sit back down next to him, his jaw still hanging open.

He shakes his head and stands taking a deep breath. He wraps his arms around Theresa and squeezes. "I'm really happy for you guys, T."

"Thank you," she whispers. "You're not invited to the wedding though," she teases making him laugh. "Well alright, if you're going to be so pushy you have to be in it," she adds smiling widely at her brother. "You too, Christian."

Both Matt and Christian nod attempting to hide their emotions. I link my fingers through Matt's and squeeze. He sighs and glances behind him towards Jason walking over with Sara and Holden. I know he's about to make some kind of joke the moment he opens his mouth. "Jason's not going to be in it too, is he? I can't do it if he's there."

"Do what?" Jason asks, his eyebrows drawn down in confusion.

"Be in our wedding?" Theresa asks sweetly.

Jason and Sara congratulate them and Matt jokes, "So it's an all men wedding to take away attention from the groom?" I just shake my head as Holden climbs up between Matt and me.

I tune out their banter as Holden cuddles between us. I love cuddling with my boys, my family and I couldn't be more grateful. At times like this, I can't help but think Micah really may have been the one to bring Matt back to me, to us, making my heart clench with both love and sadness.

Matt looks down at Holden and me and smiles, nodding his head towards our little man, whose eyes droop with exhaustion. "Why don't you close your eyes for a few minutes before dinner. I promise I'll wake you," I suggest quietly. The excitement of Christmas is finally catching up to him. He stops fighting sleep and falls completely into Matt's side like a ragdoll. Carefully, I slide a little behind him, so I can curl into both of them a little better.

Matt drops his head to mine and whispers in my ear, "Thank you, Sade."

"For what?" I question softly without moving.

"For granting me the most amazing wishes I never knew I had. I honestly couldn't ask for anything else. I feel so blessed to have Holden, to have you. I love you so much, Sadie."

He lightly brushes a tear from my cheek with the back of his hand I didn't realize had fallen. "How can you be so sweet to me and always make jokes with your family when you start getting emotional?"

He chuckles, shrugging. "I don't know, maybe you're just special."

I sigh, my heart feeling full and content. I don't think I have ever felt this happy. "I love you, Matt." He tips my chin up and lightly brushes my lips with his, sending chills down my spine. I don't believe I'll ever lose that feeling with him.

I'm grateful he's my unforgettable one.

The End

What's Next?

The next book in The Unforgettable Series was never meant to be, but I have always known her story. Now, fans have a chance to find out how Amy became the woman everyone loves to hate. Will Amy find her own happily ever after in Unforgettable Mistakes? Unforgettable Mistakes is book 6 in The Unforgettable Series. Each book in the series is a stand-alone novel, but better read in order.

The Unforgettable Series in order includes:
The Unforgettable Summer
Unforgettable Nights
Unforgettable Dreams
Unforgettable Memories
The Unforgettable One
Unforgettable Mistakes

An Unforgettable Spin-Off:
Breaking Cycles

Or check out a different town with new characters and new stories in
The Home Duet:
Dreams Lost and Found
Finding Home

Acknowledgements

Being able to completely convey my *thank you*, definitely becomes harder every single time. I will leave most of my original ones in here, with a few added for this edition. I want to start by thanking my family for their continuous love and support! As always, thank you to my mom. Without you and dad (I miss you, Dad), I don't know if I would be where I am today and I'm forever grateful. Thank you to my husband for encouraging me. Thank you to my kids for all their smiles, hugs and being my inspiration without even realizing it. Thank you for putting up with the times I say, "Just a minute," to finish a thought, idea, sentence or even a chapter. I love you all so much!

Thank you to my friends, my forever sisters of the "BRU CRU" for sharing some memories and inspirations. You're definitely a fantastic panel of experts! I love you and miss you all!! A special mention is needed for our unexpected loss this year. I know this hit every single one of us like a truck. Cheers, Heather. We love you and miss you more than we can express.

Thank you to all my editors and beta readers. I want to say a special thank you to Kelley for being there for me from the very beginning and always willing to help me out. I just hope you know I'm always here for you, just like you are for me. I'm forever grateful to have you in my life! I also want to say thank you to Nancy for helping and supporting me in every way you possibly can. I'm so thankful for your friendship and your assistance. Thank you to Dinzy Finzy Publishing for your expertise.

I'm absolutely thrilled with this gorgeous new cover, and I have a few people to thank for it. Thank you to my gifted photographer, Violette Wicik of Violette Wicik Photography. She also photographed and designed the stunning covers for both books in my Home Duet; Dreams Lost and Found and Finding Home. I always love working with you! Thank you to the talented and beautiful cover model, Kerry Mannix, who I always enjoy working with on set. I was so excited when she agreed to portray Sadie on this cover. Now, you can also catch her as a multimedia journalist with KVIA ABC 7 in El Paso, TX. Thank you again to Jessica of Uniquely Tailored for designing my beautiful new cover, as well as all the new covers in The Unforgettable Series! I love your incredible work and I'm so grateful!

I definitely wouldn't have my fifth book out in The Unforgettable Series if it weren't for all my readers. I greatly appreciate each and every one of you and hope you enjoyed reading this book and the rest of the series as much as I enjoyed writing them. I've really enjoyed meeting some of my fans and I look forward to hopefully having more chances to do that! I have to admit that feeling is incredibly surreal, but I really enjoy it!

I know I'm going to miss the Emory family, as they have become a part of me. I'm not saying the Emory family is gone for good, as I've already received requests to hear more from them, but please keep an eye out for what's next! As you now know, a fan driven novel follows this one. That fact alone, blows my mind. Thank you all so much!!

Unforgettable Playlist

Songs from The Unforgettable Series
Books #1-5

"Summertime" by Kenny Chesney
"I Cross My Heart" by George Straight
"A Thousand Years" by Christina Perri
"You Save Me" by Kenny Chesney
"Don't Ya'" by Brett Eldredge
"Beat of the Music" by Brett Eldredge
"Uptown Funk" by Mark Ronson
"I Hope They Get to Me in Time" by Darius Rucker
"Good Lookin' Girl" by Luke Bryan
"Honey, I'm Good" by Andy Grammer
"Halfway Gone" by Lifehouse
"Hotel California" by The Eagles
"Poison and Wine" by The Civil Wars
"Die a Happy Man" by Thomas Rhett
"Maybe" by Sick Puppies
"Simple Man" by Shinedown
"All In" by Lifehouse
"At Last" by Etta James
"Last Name" by Carrie Underwood
"Thinking Out Loud" by Ed Sheeran
"It's Your Love" by Tim McGraw and Faith Hill
"Making Memories of Us" by Keith Urban
"Who You Love" by Katy Perry and John Mayer
"Stealing Cinderella" by Chuck Wicks
"Today" by Brad Paisley
"Beautiful Day" by U2
"Play It Again" by Luke Bryan

Connect with the Author

For more Adult Contemporary Romance, read more by
Nikki A. Lamers. Connect with her here:

Official Author Website
www.nikkialamersauthor.com

Linktree for All My Author Links
https://linktr.ee/NikkiALamersauthor

For Clean Contemporary Romance
Read books by Nicole Mullaney. Connect with her here:

Official Author Website
www.nicolemullaneyauthor.com

Follow Her on Instagram
https://www.instagram.com/nicolemullaney/

Author Facebook Page
www.facebook.com/Nicole-Mullaney-Author-
103006415283835/

BookBub
@NicoleMullaneyAuthor

About the Author

Nikki A Lamers has always had a passion for reading and writing, especially romance. She grew up in Wisconsin with her sister, mom and dad. She always loved reading romance books and watching romance movies with her dad, something they both enjoyed. After college she lived in Florida for a few years working for the "Happiest Place on Earth," where she met her husband. She now lives on Long Island in New York with her husband and two kids. She spends her free time reading or hanging out with friends and family. When she's not writing, she works as a script advisor and supervisor in television and film. She would love to spend more time traveling, visiting new places and meeting new people as well as continue creating stories, each of her characters becoming part of her family.

Made in the USA
Middletown, DE
14 July 2024

57299076R00195